Stephen Sim lives in Scotland, where he studied at
the University of the West of Scotland achieving a
BA in Filmmaking & Screenwriting. This is his first
novel in a series of three, centering on the mercurial
character of Guinevere, Queen of ancient Britain.

Acknowledgements & Dedication

I would like to thank Carol Hughes for her help and encouragement in the process of writing of this novel.

I dedicate this book to the memory of Ada Harding Brownlee (1926-2005)

TREASURE

OF

AVALON

A novel by

STEPHEN SIM

FIRST NOVEL IN THE GUINEVERE SERIES

TREASURE OF AVALON

THE FIRST NOVEL IN THE GUINEVERE SERIES

Published by Create Space in 2014

1st Edition

This book is set in Georgia Type Set
Printed in United States of America
Edition   2014
ISBN 13: 978 1494363369
ISBN 10: 149 4363364

MAIN CHARACTERS IN THE NOVEL

ACCOLON – SERVANT TO KING LOT

KING ARTHUR – HIGH KING OF BRITAIN

LADY ELAINE – SISTER OF MORGAN LE FAY

EROS – KING OF THE FAIRIES.

FRITH – LEADER OF A GANG OF THIEVES

GAHERIS – SON OF KING LOT

GALAHAD – SON OF LADY MORGAN & KING ARTHUR

GALLIA – DAUGHTER TO A BLIND MERCHANT

GAWAIN – SON OF KING LOT

GERMANUS – PAPAL ENVOY

GUINEVERE – QUEEN OF BRITAIN

LADY HELENA – LADY AT COURT

LADY OF THE LAKE – GODDESS OF AVALON

LANCELOT – FAMOUS WARRIOR

KING LOT – ONE OF THE FIVE KINGS OF
BRITAIN

MERLIN – SORCERER, ALSO KNOWN AS
TALIESIN

MORDRED – DISABLED SON OF KING LOT

MORGAN LE FAY – SISTER TO KING ARTHUR

MORGAUSE – SISTER TO MORGAN, MARRIED
TO LOT

NEMUE – APPRENTICE TO LADY OF THE LAKE

OLWEN – DAUGHTER TO THE GIANT
YSBADDADEN

TITIUS – ROMAN COMMANDER

YSBADDADEN - GIANT

PROLOGUE

The King's Sister, Morgan Le Fay knelt in the small boat and watched the blind ferryman steer it along the narrow channel towards the land of the Gods. She could not see the magical Islands of Avalon, for the mist hung low obscuring her vision. The boatman guided the vessel successfully to the shore, but remained seated and did not speak. Morgan moved towards the center of the boat and pulled away a white cover, to reveal the body of a young woman. She placed her hands onto the woman's face. 'Elaine,' she whispered, 'we have arrived.'

The face of the young woman was unblemished; her skin was fresh and full of color, her hair was neatly brushed and shone in the speckled sunlight, while her mouth gave the impression of quiet contentment. The picture that Morgan saw before her was misleading, for her sister was no longer alive but had been murdered the previous day.

Morgan looked up from the boat and peered through the clouds to see blurred images of green and gold. It did not take long before a God emerged through the mist to stand before her. His face was strong, like that of a Greek warrior and his name was Mider. He was one of the six Gods that ruled the Islands called Avalon. 'Who dares to approach our kingdom?' he thundered.

The lady stood resolutely before him. 'I am the Lady Morgan of Tintagel. I come to make a bargain with the Gods.'

Mider smiled. 'The Gods do not make bargains.'

'I will not leave, until you hear what I have to say.'

From the corner of his eye, Mider saw the body of Elaine in the boat. He was intrigued to find out what the lady wanted to say. 'You must be a brave one to dare come here.'

'I want to propose a trade. I will restore the sacred chalice stolen from this land, in return for the resurrection of my sister.'

Mider's eyes narrowed. 'What do you know of the chalice?'

'Only what others say.'

'And what do others say?'

'That it is a rare object, held dear by the Gods.'

'The chalice, like the rest of the treasure, must be returned. If you could retrieve it, then we would be grateful.'

'Grateful enough to bring my sister back from the dead?

'Return the chalice, or any of the other objects stolen and I will restore your sister to full health.'

'Can you really bring the dead back to life?'

Mider assured the lady he could. However he admitted there was a problem. 'The problem is keeping your sister alive, without awakening her from her death sleep.'

'Tell me what I must do,' pleaded the lady.

'You must bathe her from head to toe with an ointment everyday.'

Morgan acknowledged she would do this without fail.

'You must not miss one single day, or the skin will corrupt and she will never return.

1

To Morgan's relief, her sister Morgause arrived at first light with her entourage. She arrived with a great deal of ceremony having travelled all the way from Lothian. The journey had taken four days, and had left her in a foul mood. A message sent by Morgan by raven, had reached her sister only a day after the tragic event took place. She left her isolated castle to travel without her husband's permission, first by boat, then cross-country on horse to her mother's castle at Cadbury.

Morgause resembled her younger sister in likeness; her hair was equally long and fine, her complexion was healthy. Morgause's real difference was in her manner and not her looks. She saw herself as being highborn and important, even though she had no real power. Men had the power. She had learnt early in her marriage that the only power women came by was through their bodies. This power had made it possible for her to bear healthy sons for her husband, and for the King. Now that her childbearing days were over, the lady's influence had faltered and her husband's interest in her had likewise.

Having exchanged condolences, Morgan arranged a private meeting with her sister to reveal her bargain. Having listened patiently, Morgause began to walk around the room. 'My dear sister, Elaine's death has clearly unhinged your mind.'

'You've seen the proof yourself, her face is still unblemished.'

'You have a healing touch.'

'Don't be absurd, I can not stop decay.'

Morgause took her hand away from her face. 'This Merlin, what do you want with him?'

'You must remember him? His powers can help me track down the treasure.'

'I remember him as being scary.'

'While I'm away, I need you to look after Elaine and stop mother from putting her in the ground.'

After a deep sigh, Morgause agreed. 'I'll keep the priests and mother at bay.'

'You know what to do?'

'Yes I know. It sounds ridiculous, but if it will keep you happy.'

'It's imperative you never miss a day.'

'I'll do it, stop worrying.'

'Thank you. What about your husband?'

'I doubt he will even have noticed I've left.'

With her sister on guard duty, Morgan left her mother's castle to go in search of the mysterious Merlin, one time sorcerer and friend to the late King Uther. She was riding through the forest, on her magnificent white horse named Du, on her way south to Castle Dore. The horse carried the lady with grace and ease even though she had no reins or instrument to coerce the beast. By contrast her companion, Accolon, a young man of slim build and ungainly posture, found it difficult to control his horse, a spirited black mare. The two riders had come to the end of a clearing and were now at a place where the road forked into three separate paths.

Morgan stopped Du, and studied the routes at her leisure. She looked over her shoulder to see Accolon looking uncomfortable. The lady wished she had not given in to her mother and agreed to be guarded by this young and incompetent servant.

'What are you looking at?' Morgan asked.

Taken by surprise, the young man mumbled his reply. 'Bandits...'

'Bandits?' questioned Morgan.

'I hear this is notorious bandit country.'

'That's why you are here,' she replied.

The boy looked lost and the lady realized she would probably be the one doing the protecting. She saw the humor of the situation. 'I have no fear, for I am sure you are a great swordsman.'

The young man blushed. He wondered if the lady was making fun of him.

'What path should we take?' Morgan asked.

Accolon studied the three paths and gave his opinion. 'The one on the left,' he stated with authority.

Morgan looked along the left path, seemed unsure. 'Surely that path will lead us back into the forest.'

A hand went up to the young man's face. He tried not to engage the lady's eyes. He felt her gaze would make him feel even more foolish. 'Sorry, I meant to say to our right.'

Morgan seemed to agree. She gently whispered something to Du and led the horse down the right path. The young man followed, but continued to look over his shoulder.

The lady glanced behind her. 'We need to quicken our pace. It will soon be dark and we must arrive at Wroxeter before that.'

Accolon acknowledged. He realized his poor horsemanship was making the lady feel uneasy.

It took awhile before Morgan glanced behind to find the path empty. She retraced her steps to find Accolon lying face down on the dirt. His horse had pulled up some distance away, and was nodding her head as if she was proud of her actions. The lady did not feel compassionate. 'What happened?' she asked. Her tone sounded robust. He got to his feet, wrestled some dirt from his body and tried to stand up straight. 'You were riding too fast,' he complained

Morgan witnessed the young man's clawed face and her manner eased towards him. Having caught some broken branches, Accolon now had some nasty cuts along his cheek. Morgan jumped down from her horse and came towards him. 'Let me take a look at your cuts.'

The man shook his head. She took from her pouch a green paste substance and offered her services as healer.

He looked at the substance and again tried to dismiss Morgan's help. 'I am fine, my lady.'

Morgan could tell he was rather fearful of her medicine, but she insisted in applying it. She administrated the paste to his face, her gentle touch and the cool feel of the wet substance had an immediate effect on the young man's senses.

Having twitched when the paste was first administrated, Accolon now wished for the lady to take her time. He felt her gentle fingers caress his face and felt almost overpowered by her sweet touch. He fought the terrible desire to take hold of the lady in his arms. Her eyes caught his and the young man went red in the face. As he pulled away, his hand went up to touch the paste.

Morgan tried to finish her work. 'Don't touch it, let it do its work,' she said.

'What is it?'

'Only some herbs, they will stop the cuts from getting poisonous.'

The youth acknowledged her kindness with a nod of his head and moved towards his horse. Morgan put away her medicine and moved back to Du. She remounted without a fuss, but Accolon struggled to regain his mount. The young man kicked out at the horse that was making him look so foolish.

Morgan saw the incident and chastised him. 'Never hurt a noble beast,' she scolded.

Accolon wasn't in the habit of making a fool of himself, but this lady made him nervous. Her name was as famous as King's. He asked her forgiveness and tried to change the subject. 'I have heard such stories about you, my lady,' he began.

'What kind of stories?'

'They say you have magic powers...'

Morgan interrupted. 'I do not practice magic,' she said angrily.

'I didn't mean to suggest...'

Morgan pushed her horse forward as her temper returned. 'Do try and keep up and do try not to fall off your horse again.'

With accommodation scarce, Morgan was forced to share a room with her servant in the inn at Wroxeter. The lady was tired, but after preparing for her sleep from behind a screen, she approached the bed to find it was already occupied. Accolon had collapsed on the bed and had immediately fallen asleep

The lady shook her head, but decided not to awaken him from his slumber. Finding an old chair she curled up in it and took a letter out from the pocket of her nightdress and began to read. The letter was addressed to her in Latin. It had been delivered by hand the day of her journey, but she had not yet had a chance to read it. Morgan broke the sealed wax of a mighty ring of the Chi-Rho symbol and began to read the letter in the poorest of light. The letter was written by a bishop by the name of Germanus. The lady had never met the man, but had heard his name mentioned around court. She had heard rumors that he had been sent by Pope Celestine to Britain to help spread the word and to find ways of stamping out the last remnants of paganism.

To her horror Germanus had found out her secret and threatened to exposure it to the nobility. He demanded she come before him and beg for forgiveness. Only through repentance he asserted, could she find salvation before God. The threat from Germanus, Morgan knew was real, but this also concerned the King. She decided to write a letter to Arthur and wondered if the bishop intended to slander the King's good name also.

The lady brought out from her saddlebag, her parchment and quill and scribbled a note to accompany the letter. She rolled the two together and put her own seal on them. All she needed now was a trusted messenger to take the document to the King in Gaul. She was many leagues from any of her band of supporters, and then she spied the youth asleep on the bed and sighed. She had no choice but to send him. Could he be trusted, and more importantly could he find his way without getting lost.

2

Arthur's army travelled quickly towards the town of Aube, with the objective of securing the town and all the high ground around it. He had decided this was the perfect place to engage the enemy. He had sent word to all his brethren to meet with him and to muster every able bodied man they could find. His mind was focused on the days ahead when Gawain, the youngest son of Morgause and King Lot, rode his horse up to the front of the line to address him. 'Well uncle, when shall we see some fighting?' he asked.

The King liked his nephew, although he reminded him of how young he had once been. 'Don't be in such a rush,' Arthur answered sharply.

Gawain continued in his happy mood. 'Why do you look so miserable? I would have thought the young lady's presence would have put a smile on your face.'

Arthur shot a piercing glance at his nephew. 'What young lady?'

'The Lady Helena,' answered Gawain.

'The lady is here?'

'Yes my lord. I found her...amongst the camp followers.'

Arthur cried out in anger. 'Damn the woman.'

Many of his men looked at him, but none spoke a word.

'She is no longer with the others,' informed Gawain. 'I took the liberty of giving her the protection of my caravan.'

'Thank God for that at least,' the King gasped.

'What will you do with her?' Gawain asked.

'I must send her back.'

Arthur studied his young nephew. He was a little headstrong, but he knew that in time he would settle down and become a fine leader of men.

'I put the lady into your care,' he told him. 'Take two of your men and deliver her back to Paris.'

Gawain protested.

'Don't worry, we'll save a few Romans for you to kill,' Arthur jested.

Gawain's happy mood was smashed and by all things a woman, and not even his. He cursed the lady under his breath. He realized Arthur was addressing him.

'I guess I better see her, bring her to my tent when we stop for the day,' Arthur commanded.

'Yes, my lord.'

Gawain bowed his head, turned his horse around and returned down the column of men a dejected figure.

Accolon was bundled off to the coast, to find a boat and to travel over the sea to Gaul. He had been given the letter and some maps to lead him to the King's position. He realized he could not argue, although he pleaded with the lady to wait until she had found Merlin. She explained the news in the letter was urgent and too delicate to trust to a raven. So he agreed and galloped away from his charge towards the coast.

Castle Dore had once belonged to the Gorlois family, but had passed to the King after Morgan's father had died. To the lady it felt like going home, but she was in for a surprise, for the King had never visited the place and it had fallen into disrepair. The caretakers had been allowed to pillage the castle's supplies and the place almost looked like a ruin.

Imagine the servants' surprise when a lady of distinction from the court of Caerleon suddenly arrived unannounced and un-chaperoned. Their fears were enhanced when they realized the lady was in fact the King's sister and had previously lived at the castle.

Of the four servants, a steward by the name of Fergus seemed to be the most upset. He had made a nice living out of the mismanagement of Castle Dore, but was now in a panic since the lady's arrival. He thrashed about, shouted at the other servants and tried to convince Morgan that their laziness was the reason the place was in such neglect. The lady really didn't care about the crumbling castle; all she really cared about was finding Merlin.

None of the servants had heard of such a man and concluded the lady's information was wrong. Although disappointed, Morgan was determined to explore the area nonetheless. She told the servants to ask everyone in the local villages and towns and wandered around the area herself in a faint hope of finding some useful information.

The servants' attitude of sullenness and tardiness was not lost on Morgan. The lady wished she could dismiss them all, but remembered she wasn't their mistress. With Arthur abroad, she would have to get in contact with Guinevere to ask her to replace the indolent servants and that was never going to happen. In her opinion the woman who ruled in Arthur's stead was cold and dangerous as any snake. Her poisonous venom spread throughout the land in the guise of her many spies and informants. For all she knew, one of the servants, perhaps Fergus was one such spy.

Awakening with an aching head, Accolon looked to his surroundings. They were bleak. There was a prison gate, made of iron bars on one side, while the other three walls were made of solid stone. He soon realized how cold and damp it was, as he shivered beside the only item in the cell, that of a wooden bucket filled with water. His dungeon seemed impregnable and yet his thoughts turned to escape.

He remembered a figure had come at him with a sword, forcing him to be unseated from his horse. What happened next was a bit hazy, but he remembered being dragged along the ground until he lost consciousness. It wasn't just the young man's head that hurt, in truth it was his pride also.

It wasn't long before his attacker came down the steps to stand before him. Gruffydd, looked strong, like the seasoned warrior that he was. Standing at the prison door the man had a grim expression as he stared at his captive.

'My mistress will see you now,' he announced in his deep hoarse voice.

Gruffydd opened the cell and asked Accolon to follow him. The young man followed his jailer up the winding stairs, until they came to the entrance of a large room. Gruffydd opened the thick wooden door and ushered Accolon inside. The room the young man entered was full of magnificent furnishings. A large wooden bed took up a considerable space in the room, it was ordained by beautiful drapes of crimson red. The storage cabinets stood against two of the four walls and were enriched by a vast array of cauldrons and chalices. These were arranged with great care and immediately attracted the viewer on entry. The young man was impressed by the grandeur of the place, but his thoughts remained fixed on rescuing the letter and somehow escaping. He heard a noise and turned to see a figure enter the room. The figure was small and walked like a woman, but it could easily be a young man or even a boy he thought.

As the figure came closer the young man had little doubt that it was a lady. She wore a white monk's habit that covered nearly all her body. Accolon waited for his host to speak, all the time trying to peak a glance at the lady's face. Gruffydd motioned for him to sit, but he declined and slowly moved towards the lady. This the lady did not like and she glanced at Gruffydd, who quickly stood in front of the man to halt his approach.

The young man protested. 'Why was I brought here?' he demanded to know.'

From behind her cloak the lady's eyes seemed to be studying her guest.

'What do you want with me?' he asked.

'We will come to that in a moment,' the lady replied. 'First I want to know how long you have been working for Lady Morgan.'

He found her voice quiet and refined. He was in no doubt the lady was from the nobility. 'Only for a few days,' he told her.

'Are you a loyal servant?'

'Yes, I am employed by King Lot...'

The lady nodded her head. 'Yes, yes but are you loyal to your new mistress?'

'Why would I not be?'

'The lady has a sharp tongue I hear. Perhaps you could do better elsewhere.'

'I'm quite happy thank you.'

The lady took a few steps closer to young man. 'Think carefully, do you really want to be a servant for the rest of your life. You could work for me and earn a great deal of money.'

'My master and mistress treat me quite well...'

'Master...you have a servant's mentality. Do you not want to be free?'

Accolon was happy taking orders and thought he would be lost if he had to make decisions for himself. 'I am quite happy...'

'I can make you a rich man and all I ask in return is for you to communicate certain things that might be of interest to me.'

'You want me to spy on my master and mistress...'

The lady took in a deep breath and continued. 'I am not in the least bit interested in them. I want you to spy on the Lady Morgan and report to me regularly. In return you may have the letter back unopened and ten pieces of silver. That will be repeated on every occasion you produce information to my satisfaction.'

The lady looked to Gruffydd, who produced the letter from inside his shirt and handed it to her. Accolon could see for himself that the seal was unbroken and he began to waiver. He hated to admit to himself the offer was tempting, for in the past his existence had often been precarious. Sometimes he was forced to eat the leftovers and sleep rough on cold floors or even outdoors. Then the boy's integrity reared its head and he declined the lady's offer out off hand.

The lady's eyes turned to Gruffydd, who immediately raised his sword from its sheath.

'That is a pity,' she declared.

Gruffydd's eyes turned to the lady. 'Where will I dump the body?' he asked.

She turned, as if to make for the door. 'The nearest wood is not far,' she told him. 'Just make sure he is not found in a hurry.'

It was the coldness of these words that panicked Accolon into a change of heart. 'Wait,' he cried. 'What kind of information do you mean?'

The lady turned and came back to the two men. Accolon could see Gruffydd's sword glimmer in the sun's light and it became a clear reminder of his true position.

3

Morgan sat alone at the great table and pondered her situation. She had an uneasy feeling concerning the servants, whose manner was becoming more suspicious by the day. Servility had been replaced with downright hostility. She felt uneasy as she began to eat her ill prepared meal and after a few mouthfuls, a sudden chill struck her stomach making her feel sick. A sharp pain then shot through her as she leant forward and tried to speak. The sound the lady made was garbled and incoherent, as she tried to rise from her chair. The lady's legs gave way and she flopped down by degrees onto the cold stone floor.

Morgan fell in and out of consciousness. When she was conscious she was aware the servants were present in the room and that Fergus was issuing orders to the others. Her thoughts were confused, although it seemed likely to her that the servants of Castle Dore wanted to do her harm, she could not understand why.

She realized she was no longer at the table, but on her back on the floor. The window of the room was open and she could hear the sweet sound of birds chirping. She turned her head and to her surprise she saw her father, Lord Gorlois's bulky figure standing beside her. He was smiling and offered her his hand, but she was unable to move. He opened his mouth and began to speak, but she could not hear his words. She tried to speak herself, but similarly her words were silent. As she closed her eyes, the image of her dead brother Owen then appeared. He was in full battle gear, his sword and shield by his side. He opened his mouth to speak, but again she could not hear what he said. The pain that had died away returned and she gasped for relief.

She raised her body a little. 'God, help me,' she pleaded.

The release of her pain seemed to be God answering her prayer, as she relaxed and fell back. She opened her eyes, and again it was her father who was by her side. This time she could hear his words, they were soft and gentle, the way he used to talk to her when she was a young child. 'Morgan, it is time for you to come.'

She then heard her own voice as a child of six, make her reply. 'No father I can not come. I must look after Elaine, she needs me.'

Gorlois smiled and bent down to gently touch her hair. 'You will not come with me then?' he asked.

Again the child replied. 'I must find the strength to carry out my duty.'

'Then may the Gods give you that strength, child.'

Gorlois disappeared and a sudden darkness replaced his figure.

Standing over Morgan were three people, Fergus and two female servants, Angharad and Ruth. It was Angharad who spoke first.

'What have you done?' she accused Fergus.

Fergus looked down at the body of Morgan and his right eye began to twitch. 'I've done what my mistress asked of me,' he stammered.

'She told you to kill the Lady Morgan?' Angharad asked.

'She told me to put the potion into her food.'

'You must have used too much,' Ruth said.

'How did you get the potion?' asked Angharad.

'It came by a raven, along with my instructions.'

'When did it arrive?' Angharad continued.

'Why are you asking me all these questions?'

Angharad took Fergus by the arm and walked with him a short distance. 'I don't think you realize, but you have murdered a member of the High Council and the sister of the King.'

Ruth bit her lip, looked to her two companions. 'We can't leave her here,' she told them.

Angharad continued to ask about the message and Fergus went to his room and came back with it. He gave it into her hand. After her inspection, she declined her head. 'It is her writing for sure, but she has not signed it.'

'You must help me bury the body,' Fergus informed them.

They were reluctant, but it was clear Fergus could not dispose of the body himself. So they wrapped Morgan up in a large sheet and carried the body down to the rear of the castle. Angharad addressed Fergus again. 'We will keep the note, in case we are found out.'

Fergus agreed and felt a little less uneasy.

It was on one of his rare outings into the village of Cunomorus that Merlin heard his name mentioned. This was unusual, for all the inhabitants of village usually just laughed at him and would call him by derogative names, such as the *'green man'*. He lingered for awhile in the inn and learnt that a certain important lady was looking for the outcast Merlin. He heard the name Morgan, but did not at first associate it with his past life and the court of Caerleon. It was only when he was kicked out of the establishment and was wandering along the cliffs towards the cave he called home, did he remember the young lady.

It must be the same one, he thought. She was two years older than the young Prince, but could beat him in everything; swordplay, language, horsemanship and even hand-wrestling. Her star burnt so bright that it dimmed everyone around her, including Uther's son. In his opinion she should have been the heir to the throne, but a rather dim witted lad called Arthur had been groomed in her stead. He had become the High King and had led the Celtic people to more bloodshed and warfare.

Merlin began to retrace his steps, hurrying now towards the old Castle of Dore. He remembered hearing someone say she was there making a re-acquaintance with her past home. He wanted to see if the young girl had matured into a great lady and to perhaps have an intelligent person for once to converse with.

The vagrant bumbled along the ragged road eagerly awaiting the encounter, when he suddenly realized just what a state he must look. He could not expect the lady to receive him looking like a poor beggar. Yet he could not transform himself so easily, unless he resorted to his old ways, the ways that had got him into so much trouble. Magic could transform him, but did he dare use the power again. He had taught Morgan many things, even magic, but she was reluctant to put her power to the test for fear of being denounced. Her instinct had told her of its danger, how he wished now he had listened to the young maiden.

He came upon the once mighty castle and looked up at its crumbling turrets and decided to venture to its rear and to the servants quarters. There he hoped to sneak in without being seen. He increased his pace and found himself by the lower gatehouse. There was no one around so he entered and began to climb some stairs. He heard soft moans of a woman crying and went to investigate. The sound got louder as he found an open door and entered. He saw a young maid slouched down on the floor, her hands over her face. She wept into an old cloth, before looking up at the figure standing before her.

Merlin's clothes were torn and dirty, his hair long, but for all that his words were spoken like a nobleman. 'Why do you cry child, what has happened?'

'Oh sir, it is terrible thing they have done,' she told him.

He asked her to explain.

'Why those heartless villains, they have killed Lady Morgan.'

'Why would they do such a thing?'

'Oh sir they are bad, especially that wicked Fergus. He has been stealing from the King for years and he must have panicked when the lady arrived unexpected.'

'Where is the lady?'

'They've taken the body out to the woods to bury it.'

'Did you see which way they went?'

'They used the back entrance from the tower,' she told him. 'But it is too late, the lady is dead, I heard Fergus say so,'

'You must show me,' Merlin told her. 'Do not be afraid, no harm will come to you.'

Young Mary nodded her head and led the old man back the way he had come. They left the castle by the back entrance to the tower and into almost total darkness. Having forgotten to bring a light, Merlin was guided by the young girl over some fields and into the forest. They stopped and listened, and after a moment they picked up the sound of something hitting the ground. Merlin looked in the direction of where the sound came from, before addressing the girl. 'You stay here and do not be frightened.'

'Oh, be careful sir, they have already committed one murder tonight.'

Merlin smiled at the girl. 'I'll be careful. Lie down on the turf and don't move.'

The girl did what she was told.

Merlin followed the sound as he entered the forest. He did not have a plan, but his anger was growing in intensity. He would strike down the evil beings responsible for the death of the lady and bring about some kind of justice. He arrived at the scene to find Fergus wiping his brow of sweat. It was clear the man was not used to manual labor for he had hardly dug away any soil. His two companions were watching him close by. Ruth was sitting on the ground with her hand on a fire torch, while Angharad was standing by a tree directing the operation. 'We haven't got all night,' she complained to Fergus.

Fergus glared at her, picked up the spade and started to dig again.

Merlin saw Morgan's body wrapped in a sheet, some yards from the proposed grave. He thought it might just be possible to steal the body from under their noses. The biggest problem was not so much Fergus who was busy, but the two women. Then he remembered Mary, if she was willing she could act as a decoy. If she could make a noise from the other direction, hopefully their attention would draw them away and he could rescue the lady. The girl was amenable and his plan was set in motion.

The plucky young Mary walked in a circle until she was standing directly opposite Merlin. She whistled like a bird, to let him know she was ready and in place. His plan could not have worked any better, even though he underestimated the difficulty of carrying a human body.

Mary broke several twigs and waited for the women to react.

Angharad walked in the direction of where Mary was standing. If the girl was frightened she did not move from her spot. She put her hands to her lips and did a very good interpretation of a rook crowing.

'It's only a bird,' Angharad announced.

As she began to walk back, Mary broke more twigs and Angharad turned and ran towards the sound. In her haste, she fell over and hurt her leg. Ruth went to her aid, giving Merlin his chance to snatch the body. Fergus must have heard him, for he put down his spade and looked in his direction. If he did witness Merlin carry Morgan's body away, he did not react. His inaction gave the man time to carry the lady out of the forest. Puffing and panting he found the clearing more with luck than with good judgment. He carried her as far as he could, before resting her down on a hilly bank.

To his surprise no one came after him, neither the man nor his two accomplices exited the forest. This gave him the time to pull away the cover and with the help of the bright moon see the lady's face. To his surprise, the lady's features had not changed much, her face still remained striking. Her skin gleamed in the pale moonlight giving her a luminous quality.

Laying his hands on Morgan's heart the man listened in the faint hope her heart still had a beat. The young maid had been correct, they had killed her and now all that remained was to put her in the ground. Or could he remember some miracle spell to revoke death and bring the lady back the life. His kin on Avalon had empowered him with such a gift, but that was a long time ago. Could he remember? Could he believe in himself and trust his instincts and power once more? Time was everything. Only a truly powerful God could revoke death after a day or more, so he knew he could not wait. Putting his hands back on Morgan's chest he lifted his voice and began his oratory.

Merlin said the magic words over and over again, but still the lady did not move a muscle. A short time had elapsed and although the two women had not re-appeared, the male servant Fergus had found the clearing and was standing close by. He watched the old man's animated actions over the corpse, his shouting, his strange words and his hysteria and thought the man must be mad. Like many people when confronted with madness he showed restraint, even fear, so he approached with caution.

Fergus got within a few paces, when suddenly Merlin turned his head and fired a volley of abuse in his direction. The old man pointed his finger at the servant and shouted his spell of vengeance. The words he used were of an alien nature, but their effect was immediate. The man's body turned instantly into a grey colored stone. Fergus was frozen like a statue, his arms and legs which had been in the middle of action were now stranded in an unnatural pose.

Merlin looked inordinately pleased with himself. 'Well who would have thought,' he muttered. He turned again to Morgan's body and with renewed vigor repeated the spell once again. He placed his hands over the lady's heart and pushed several times. He looked into Morgan's eyes and could see for the first time a glimmer of life and after a few more pushes Morgan gasped and exhaled air from her body.

4

Having accomplishing his task in returning Helena to Paris, Gawain lost no time in returning to Arthur's camp. Aube was awash with soldiers, they overflowed from the town onto the surrounding countryside. The poor inhabitants of the town had no say in what was occurring. Many feared they would be caught up in the forthcoming carnage, although others were quite happy to reap the benefits of increased trade and commerce. It took Gawain some time to find Arthur, as the King had wandered off on his own and was observing the town from a high hilltop.

Arthur's success in battle was down to his meticulous planning and his cunning in setting traps and ambushes. He did not believe in the etiquette of warfare, winning was all that mattered. There was another reason for his success, this was a gift left for him by a mysterious benefactor. The gift was that of a great sword, which arrived on the day of enthronement. Suspecting Morgan was behind the gesture he praised the object, swearing to wear it always in battle. He kept to his word and reaped the reward as the sword became legendary. The blade did more than cut down his enemies; it somehow prevented him from ever losing blood in combat.

Many blows struck the King over fifteen years of warfare, but each blow failed to draw his blood. In the heat of battle no one had time to witness this anomaly closely, although some close enough on occasions, must have suspected magic. Everyone else suffered wounds, but never the King. The gift had not come from the Lady Morgan, but from another quite different lady.

Gawain climbed up the twisted path towards the King. As he climbed, he noticed that Arthur had unloosed the sword from its scabbard and had left it resting upon a rock. This gave the young lord a chance to pick up the celebrated object and have a good look at it. He had always wanted to hold Excalibur in his hand and now his chance had arrived.

After a moment's hesitation, Gawain, sword in hand began to practice his thrusts and counter-trusts. He was astounded by the weight, for it was heavy, far heavier than his own blade. From the corner of his eye, Arthur witnessed his nephew wield his precious possession and reacted swiftly. He bounded down the path towards his nephew in a rage, but prudence made him slow his pace, for Gawain held the upper hand with Excalibur at his disposal. 'Put it down,' Arthur commanded him.

A smiling Gawain went to hand the sword by its hilt to his uncle. Arthur snatched it from his grasp. 'I did not mean anything, uncle; I have always admired it so...'

Arthur could see he had been in no danger and relaxed. 'Forgive me, nephew. You really shouldn't sneak up on people.'

Gawain agreed. 'Could I use it sometime, that is when you do not...'

'No, I can not allow that, but if I ever did it would be to my favorite nephew,' he acknowledged with a smile.

Gawain accepted the compliment. 'It is heavier than I imagined.'

'A heavier man needs a heavier sword.'

Gawain nodded that he understood.

'I assume you have a report to give to me,' Arthur inquired.

'Yes. I returned Lady Helena to the castle...'

'Was she any trouble?'

'Apart from her verbal abuse the lady behaved herself.'

'Good, we can not have our womenfolk subjected to the coarseness of battle.'

'Talking of coarseness, the lady's choice of words sometimes was quite shocking.'

Arthur laughed. 'She did not learn them from me.'

'She must have picked them up in some tavern.'

'I hardly think the lady frequents such places.'

'Then her brothers?'

29

'She has no brothers. She is happy to remain in Paris?' Arthur asked.

'I warned her of your wrath if she disobeyed you again.'

'Good. Is there any other news for me?'

Looking startled Gawain swore. 'I almost forgot. I have a letter from Lady Morgan.'

Gawain produced the letter from inside his shirt and handed it to the King.

Arthur took it from him, witnessed the seal and looked up at Gawain. 'Did this arrive by raven?'

Gawain looked surprised by the question. 'No uncle, it came by a messenger.'

Arthur opened the letter and studied it. He lifted his eyes to look at Gawain again. 'Did the seal look like it had been tampered with?'

'No, I'm sure it has not, your grace.'

'This messenger, do you know him?'

'Yes, he is my father's manservant.'

'So he is trustworthy?'

'He's very loyal.'

'Is he here?'

'Yes, I thought it best to bring him along.'

Arthur nodded. 'I will have a word with him shortly, but first I might need you to go on another errand for me.'

'No my lord,' begged Gawain. 'You seem determined for me to miss all the fighting.'

'What do you know of the bishop of Auxerre, a man by the name of Germanus?'

'Nothing my lord, I have never even heard of him.'

Arthur read the letter a second time then folded into his shirt. 'Perhaps you are not the man for this particular job.'

'If it is about religion you should send for Mordred, he is quite a scholar on such matters.'

Arthur nodded. 'I might just do that.'

Inside the walls of Castle Dore, Morgan was recovering with the help of Merlin and the eager young Mary. She had confided in the old man, telling him about Elaine's death and the search for the God's treasure. He listened and said nothing. The lady had opened her heart and was a little disappointed by his lack of reaction. 'I could do with your council,' she remarked.

At first he seemed reluctant to speak, but after a lengthy stare offered his thoughts. 'You must find the treasure first – Elaine's killer will have to wait.'

The lady agreed.

Merlin stroked his long beard up and down. 'Only one man would dare...'

Morgan got to her feet and walked towards him. She didn't need to ask who that man was. 'I have written to him...'

'Would he tell you?'

'But Elaine is family, he surely...'

'Why did he risk so much for mere trinkets?'

'How do I know? There must be items of importance I guess...'

'Yes. There must be items of importance for the Gods to make a deal with you.'

'I did not know about the treasure, I had only heard about the chalice.'

'It must be the chalice that is important,' Merlin conjectured.

'But the God made little of it.'

Merlin smiled. 'I know for a fact that the Gods hold the chalice as both a sacred vessel and an item of power.'

Morgan stared at Merlin. 'Power?' the lady questioned.

King Lot of Lothian and Orkney was a Norseman and uneducated. He had won his lands through cunning and his loyal patronage of King Arthur. If the man could be brutish in his manner sometimes, he was nonetheless a good family man. His wife's actions had made him look foolish yet again, but he was used to that by now. He had travelled on horse to Cadbury Castle to enquire after her and to pay his respects to Lady Ygerne on the death of the Lady

Elaine. The Lady Ygerne met him in the courtyard and assured him that Morgause was well and looking after Elaine. Looking confused the man asked when the funeral was to be held. When Ygerne deferred his question the man became concerned.

'My lady I would not keep the body too long...I have seen what happens...'

The man did not get a chance to finish. 'Do not lecture me, young man,' she scolded. 'I am quite aware what happens when a person dies.'

Lot tried not to smirk, but the thought that he was still a young man made him smile inside. Now well into middle-age, the man's body had begun to creak under the strain of his tired limbs.

'Can I be of any help?' he asked.

'That's kind of you, but everything is under control.'

The King was not one for small talk and after spending an uncomfortable few moments with his mother-in-law, he sought out his wife. He approached Lady Morgan's bedchamber where he had been told to find her, but as he reached the entrance a guard blocked his path.

'Get out of my way you fool,' he yelled.

Hearing the commotion outside the bedchamber, Morgause exited from the room to be met by her angry husband.

'Tell this fool to get out my way,' Lot cried.

With a nod of the lady's head, the guard moved back into line and stood motionless.

'Do you always have to be so loud and uncouth,' the lady remarked.

'What do I have to do to get an audience with my own wife?'

An annoyed Morgause dragged her husband into the room and told him to keep his voice down. The man did not see why he should, until he remembered her dead sister. 'I am sorry for your loss,' he stammered.

Now in the room, the man was immediately shocked to find the body of Lady Elaine lying fully dressed on top of the bed. Morgause saw his stare and sighed. 'You will have to be told, but whatever you do, do not breath a word to a living soul.'

The man turned his head to stare at his wife. 'What the devil are you talking about?'

5

Mordred was the second son of Lady Morgause and King
Lot and the one most people talked about. He was tall,
gaunt, with a body that was twisted in shape and a mind
twisted in suspicion. He rejected the love of his mother and
father, believing that his conception was unlawful. In effect
he believed he was a bastard. This factious state of mind
soured his relations with his family including his three
brothers, Gaheris, Agravain and Gawain. The latter he
hated for his ability to win everyone's approval and to be
always by the King's side.

Their rivalry was famous and being the weaker in
body, Mordred was the one who suffered the humiliation
the most. He could not compete with his brothers in battle
so he turned instead to study and to prayer. With the help
of Lady Morgan, he poured over every manuscript he could
find and learnt every language the lady could teach. She
became like a surrogate mother to him, treating him on an
equal footing. She found him more interesting than most of
her kin, often praising him to the King for his wisdom and
good sense. The King wanted warriors and not scholars so
the man was ignored most of the time, but not today. The
King had summoned him to give him his council.

The King was in his tent, issuing orders to several of
his commanders when Mordred appeared. To everyone's
surprise the commanders were quickly dismissed. All alone
with the King, Mordred became timid and nervous. Arthur
sensed this and offered him wine and spoke of everyday
things, before coming to the point. The King asked his
nephew if he knew of a bishop by the name of Germanus.
Mordred's face grew paler as he failed to answer.

Arthur pressed him. 'I can see you know something
about him.'

'He is the most feared man in the Christian world,'
Mordred declared.

'Why is he so feared?'

'He has the ear of the Pope...'

'You overestimate the power of the Pope. It is through battle that real power is achieved.'

Mordred bowed his head to accept Arthur's wisdom, but he could see the King was worried. 'He has a reputation for ruthlessness. He was once a soldier of note, but turned to the church. Some say he manages to combine the two in his new post.'

'A holy man that fights, I really must meet this fellow.'

'My lord, I pray you do not...'

'You are scared of him...why?'

'You have reigned in a tolerant manner when it comes to the religion, he would have you change this...'

'He has no say in anything I do...'

'I hope that remains so.'

'You give him powers he does not possess.'

'He has a reputation for manipulating people. Blackmail and torture are the tools of his trade.'

The King offered his nephew a chair and the two men continued discussing the holy man. 'I want you to meet with this Germanus,' Arthur commanded.

The look of horror came upon Mordred's face, this amused the King and he smiled. 'I want you to take him a message from me, but before that I must emphasize something to you. When you meet him, it is you who will have the power over him. If he is unreasonable you can arrest him.'

Mordred was now the one smiling. 'I am not a soldier, I can not arrest people.'

'On my business you can. I will give you a decree that will give all the power you need. Of course you shall have a body of men with you to enforce this power.'

'Do you really want me to arrest this holy man?'

'I will give you a letter to give into his hands, only into his hands. After he reads it, if he does not give his word to be bound by what it says you will arrest him in my name.'

Mordred shook his head. 'Please give this assignment to someone else. I fear I will fail you...'

'You will not. I have given it to you because you are the best man for the job.'

Mordred and Arthur continued to talk until the night came upon them and several of the King's commanders sought out their commander-in- chief.

'Do you know where he is?' asked Arthur.

'Not for sure. He wanders from church to church, from town to town.'

'But he is in Britain?'

'Oh, yes uncle. He could be at Canterbury or maybe Chichester. He likes the wine of the south.'

'You shall leave at first light. I will have the letter and more instructions sent to you before morning.'

Mordred left the King and sought out Gawain to boast of his new found importance. Gawain only laughed and implied he was a fool, but only Mordred suspected the mission's true importance.

Morgan and Merlin set off for her mother's home in Cadbury. Unknown to the lady, the old man was full of trepidation about seeing the woman he had once tricked. After some protest he allowed Morgan to cut the hair on his head and on his face. This set about a transformation that was truly remarkable, for even with many years of degradation, the man still looked younger than his years. His face was rather handsome, even if the rest of his frame was mostly skin and bone.

Merlin refused to talk about himself, preferring to hear all the news and gossip from the lady about Caerleon.

Morgan left out some of the more intimate details concerning the King and his unhappy marriage, but related the general position at court. She was praiseworthy of many, but when she talked about Guinevere, her hatred was easy to witness. He quickly steered the conversation away from the Queen and asked about her mother instead.

'She is well, although sad,' Morgan stated.

'Does she remember me?' asked Merlin.

Morgan hesitated. 'She was not keen in me seeking you out.'

The news appeared to depress the man, as his conversation began to falter.

The conversation was stilted over supper, which Morgan put down to her sister's matrimonial situation. The reality was quite different for it was the awkwardness between Merlin and the Lady Ygerne that was the cause of the uncomfortable atmosphere. Their re-acquaintance had brought back hurtful memories and both parties suffered the torture of regret. To Morgan's surprise Merlin announced his departure at dinner. He gave a polite reason for his going and promised to keep her informed of any news he might pick up about the treasure. The lady felt disappointed in the man who was abandoning her so suddenly.

He left early in the morning, leaving one woman at least relieved. Unknown and unseen to Merlin, Morgan had employed a spy to follow the old sorcerer. The young man was called Yvain, the illegitimate son of King Ursien and a lady of god. He was a man of few words, whose loyalty to Lady Morgan bordered on fanaticism. A master of disguise, he could change his appearance when called upon. Yvain was an expert in sleuthing and remained unseen by the time Merlin reached Wroxester. There Merlin stayed at a cheap inn and left early the next day. He changed horses and rode northward along the west coast, towards the land of the Picts

6

Helena of Benoic had the most beautiful of blonde hair, a girlish laugh and a certain artless charm. She also had an unwavering determination to get her own way. This willful streak in her character many failed to recognize, including the King.

The lady's horse had gone lame and was refusing to go any further. She tried to coax the stubborn beast by coercing it with kicks and slaps, but this only made him more willful. The lady dismounted from her disobedient beast and studied her immediate surroundings. She began to walk though the field, aimlessly heading in an eastern direction hoping to find a village or a landmark. She knew Aube was near, for a stone had indicated it was some five leagues away. That had been last evening and Helena was sure she had travelled that far by the early hours of the morning. With the day now upon her, she expected to stumble upon the army at any moment and hopefully a not too angry King.

The lady began to hear a noise in the distance, sounds although garbled suggested a large gathering of people. She followed the noise until she got to a plateau and looked down. The spectacle she saw was truly spectacular. The lady felt a little intimidated, as she witnessed a colossal army of men encamped in the valley below her. Helena was hopeful she would stumble upon her friends and countrymen, but when she studied the troops and their armor they appeared more Roman than Celt. She was contemplating her best course of action, when she heard movement behind her. As she turned, she saw four soldiers standing over her, with broad smug smiles. They were attired with body armor, white tunics and short swords that made them easily distinctive as members of the Roman army.

Unlike previous Roman armies, their dress was unclean as were their hair, hands and faces. The discipline of previous Roman armies was now a distant memory, and what Helena now saw before her, were mercenaries from the four corners of a crumbling empire. Desperate and brutal, these men were paid to kill and they really didn't care who it was that they ran through.

Helena could not retreat, her only hope she surmised was to bluff her way out of her situation. It was the tall scrawny eastern looking Roman who first approached her. His deformity came in the form of a black patch which covered his right eye. No doubt he had lost this in some battle or other, but his disfigurement only increased Helena's fear of the man.

'Well, my fellow brothers, look what our enemy has given us,' Fabius exclaimed.

The other three soldiers moved forward, making Helena's escape impossible.

'Please, I'm just a peasant girl,' she said.

She spoke in Latin, a language they all understood.

'A peasant girl who speaks our language,' Fabius remarked.

The soldiers were all sturdy looking with exception of Fabius whose muscles were confined to his broad shoulders.

'I think you are a lady,' Fabius remarked.

'What should we do with our prize?' the second soldier asked.

'She's one of them, we should do what they did to us today,' suggested Fabius, as he laughed and grabbed at Helena's dress.

Part of the material tore as she struggled and kicked against her attacker. The other men watched as she clawed away at his body, tearing at his neck and face with her fingers. This only angered him and he threw her down onto her back and jumped on top of her. It was at this juncture that the other men heard a noise and turned to see another soldier come amongst them. Standing in front of them was Titius, their Legion Commander.

Titius stared at his comrades, his face showed his disgust. 'What goes on here?' he demanded to know.

One of the soldiers muttered an excuse. Titius pushed past the three and grabbed Fabius around the neck and threw him off the terrified Helena.

While the three soldiers continued to mouth their pitiful excuses, Fabius got to his feet and looked as if he was about to draw his sword on his commanding officer. He had his hand on its hilt, but did not draw it.

'It's just a pagan slut,' Fabius declared.

'You'll get your chance to fight the Celts on the battlefield,' Titius remarked.

The commander turned his head to look at Helena. 'Who are you? What do you want here?' he asked.

Helena quickly got to her feet and tried to cover herself up with the rags that were now her clothes.

'I am lost my lord. I am in need of your protection,' she asked.

'Then you shall have it my lady,' Titius assured her.

Helena held out her hand to Titius, while her other hand kept her modesty at bay. He took hold of her hand and began to lead her away. They had only walked a few paces when Fabius cursed and spat on the ground. Titius turned, looked at his men with an eye of a patriarch looking disapprovingly at his offspring.

'I know who you are, you need not worry, you will all be punished,' he told them.

Fabius wasn't in the mood to be given a lecture and swore at his commander. 'Why should you get the spoils of war?' he asked him.

'Report to the Commander of the Guard,' Titius commanded.

Standing defiantly, with both his arms by his side Fabius challenged his commander's authority.

'Why don't we fight for her?' Fabius suggested.

'This is not the time,' Titius assured him. 'But if we are not dead after the battle, then we will settle this privately.'

Fabius looked at his fellow soldiers, he could tell by their faces they all were impressed by Titius's answer. He nodded his acceptance and Helena and Titius walked away towards the Roman encampment.

Helena had recovered her composure and was warming herself in front of a fire outside the Commander's tent. Titius brought from the tent a cloak and put it around the lady's shoulders. 'Are you warm enough now, my lady?'

'Yes, thank you.'

'Are you with the Celtic army?' Titius inquired.

'In truth sir, I am lost.'

To her surprise the lady felt safe in the company of this stranger, a man who quite possibly should have be her enemy.

'I never really thanked you for coming to my aid,' she began, 'I thank God for your intervention.'

Titius smiled. It had been a long time since he had been in the company of a lady and he was having trouble thinking of things to say. 'I apologize for my fellow countrymen,' he stammered.

'War must be harsh. It must make men brutal.'

'I guess that is true, but the army is all I know.'

'How long have you served?'

'Thirty years, my lady.'

'You're surely not that old?'

'Five more years and I will retire with a good pension.'

'What will you do then?'

'Oh, live out the rest of my days on the island of Sicily.'

'God willing, you shall see that day.'

Titius acknowledged her kind words.

A Roman soldier carrying a piece of parchment approached Titius and handed him his document. Titius acknowledged the soldier, opened the parchment and read its contents. The look of relief upon his face indicated it was good news. He did not forget his guest, assigning two of his men to stand guard over her, while he attended to his duty. 'I will be back soon,' he told Helena.

The Roman army had made camp two miles from Aube and on low flat farmland. They were in a fairly weak position compared to the Celtic army, which held the high ground to the north of the town. Arthur had sent out scouts to see the full extent of the Roman strength and was surprised to find that many of their eastern troops had not yet arrived.

From intelligence he was aware that the Libyans were on their way led by Vulteius and that he would be arriving in a few days. He had made his decision, but he had left it to the younger generation to deliver his message to the Romans. He had made arrangements to meet the Roman delegates on a hill over looking the two armies. This hill stood approximately a mile from each camp.

He had given the command of the delegation to the son of King Bors of Benoic, simply called young Bors. He in turn picked two others to accompany him on their rendezvous, Gawain and a soldier of little experience called Gerinus. These raw solders all had a reputation for recklessness and many were alarmed by the King's selection.

The six soldiers all on horseback arrived on the mound at the same time, three from either side. The Roman three were; Quintilianus, Mucius and Titius, they saluted their opposites as Bors came towards them. He had in his hand a parchment from Arthur, which he handed to Titius. The Roman Commander studied the parchment, as everyone else looked on. Gawain's horse seemed nervous and would not stay at peace. The noble animal's senses were on edge, it was almost as if the beast knew the contents of the note.

Titius finished reading and looked across at the three Celtic warriors. His expression remained the same, but Quintilianus glanced in his direction, his gaze asked the question the rest anxiously waited for.

The parchment was passed to each of the Roman soldiers. It was Gawain who broke the silence. 'So it would seem our King wants you to hurry back to whence you came.'

Quintilianus took exception to the discourteous statement and cursed at the young man. Gawain only smiled and cursed back at the Roman.

'You Britons are fools,' Quintilianus stated. 'You make war with threats and idle boasts.'

'You will see shortly that they are not idle my friend,' said Gawain.

'We Romans do our talking on the battlefield,' Quintilianus scorned.

Gawain's actions were so quick, that the others seemed suspended in time, as he withdrew his sword and struck Quintilianus a fatal blow across the man's upper body. His sword sliced through the Roman's head and almost decapitated it from his body.

Everyone was in shock until Titius and Mucius drew their swords and were matched by the Celtic soldiers. A mini battle began on the mound in clear view of the two armies. The warriors engaged in close hand to hand combat, but as they fought with tenacity and skill it soon became clear that three would soon get the better of two. Gawain struck Mucius a vicious blow on his side and the Roman fell to the ground. Gerinus finished him off when he struck his spear through his body armor. Bors and Titius hacked at each other, many of the blows would have felled most men, but when Mucius died, Titius knew his time was up.

Gawain came at him from one direction, while Gerinus came from another. It was Bors, or rather his horse that saved the Roman's life. The horse moved forward and forced Titius's horse backward, throwing the Roman onto the ground. To his surprise the Celtic warriors did not finish him off, but rode away from the scene. He glanced over his shoulder to see thirty Roman Cavalry ascending towards the mound.

The three Britons galloped back towards their camp, followed by an ever increasing number of Roman youth. It was Gawain who directed them towards the dark valley and

43

the cover of the forest. They reached the forest not a moment too soon, as Titius struck his sword down on the shoulder of Gerinus and the Celt fell from his horse. Bors and Gawain had no choice but to try and stay ahead of Titius and the rest of his men.

The Roman warriors were now at the entrance to the forest and in close pursuit. Gawain seemed to know his way as he dragged his pursuers towards an opening perfect for an ambush. The King and several hundred of his men were waiting to greet the youth of the Roman war machine. The carnage resembled more a slaughter than a battle, as the Celts hacked down their opponents. It was an object lesson in guile and a lesson to all commanders not to let emotion overpower judgment.

Arthur and the Celtic army drew a pincer movement to cut through the weakest point of the disorganized Romans. This would allow them to exit the forest before their enemies could arrange reinforcements. However as they began to make their escape the Roman cavalry commander, a man name Ydernus, broke through their lines with a Legion of his men and began to cut off their retreat. The battle could have been lost in that moment, if it had not been for Lancelot who burst forth with his cavalry to smash Ydernus and his men from the rear.

7

The Pictish land had no official border and their people were so diverse that they included Irish in the Western Islands, Celts in the lowlands, and Picts everywhere else except Orkney. Merlin knew his way around this area and travelled without incident to Dumbarton in the central lowlands. He found the people there friendly and like minded. What did surprise him was the influx of foreigners, since his last visit. They seemed to make up a quarter of the population, mostly Saxons with a few blonde haired Angles. He rested in a good clean dwelling and sought about hiring a servant to look after his person. After much debate he settled for a man who was quiet and polite. He was a Celt, with a good command of both Latin and Goidelic, a strange and unusual attribute for a manservant. The name he gave was Yvain. He was efficient and asked no questions.

Merlin and his servant successfully move up the western coast of the land of the Picts. Merlin told anyone who asked them, that they were on a pilgrimage to visit Columba in Iona. This was indeed true, for he was a good friend of the priest's. Columba was in fact in exile, banished for his opposition to the Irish King. He was of royal lineage, and a member of the Cenel Conaill, whose high king ruled at Tara. He was a man of great importance and a possible threat to the King of Ireland. His threat was totally illusionary on the part of the Irish King, for his settlement represented peace and tolerance.

The Irish came over to Argyll and set up in three regions, the largest being Dalriada. The land was under constant attack; from the Picts, the Angles, and the Britons. The Irish were constantly on the look out for spies and anyone who looked suspicious. A clean-shaven Merlin and Yvain happened to fall into that category.

Yvain climbed upon a rock and peered across the land in the hope of spying Iona in the far distance. A sudden sound made him glance to his right, to see six men standing around him. Their cloaks and shawls were made from tartan cloth which draped over their shoulders. They all carried a large lightweight shield and a large broadsword which most carried on their backs. Two of the men had their swords already drawn and challenged Yvain. 'Where is the other one?' the first man asked.

Looking dumb, Yvain shrugged his shoulders. The Irishman asked again, but got no answer. 'It doesn't matter, we will find him. Take him.' The rest of the Irishmen manhandled Yvain, pushing him forward until he fell to the ground. He got to his feet and stumbled along beside his captors, listening to their taunts and curses. They took him to their small community and a series of brochs. The broch he entered was a wooden lean-to structure building, erected against an inner wall of unmortared stone. He was led through an outer wall and gatehouse and into a larger building that was totally round in shape. Finally he was taken down a few steps into a dark chamber, where he was thrown into a caged pit. In his solitude, he contemplated how useless he had been in the service of his lady and cursed his misfortune.

Merlin had escaped capture by becoming invisible, just before the men had surrounded the helpless Yvain. He was in a good position to see everything that transpired. Having no loyalty to his new servant, he did not see fit to intervene. He soothed his conscience by telling himself his mission was too important to risk capture or delay. He left the man to fend for himself and managed to make his way to the coast.

After bantering with a fisherman, he secured a small coracle and headed to the Island of Iona. He arrived as the sun was going down, and was met quite by chance, by a group of young monks walking along the beach. They took him to the abbey if it could be called such, as it was nothing more than a long broad building made of wood. It had two smaller buildings by its side, one of which was a watchtower.

They entered the abbey to find it busy, with a curious mixture of artists, pilgrims, monks and dignitaries from many different lands.

The new visitor was fussed over and given some bread and wine. A young monk ran away to another part of the building and brought back with him a middle-aged man wearing a white robe, brown pants and worn sandals. The two men stared at each other, before embracing each other. 'You drunken sinful man, what brings you to this part of the world?' Columba quipped.

'Not your god-awful wine that's for sure,' Merlin replied.

'Since when have you been careful what you put down your throat?'

'I have been reborn,' Merlin advised. He showed off his clean face to prove the point.

Columba put a finger up to his mouth. 'You have travelled all this way to see me?' he inquired.

'I come in need of your help.'

After Merlin had finished his meal the two men went for a stroll along the shore's edge. Columba's expression had changed. 'We both have fallen foul of Kings my friend, but for my part I am content to remain in exile...'

'Did I ever mention the Lady Morgan before?'

'No I do not recall you mentioning her.'

'She's in need of my help and I thought you might be able to help her acquiring a certain item.'

'I live a humble life; I hardly think I can help you.'

'The Gods have had a sacred chalice stolen from Avalon.'

'Not you my friend?' asked Columba.

'I wouldn't dare. I suspect only King Arthur could have been so reckless. I remember what the chalice looked like and I was wondering with your help, could we exchange your chalice in its stead.'

The idea was met by groans of disapproval. 'You don't realize what you are asking.'

'I do, but without my help you would still be rotting in some jail in Tara.'

'This Morgan must mean a lot to you?' the priest suggested.

'Yes she does, but so does our friendship.'

Columba agreed to think about, but his demeanor suggested to Merlin that the object was too precious to give up.

Accolon, with the King's message safely on his person, left Castle Dore after seeing Mary and hearing of her tale. She had told him in vivid detail the episode concerning his mistress and the attempt on her life. This tale was so shocking to the young man, that it reminded him of the danger of his own duplicity. His betters played all manner of power games and were capable of terrible deeds, yet he was not brave enough to make his own way into the world. He remembered Lady Morgan's gentle touch, as he put his hand up to his face and relived the moment she had touched his cheek. He could not abandon such a lady he thought, danger or not.

On his return to Britain, he was forever watchful for ambush. The lady in the white habit had told him she had eyes everywhere and he quite believed her. The young man felt those eyes peering from behind every tree, every building he pasted. He travelled through the villages and small towns heading towards Cadbury, ever watchful. When strangers inquired anything from him, he became reserved and unfriendly. Still with many miles left to travel, the young man decided to risk a stay overnight in a small inn. He was halfway between Castle Dore and Cadbury in a small town called Maiden.

The inn was small with only two rooms beside the landlord's and so he was forced to stay with another. The man he stayed with was slender in statue, with short hair and clothes that did not seem to fit him properly. He seemed as young as Accolon, for his face appeared boyish and doleful. The two young men did not exchange names and both seemed resentful at having to share a room.

Accolon's companion bedded down for the night on the floor next to the window. In truth Accolon was quite relieved not to make conversation, but his companion's secretive behavior left him worried for his safety.

With the King's letter sewn into his shirt and his dagger under his headrest, he tried the best he could to succumb to his tiredness.

It was sometime in the early hours that Accolon was awakened by a noise from outside. The lack of light made it impossible to see clearly, but he made out the figure of his roommate kneeling beside the window. He seemed to be whispering to someone, but Accolon could not make out the figure from the other side. He was frightened to move, but deliberately listened with all his might. He had learnt to listen at doors and windows, often picking up important news for his master King Lot. He was a touch paranoid after his ambush and believed quite wrongly that the plot was against him. As he listened he heard two voices, that of a woman's and that of a man's. The female voice seemed to come from within the room and was the most clear, the other was more distant and broke up from time to time. This made it hard to understand all of their conversation.

The female voice sounded foreign, the lady's speech was punctuated with pauses and sighs of anguish. 'Tell me more about this man?' the lady whispered.

'I have...he is Gaheris son of...Lot and the lady...'

'Can you find out more about him?

'Yes, but he is a soldier and has gone off to join King Arthur in Gaul.'

'I must know why he is looking for me?'

'Do you want me...?'

Accolon missed the end of the sentence, but assumed the man was asking if he was to follow Gaheris to Gaul.

The lady seemed to ponder, for there was a lengthy pause. Finally the lady sighed. 'I wish my father was here to guide me...'

The man interrupted her. 'He would not want me to...'

49

'So be it, then stay...'

The lady turned her head and looked at Accolon asleep on the bed.

'I fear to sleep...for I might not awaken. What if he was sent by them?'

The man offered to climb into the room.

'No I am awake now, I shall not sleep anymore.'

'I could cut his throat?'

The lady was adamant that no one was to be harmed. 'If I am to die, I will not have the blood of others on my conscience.'

The man's voice choked with emotion. 'I will be bold enough to tell you what your father told me the day you were born,' he said. 'Look after her he commanded me, for she is the embodiment of everything that is good in this world. Make me a promise to die for her if need be. I so made that promise...'

The lady's voice lowered and became broken as she fought back tears. 'Dear faithful John, I would not have you die for me.'

The man's voice remained passionate. 'I have no intention in dying just yet, my lady. Not when you are still in this world.'

The exchange ended shortly after this and Accolon tried to return to his slumber, but he could not get the lady's soft voice out of his mind. She sounded so afraid and so tired. He wondered how long she had been hiding from her pursuers and just how real the threat was to her. He kept asking himself who would want to hurt such an innocent and why. Her voice sounded like an angel's, sweet, pure and full of compassion. He wished he could stay and be of service to her, but this was not possible. He had enough problems of his own to sort out.

By the time Accolon had arisen, the young lady had already dressed in her manly attire and was looking out of the window. He could not see the figure from the night before although he was sure the man was nearby. He dressed quickly and was about to leave, before realizing that the lady looked paler and more tired than ever. He

50

reached into his pockets and with a dash of humanity pulled out two bronzed coins. 'Do you have money for something to eat?' he asked his fellow boarder.

A flash of fear came into the lady's eyes as she turned to look at the young man. He felt she wanted to answer, but was afraid she would give her identity away so she merely nodded her head. Accolon should have left it there, but he was intrigued to find out who the maiden was. 'My name is Accolon. I am a manservant to King Lot of Lothian.'

The lady's eyes opened wider as if startled by the statement. She lowered her voice, and tried to speak as a man might. The tone of her voice remained soft and feminine however. 'King Lot...you are his servant?'

'Yes, although I am on the service of the Lady Morgan at the moment.'

The lady cleared her throat and put her hand over her mouth to muffle her voice. 'Do you know the King's son, the man called Gaheris?'

Accolon smiled. 'I know all his children, he has four sons and...' He paused before revealing the man's two illegitimate daughters. He continued in a more cautious manner. 'You could not meet four men more different...'

The young lady interrupted him. 'I am only interested in the man called Gaheris.'

'He is the quiet one of the family,' Accolon stated. 'He is thoughtful...you would not get a rash or an unprepared remark from him, he thinks before he speaks.' The young man paused to study his companion. She still had a certain look in her eyes perhaps not of fear, more a look of curiosity. 'What is your interest in this man?' he asked.'

The lady's eyes lowered. 'I had heard some things concerning him.'

'Good things I'm sure.'

The lady lifted her head sharply. 'He is a good man then?'

'Since you asked me, I think he is the best of men.'

This remark seemed to please the lady, for she tried to hide a smile.

Accolon reminded himself the lady was playing a part and decided to continue with her charade.

'I hope he has not stolen your lady...or anything of that sort?'

The lady looked confused for a moment, before shaking her head. 'Is he one for the ladies?' she asked.

'No, he is a loner. He often goes off for long periods by himself.'

The lines above the lady's eyes increased. 'Is he looking for someone?'

Accolon shrugged his shoulders. 'No one knows. Some say he is on a quest for the King, others that he is looking for some woman.'

The lady's hands began to tremble as fear returned to her eyes. Her voice stuttered a little. 'He would not hurt a lady...'

'He is bold in battle, but timid and shy with the fairer sex.'

The lady looked sicker than ever. Accolon went to her and offered his services. He made her lie on the bed and promised to return with some food immediately. The lady protested, but her weary body collapsed onto the bed and seemed unable to move. Accolon hurried and return within a short time, but by then the lady had fallen asleep.

8

Yvain had tried to escape on his first night of capture, managing as far as Dunollie. They came after him, recaptured him and beat him for his trouble. He vowed to try again the next night and every night until he had managed eventually to escape. He would endure their taunts and threats and await his chance. He saw for himself the harsh reality of life in the Irish community and was forced to do many horrible jobs; he was made to slop out their pigsty, to collect cow manure for fertilizing and take part with their women in the making of their stinking glue. After only a day, he quickly looked disordered, smelt of manure and resembled his captors.

Nemue was not like the rest of her Irish émigrés, perhaps because her blood was mixed, her father was Irish, but her mother was a Pict. She looked after her mother who was sick, but felt only hatred for her father, who lived in fear of his daughter. Ever since Nemue had turned six, she had shown certain powers. These powers came and went, but they could rear up at anytime, so people in the settlement generally kept their distance from her.

Yvain was sitting on the ground outside the smallest of the broch's, when he first spotted her. He realized immediately that she was different from the rest, for her clothes were clean and she walked with a certain stature unlike the rest of the Irish who seemed barbaric by comparison. She was carrying a basket of herbs and his attention was focused on her face and not on the two men to her right, who were heading in his direction. The men had their swords drawn, ready to inflict damage on his person.

The first man was called MacRoth; he was tall, broad, with a mass of red hair and a nasty habit of spitting on the ground. He came up to Yvain, spat at him and ordered him to his feet. Yvain pretended he did not understand and remained seated.

The second man was called Conall; he was even broader than his friend, with massive hands and a stoop that made him look smaller than he really was. He raged at the Celt. 'Get to your feet you lazy bastard.'

The power of his address reached Nemue, who ambled over to the scene to witness the encounter. MacRoth continued with similar abuse and kicked Yvain on his side. Yvain looked up at his abusers and said nothing. MacRoth went to kick him again, but Nemue's voice bellowed out at him. 'Leave him alone, he's not doing you any harm.'

MacRoth swung his head to the side, to see who had dared to intervene. He saw young Nemue and his manner changed. Yvain could have sworn he saw a look of fear in MacRoth's face. Conall also turned to look at the young woman. Neither man said a word, but both glanced at each other. To Yvain's astonishment, the men then took a tongue-lashing from the girl before moving away. Could it be he wondered that these strong men were afraid of this diminutive young maiden? He got to his feet and was about to thank her, when he noticed her eyes. They were bright blue and shone with an intensity that startled the viewer of them.

With a look of astonishment still on his face, Yvain spoke. 'Thank you, I could have handled them...but it was...'

'Of course you could have. With bullies, all you have to do is stand up to them.'

The girl began to move away. Yvain followed. 'Wait, I must talk with you.'

Nemue continued to walk at a quick pace, forcing Yvain to hurry. 'Why are you in such a rush? he asked.

'My mother is sick; I do not like to leave her alone too long.'

'I have to escape here...'

'Then escape,' the girl told him.
'I've tried...its not so easy.'

Nemue stopped, looked at Yvain. 'You want me to help you?'

After a moment's hesitation, Yvain admitted he did.

'You are rather weak.' Nemue took her right hand and placed it on the man's left bicep. 'You are not used to fighting, or doing manual labor?'

'I am a servant...'

'What do servants do?' the girl asked.

'Cook, run messages, look after horses...'

'You must be brave and learn to fight like a man, before I can help you to escape.'

'I've no desire to become like your friends...'

Nemue began to walk again. 'They're not my friends.'

Yvain caught up with her. 'If you hate them, why do you stay?'

'My mother needs me.'

'Will you help me?'

The girl stopped again, looked into the man's eyes. 'Yes, I will, but only if you do what I say.'

It was late and the sky was black and grey, only a sprinkling of light from the stars shone an uneven blanket over the encampment. Arthur had been abroad for some time and was near exhaustion by the time Lancelot came upon him. The two men were of similar age, but the burden of being King had left its toll on Arthur, who looked a good ten years older than his warrior friend. Lancelot, until his infatuation with Guinevere, had been fortunate to live a carefree existence. His friend's association with his wife could have proved a possible source of conflict between the two men, but Arthur seemed strangely uninterested in his wife's affairs.

Lancelot had become the lady's champion on the battlefield and in the bedchamber if you listened to rumours. The Queen had given him a ribbon of gold to wear around his arm, whenever he went into battle. This emblem of love was a token, often handed out by the noblewomen of the land to their champions. This token was not lost on the members at court and much gossip spread through the five kingdoms concerning it. Arthur surely knew about his wife's blatant act of betrayal, but he never commented on it.

Arthur saw his friend approach and spread out his arms in welcome. The two men embraced and smiled at one another.

'You always did have remarkable timing, my friend,' the King observed.

'Pure luck,' Lancelot replied.

Arthur agreed. 'How is my oldest friend?'

'I am well, but you look to be in need of more exercise.'

Lancelot patted the King on the stomach and chuckled.

Arthur laughed, as the two men walked away from the wounded.

'How is the Queen?' Lancelot asked.

'No idea, she doesn't seem fit to tell me much these days.'

'Women,' exclaimed Lancelot.

The King lifted up the canvas of the tent and ushered Lancelot inside. The tent was empty, but for a sleeping roll on the floor and a small table, that housed several maps. After drinking some inferior wine, the two men opened the maps and began to plan.

'You favor a quick and decisive attack?' asked Lancelot.

'Strike now and we destroy them before reinforcements arrive,' said Arthur.

Lancelot hesitated, turned his gaze away from the King's.

'You disagree?' asked Arthur.'

'No, it's not that. I don't understand why you picked a fight with the Romans, in the first place.'

'Your information is wrong, they picked the fight...'

'They were concerned at your sudden expansion...'

'I have not entered their territory...'

'Not yet, but it looked likely.'

Arthur's fists were closed as he put his hands down on the table with a thud. Lancelot knew his anger from old, but he also knew his King had too much sense to continue on into Egypt, Syria and beyond. After a long silence Lancelot offered an answer to the King's problem.

'Let me see if we can negotiate an end to the hostilities?'

'After what happened today, do you really think they'll accept peace now?'

'A long war with the Romans would be a godsend to your other enemies.'

Arthur swung his head round to stare at his old friend. 'Have you heard something?' he inquired.

'Nothing specific, just rumors...'

'What rumors?'

'There's talk of unrest in the north.'

'There's always unrest there, I'm sure Lot can handle...'

'No I didn't mean in Lot's kingdom. My informants tell me King Pelles has been stirring resentment against the Saxons in his area.'

'Pelles is a fool.'

'Yes, he is,' a smiling Lancelot acknowledged.

'You think someone else is responsible?'

Lancelot hesitated.

A thought occurred to the King. 'Have you ever heard of a bishop by the name of Germanus?'

'No I haven't. Do you think he is behind it?'

The Lady Morgan read the message, as a devoted nun reads her scriptures. She devoured every word, every syllable and reread it several times over, before finally crumbling it in her hand in disappointment. The lady knew that too often in the past whenever the King needed to be strong, he would dither and be indecisive. He swore he knew nothing of the theft from Avalon and did not see any reason for his immediate return. Morgan felt abandoned by her brother, just like so many others of his loyal subjects the length and breathe of the kingdom.

With her mood becoming darker, a servant entered her chamber to bring her news that Merlin had returned. She was informed he had brought a visitor with him. The Lady Ygerne received her guests in the great hall of her dead husband's castle. She welcomed Columba to her home, and spent a long time discussing his unique community with him. This allowed Merlin to make a full report to Morgan on his unsuccessful journey and to make one surprising suggestion to her. He volunteered to go to the King and plead for the treasure directly. 'Give me a message and I will make him listen to reason.'

'I should go, I am his sister...'

'You are still too weak. Let me do this for you.'

'You have no doubt that Arthur stole the treasure?'

'Do you?' asked Merlin.

The lady shook her head.

'I only hope he will listen to reason.'

'I shall make him listen, my lady.'

'He might arrest you and strap you in irons.'

'I am prepared to take that chance.'

'You surprise me with your courage.'

'When you have nothing else to live for, courage seems hardly to matter.'

'When we retire, I will send you my correspondence.'

Merlin nodded his head.

9

Helena's fear had returned. Titius had not returned and the night had fallen, bringing with it, its strange noises. The lady stayed in his tent and every now and again looked out to see if the guards were still present. They had not moved, but she heard a great deal of chattering between them. She could make out that the army had been embroiled in a scrimmage, and that things had not gone well.

The thought that her protector had perished, filled the lady with dread. At any moment some Roman soldier might enter and thrust a sword through her body. This was her situation as she waited for the dreaded moment to arrive. She heard a commotion, but before she could investigate two soldiers carrying Titius entered the tent and laid him down on his bunk. The lady did not wait to offer her help, she directed the soldiers to bring her what she needed, which was water, a cutting knife and some ointment to bathe the man's wound. They did what they were told.

This was the first time she had ever treated an injured man before, but she had witnessed physicians on several occasions. Her care was surprisingly proficient and the lady had bandaged his leg by the time a Roman physician arrived on the scene. After examining the wound, the physician declared Titius would make a full recovery and that his leg was not in danger of infection.

The lady was alarmed at the degree of emotion she felt concerning his welfare. Was it just for her own safety that her feelings were excited, or did she feel some attachment to this man? Titius swore at all present and dismissed everyone from his tent except the lady. He pointed to a cabinet beside his bed and asked the girl to open it. Helena did what she was asked.

Inside the cabinet was a bottle of liquor, which the girl took out and gave to the man. Titius took two swigs from the bottle, then heaved a sigh and fell back on his bunk. He turned his head to look at the young woman. 'Your people don't believe in playing by any rules,' he declared.

'I'm sorry. I didn't know war had any rules,' the girl replied. Her voice was so full of compassion that the man reached out his hand to touch hers. She saw no reason to withhold it and took the man's hand in her own. 'Does it hurt awfully?' she asked.

'You must think I'm rather a poor warrior.'

The girl smiled, shook her head. 'I think you men are crazy for hurting each other so.'

Yvain had soon mastered all the basic moves required by every soldier in any army. To his surprise he learnt what Nemue taught him quickly. She was patient and took her time in explaining every move and every counter move. She also managed to smuggle him food every night, to help arrest his growing hunger. This had the effect of improving his physical condition, but unknown to the man she was feeding him more than just potatoes and meat. She mixed in some special ingredients of her own, that had the effect of building up his muscles and caused him to be more alert. As the days passed he got stronger, but this did not stop his tormentors, as they continued as before. MacRoth in particular would not leave him alone with his verbal and physical assaults. He made their encounters ever more acrimonious, until Yvain wondered if he had a private reason for hating him so.

MacRoth followed Nemue one night, as she made her usual rendezvous with Yvain. He waited behind a wall and watched, as they fought with their wooden swords. He witnessed a certain amount of affection between the two and his belly filled up with jealousy. The unattainable girl that everyone feared had always fascinated him. His love had been twisted inside of him over the years, until he felt nothing but hatred for her now. The sight of her, enjoying the company of this Celtic pig, only made his anger grow more.

'Come away with me?' Yvain pleaded.

Nemue stopped fighting and said nothing. She looked down at the ground at her feet.

'You still do not use your feet properly,' she attested.

'Is your mother not strong enough to travel?' the man asked.

'I feel she is close to death.'

'I wish I could help you.'

Nemue smiled at the Celt. 'The beast that is MacRoth will take me once you leave this place.'

'How do you know this?' Yvain asked.

'I can see it. I have the ability to see things still to happen.'

'How is that possible?'

'I do not know, but it has happened before.'

'Will you not change the future if you leave with me now?'

'I can not leave my poor mother to die here all alone.'

'Are you sure there is no other way?' Yvain asked.

'If you fear retribution afterwards, I can assure you no one will find his body. MacRoth, even the sound of his ugly name makes me shiver with fear,'

'I am ready to carry out the task.'

Yvain moved closer to Nemue and kissed her on the mouth.

MacRoth was aware that his breathing was louder and his hands were covered in sweat. He had overhead a plot to murder someone and realized suddenly that the plot was to murder him. Without thinking he decided to confront his would be assassins and turn the tables on them. He ran forward with his sword drawn, ready to strike down Yvain where he stood. Luckily the girl's reactions were quick and she pushed Yvain out of the way and stood ready to defend the assault with her wooden sword. Nemue's wooden sword was no match for MacRoth's steel, but her quickness of feet kept the girl alive long enough for Yvain to grab him round the waist and wrestle the man to the ground.

As the two men struggled on the forest floor, Nemue reached into her belt and withdrew a dagger. She rushed forward hoping to help Yvain, but the two men tumbled around in the dirt, making it impossible to tell one from the other. Finally the Irishman knocked Yvain backwards and the young man seemed unable to get back to his feet. Nemue could see that one lunge from MacRoth's sword would finish her friend, but the girl was quicker than her opponent and plunged her dagger into the man's side before he could strike the fatal blow. Nemue had used all the strength in her slender body to stab him, but saw that one blow was not enough. She grabbed the man's sword from his grasp and forced it into his body, like a seasoned warrior. He gasped for breath for a moment before keeling over on his side, dead.

Guinevere waited until first light, before issuing orders to all Christian warriors at Caerleon to make ready. The lady felt better for taking action and not having to wait for men to make decisions. The unrest in Corbenic had given her the excuse to go into that region and drive out the heathen Angles. Once that had been achieved, then the conquest of righteousness would continue throughout the north cleansing the land of paganism she hoped forever.

She had not informed the King, nor did she intend too. Morgan was busy with a private affair, while Pelles and Ursien had given their support for the venture. Having often complained to Arthur about the foreign threat, the Kings gave their support readily in the hope of quelling the increase of more immigrants.

As she sat eating her simple meal of oats and milk, her thoughts turned to her two biggest foes, Arthur and Morgan. She would take Gorlois's castle at Cadbury and imprison all those within. A little insurance might come in handy she thought. For many years the women of the Gorlois house had been a thorn in her side; Elaine had tried to possess Lancelot, Morgan had tried to surpass her as Queen, while Ygerne had tried to poison Uther against her, even before she had come to the throne.

The Lady Elaine had already paid a terrible price with her meddling; now the others would feel the wrath of her vengeance too.

An attendant entered the room to inform Guinevere that everyone was ready and awaiting her appearance. She got up from her seat, told the attendant to saddle her horse and went to her bedchamber. In entering her room, she sank to her knees and stretched her hand to reach a lever. She pulled the lever to release a secret door behind her bed. She entered her secret chamber and pulled another lever from behind the wall, to close the door behind her. She felt happier, more secure in her private sanctum, away from prying eyes.

The room was small and dark, only one torch hung on the stone wall. The defused light still allowed the Queen enough light to see the contents of the room. On one side of the room was a chest of drawers, where a large amount of clothes lay neatly folded. The largest part of the room however, was taken up with what can only be described as a private armory. Two large wooden cabinets housed a vast array of arms, from swords and spears, to daggers and shields of every description. Several items were Roman, but others came from further afield, such as Carthage, Antioch and Palestine.

This was a rare assortment of warfare, put together by someone with an ardent interest in the subject. This secret side of the Queen's nature had remained hidden, just like her private chamber. She looked and behaved as a woman in society, but her nature was somewhat different from most other women. She hated the silly talk that her own sex often indulged in and craved the company of men. She reveled in their stories of heroism and longed to go forth with them whenever war broke out. She knew God had made a terrible mistake in making her a woman, but he had made her strong for a reason. That reason she believed was to be a leader of men, a leader to all her subjects.

She quickly changed from her usual courtly dress to her new attire of a man's warrior dress. She wore over her upper body, a suit of chainmail beneath her plain colored shirt. Around her waist the lady wore a belt of silver, adorned by a Christian cross. Attached to the belt was a silver sheath which housed the finest of Roman swords. A Queen could ride out to battle looking just as magnificent as any King she thought.

10

After her conversation with Merlin, Morgan went for a walk alone around the grounds she knew so well. She was hoping for some time alone, but the bustling figure of Lot came towards her to disturb her solitude. He stopped by her side and sought to engage her in conversation. 'I am glad to have a chance to converse with you, my lady,' he said.

Morgan suspected the man was going to give her a lecture concerning her sister Elaine, but she was mistaken for the man broached the subject of politics.

'I didn't just come to find my wife...I also came to converse with you on matters of state,' he informed the lady.

Almost as if someone had shaken her, Morgan suddenly appeared more interested. 'This is not the place for such things,' she advised. 'You could put your information before the full council at the harvest feast.'

'This can not wait until then,' he told her.

King Lot was a blunt man and blurted out his reason in addressing the lady. 'The King is under threat from forces within,' he told her.

Morgan had no idea what he meant. Her reaction to his startling statement confirmed his suspicions the lady was ignorant of any conspiracy.

'The Queen has raised an army and has set in motion a plan I believe to oust the King.'

'She must be mad. She could never succeed in such a thing.'

'You know of the unrest in Corbenic?'

'Yes, something of it, but that is surely nothing new...'

King Lot stared at Morgan. She in turn stared back. The two were measuring each other and contemplating whither they should trust one another.

'It is not what it seems. The Queen means to smash the Angle settlement there.'

'In what pretext can she do that.'

'The trouble started because of Pelles's insistence in banning all religious ceremonies that were not Christian.'

'And the Queen has backed him?'

'I believe the suggestion came from her.'

Morgan laughed. 'Yes that would be like our tolerant Queen. I have reason to believe she has her heart set on destroying me also.'

'We must do something to stop her, my lady.'

'I will send word to Arthur to return at once.'

Lot seemed relieved. 'Will he come?' he asked.

She spoke while nodding her head. 'This day's been coming for some time. Merlin will insist on him coming back home.

Mordred landed in Britain at Dover and travelled with his fifty men towards Londinium. He felt for the first time in his life alive and full of his own importance. Just the thought that the King had asked for his help, had reinvigorated his own existence. He was determined to prove to his brothers he was their equal. The man cared only for one of his brothers, his name was Gaheris. His brother was a studious man and known for his learning as well as his fighting skills. He was three years older than Mordred and very popular with his men. His choice seemed perfect, for no one had a better awareness of the every changing face of the Christian church than he.

Londinium seemed a good place to start looking for the bishop. It was a provincial capital and almost as important as York or Canterbury. It also housed the best wine in the country and the good bishop was renowned for his love of the claret. Two days and nights were spent looking in taverns, churches and brothels, but this brought no reward. Mordred moved further inland and scoured the countryside, but no one admitted to having seen or heard of the man.

It was Gaheris who suggested sending word to all five Kings, asking for their assistance. Even with some of the Kings abroad, their kin would know if such a man were amongst them at their court. This would take some time and so Mordred and his men decided to find a base and await word. He had no thoughts on the matter himself, so he left the details to his brother. For reasons only known to Gaheris, the band of men moved further west to the town of Cirencester.

Mordred did not query this and while his men found accommodation in shabby inns or small farms, he, Gaheris, and a priest called James stayed at the nearby castle.

His host, the Duke of Mador was not at home, but his wife Hester entertained them with good wine, food and a song or two. There was something about the lady's manner that suggested to Mordred that their visit had come at an inconvenient time. Hester was the Duke's second wife and still young, perhaps that was the reason she appeared nervous and a little ill-temperate, thought the young man. He had the impression the lady was concealing something and speculated just what that could be. He could see the lady's hands trembling and concluded that maybe she was hiding a young lover.

With his daydreaming complete, Mordred began to take an interest in the conversation between Lady Hester, her step-daughter Megan, and brother James. Megan was asking the good brother a question. 'Do you think it right...that a young girl should be forced to marry before she is of age?'

The priest's face was a study as he shook his head. 'No I believe the King is right to put a stop to the unholy practice of marrying children to older men. What age are you, child?' he asked.

'I am thirteen, but my father has already arranged my marriage.'

Hester cut in. 'The man is of good family of course and has land of his own.'

'The King views such marriages as unhealthy and has attested that the age of consent should be fifteen.'

'Yes, but does not the church contest this, brother?' Hester asked.

'Only the more radical clerics, but I am happy to say I am not one of them.'

Gaheris's attention seemed to wander and he waved to a servant present to come to him. Mordred couldn't hear what was being said, but he was intrigued by his brother's secrecy. The servant bent his head forward and listened as Gaheris whispered in his ear.

'Have you any news on the girl?' Gaheris asked.

'No sir, the last word I heard was of a possible sighting of two men headed towards Glastonbury.'

Gaheris looked confused.

'One of the young men was particularly boyish in appearance...'

'I see.'

'I gave the order for your man to follow and investigate.'

'Good. Once my business is finished here, I hope to spend a little time in Britain. I will want full reports from all my scouts.'

The servant nodded and moved away from Gaheris.

Guinevere found the precaution for attack at the Cadbury Castle to be nothing short of a disgrace, and the Lady Ygerne's humble forces a shambles. So much the better from her point of view of course, for it made the capture of the lady's castle little more than a formality. The Queen, in full battledress, stormed through the doors of Ygerne's great hall with a dozen of her most trusted men and quashed the last remaining resistance.

The Lady Ygerne was alone apart from Morgause, having said goodbye to Morgan and all her guests the day before. Lot had promised to return in a few days, after concluding some business in Glastonbury, while Morgan travelled some of the way with Merlin, before leaving him to travel to Tintagel. The sea breezes of Tintagel would help her recover and let her think, while the soothsayer tracked down the King. She had given him a fine pair of ravens, her trusted birds and her carrier of messages if he was in need of her assistance.

Ygerne was standing alone by the window, looking out over the ghastly picture of wanton destruction, when the Queen entered. Guinevere was the first to break the silence. 'You do not bow before your Queen?' she shouted at the lady.

Lady Ygerne was slow to turn and face her sister-in-law, when she did she had a broad smile on her face. 'I do not bow before traitors,' she replied.

The Queen walked towards her, stopped a few feet away, drew out a dagger and held it close to the lady's face. The point of the dagger rested firmly at the lady's chin. 'I have waited a long time for this moment and I intend to savor my victory.'

The Lady Ygerne did not flinch, but continued to smile. 'Enjoy your moment, for that is all it will be, once my son gets home.'

Guinevere took the dagger away from the face of the lady and returned it to its sheath. 'He is slightly distracted at the moment by thousands of Romans,' she informed the lady.

Ygerne did not answer.

'Perhaps he shall not return this time, after all his luck must run out sometime.'

The Lady Ygerne had the distinct feeling the lady was referring to some forthcoming disaster.

'Do you plan to kill my son and take the throne?'

Guinevere laughed. 'My, you do get to the point, lady. I'd thought I would leave the Romans to take care of him, they are better at killing than I. As for the throne, well I am but a feeble woman. Of course there might be better claims...'

'The Kings would never agree to you being put on the throne.'

'Wouldn't they,' Guinevere contested, 'strange then that two such Kings have already pledged allegiance to me. I feel the others will soon follow...'

'Morgan would never agree.'

'Alas, her days of power are coming to an end.'

The Queen began to stroll amongst the fine furniture and ornaments that decorated the main room in the castle. 'It's nice here, but I could never understand why you chose not to live with us at Caerleon?'

'Couldn't you,' Ygerne stated sharply.

Guinevere wasn't sure just what she was going to do with the Lady Ygerne, but her taste veered towards the exotic and the painful.

Ygerne stared at the lady's strange costume; her face was a mixture of contempt and bewilderment. 'A chameleon may change its appearance, but a snake never can.'

The Queen pretended to laugh, but inside she was seething. 'That tongue will be the death of you, lady.'

Guinevere made a sign to two of her guards, who then forced the Lady Ygerne to the table. She sat at the head of it, as a quill was dipped in dark dye and forced into her hand. Guinevere took from a satchel, a piece of parchment and placed it down beside Ygerne on the table. 'You will sign this and then you can take up your new residence in the dungeon.'

'I will sign nothing,' Ygerne asserted.

'I shall read it to you. It states that you and your daughter, the Lady Morgan plotted to overthrow the King.'

'I plotted against my own son, who would believe such nonsense.'

'It doesn't matter what anyone believes. It will give me the legitimacy to hang you and burn the witch for treason.'

'You can not make me sign this,' Ygerne cried.

'Oh, didn't I say. If you do not I will be forced to kill every member of your staff. '

'I don't believe any woman bore you, only a mad dog could have conceived such evil.'

Taking out her dagger again the Queen slammed it down on the lady's left hand. Blood oozed over the table as Ygerne screamed.

70

'Sign it now, before I tear your hand off,' the Queen screamed.

Still Ygerne refused to sign. Just before the Queen withdrew her dagger from the hand of Ygerne, one of Guinevere's men entered the great hall. 'Your grace, I have found something quite peculiar,' he stated. His expression was hard to read, but his brow was tight and his face looked spooked.

Sounding irritable the Queen asked what he meant, before yanking her dagger from Ygerne's hand.

Lady Ygerne screamed in pain before shouting abuse at Guinevere.

The soldier answered his Queen. 'I have found a body, my lady,'

'And what's so peculiar about that,' the Queen shouted.

'It's the body of the Lady Elaine.'

'Don't talk nonsense – the lady has been dead for more than ten days.'

'I think you should come and see for yourself,' the man asserted.

As Guinevere turned her head to look at Ygerne, it was not pain she saw in the lady's eyes but fear.

11

Several hours had pasted since the recommencement of the battle and Helena was seated alone in the Roman commander's tent, praying for his safe return. Titius could hardly walk, but still managed to mount his horse and ride at the front of his army. With a terrible uneasiness, Helena finally exited her safe haven and strode onto the desolate battlefield. The bodies were stacked up on carts, like dead fish waiting to go to market. She witnessed hundreds of carts and hundreds of bodies, and some wounded men hopping about as much in a daze as she was herself. There was noise everywhere, of men weeping, yelling and cheering. The voices of the Celtic army were bellowing their victory, while the defeated Roman army was whimpering in pain and despair.

The yelling increased in intensity and the lady looked in the direction of whence it came. She was shocked to witness a group of Celtic soldiers fixing ropes around tree branches. It was clear they meant to hang as many of their captors as they could possibly find. A series of nooses hung tantalizingly above a group of helpless prisoners. Helena didn't want to watch, but her eyes could not be torn away from the ghastly sight. She fixed them on the helpless row of lifeless captives and saw to her horror her rescuer. The man was calmness itself, and did not make a sound; he even had a smile upon his face. It was clear to the lady that the man had made his peace with God and was ready to meet his maker.

Helena ran forward towards the ghastly scene, yelling for the men to stop, but a Celtic soldier swung a blow at her and with the butt of his sword struck the lady across the face. She cried out in pain, as she fell to the ground. The soldier thought his eyes had deceived him, when the lady staggered to her feet and whipped the blood from her mouth. Just as the soldier was about to repeat his actions, a blow from a sword ripped the man's head clear from his shoulders. His head hit the ground with a thud. Helena quickly turned her head to see King Arthur on horseback beside her, his sword dripping with blood.

'Take down those ropes you miserable sons of bitches,' he yelled. Arthur turned and looked at the blooded maiden. 'Why do you never do what I say?'

'Is this how you treat your prisoners?' the lady cried.

'They are far too valuable to die like this,' Arthur retorted.

'What do you mean?'

Arthur was tired of all the bloodshed and wanted to clean the blood from the maiden's mouth. He got off his horse and went to greet the lady, but if he expected the lady to rush into his arms, he was sadly disappointed. Instead she brushed past him and marched up to the band of prisoners and started giving orders to all the King's men. Arthur's men all looked to their King for guidance.

Nemue stood alone, near the edge of the cliff, as the rest of the village stood some distance back from her. Many feared her anger, for the girl had just lost her mother and was desolate in her bereavement. The whole Irish community had gathered to look upon the spectacle that the outlander was delivering. It had been a few days since the disappearance of MacRoth and Yvain and people were still chattering about the affair. Most felt MacRoth had gone after the Celt and would bring him back beaten and exhausted within a day or so. When that did not happen, more colorful suggestions then followed, including the suggestion of murder.

The young maiden had painted her face with different colored dyes, crimson, amber and blue and was standing completely naked looking out to sea. Her nakedness attracted a great deal of attention, particularly from the youthful males of the village. Nemue's voice vibrated into the air, her voice sounded strangely powerful in the language of the Picts, a tongue no one else in the camp could understand. She was standing in front of a wooden and stone built vault that looked somewhat improvised. The wood somehow held together the pile of loose stones that were haphazardly arranged around the structure. The grave, for that is what it was, stood some feet from the edge of a cliff facing out to sea. The words that Nemue spoke over the grave were roughly these:

'I will not forget your beautiful head, or your beautiful smile that warmed my very being. Nor will I forget all the kind words we exchanged together over the years. I choose to remember the times we laughed and not the times we cried and I choose to tell my unborn children how unfortunate they are never to have witnessed your warmth and kindness. I call to the Gods to lead you from this darkness, into the light that is their kingdom. I hope to see you again my beloved mother.'

Nemue raised her arms outwards and began to chant a dirge. She sang for quite awhile, until her voice became soar and she could not sing anymore. When this time came, she put her clothes back on and moved towards the Irish camp.

All but a few people had lost interest in the spectacle, but standing waiting patiently was her father Capa, with Conall and a few other men, who were members from the settlement council.

'I am sorry for your loss,' Conall told the maiden.

The girl waited for her father to speak, but he held his tongue.

'I thank you for letting me send her off in this way,' the girl acknowledged.

All the men greeted her words with approval, before her father addressed her. 'Daughter, the council has made a decision,' he stated.

'I know your decision,' Nemue said. 'You are frightened I will kill you all in your sleep.'

'We fear your magic and your temper,' Conall admitted.

'You have never seen my anger or my magic,' she told Conall.

'No, but your father has. He has told us of a time you threw him through the air and he couldn't walk for a week.'

'Did he also tell you the reason why?' the girl asked.

The men all looked uncomfortable and Conall even began to sweat.

'I never imagined I would be welcomed to stay,' admitted Nemue. She then stared at her father, before addressed him alone. 'I will never forgive you for the cruelty you handed out to my mother. If our paths ever cross again I will strike you down where you stand.'

There was terrible silence and Capa couldn't tell if the men beside him stood in judgment of him or not. He waited for some indication of support from them, but no one spoke up for him, perhaps they felt his daughter's wrath was justified.

Having finished what she had to say, the young girl then went inside her broch and took her few possessions and was about to leave when Conall entered.

'I never knew,' the man said. 'We never knew he was such a harsh father or husband.'

'Would it have made any difference?'

'Perhaps I could have said something to him.'

'It doesn't matter now. I am free of him for good.'

'Where will you go?'

'I don't know, but as far away from here as I can.'

Conall took from his skin coat a small bundle and offered it to the girl. A look of bewilderment flashed across the girl's face.

'What is this?' the girl asked.

'It isn't much. A little food, a small knife and three silver coins.'

Nemue opened the bundle which was wrapped up a clean piece of cloth and saw the contents that Conall described. Her eyes looked up and stared at the big cumbersome man standing before her. She was waiting for an explanation while he was looking for some words to hide his embarrassment.

'The food is most welcome, as for the knife I'm sure it will find a use for it, but where in the name of the Gods did you get the coins.'

'The Celtic youth, he had it on him when we caught him. I think they use it to trade in their lands.'

Nemue looked down at the items in his hands and took them unto her own.

'You liked the youth and if you were thinking of living in their world, the coins will be most useful.'

The maiden's eyes looked into Conall's, her tears trickled down her cheeks.

'This is a sad day, but you have put a little joy into it. I thank you for that.'

The maiden put the bundle into her satchel and prepared to leave. She left the settlement in a hurry, running to her horse and not turning around. She jumped up on the animal and was riding away from the camp before Conall could say his last farewell.

The Celtic army was in good spirits for they were heading home a great deal wealthier, with hostages, gold, jewels, and weapons. One Celt however was not happy and that was the Lady Helena. The lady refused a wagon and was riding side-saddle behind Arthur and his leading group of riders. Her companions at her side were the younger warriors, Bors, Agarvain and Gawain. As the party continued onwards in the harsh sunlight, Helena continually glanced over her shoulder towards the cages where the prisoners were held.

Seeing the lady's interest, Gawain was curious and moved his horse alongside the lady's. 'Is there something back there that interests you, my lady?' he asked.

Helena looked away from Gawain and did not answer.

He smiled, seemed to think her interest was amusing so he pursued the matter further. 'Don't feel sorry for the prisoners, the enemy treat our prisoners far worse.'

Helena turned her head and stared rigorously at the young warrior.

'They did not treat me badly. They did not cage me like a wild animal.'

The vigor that the lady spoke rather took Gawain by surprise and he found himself at a loss to rebuke her statement.

Bors came up on the opposite side to Gawain and engaged in the discussion. His manner was more matter of a fact. 'We treat our prisoners humanely, we give them food and water and we do not beat them.'

Helena now turned to look at Bors. 'I can't help but notice that we keep women and children in these cages.'

'They would run off if we did not,' the man informed her.

'Why do we need them, surely they are of little value? 'she proclaimed.

'Some have importance, members of their nobility for instance. They will be exchanged for our own prisoners or sold back to the Romans for gold.'

Helena's stare became more pronounced. 'We sell people?' she questioned.

'It is a common practice. I believe it was the Romans who started this particular profitable practice.'

'And the rest, the ordinary prisoners?' the lady asked.

'They will be sold as slaves, probably in Paris.'

Helena's reaction to this piece of information left Bors in bewilderment. He could not understand why the lady was so interested in the enemy's wellbeing.

Bors and Agarvain excused themselves a short time after, leaving Gawain as the only representative of Celtic manhood left to defend their honor. He tried once more to placate the lady, but she was adamant in her condemnation.

12

Nemue travelled over land and sea and was now approaching her final destination, the Isles of Avalon. Although the group of Islands was out of bounds to all humans, the lady of the lake had given her precise instructions to avoid detection. Sitting low in her small boat, she managed to hide below the boat's rim as she passed the other Islands. She could hear her heart beat as if it was about to burst from her body as she approached the final Island, the island called Foaine.

The Island was empty of animals, vegetation and humans, only one God called it home, although fairies from the underworld visited the lady every day. This last Island was a good distance out from the rest and had two important features; the first was a huge rugged rock carved out by nature, this massive structure stood to one side of the Island and towered over everything else, the second feature was a lake unlike any other. It was sheltered thanks to the mountain and devoid of any real breeze which made life extremely pleasant for the lady that reigned there.

The God that the young Nemue had come to see had not revealed her name, so the girl called her simply the lady of the lake. No human other than the girl knew of her existence, not even Arthur who had benefited from her magic.

The lady of the lake had come to the young maiden in a dream some time past and had summoned her to visit her magical Island. This was Nemue's first visit, as the boat navigated around the huge rock its sharp features appeared through the mist, startling her in its scale. Although a good sailor, the girl had no need to guide the boat, because it glided itself towards the middle of the lake, where it suddenly stopped.

The Goddess erupted like some volcano from the lake, splashing the waves over the small boat, making it rock from side to side. Nemue was fortunate not to fall overboard, as she stood transfixed by the creature that appeared before her. The lady of the lake appeared at first sight, like any young woman; she was completely naked down to her waist, her breasts were small, her hair was long and swept below the water, her face was serene with soft lines, her cheeks were crimson, like a fresh apple's. Nemue's eyes could not see beneath the water, to see the lady's legs and feet. What she would have seen was not like any human form, for the lady's body was completely amphibious below her waist; she had skin on the upper part of her body, but scales and a tail of a large amphibian creature on her lower body.

The lady of the lake was a creature of the water, completely happy to live in her own small domain away from all humans. Untroubled by any predators of the sea; her reign over her kingdom was unchallenged. Around her head swarmed a cornucopia of noise and movement, as fairies buzzed and hovered over the lady's face and body. These creatures were like her children who fetched and carried for her, keeping the lady informed of the world outside her realm. The fairies' wings flapped through the air, making a constant humming noise. Their wings gave them access to the human world which was useful for their mistress.

Nemue seemed aware that the lady was not in the best of moods by the fact that her lips were tightly shut and she did not welcome her young protégée with a smile. The lady's hand swiped at the fairies around her face with air of displeasure. 'Get out of my face you band of pixies,' she scolded.

Nemue smiled at the fairies, as they changed their aim of attack and began to circle around her now, with their squeaky language of senseless chatter. The girl couldn't understand what they said and asked the lady to interpret.

'Oh, don't encourage them, they're been in a ghastly mood all day,' the water goddess warned.

79

'They are adorable,' Nemue articulated.

The lady rebuffed the statement, but answered the girl's question after a short pause. 'They think you are nice and should stay with us awhile to keep us company.'

'Can I?' the girl asked.

'Stay as long as you want, but remember if you stay too long you'll begin to lose the power of your limbs and become a creature of the water.'

Nemue thought that might be fun and was happy to declare as much to the others. The lady finally managed to convince her that it was premature to abandon the world of the humans.

The fairies were banished to the shore by the lady, so that she could talk to the girl in quietness.

'I came as soon as I could,' Nemue stated.

'Yes, I heard an alarming tale concerning the death of a man at your hands.'

Nemue lowered her head.

'Is the tale true? 'the lady asked.

'I'm afraid it is, but I did not have a choice,' the girl pleaded in her defense.

'I know the basic facts and I do not find you at fault. There is a problem nonetheless if stories like this get known. You understand what I mean?'

'Yes, that is one reason I left the settlement.'

'Yes that was wise. Where will you go child?'

'I will find my way.'

'You have given the boy Yvain, something that once belonged to me.'

Nemue's head looked up at the lady. 'Forgive me! I knew I could always find him again no matter where he was.'

'He means that much to you?'

'I have never been in love before, but the ache I feel must mean something.'

'It means you are human, and like all humans prone to displays of irrational emotion.'

'I'm sorry if I have displeased you.'

The lady smiled, offered the girl something that she took from around her own neck. The necklace she gave away was dripping wet and looked very like the one Nemue had given to Yvain.

'You will not part with this one I hope?' the lady asked.

Nemue took the necklace and put it around her neck.

'I will not part with it, I give you my promise.'

The lady accepted the girl's pledge, but still looked anxious.

'You have been practicing your skills I hope?'

'Yes, but it has not been easy,' the girl stated.

'Forgive me, I know about your misfortune. It is not easy for me to understand this human affliction called death.'

'It is a dark and fearful thing,' the girl told her.

'Would you like to forgo ever having to go through it?' the lady asked.

'Is that possible?'

'If you did commit to this life, you might not have to be a creature only of the lake.'

'I don't understand?'

'The fairies go back and forth from the land of the humans and this land. It might be possible for you to do likewise.'

Nemue's eyes opened wider, the idea seemed to intrigue her.

'It sounds wonderful, but would I lose my legs?'

'No Nemue, you would have the best of both worlds. The wisdom and magic I can bestow on you here could help you in the other world too.'

Nemue agreed to the lady's plans. She longed to know more about the lady's magic and to explore the lake. The fairies came back and a party full of merriment and joy then lasted until the night began to fall.

Before Nemue set out to return to the mainland, the god asked her to pay a visit to Tintagel to persuade Morgan to visit her. 'Take the fairies with you. They can help the lady to come here unseen.'

'Do you wish me to return with her?'

'No, you can spend sometime with your young man, just be careful not to mention me in any of your conversations.'

Nemue was happy and told the lady she would do as she wished.

13

As the night fell upon the army, and the tents were being erected, the soldiers were settling in for their quiet night under the stars. The air was sweet after a rainstorm, but the grass was still wet and the ground was more than a touch muddy. Helena disguised herself the best she could, wearing a hooded cloak and a servant's costume and began to wander through the camp. She saw for herself that the prisoners were guarded well and particularly the ones deemed of special value. Titius was not alone in his cage; he had another soldier with him, which meant she would be releasing two prisoners and not one. The worry of this quickly vanished, when she witnessed for herself the guards in situ and how they were armed, with swords and spears.

She had hoped the darkness would help, but it was a clear night and the stars were shining brightly. The majority of the soldiers were now asleep, as Helena took her time and moved within a short distance of the prisoner's compound. A guard came up to her and advised her to move away. This she did, but only by moving a short distance. She dropped to the ground in-between two warriors who were fast asleep. She was aware that timing would be all important, and she waited.

As the night unfolded, the air grew cold and the guards longed for the day to come and their duty to end. The guards nearest to Titius's cage began to whisper amongst themselves. Helena strolled up to them and asked their help in a wager. The soldiers seemed interested in finding out just what this wager was and in the lady herself.

Keeping her hood up, the lady was clever enough to show various parts of her young and perfectly formed body to the men. While the men were half listening and half watching the lady's legs, she asked for their opinion. She had two wooden cups, one in each hand and she offered them to the guards. 'I can not tell which of these two brewed drinks taste the best?' she declared.

The guards both smiled. They could be forgiven in thinking that they were living some wonderful dream. Both the men sipped from one cup, then swapped and tasted the brew from the other. They both looked at each, seemed to agree that one was better than another. The taller of the two men pointed to the cup in his hand. 'This I think is the strongest and the best.'

His friend disagreed. 'Mine tasted sweeter, mine is the best.'

Helena seemed interested in their judgment. 'Perhaps you both should finish each others just to make sure you haven't misjudged.'

The men agreed and swapped the cups again and drank the last of the brewed concoction. They both agreed that their elixirs were strong and they were correct, for both contained a strong drug that the lady had persuaded a physician to give to her, to help her sleep.

It was not long before one and then the other fell asleep and flopped to the ground. The sound they made when falling might have alerted their fellow guards, but they either did not hear, or were half asleep themselves for they did not stir. Helena searched the men's bodies and found a bunch of keys. Without jangling them too much, she tried one set, then the other. The second set opened the cage and the lady found Titius was awake, although his compatriot was not. As he stepped out of his cage he wondered who it was that was offering his freedom.

Helena stood back expecting him to run for cover.

'Who are you?' Titius asked.

Helena was reluctant to answer. 'You must run towards the trees to your right,' the lady advised him.

Titius smiled. 'It is you my lady,' he announced. 'Do you realize what you are doing?'

Helena lowered her voice and came up close to the Roman. 'Please run now, before the other guards suspect something.'

To her amazement the man refused to budge.

'This will not go well for you. They may put you in prison.'

'The guards will never recognize me,' Helena assured him. 'It will be alright, so long as you go now.'

'Will I ever see you again?' he asked.

'Who can say,' the lady replied.

The man kissed the lady on the cheek and ran towards the forest. Helena watched as he ran with like a primitive animal twisting its way through the forest to safety.

The decision to bury Elaine was given by the Queen as the sun was about to go down. She had no ceremony and allowed only a few witnesses to see a local priest give his blessing. Elaine's short burial took place on the grounds of the castle, but her mother was not present. She was chained like an animal in the dungeon in almost total darkness. Before sunup either Ygerne or Morgause would have to administer the ointment to Elaine or her body would rot and turn to dust. As Ygerne contemplated her dilemma she fought her mounting despair to somehow remain optimistic. Her only hope she realized would come when the Queen left, and one of her servants might help her to escape. As luck would have it, for some reason Accolon was not imprisoned or killed. He might be the only servant capable of instigating her release.

With the Queen gone, Ygerne called the guards to her cell and pleaded for her release to no avail. A short time later she complained of feeling sick, saying that the cold and damp of the cell was making her unwell. At first this did not work either, but when she started coughing uncontrollably she was allowed to leave and go to her room.

The guards kept a constant guard outside her door, but after complaining some more, they agreed for her maid to attend upon her. When her maid, Catherine finally appeared, Ygerne gave her instructions to find the burial place of Elaine and to apply the elixir over her body. The maid gasped for breath, she could not take in this strange request and shook her head at her mistress. 'No my lady, I can not do such a thing,' she told her.

'But you must. I command it.'

'I can not defile a body.'

'You do not understand. The Lady Elaine is not dead, but she will be turned to dust if you do not do as I ask.'

Still the peasant girl refused and nothing her mistress said could get her to change her mind. In despair, Ygerne asked her to contact Accolon and get him to come to her. Catherine was more than pleased to do this and hurried off to find the young man. Accolon bribed his way into the lady's room and was standing at attention before her. Ygerne had cleaned her person and was looking more like her true self again. Just as she was about to speak, a terrified young man fell to the ground at her feet. 'Oh great lady forgive me, I had no choice the Queen forced me...'

Ygerne helped him back to his feet and asked for an explanation.

'The Queen wanted to know where the Lady Morgan was...and I had to tell her...'

'Is that all,' Ygerne sighed. 'Do not fret; I have more important business for you to attend to.

Ygerne explained for a second time, the job that was needed to be done. Accolon said nothing, his reaction was similar to the maid's and he was equally reluctant to comply.

'Of course I will do this thing, but...' the young man hesitated.

He was invited to go on by Ygerne.

'Do you mean for me to dig her up and then put her back in the grave?'

Ygerne was perplexed with the question. After a moment, she shook her head. 'You cannot wait. You must cover her body with the elixir immediately, then you must find a safe haven for her to stay, someplace away from prying eyes.'

The young man wondered if there had ever been a more bizarre request made to a servant. 'I will do what you wish my lady, but I fear it is doomed to failure.'

'You must try, and do not worry on the other thing. I will make sure Morgan knows of your sacrifice this day. You will take some of Elaine's clothes and dress her once you have applied the elixir.'

To dig up a body and then to bathe it and to dress it was bad enough, but the young man was so innocent that he had never seen a woman naked before. He would see everything and this made him nervous, and then there was the chance of discovery. How could he explain what he was doing with a dead woman? A shiver went through his body as he listened to more instructions from the Lady Ygerne.

'I wish you luck, I am depending on you.'

Accolon wasted no time in finding the burial place of Elaine. The grave had no burial mark or stones, but only a bouquet of wild flowers lying on it. He worked like a laborer and dug up the lady from the ground without being seen.

With his hands, he whipped away as much dirt as he could to view the lady's face. She looked strangely peaceful and Accolon wondered why her family could not let her rest in peace.

Being aware that when the clouds dissipated a little, he might be seen, he carried Elaine in the direction of the river. He found the body heavy as he trampled along the riverbank, until at last he fell to his knees exhausted. He bathed Elaine the best he could, before pulling out from his pocket the elixir and applying it as instructed. He had never seen death at close range and something inside him almost quaked with emotion as he touched the lady's skin. Having fulfilled his duty, he breathed a huge sigh of relief.

14

Ursien, King of Gore was not a young man anymore and since his wife's death seemed only interested in the siring of a son. He had scoured the country looking for a new Queen suitable to his taste and highborn enough to please the hierarchy of his court. His eyes had spied many young maidens, but their lack of position or breeding had made their choice unsuitable.

There was one woman that fitted his needs perfectly, but that lady was above all others. She was no longer married and was regarded by many as having a great intellect. She was also still good-looking enough to attract the eye. As he sat waiting for the arrival of Guinevere he started fantasying about the lady. He pictured her in his bed, her slender body entwined with his. She had long dark hair and a skin that looked pale like marble, but her presence was anything but cold. She would rage into a passion on a subject that was close to her heart and would captivate her audience with her eloquence. He had never known a woman whose passion could stimulate him so. Under his breath he whispered her name, *Morgan, Morgan...gods above, what a woman she was*. He had to admit he had grown hot at the thought of bedding her, but then again what full-blooded man in the realm hadn't.

His fantasying came to abrupt end, when one of his stewards entered to announce there were visitors enquiring an audience with the bishop. Ursien grunted, got to his feet and came towards the man. 'Why do you bother me with this?' he asked.

'It is just I can not find him anywhere.'

Ursien laughed. 'Perhaps you're not been looking in the right place.'

The steward informed his master of all the places he had looked. The King of Gore smiled. 'Have you tried the maid's quarters, by any chance?'

The steward looked dumbfounded.

'Come...we shall seek him out. Let's catch the man unawares.'

Ursien went with his servant down towards the burrows of the castle to the servants' quarters. After entering unannounced in two rooms, it was in the third room that they found their man. He was not alone, but was with a young kitchen maid. They were both naked and sweating to excess. As the bishop forced the maid from his arms he looked up at the intruders. The steward yelled at the poor girl, calling her names and suggesting she look for work elsewhere. Ursien just laughed and yelled at the steward. 'Leave the girl alone,' he told him. He slowly approached the holy man and pretended to be shocked. 'I do hope my young servants are to your taste, your holiness?' he inquired.

'I have no complaints,' Germanus replied with a hint of a smile on his face. He looked up at the King. 'Has the Queen arrived, my lord?'

'No, it is not the Queen.' Ursien looked at his steward. 'Who wants to see him?'

'Two envoys have arrived with a message from King Arthur,' the steward replied.

'Your importance grows,' Ursien announced, 'messages from Kings, audiences with Queens, no wonder you are conceited.'

Germanus while quickly putting on his clothes, kept an eye on his host. He found the look of smugness across Ursien's face annoying. 'What you perceive as conceit is merely dedication.'

'My own chambers are at your disposal, you can entertain them in complete privacy. Only pity they are not female, eh.' The King of Gore looked to his steward again. 'I take it they're not?' he asked the man.

'No my Lord, they're the sons of King Lot.'

Ursien looked once more at his steward, his face glowed with hate. 'Not that arrogant pup?' he inquired.

'No my lord, Gaheris and the...'

'Yes?'

'Well...the bastard, Mordred.'

'Gossip mongrels,' Ursien growled. 'How do you know he's a bastard, were you present when he was conceived?'

The steward shook his head, looked as meek as he could and escorted Germanus towards the King's private chamber.

Gaheris was well aware of his role as he and Mordred were escorted to into a small but lavish bedchamber. His position was clear, he was here to observe, while his brother was the one who would do the talking. This was Mordred's big moment. His brother had in his hand the document that the King had given him. For the first time Gaheris wondered at its contents and why this member of the church was so important.

The brothers entered the room to witness the holy man in deep contemplation. They were not expecting to see someone ordinary and found themselves somewhat taken aback by the sight of the man. He was small, his head was clean shaven as was his face and he wore a long black robe. He held in his hands a crucifix, which he turned over in his hand several times. He was perched on the end of a table, his face staring down at the ground while he mumbled some Latin from the sacraments.

The two men waited until he had finished before uttering a sound. 'We come from the King,' announced Mordred in a voice that sounded good and strong.

'Indeed, I was expecting you,' Germanus replied, lifting his head to see who stood before him. 'What took you so long?'

This response had Mordred somewhat at a loss for words. Gaheris however looked calmness itself. He looked at the bishop and found the man was looking back at him. 'You were expecting us?' Gaheris asked.

'Why of course, you bring me news from Lady Morgan...'

Mordred shook his head. 'No my lord, we...'

Smiling, Germanus interrupted. 'Your grace is the correct term. My lord can only belong to our holy father.'

Mordred bowed his head, bit into his lips and moved closer to the bishop. He reached out his arm and offered him the parchment. Reluctantly Germanus took it, broke the seal and looked at the contents of the document. As he was reading Mordred continued. 'You will abide by the King's commands?'

Germanus looked up from reading the document to challenge Mordred's question. 'You have read it?' he asked the young man.

'No, I have been given orders...'

The bishop interrupted. 'I think you are mistaken, your King can not give me orders. I am here on the business, for his holy father Pope Celestine. I take orders only from him and God of course.'

Mordred's face was flushed as he tried again to finish his statement. 'If you do not agree to abide by the commands written in the document, I will be forced to arrest you...'

The right hand of Germanus rose in the air as he finally finished reading the note. 'Arrest me, on what charge?' he demanded.

Again Mordred seemed lost for words. Gaheris stepped in. 'We have a decree from the King...'

Germanus threw the parchment on the floor and got to his feet. 'Your King has no power over me. Your decree means nothing.'

'We have force,' Mordred announced.

'Don't be fools, I am surrounded by men.'

'If you mean King Ursien's men, can you be sure of his support in this matter?' questioned Gaheris

Germanus opened his mouth to belch out a thunderous laugh. The brothers looked to each other, their faces drawn in shock. After a few moments the bishop regained his composure. 'I have no quarrel with your King. I only wish to give to him and the good lady a chance to cleanse themselves of their sins.'

Neither man knew what the bishop meant by that and their innocent faces told the holy man that they were ignorant of the contents of the letter and what their mission was all about.

'Will you come quietly?' asked Mordred.

'I do everything quietly, but where were you thinking of taking me?'

Mordred glanced at his brother. Gaheris offered a suggestion. 'You can remain here under guard, until the King sends for you.'

Germanus seemed amused. 'I'm not going any place, but I assure you it is more likely the King and the lady who will come to me.'

Gaheris had taken a huge dislike to the arrogant holy man and wanted to clap him in irons, but he wondered what gave him the right. Before the on surge of Christianity the religious practices of the old religion were common place. He had heard of stories of animal sacrifices and even human ones. In his short life time these practices had been outlawed, thanks to Arthur's father King Uther. His aversion to the old practices made him aware of the importance of the Christian church and the importance to its leaders, such as this bishop before him. 'We will communicate with the King. In the mean time I would prefer it if you do not leave here.'

'I hate to repeat myself, but I will go wherever I please. Please convey these utterings to your King.' Germanus walked behind a desk and took some parchment and a quill and was about to write. 'Better still I will give you messages for both Arthur and Morgan.'

As the bishop began to write, Mordred's face grew red as he began to give in to his anger. 'I arrest you by the order of King Arthur and command you accompany us to Paris.'

Germanus did not look up, but continued writing. Mordred began to repeat himself. 'I heard you the first time,' the bishop muttered. He finished with a flourish and threw the quill over the desk before getting to his feet. He then burnt some wax over the letters and using his ring from his hand he pressed his seal over the wax, to seal them.

'There...you shall give this one to the King,' he handed one of the letters to Gaheris, 'and this one to Morgan.' He gave the other letter to him also. 'Be sure not to mix them up, it could be embarrassing.'

Gaheris took the letters, looked at them briefly and saw one was marked with a large letter m.

Mordred looked to his brother for guidance, but Gaheris much to his annoyance accepted the letters and agreed to deliver them. It was galling to him not to arrest the bishop and fulfill his duty.

As the two brothers left the room, Mordred grabbed hold of his brother's arm to ask him the reason for his capitulation. Ushering Mordred from the room Gaheris explained his reasons. 'We have fifty men, Ursien has several hundred,' he whispered. 'Besides he is a holy man and unless he has committed treason the King has no right to arrest him.'

'The King gave me my instructions...'

Gaheris interrupted. 'We might still arrest him, but first we should seek out the Lady Morgan and deliver her letter.'

'I don't understand any of this.'

'That is our problem. The King did not see fit to tell us what this is about, but perhaps the lady can tell us.'

From behind a wooden paneled insert, Ursien had seen everything that had transpired and like the two brothers, was baffled at what it all meant. He was more intrigued than he might have been, because he knew it concerned the Lady Morgan.

15

Gaheris had finished collecting his possessions prior to leaving, when he heard the sound of men on horseback approach the castle. His curiosity had him peer from the slit of the window to see what he could. What little view he had, indicated to him that a great many soldiers had just arrived. What their purpose was he could not tell, for Ursien had plenty of his own men and did not need any more. He left his room to investigate and to find his brother.

Mordred was still seething with rage as he entered the stables to check on his horse. The beast had been well looked after by a groom who loved his charge. The animal was well rested and fed and was feeling rather too comfortable to set out again so soon. Mordred was sheltered behind several horses when the influx of riders came thundering to a halt just outside the stables. He listened to the orders given to several grooms. 'Look lively there, you lazy lot, the lady wants her favorite washed and fed immediately.'

One of the grooms accepted the charge and swore it would be done. 'And look after as many of the others as you can.'

Again the groom agreed.

Mordred moved closer to the door of the stable to see what was happening. He saw a soldier climb down from his horse and whisper to the man who had given the orders. The figure's face gleamed just enough in the moonlight for the man to see their face. To his amazement he saw the face of the Queen, the Lady Guinevere.

Gaheris had his ear to the floor in an attempt to hear the conversation below him, between the Queen and the bishop Germanus. He was unable to see what was happening, but he could hear a little. Unknown to him, his host had the same idea and was watching and listening from his secret panel as he had earlier.

Guinevere was in good heart and began by relating her precautionary action against Morgan and her family. For a man of god, the bishop seemed devoid of compassion for the unfortunate Lady Ygerne. The Queen was studying the man before her. She was well aware of his reputation and felt he was the only man likely to take up the reins of any Holy Crusade. The lady was sure the Christian faith needed such a man to crush all paganism from the land forever. She was putting her faith in his hands. 'Your grace is well?' the lady asked.

Germanus came towards the Queen. To Ursien's surprise it was Guinevere who bowed and kissed the ring on his right hand. 'You look changed my lady. I almost didn't recognize you,' the man told her.

'This is practical for what I must do,' the lady replied.

Germanus smiled. 'I have never met a lady such as you. Your resolve is so...absolute.'

Guinevere was not a lady who took kindly to flattery, often suspecting a deceitful purpose. 'I need three things from your grace; money, the support of the church and the whereabouts of a certain young man.'

A sudden look of embarrassment flashed across Germanus's face. 'Well, if you had come yesterday, I could have provided you with all three...but unfortunately I can only give you the money and God's blessing.'

'You promised me you had found the young man.'

'Indeed I had, but I heard only a short time ago that someone had abducted him.'

'How was that possible?'

'All is not lost. My contact at the monastery saw everything that took place. Unfortunately he is a devout coward and took no action to stop the abduction.'

Guinevere stared at the bishop. 'This better not be a deception,' she advised him.

Putting his hands across his chest, the bishop indicated he was hurt by the suggestion. 'I have no use for this young man, although I hear he is well read on all aspects of our religion.'

'In that case he might be inclined to our way of thinking.'

'That is possible.'

Guinevere could not hide her disappointment.

'Do not fret my lady, my contact may be a coward but he is not stupid. He followed the man and is close behind as we speak.'

'How do you know this?'

'I have more than one friend at the monastery.'

Guinevere smiled and her face became more relaxed. 'I was looking forward to meeting the young man. You have seen him?'

'I had a brief interview with him.'

'What is he like?'

Germanus put his finger to his mouth and smiled. 'He is a rare breed. He is totally idealistic and practices what he speaks...'

'It sounds as if you admire him.'

'Indeed I do and so will you, but all that idealism comes at a cost. You will not meet a more naive or unworldly man in all Christendom.'

'He has spent all his life in the monastery?'

'Yes, but many do, my lady. I do not believe he has felt like a prisoner at any time.'

Guinevere seemed to be waiting for a question from the bishop. They both stared curiously at each other.

'Your part of the bargain?' he inquired.

'I have it...'

'With you,' asked Germanus.

'No, but I can produce it within a few days.'

'Then I shall have it in my hands soon?'

'Providing you can supply me with...'

'I shall, but I beg you not to take part in the attack tomorrow...'

'I must,' declared Guinevere, 'no one can stop me.'

'And if you succumb, what happens to our bargain.'

'There is little chance of that, besides we have too much still to do.'

'I hope God feels the same way about that.'

'Do you doubt him, your grace?'

'I never doubt him my lady,' Germanus said smiling. 'Like you I am curious, what does the chalice look like?'

'It is simple, but exquisite.'

'I can not wait to hold it in my hands.'

'Can you be sure it is the one you seek?'

'Oh my lady, do not make me doubt now.'

Young Galahad was washing himself by the river, while King Lot was standing over him urging him to make haste. 'For God's sake, how clean can one man want to be?' cursed the King.

Galahad continued to bathe, but turned to look at his companion. 'Do you think it appropriate to speak of God in that way?' he asked.

'We haven't time to stand here and talk of God, we need to keep moving.'

'I can't help but feel you've made some kind of mistake. I can't think why anyone would want to abduct me?'

'I have my orders...but you are in no danger.'

'So you keep saying...'

'My lady must have acted for a good reason.'

'Your lady?' the young man asked. 'Please tell me who she is and what is her connection to me?'

'You ask too many questions, young sir.'

'You must know who the lady is?'

Lot's face scowled. 'I see no reason in withholding her identity. The lady in question is a member of my family, the Lady Morgan.'

To his surprise the name registered with the young man. 'My lady is well known and respected,' Lot assured him.

'I know, even within the cloisters, the monks know of this lady.'

'Well, get your things together. We should reach our destination by first light.'

While drying his face the best he could, Galahad sat down on a rock and continued to question his abductor. 'Is the lady very beautiful?' he asked.

Lot growled again. 'Yee Gods, do you never stop with the questions.'

'Other than seeing a young girl, a seller of fruit, I have never seen a woman before and I wondered what women were like.'

'They're nothing but trouble young man. You stay well clear of them.'

'That doesn't include Lady Morgan, I assume?'

'Well, she is special.'

'How is she different?' Galahad asked.

'She has a commanding presence, a dignity that is hard to explain, you will see for yourself.'

'Will I see her tomorrow?'

'You won't meet her tomorrow, but soon. In the meantime I am to take you to see her mother.'

Lot put out his arm for the young man to get to his feet. Galahad became aware of how powerful the man was as he lifted him up. 'Are you a great warrior my lord?'

'A great fool more like,' the Norseman joked.

'Would you teach me to fight?'

'Certainly not, I'm sure you're destined for the life of a scholar.'

They went to their horses and were about to ride off when Lot heard a sound of footsteps approaching. He strained his eyes in the dim light and saw what looked like a beggar stagger towards them. Taking no chance he withdrew his sword and waited to see the man up close.

The beggar had his hand out and in a barely audible voice pleaded for some money. Lot told him he had none and told him to move away. The beggar in an act of foolishness then tried to take hold of the reins of one of the horses.

Lot took the hilt of his sword and cracked it across the beggar's head and the man groaned and fell to the ground. The King went to turn his head, but a butt of someone's sword struck him across the side of his face. He struggled to keep his eyes from closing as he fell to the ground with a thud. He lay motionless on the grass as he looking from his low angle to see two figures, drag a reluctant Galahad away.

16

Merlin reached Dover within two days, but he was unsure whether to hire a boat and travel across the sea to Calais or to wait for the King and his men to arrive this side of the water. He knew Morgan had summoned the King and felt it was just possible they might miss each other in the crossing, so he waited in an inn close to the shore. The port was quiet, but in a short time the place would be crammed with soldiers and then he would gain accurate information about the whereabouts of the King.

His thoughts turned to the past and the betrayal of the Lady Ygerne. The deed had been done for the best interests of the realm, so he had been told and yet he should have known better. Kings use people, and Uther had used him and the lady most grievously. Arthur never forgave his father or Merlin for his participation in the rape of his mother. He couldn't blame the man, more importantly he couldn't forgive himself either. His shame reached down into the very bowels of his soul.

'Have you come far?' a woman's voice asked him.

Merlin looked up to see a before him a woman in her middle years. She did not look like a prostitute or a lady of standing, but just a hard working woman, used to toil and hardship. He witnessed her hands which were full of scars and burn marks. In her right hand she held a tankard which was full of mead. 'I bought you another drink,' the woman said.

She put the tankard down on the table beside him. 'You have been here a long time and the landlord was getting suspicious,' she whispered.

Merlin was not used to social chatter and his slowness to react made the woman turn to go. 'Wait, don't leave,' he said. The woman turned and came back to the table.

'Would you like to join me?' Merlin asked.

The woman looked unimpressed with this suggestion. 'I didn't do this with that in mind.'

'Oh, please don't think...I am waiting for someone and have nowhere else to go.'

'I can't stay long, for like you I am awaiting for someone.'

The woman brought her own drink with her to his table and sat down opposite. The man struggled to make small talk and the conversation was both awkward and trivial. He stared at the woman for quite awhile until a smile came upon her face. 'I don't mind your stare, but it's your eyes, they are so strong that I feel them reaching into the back of my head.'

'Forgive me. I do not see many people and I've forgotten my manners.'

'I too know what it is to be lonely.'

Merlin scowled. 'I did not say I was lonely.'

The woman sighed. 'Perhaps I should leave you in peace.'

The lady got to her feet, but Merlin took hold of her arm and persuaded her to sit back down again.

'What is your name?' the man asked.

'Gallia,' the lady replied. 'I am...a simple trader.'

Looking interested Merlin asked what her business was, but the lady refused to be explicit.

'And you my lord, what is your name?'

'The name I was born with was Taliesin.'

'A curious name, but it suits you.'

'We both have unusual names,' stated Merlin. 'I suspect your name to be Greek in origin.'

As they chatted he realized the lady was more educated than he first thought. Her name, which was indeed Greek was not a name given to a peasant girl. He had heard the name only twice before, once when he scoured the world after his banishment in the city of Antioch. The lady in question in that place was the daughter of a rich trader of olive oil. She would now be in middle age just like this lady, but the coincidence was too great for it to be possibly the same person. The other lady

101

was the wife of a Roman Senator by the name of Cassiodorus, a lady of much grace and wisdom who was also a scholar like her husband. She would be much older than this woman.

'You seem strangely out of place here,' Gallia remarked.

'I am out of place everywhere,' Merlin commented.

'This friend you are waiting for, is it a woman?'

'No, you might not believe it but this place will soon be swamped with Celtic soldiers.'

Gallia laughed. 'Are you a prophet then?'

'Yes something like that.'

Merlin liked the lady's laugh and was just beginning to enjoy her company when he heard her name being called. The lady turned her head and saw a man sitting at the table nearest to the door. He was not alone, for another man was seated opposite him. The man who was staring at Merlin was large and pale: his sandy hair was turning a little grey, the rims of his eyes were red and his thin lips seemed somehow cruel, but worse than this was his sinister eyes.

That so primitive a man should be associated with the lady shook Merlin at first, but he knew it was none of his business and was happy to say his farewells.

Gallia turned her head to look at the man and acknowledged his address with a slight nod of her head. She made her excuses to Merlin and made to leave the table.

'Do you have to leave, I was enjoying our conversation,' Merlin informed her.

Gallia bit her lip. 'Forgive me, but I have some business to attend too.'

The lady left Merlin and went over to the table occupied by the two men. They both got to their feet and offered her a seat beside them. Merlin had in a short time become interested in the lady and now more than ever because of the company she kept. Once or twice the men glanced in his direction and particularly the man with the sinister eyes. Merlin in turn kept glancing at the group, but only once did the lady return a glance in his direction.

Accolon had found an empty barn and had left the Lady Elaine there to explore the immediate area. He was looking for King Lot, having been told the King was due to return to Cadbury soon. He wanted to warn him about the imprisonment of Lady Ygerne and to stop him walking into a trap. As the morning sun broke through the trees, he found himself in an area he was not accustomed too.

People were just beginning to go about their business and the young man realized that the area he thought was quiet was instead a busy hub of activity. He had left Elaine in a barn that housed nothing, except hooks attached to its walls and some bails of hay. The thought just occurred to him what the barn might be used for and if he was correct, then the lady might soon be discovered. He ran back to the barn as fast as his legs would carry him. As he approached he saw two men carrying animal hides towards the barn. 'Kind sirs, Accolon cried, 'Can you help me please?'

The two men swung round to see the frantic youth stand before them. The youngest of the men addressed him. 'Pray tell us how we can help?'

Still a little out of breath Accolon had to think fast. 'I need all the local men to gather what weapons they have and come with me to Lady Ygerne's castle.'

The older man laughed and began walking towards the barn again.

Accolon continued as before. 'Your Queen needs your help.'

The older man stopped and turned his head. 'No offense but the Queen can sort out her own problems.'

'Does she not protect you, and treat you fair?'

The young man nodded his head, but the older man who was still carrying a load of hides moved closer to Accolon. 'She looks after her own and we do the same...' The young man interrupted. 'Father, she is fairer than most. She provides us with a great feast at harvest time.'

'She might be fair, but she would not have her privileged position but for people like us.'

Accolon agreed with the fellow and pleaded that the lady would be forever grateful for any assistance he and his fellow subjects could give. 'I should not wonder if the lady will shower you with land and even gold,' he attested.

'Father, just think what we could do with gold...'

The older man spat once more and relieved himself of the bundle from his back. 'Just what do you think we can do?' he asked Accolon.

'Some guards have taken her prisoner in her own castle and have locked her in her room. I can sneak the villagers into the castle by a secret entrance at the rear of the castle.'

The older man shook his head. 'We are not soldiers, why should we risk our lives?'

'Why have the guards locked her up?' asked the younger man.

'The guards belong to one of her enemies, who mean to do her harm. Do you not want to help save the good lady?'

The younger man seemed willing, but his father still shook his head. 'There is something strange about all this. Why has someone done this?'

Accolon wondered how popular the Queen was in this area and taking in to consideration the risk involved, decided to tell the truth.

'Queen Guinevere is not someone I would like to cross,' the older man stated.

17

Morgause had languished in a cell just like her mother and she too had complained, until she was allowed access to her bedchamber. She had guards put outside her door, but still found ways to communicate with the servants of the castle. She could not communicate directly with her mother, but one of the maids assured her that the lady was quite well. She managed to send back and forth messages to the kitchen and from these messages a plan was set in motion.

The cooks of the castle were the best in the land and the Queen's men had the night before gorged themselves on large portions of wonderful food to their hearts content. They were not used to feasting on such delights as pheasant, duck and sweetbreads, and when the time came to change the guards, the new men did not arrive at their posts. With no sign of their replacements the guards on duty were becoming restless.

Morgause's plan was simple. She had issued orders to the cooks, through her personal maid, to put something unsavory in the evening meal. That something was a drop of cowbane, not enough to kill anyone but enough to make all who ate extremely sick. As was the case in most powerful family establishments, a good supply of herbs and plants were kept in a safe place in the kitchen, including plants that were poisonous. Her mother's food was delivered with a note place in her first course, that of fish with potatoes.

Ygerne read the note and knew not to eat anything of the meal. She declared she was not hungry and pushed the meal away.

It was just before dawn when Morgause implemented the second phase of her plan. She had her servants steal the two keys needed from the ill soldiers and proceed to the rooms that housed herself and her mother. The guards standing waiting for their comrades were impatient and were pacing the stone floor outside both doors.

Morgause's personal maid Ina was a sweet faced girl of twenty, who would blush at the mere sight of a man. She nevertheless came up to the soldier standing outside her lady's bedchamber and began to flirt with him. She giggled and whispered something in the man's ear. 'My lady does not let me speak to men,' the girl advised him.

'That's a shame...we can be quite useful.'

Ina giggled again. 'My lady has told me what use men are.'

The soldier wasn't sure if the girl was jesting, or if she was a little naive. Ina carried a tray with some meat and fruit and the man's eyes swelled up with desire. Ina saw his mouth water and offered him the contents. 'Will your mistress not want her morning meal?' the man asked.

Ina shook her head. 'The poor lady is in mourning. She hasn't eaten anything for days.'

The man's eyes wandered through the contents of the tray as Ina's eyes hinted at the chicken. 'I had some earlier,' she told him, 'it was quite delicious.'

The man could not stop himself and he lifted a piece of white meat and ate it with a great deal of relish. Ina giggled and encouraged him to eat some more.

Accolon led his men into the castle by a secret passage known only by a few. They expected to be met by the Queen's men and to have to fight their way in with what basic weapons they had. Their armory was a strange mix of the norm: a few swords, an axe and a spear and the exotic: several pitchforks, shovels and even some small hammers. They could not believe how easy it was as they climbed stairs and entered rooms without being challenged. At last they came to the main rooms in the castle that housed the Lady Ygerne and the Lady Morgause. The men charged forward into these rooms with their weapons extended, expecting a fight, but found instead a peaceful scene of women sitting around a fire.

Lady Ygerne jumped back in horror. 'Good lord what now,' she cried.

Accolon was at the front of the line and fell to his knees before her. 'My lady, we came to rescue you from your captivity.'

Ygerne smiled and got to her feet. She took her time as she spoke with all who had come to her rescue. 'I am pleased with all of you and you will all be rewarded. As you see I am safe, but your help is still needed.'

Accolon offered everyone's services.

'The Queen's men are all scattered about the castle, they are all ill and of need of a purgative. I will be glad to give them this, when your men help us to lock them all up in the cells below.'

The men all agreed and Lady Morgause organized the enterprise. Ygerne took hold of Accolon as he was about to leave with the others. 'My daughter, you have her well hidden?'

'I have her hidden, whither it is secure I do not know.'

'Where is she?'

'Not far, I can take you there now if you wish?'

The lady agreed and after confiding in Morgause, they rode out from the castle.

It was morning and the birds had awakened the brothers from their slumber. To their surprise Guinevere had not wished to see them or asked after them the night before. They concluded that the bishop had told her everything that had transpired between them. Still Gaheris was in a state of panic. Whatever had upset his brother Mordred had tried and failed to get him to confide in him. Instead Gaheris pleaded with him to forget the King and his assignment and go in search of the Lady Morgan.

'Where are you going?' Mordred asked.

'I haven't time to explain, but we must leave together as we had arranged. They must not think we are about to go our separate ways.'

'Shouldn't we stay and greet the Queen?'

Gaheris was daydreaming and not listening to what Mordred was saying to him. 'That's if she will let us leave at all...'

'Not let us leave! What are you talking about?'

Gaheris tried to smile.

'You are acting very strange. Are you on some secret mission you can not divulge?'

Gaheris was slow to answer. 'Yes, I am, and one day I will reveal everything to you.'

Mordred seemed a little placated. 'It is not odd that the Queen should visit this place?'

Gaheris agreed.

'We must say our farewells to King Ursien.'

'What do you make of him?' Gaheris asked

Mordred pondered. 'I like him, he's a little unrefined.'

'Raw,' suggested Gaheris.

'Yes, you could say that, but I feel he is an honest fellow.'

'Do you think he would betray the King?

Mordred looked shocked at the suggestion. 'No, he is loyal, hasn't he proved it many times in the past.'

'Perhaps he will have to prove it again and soon.'

'More riddles. Let's get out of here so we can breathe the clean air, this place stinks of intrigue and plots.'

The bishop stinks of intrigue, thought Gaheris, as the brothers made their way to the King's Hall to say their farewells. They were in for a surprise for the only one sitting down eating his morning meal was Germanus. 'Ah, good morning young men,' the bishop welcomed them.

'We came to say our farewells,' Mordred advised the man.

'Is the King still asleep?' Gaheris asked.

'You must stay and have some food, the sweet meats are delicious.'

The brothers declined the offer. They waited for Germanus to reply to Gaheris's question.

'Oh, you are too late. The King left with Queen Guinevere at dawn.'

Gaheris came forward and stood beside the bishop. 'Where could they be going at such a time? 'he asked.

Germanus finished eating some meat and looked up at Gaheris. 'I'm afraid they did not confide in me. I believe the Queen mentioned something about affairs of state. I don't envy her, her burden, although she never complains.'

'You did not mention to her that we were staying here as guests?' Mordred inquired.

'I believe the King mentioned something.'

'Did she not see fit to see us?' Gaheris queried.

The bishop wiped his mouth with a cloth and stared at Gaheris. 'I can see you are upset. It went clear out of my mind. The Queen did give me a message to give to you.'

Gaheris stared back at Germanus, his frown might have appeared threatening, but the bishop only smiled. He got to his feet and stood eye to eye with the young man. 'She wanted you to know that your secret hoard is no longer a secret. Needless to say I do not know what she meant by that, but I hope the message has some meaning for you.'

Germanus saw the look of panic on Gaheris's face and turned to look at Mordred. He waved his hand for Mordred to come and help his brother who seemed to be having trouble with his breathing. The bishop's reactions told its own story, for whatever the message meant the Queen hadn't seen fit to inform him of its meaning.

Mordred poured his brother some wine and forced him to drink it slowly. The bishop kept his distance, but showed signs of concern. 'I hope you are not coming down with some malady?'

The wine had done its work and Gaheris's color had returned to his face.

'Your Queen is quite a woman. I have never met anyone so dedicated,' the bishop declared.

Gaheris let the goblet of wine fall from his grasp and turned to address Germanus. 'Dedicated to what, your grace?' he inquired.

18

Merlin was contemplating the night that had just past. The King's men had started to cross the narrow sea, although Arthur was not expected until the following day. Rumors of the King's ill-health reached the coastal town, a chill had apparently reached his stomach making him too weak to travel that day. Merlin's thoughts were not on Arthur, but on the woman he had met the night before. The encounter was random, but for some reason he was moved to want to help her. Maybe it was the lady herself or maybe it was memory of those desperate days in Antioch, or the realization that there was someone like him, broken and afraid. Whatever it was, it had led him to follow the lady and her companions from the inn to the seashore. He made himself invisible and followed some paces behind in a hope of hearing some of their conversation.

The man with the sinister eyes, whose name was Frith, was doing most of the talking and he was venting his bile at Gallia. 'You knew we were meeting and yet you still sat and talked to a complete stranger. You want me to believe such bilge.' Gallia, if she felt intimidated did not show it. 'It was either that or be pestered with every man in the place. The establishment is a well known den for prostitutes.'

'What did you talk about anyway?' Frith asked.

The other man, whose name was Grim, offered his opinion, 'Did you talk about the weather?'

Gallia glanced at him, before returning to look at Frith. 'He was kind and lonely and we shared a few reminiscences of happier days.'

'What kind of reminiscences?' Frith wanted to know.

'What do you mean?'

'You didn't relive your happier days in Antioch for instance?'

'No. I swore to forget those times.'

Frith had a leer of a smile on his face. 'Just remember my lady, without the money you make with us, your father would most probably be dead by now.'
Gallia accepted this was true and acknowledged as much. 'What are you buying tonight' she inquired.

'We need your expertise to verify if certain goods are real and not cheap fakes,' Frith acknowledged.

The three of them came towards an isolated boat, which was old and clearly not seaworthy. Frith put his hand out to stop the others and listened. A faint noise was heard onboard the vessel. The captain, a man by the name of Mosca, cursed before coming on deck. He saw his buyers standing on the quay and welcomed them. 'Come on board, there's just enough room,' he told them.

Grim volunteered to be the lookout and he stayed on the pier. Frith helped the lady on board and Merlin, still invisible, came on board directly after her. If the boat rocked a little with his weight, no one spotted the difference. Gallia and Frith followed Mosca to the stern of the boat. It took the captain a few moments to take some items wrapped in cloth from a small wooden chest. He carefully tore away the wrapping of the first item, to reveal a large bronze cauldron, studded with gold braid and red jewels. The object even at first sight appeared most fine. There were six panels all depicting elements from Celtic and Thracian mythology. It was Gallia who broke the silence. She glanced at Mosca. 'This is a most beautiful object,' she advised him. 'I wonder where you found such an item.'

'That is my business,' Mosca replied curtly.

Frith glanced at the lady, who had the cauldron in her hands. She turned the object slowly, examining it in great detail. 'Well?' Frith asked impatiently.

'I would speculate that the cauldron is between one and two hundred years old.'

'Not earlier?'Frith enquired.

'I'm sure it was made for Christian worship some place in the east, perhaps to be used to serve the Eucharist.'

Mosca nodded, as if he agreed. He took away the wrappings from the second item, to reveal a fine looking silver chalice. This had the appearance of greater age and was made from the finest plain silver. Gallia again held this item up to examine. Frith raised his arm too and touched the chalice with his hand, but did not take it from the lady's grasp.

Gallia studied the chalice at length, while Frith's impatience grew. At last he could not wait any longer. 'Well, tell me how old and how valuable.'

Gallia took her time and examined both the inner and the outer engravings of the vessel: she saw the fruited grapevine form around the gilded shell; this was inhabited by birds and animals, which included an eagle, a lamb and many others; this was not all, for further down towards the base were twelve human figures holding scrolls, one figure stood out from the others and seem to depict Christ, while the others looked upon him with reverence.

Gallia saw from the corner of her eye, Frith's fascination with the object. 'I am as sure as I can be that this chalice is about four hundred to five hundred years old.'

Frith smiled. 'How much is it worth?' he asked.

'It's impossible to say...'

'You mean it is priceless?' inquired Frith.

'Everything has a price...'

Frith laughed. 'Yes, as you can attest to that.'

It was the relish of this statement that angered Merlin. He saw Gallia's face turn white and watched her bite at her lip. It was as if Frith had thrust a dagger through her heart, for the lady stood still as death.

Frith's expression did not indicate what was just about to happen next. 'We will take both,' he announced to the happy Mosca.

Mosca began to re-wrap the objects with care. He hinted about a price, but was rather timid in offering an amount. Finally he ventured a figure. 'How about one hundred silver coins?'

Mosca partly turned his body to look at Frith. With a cruel smile still upon his face, Frith drew out his dagger and thrust it hard, twice upwards into the Jew's body. The man's eyes opened wide, before he collapsed in a heap at Gallia's feet. Some blood splattered over the lady's face.

Frith had acted so quickly, that Gallia and Merlin had not moved. The lady wiped some of the man's blood from her face, before attacking her colleague verbally. 'You fool, you didn't need to do that,' she cried.

Frith was heartless and spat at the dead man's body. 'How do you think he got them? 'he asked.

Gallia's shock had been replaced with anger. 'It takes a cutthroat to know a cutthroat I suppose.'

The look of hate flashed across Frith's face. 'You are not irreplaceable, lady, do not forget that.'

Merlin thought about killing the man where he stood, but he wondered what was going to happen next. After withdrawing his knife from the dead man's body, Frith took the prized objects from the deck and was about to leave. Gallia hadn't moved and was staring down at the unfortunate man. 'Are you just going to leave him here?' she inquired.

'We could throw him overboard, but the splash might be heard.'

Frith turned and climbed back onto the jetty, where he found Grim waiting, anxious to see the treasure. Gallia followed behind. Although her breathing sounded heavier she did not display much outer emotion.

Merlin followed as before and was surprised to find the glee of the men as they discussed the murder between themselves. Gallia's reactions to her companions told of her disgust and yet she was party to it, she had witnessed a cold blooded murder and it would seem was not going to do anything about it. What hold did these villains have on her, he wondered? What could make a decent woman fall in with such vile creatures? He decided he had to save her from these villains. Merlin followed her and her companions to a cabin in the woods, just west of Dover, where he contemplated what to do next.

By the time Lot got back on his feet, the men had carried Galahad away. He looked around for clues as to where they had gone and found a trail to follow. He was on foot and the robbers were now on horseback. Despite this, he followed the tracks through the forest the best he could. To his surprise they appeared to be going towards the Lady Ygerne's castle. He walked at a quick pace and hoped that by some miracle he might catch them up. He had no idea who had captured the young man, but he believed they might have some connection to Guinevere.

The men, who had carried off Galahad, had been given instructions to await their master in Queen's Ygerne's castle. They took the poor decision to ride the horses and have the young captor walk beside them on foot. Galahad did not take too kindly to being kidnapped for a second time in a day and his attitude to them was petulant. He complained of sore feet, of being tired, of the rope tied to his wrist of being too tight, in fact he complained non-stop.

At last one of the men got off his horse and offered the youth a chance to ride beside him. With a smile on his face Galahad decided to sit behind the man on the horse, a choice that bore dividends almost immediately. Before the horse of the hapless kidnapper had gone a few paces, Galahad had stolen the man's dagger and had it around his throat.

'You would not cut me with this weapon,' whispered the man.

'Don't think I do not know how to use it. I have gutted many a rabbit in my time,' Galahad informed the man.

'But you're a man of God, you do not believe in killing,' the man continued.

'How do you know this?'Galahad asked.

The other man ventured his horse closer. 'We know you have been living as a monk at the Church of the Virgin Mary in Glastonbury Abbey.'

Galahad reminded the man that he had a knife at his friend's throat and warned him not to venture nearer. The young man had never harmed a living soul, but his abductors were a spineless pair and did not want to risk their worthless necks. The situation might have been different if the men were working for a cause, but they were only paid lackeys.

To Galahad's surprise one man allowed his friend to tie him up, while he tied the other to a tree. The young man, after achieving his goal, rather wondered what to do next. He questioned them on the identity of their master. At first they were a little reluctant, but when Galahad produced the knife again, the skinny man told him they were on an errand for the bishop Germanus.

After finding out all he could about the bishop, Galahad decided it was time to leave. 'If you have nothing else to tell me, then I will take my leave.'

'You can't leave us here,' they both screamed.

Galahad mounted one of the horses and tied the other to his waist and was ready to move away from the scene. Feeling rather pleased with himself, he said farewell to the men and disappeared through the trees. He was heading back the way they had come, in the hope that he might come across Lot. He had lots of questions for the man, questions about bishops and great ladies and why such people should be interested in him.

19

A full day of rest and quiet contemplation had help Morgan
to regain her strength as she waited for Merlin's return.
The morning mist had cleared, letting in the fresh but cool
sunshine. The summer was at its end and the autumn
breezes were filling the air with just a hint of a chill. It was
Haligmonath – holy month –as the peoples of north called
the old Roman month of September. The time of plenty
would soon be replaced with the need to store and prepare
for a long winter. Recent harsh winters had taken too many
of the old and weak, making Morgan more determined
than ever to draw up fresh plans to preserve the country's
stock of grain and barley.

As she walked towards the sea, she became engulfed
in what she assumed was a hive of bees, for many objects
swarmed about her head. Their noise made her ears ring
and their constant movements were an irritation to her
senses, but once she had used her hand to swot the beasts
away, she realized that they were not bees at all, but
specimens of quite a different variety.

The two adult fairies rebuked their young offspring
for frightening the lady in such a way. The noise of
complaint died as Eros, the fairy King, ordered his children
to behave themselves. Morgan blinked several times and
assumed the beings were part of some dream she was
having. After closing her eyes for a moment, the lady
reopened them to see six small, delicate and rather radiant
looking beings flying in front of her face. Standing beside
the fairies was Nemue; her small stature seemed huge next
to the tiny creatures as the girl introduced herself. 'My
name is Nemue, you might know of me through your
servant Yvain.'

'Indeed, we were talking about you a short time ago.'
Nemue smiled. 'I have come with a message from a
special being, one that wants to help you.'

Morgan looked at the fairies all floating in midair and wondered who this special being could be. She studied the features of the tiny ones: their faces were small and round, like the faces of small children; their eyes sparkled like precious gems and their mouths were thin and small, which might explain their squeaky voices; the rest of their bodies were thin and light, including their exquisite multi-colored wings. At first the lady thought their features were identical, but after close examination she preserved that two of them were bigger than the rest, (adults) and that one was male and the other was female.

The four smaller fairies began to babble incoherently again amongst themselves. This time it was Sybil, the other adult that put them in their place.

Morgan opened her mouth to speak to the creatures, but found she could not find words to express herself. Sybil looked at Eros, who slowed down his wings in flight, to bow before Morgan. 'Good lady,' he said, 'our mistress has sent us to escort you to her home on the island of Avalon.'

Eros's voice was high-toned, not unlike his wife's, but his timbre was lower and a little easier on Morgan's ear to comprehend. The lady stared hard and long at the curious sight before her. She turned to the girl by her side. 'Who is their mistress?' she asked Nemue.

'She is a God like the one you have already met, but she is different too. You will see for yourself when you meet her.'

'We will escort you there,' Eros stated.

'What is your mistress's name?' Morgan inquired.

'The lady keeps her name a secret, but I call her the lady of the lake,' Nemue informed Morgan.

'I am waiting for a friend.'

'My lady made it clear to persuade you to come now,' said Eros.

Sybil hovered closer to Morgan, her face protruded so close that it almost touched the lady's nose. 'My mistress does not trust Merlin and fears his influence over you could be hurtful to her cause,' Sybil advised.

'Her cause?' inquired Morgan.

Eros glanced at Sybil, but the female fairy continued. 'Our mistress sees both the good and the bad of your species and wants to ensure that the good does not get...' Sybil looked to her partner for help.

'Our great lady has a great compassion for the humans who choose goodness over wealth or power.'

Sybil was nodding her head in agreement as her young giggled in the background.

'I will come to see your mistress, for I am certainly in need of help.'

'Good, we will make your journey pleasurable my lady,' Eros stated.

Morgan managed a smile. 'What will I say to Yvain?'

'I will stay with him and make sure he knows you are safe,' said Nemue.

Sybil smiled at the human. 'We will sprinkle angel dust over you and carry you through the air to Avalon.'

Morgan looked a little concerned. 'I am too heavy I will fall...'

'Do not fear my lady, you will be quite safe,' Eros assured her.

'Do not fear being seen either, for no human can see us,' Sybil assured the lady.

Morgan was still concerned. 'Will I not be afraid? 'she inquired.

'You will find that flying is exhilarating,' said Eros.

Sybil continued to explain. 'Time will stand still for you now and when we return you to this place, it will be as if you had not been away.'

Morgan had a lot of questions, but her thoughts were muddled and confused. She agreed and saw how that even the waves of the sea were suspended in time. There was no sound and not a drop of breath touched her face, it was as the fairy had stated, time itself had stopped.

The journey ended too quickly for Morgan's liking, for the feeling of flight was as Eros had promised, truly exhilarating. She kept her eyes open the whole time and saw the earth like never before. The view from the sky showed the land and sea at their most beguiling; she saw how green the pastures were, how golden brown the fields, how blue and calm the sea. It made her realize how wonderful the world could be if wars and strife could be eliminated.

With this thought she was brought before a great lake and to a great creature. The lady of the lake swam towards the large rock, where Morgan rested. She only partially came out of the water to appear before her guest, naked from the waist up. The lady greeted Morgan with a smile. 'You came, I am pleased,' she told her.

'You wish to help me? 'Morgan inquired.

'I'm sure you have a great many questions, but most of all you want to know who killed your sister.'

Morgan eyes were transfixed by the creature she knew to be different and yet appeared to be just like any other human female.

'I can show you just how it happened, but are you ready to witness such a spectacle?'

'I do not understand. Are you saying you can show me the person who killed my sister?' Morgan asked.

'This lake and its water are magical. Through my power I can evoke images from the past, but the image I will show you will be distressing for you to witness.'

'I do not care about that. I must know who was responsible for Elaine's death.'

'Come, look into the water where I stand, it will show you what happened to your sister immediately before her death.'

Morgan did what she was asked and stared into the water around the lady of the lake's feet. The water swirled around and changed color several times before eventually becoming clear. It was like looking into a mirror, but seeing other people instead of one self. The figure looking back at her now was none other than her sister, Elaine. She was brushing her long golden hair and staring back at her own image in a pool. Her face radiated pleasure and contentment as she hummed a lullaby, while the fingers of her left hand gently touched the water. The ripples blurred the image for a moment, before a second image stood behind the first.

The second image was of a man and he appeared taller, as if he was standing while the lady was kneeling. The man's face was partly blocked by Elaine's figure, but she smiled and did not turn her head. Elaine continued staring into the pool. The man's hands grabbed hold of her neck and pushed her face down into the water. Still the lady sensed no danger, for her smile remained as the water bubbled from her mouth. After a moment the man let go of her and Elaine's head exited the water.

For the first time Morgan caught a look at the man standing over her sister. It was a face the lady immediately recognized, for it was the face of the most famous warrior of all, Lancelot of Benoic. Elaine glanced behind her to see the man whom she had loved ever since her childhood. The couple fooled around some more around the pool and were smiling and enjoying each other's company. Everything was done with laughter and good spirits. At no time did the playfulness suggest anything sinister.

This scene continued for some time and Morgan thought perhaps the lady of the lake had given her the wrong image to look at. When all of a sudden two hands grabbed hold of Elaine and pulled her head under the water again. This time the lady struggled, beating her arms in the water with all her might. The splashes were frantic, and the noise although muttered, sounded desperate and ghastly as one human forcibly took the life of another. Finally Elaine's arms faltered and came to rest, as her face turned blonde just like the color of her hair. The water became silent again as the man's hands were released from the lady's neck. Morgan could not see the face that the hands belonged to, but presumed they were Lancelot's.

Gaheris had given both letters to his brother and had advised him to deliver them to Morgan, whom he believed to be at her mother's castle at Cadbury. Mordred was reluctant to go on his own and wondered where his brother was heading and why it was a secret. He did what was asked nonetheless and took the quickest route through the Bedegraine forest and headed towards Wroexter.

It would take the young man three days, riding fast to get to where he wanted to be. His brother had emphasized the importance of reaching Morgan, delivering the letters and telling the lady that the bishop was in league with Guinevere. He promised to do this and queried what was so important that his brother could not come with him. Gaheris did not confide his reasons for going off on his own, but promised one day he would. Mordred agreed to be content with that for now, but was displeased that so many of his family withheld secrets from him.

Gaheris galloped north towards the great Roman wall, heading to his homeland. He would travel through King Pelles's land and perhaps find out what Guinevere and Ursien were up to. His eavesdropping the night before had told him something was about to happen and that something involved some battle or raid. From the Queen's message, the man suspected Guinevere was now in possession of the treasure.

20

'I am surprised you do not want to witness more from the past,' the lady of the lake queried.

Morgan looked dazed by the lady's suggestion. 'You mean I can see anything from the past I wish?'

It was the look of wonderment upon the lady's face that brought a smile on the face of the God. 'I'm not sure about anything, but a great many things certainly. Is there something you wish to see? Remember the past is gone and can not changed.'

'Can I see the raid on Avalon, where the treasure was stolen?' asked an impatient Morgan.

'Ah, I thought you might, 'the lady replied. 'Though I must warn you not to mention to a living soul what you witness here in this place.'

Morgan promised to keep everything secret.

'That includes the other God.'

'You mean he does not know about your pool?'

'He knows of its healing qualities, that is enough. I do not wish for him to know about my visions, especially concerning the future.'

'The future,' shrieked Morgan. 'You mean you can see that too?'

'The future is different, as there can be many different versions of it. Interpreting the one that will come to pass is tricky, but not impossible.'

Morgan was dazed and waited for the lady of the lake to show her more amazing things from her magical pool. What the lady showed her made her heart almost stop. Her own brother had lied to her as she suspected, for she witnessed his tenacious raid on Avalon and the theft of the treasure from the sacred Isle. The lady of the lake could see the lady's anger and hurt.

Even after the images began to dissipate, Morgan continued to stare into the vortex of the pool. 'Where is the treasure now? 'she asked the God.

'I believe that all the treasure was given to Gaheris for safe keeping, but I have not been able to find out where the young man's hiding place is.'

'Then I must see Gaheris and persuade him to part with the treasure.'

Morgan was startled by the lady's next question. 'What if I were to make a bargain with you for the treasure?'

'I do not understand.'

'You would not have to wait. I can restore Elaine back to life immediately.'

At first Morgan agreed without reserve, but then she wondered what the lady would want in return.

The God smiled. 'You think I want to trick you?' she asked.

'I've made a bargain already.'

'Let me worry about Mider,' the lady of the lake suggested. 'The treasure means little to the others, but for me certain items have a special value. I would like those items returned.

Morgan still looked worried. The God Mider might not be so forgiving if he thought she betrayed him.

'You are worried about Mider I see, but don't be. He would not dare harm you, once I put you under my protection.'

'These items, how will I know them?'

'They are small containers that look like message carriers. They are made of a substance that looks like gold and are quite impregnable. They are distinctive, and different from the rest of the treasure.'

Morgan's hesitation came to an abrupt end, when she yelled her acceptance.

'You have the lady nearby?' the God asked.

'Yes, at my mother's castle in Cadbury.'

'Bring her to Tintagel, from there I will send our little friends again to guide you here.'

123

Morgan was overwhelmed with gratitude, as the lady of the lake summoned Eros and Sybil to her side. She gave them their instructions and Morgan wrote a note informing her family that she was heading back home with good news.

'I will find the treasure and return it to your lady, 'Morgan promised.

The lady of the lake smiled. 'I can see how pure your heart is, I know you will not let me down.'

The lady was in a mood to confide some more to her guest. 'I will reveal to you something that is a secret. Needless to say our bargain of confidence holds for this also.'

Morgan agreed not to say a word.

The lady began in a curious melancholy manner. 'It is a curse to look into the future,' she began. 'In most cases you are not able to change history by it, nor perhaps should you try, but how frustrating it is see such heartbreak.'

The lady then turned her head to look directly at Morgan and addressed her in a most matter of fact way. 'Your brother will die shortly,' she revealed.

Morgan cried out his name, but the lady of the lake asked her to listen to the rest of what she had to say.

The lady continued. 'He will die, for I have seen three separate versions of his death, all on the same day. He will die in two days from now, and neither you nor I can do anything to stop it.'

'Should we not try at least,' insisted Morgan.

'No my dear, no one can undo this,' the lady stressed. 'I wanted to tell you something else, but alas I have made a mistake in being so blunt.'

Morgan calmed herself and assured the lady she would listen without further interruption.

'A plague is coming to your lands, a plague driven by the fanatics of the religion you know as Christianity. This religion will destroy everything that does not conform to their narrow views. Soon they will wipe out the last remnants of paganism with blood and hatred.'

'We must stop them,' cried Morgan.

The lady of the lake smiled. 'You must stop them,' she exclaimed.

'Can you not send down thunderbolts and strike them down.'

The lady laughed. 'The Gods have pledged an oath not to interfere in earthly concerns. An oath countless have broken, but for reasons I can not go into I am powerless to act.

Morgan's tone had changed and the lady of the lady perceived this. She thought to fuel the lady's hatred for her rival. 'You can be in no doubt that Guinevere is behind the forthcoming death of your brother. You must kill this evil woman and stop her followers from plunging the land into a civil war.'

Morgan somehow managed to control her feelings of hatred in front of the lady. She bombarded the lady with more questions. 'Can you not use the spell to save Arthur as well as Elaine?' she asked.

'You can bring him here after death and I promise to do what I can for him, but you must promise me in return to fight against this forthcoming plague.'

'How can you be so sure I can stop it?'

'These two individuals will put in danger your entire race's future. Crush them or a great age of enlightenment will be snuffed out, to be replaced with an age of darkness and despair.'

Morgan argued for the lady's interference in crushing the forces she had described, but the lady vowed to show Morgan in the pool, just what like the devastation would be like.

'Look into the pool again and see what they will do to this beautiful land, if you do not take up the challenge and lead a revolt against them.'

Morgan stared down at the pool as the water around the lady twirled around like a whirlwind again. The many colors of the water changed as the water dissipated to leave a vision. This vision was of a village full of men, women and children, going about their everyday lives. Morgan could tell it was an Angle village by the clothes the inhabitants wore; their shabby furs and leathers and by the light colored hair, that were bound with silver and bronze wire that only the Angles wore around their heads.

A small army of fifty to sixty men rode at a gallop towards the village square. As the riders came closer, some villagers stopped to watch the men approach, never fearing for their safety. It wasn't until the fire came raining down on them, did they realize that they were under attack. Archers had lit their arrows with Greek fire and had fired them onto the roofs of the Angles homes. The crudely built thatched huts quickly burnt and the inhabitants ran out onto the road to be met by soldiers wielding their weapons of death. It was not just arrows that pierced the Angles village that day, but swords, daggers, axes and spears. The bloodletting was fierce and uncontrollable as men, women and even children were hacked to death without mercy. The sight set before Morgan was brutal, but worse was to follow.

The lady watched in horror at the picture of destruction and slaughter continued. The yells of pain and terror wrenched at her insides as she witnessed heartless men raped women and kill children before her eyes. The tears began to run down the lady's cheeks, but still she did not look away. To her dismay the massacre had not yet reached its end.

The figures of the murderers mostly wore black and kept their faces covered, but at the front of the carnage were two figures that had stopped their blood letting to dismount from their horses to study the scene before them.

The man was large in size and did not appear young, while the other was small and appeared middle aged. To Morgan's surprise the picture was just clear enough to see their faces. The large man took off his metal helmet and turned to address his companion. His companion did so likewise, to reveal a shocking discovery. The small figure was not a man at all, but the Queen Guinevere.

Ursien, the King of Gore addressed Guinevere. 'Is all this really necessary?' he complained.

Guinevere gave the man a look of contempt, before shouting to someone engaged in the massacre. 'Pelles!' she roared. 'Leave no one alive to tell the tale.'

Ursien had killed more than his fair share in battle and had cut throats, hung people, but he had never killed children before and his skin crawled at the sight.

'You have become weak my lord,' Guinevere told him.

'What does this achieve? 'he scorned.

The Queen turned her head to witness a young man cut down from behind by an axe. His head spit almost in two, as the blood spurted into the air, Ursien saw the look of triumph upon the Queen's face and felt sick. Something inside him rebelled against this holy war. He wished he had never become involved, but he was caught up in it now and he could not retreat.

'Let this will be a warning to others, to live our way or return to wherever they came from,' the lady spouted.

Guinevere set about organizing the last deeds of slaughter, by having the remaining men, women and children gathered and brought before her to be executed. Three men, two women and two children were on their knees before the Queen. The women wailed and begged for mercy, the children could not stop crying and the men stayed silent.

'In pain of death,' the Queen yelled. 'Do you abandon your heathen ways and pledge allegiance to the one true God?'

The women screamed yes, while the children continued to cry and the men said nothing. Guinevere repeated her question and again got the same result.

King Pelles took off his disguise and along with two others dragged the men to their feet and set about hanging them from the nearest tree. The women screamed and begged for mercy. Guinevere did not heed their pleas and gave her order to hang all three. One died quickly, but the other two lingered for awhile, their ghastly groans echoing throughout the village.

Now the Queen turned to the hysterical children. One girl around eight and one boy around ten and asked them again if they abandoned their heathen ways. Ursien tried to intervene, but Pelles withdrew his sword and pointed it at his chest. The two saved Angle women pleaded that the children would pledge their allegiance, but Guinevere insisted the children speak for themselves. After witnessing such barbarity the poor children could not stop crying and could not utter a word on their own behalf.

Morgan glanced at the lady of the lake, hoping for some comfort but the lady's face told her what the end was to be. There was gasp of horror from Morgan, who put her hands on her head and began to weep.

The picture dissolved and the lady of the lake held Morgan in her arms for a moment. Morgan stared at the lady. 'I must stop this from happening,' she declared.

'That is not possible. The scene we witnessed was not the future, but the past. The massacre took place earlier today in the Village of Haydon Bridge in Corbenic.'

21

Merlin's decision to keep following Gallia and her companions was taken after much thought. Lady Morgan would be anxiously awaiting news, but since the King still had not arrived, he thought about sending her a message. He did not trust messages delivered by raven, so he summoned the fairy King Eros, to ask for his help. His association with the fairies was a strange one, being part God and part human had confused the tiny supernatural creatures. Like the Gods, he could see them and summon them at his will. He also knew that they only really cared for the lady of the lake, and were loath to be used by any other. So Merlin could not be sure the fairy King would come. In fact Eros could not, but another fairy came instead. This fairy was called Daphne and she appeared beside the fallen God in the forest west of Dover.

'Oh, it is you my lord,' she said, as Merlin appeared from behind a tree.

The area was sparse of everything except trees, wolverine and wild boar. In the past the forest had been used for hunts for the nobility, but then came the wars and the place had become overrun with birch trees and wild beasts. Merlin acknowledged Daphne and welcomed her. 'I appreciate you coming before me,' he told the fairy.

'My mistress does not know I have come.'

'I have a message I must get to the Lady Morgan.'

'You wish me to deliver it?'Daphne enquired.

'Tell her I am still waiting for the King and will come as soon as I can.'

Daphne could not contain her curiosity. 'You are some distance from the coast. Pray tell me why you wait for the King here?'

Merlin did not want Daphne to know his true reason, so he said nothing.

Daphne flew up close to Merlin and looked into his eyes. 'You are here because of some woman.'

Merlin could not conceal the truth, so he laughed. 'These humans have a way of entrapping you with their problems,' he said. 'Their females are somehow enchanting...'

Daphne interrupted his eulogy. 'My lord, have you not learnt after the last time?

'You do not understand,' pleaded Merlin.

'Maybe not, but I'm not sure I should tell the lady you are caught up on some business of your own.'

'Don't tell her anything if you wish.'

Daphne flapped her wings and cursed quietly.

'I will keep my rendezvous with the King,' said a disgruntled Merlin.

'Do not look so irritable,' Daphne told Merlin. 'The lady has now made her acquaintance with our mistress.'

Merlin was shocked by the news. 'How did that happen?'

'Our lady took an interest in the matter and in the lady.'

'Go on,' said Merlin.

'The Lady Morgan has already had an audience with our good lady and has made a bargain. Our mistress has agreed to restore the Lady Elaine to full health.'

Merlin was suspicious. 'What does your lady ask in return?' he asked.

'She made the same deal with the human.'

'What about Mider, how will he feel once he hears?'

'You worry too much, Merlin. Our mistress will keep Lady Morgan safe.'

Merlin, still in disguise, had followed Gallia and her two associates from the cabin in the woods, to the Dover docks. There they travelled to Mucking on a vessel that was over crowded with passengers. The small vessel was in danger of overturning many times before finally arriving at its destination. In a rush to disembark, Frith had somehow upset the captain. The man stood on the deck of the boat and tried in vain to make a case for his special treatment.

Merlin was amused to see Frith being made to wait till everyone else had disembarked before his eyes. His enforced tenure made it possible for his two companions to leave without him. Perhaps it was this thought that made Frith sweat and become over animated.

The captain was large, muscular and looked more than capable of handling himself in a fight. Frith's constant salvo was beginning to antagonize the man and Merlin was expecting the captain to strike out at him at any moment. Sure enough, that is exactly what happened. Frith waved his arms in front of the captain when he saw his companions embark without him. The blow was quick as it was hard. Frith hit the deck with a thud.

What happened next took Merlin by surprise. As the people turned their heads to look at the violent disturbance, Gallia took her opportunity. She had the cargo of precious artifacts in her hand and when Grim turned to look behind, she smacked the bag against the side of his face. The man fell backwards onto the gangplank blocking its access. Merlin ran after the lady as she ran down the plank at a swift pace. He had to step over people, pushed his way past many to give chase. By the time he reached the quay the lady had vanished. To have lost his quarry so easily was embarrassing. Either the lady moved like lightning or he was getting old, he surmised. He had two choices, he could scour the inns and taverns of Mucking in the hope of spying his lady or he could find what her companions knew. He decided to find out what Grim and Frith made of Gallia's betrayal. He assumed the lady had planned to steal the artifacts and double-cross her associates.

Some time later, when all the commotion was over, he followed Frith and Grim to an inn called the Arthur's Crown. Still in disguise he placed himself at the table in sight of his adversaries. It didn't take long before Frith began to articulate his bitterness.

'Does she really think I will allow her to get away with this? I can destroy her at any time.' He took a slug of his drink and continued. 'I shall tell her precious father all his lovely daughter's secrets, and watch the light go out of his eyes.' He turned and looked at Grim, and spat on the table. 'I will enjoy killing the old man.'

Even Grim had a look of disgust on his face. 'If you kill him, then Gallia will come after you.'

'What would you have me do?' Frith asked.

'We have to figure out where she will take the goods.'

Frith was thinking, but at the same time he was plotting his revenge. 'I'll make her squirm before me. She will be on her knees begging for my forgiveness.'

Grim inquired about local fences.

'I can think of two or three that would gladly take her merchandise, no questions asked.'

'Then we must go to them and perhaps...'

Frith shook his head.

'They would not deal directly with someone like Gallia.'

'Can you be so sure?' Grim questioned.

Frith finished his drink and shouted to the landlord to bring some more. The landlord obliged, but his lips told their own story of his displeasure of his new guests. He did not want trouble and Frith's foul mood had him worried. 'Are you gentlemen staying nearby?' he inquired.

'Why?' Frith spat.

'It is just I am full up and if you are in need of lodgings you might need to look someplace else.'

Frith didn't like the man and told him to mind his own business. The landlord moved away, but indicated to a couple of his staff to keep an eye on the strangers.

Frith drank some more and surprisingly became melancholy. 'She once looked on me as a friend, and a confidant.'

Grim assumed he was talking about Gallia.

'She is beautiful, don't you think so?'

Grim agreed she was not bad looking. 'Not bad, he says,' grumbled Frith. 'She's far too good for the likes of you...or me for that matter...I was not always this foul beast you see before you.'

Merlin was becoming intrigued. He never would have believed that under that thick skin lurked a decent human being.

'Do you regret the life you have chosen?' Frith asked his companion.

'I was born in a stinking farm, where I stayed much of the time. No I do not regret a thing.'

'Not even, when you had to...'

'I don't think about it.'

'A man with no conscience,' Frith muttered. 'I need be careful never to turn my back on you,' he said ruefully.

A plan was arranged by the two men to try the local procurers of stolen goods early the next day.

Merlin had decided to trawl the dock area to meet the most unsavory types, in the hope they would lead him to a man capable of buying the treasures that Gallia had in her possession. He was just about to leave when a man approached the table next to his. The man bent forward and whispered something into Frith's ear. Unfortunately, Merlin could not make out what was said, but Frith and Grim left immediately. Merlin followed them again and was conscious of their sudden change in mood. It would seem the villains had located the lady and were on their way to pay their respects.

22

Galahad had been introduced to Lady Ygerne and Lady Morgause by King Lot. The King had come upon the lad in the forest and had embraced him warmly. They reached Queen Ygerne's castle late in the night, but the household was still awake after receiving the correspondence from Morgan telling them of her deal with the lady of the lake.

Neither Ygerne nor Morgause knew of their kin's secret. Lot had been told, but he would rather have had his tongue cut out than to reveal Morgan's secret.

Ygerne took Lot aside for a moment and explained what had transpired when he was away. 'The Queen was here?' he whispered.

'She had us captive, but for your clever wife and my loyal subjects we would still be locked up.'

'What have you done with her men?'

'Morgause and some of the local villagers locked them down in our dungeons below us.'

Lot laughed out loud. 'The Gorlois women are truly amazing,' he cried.

Morgause turned her head and smiled at him. For the first time in many years the man felt he had done something that had pleased his wife. A steward came forward to address Ygerne and the man whispered something in the lady's ear. She glanced at Lot and ushered him to her.

Morgause and Galahad did not see the gesture. The man was quickly by her side. 'My lady what is it?' he asked.

'A bishop by the name of Germanus has arrived unannounced. Do you know who he is and what he might want here?'

'It is rather late to expect to be entertained,' Lot commented.

Morgan had mentioned his name and Galahad had informed him he was responsible for his attempted kidnap.

What business could he possibly have here? 'What little I know of him my lady, makes me suspect he could be in league with Guinevere.'

'So he has come here expecting to meet the lady,' Ygerne surmised.

She approached the steward and informed him to show the bishop into the chapel. The young steward looked surprised, but bowed and assured his mistress it would be done.

Ygerne and Lot left the great hall and set a trap for their unexpected guest.

Germanus was on his guard, for he was surprised by the lack of warmth of his arrival and the fact that the guards on duty did not seem to be that of the Queen's. He waited in an antechamber for the steward to return. When the man did return, he led Germanus up a flight of steps to a small confined room off the main tower. This too made the bishop uneasy, but that uneasiness diminished somewhat when the man studied the room he found himself in. The room was circular and had no furnishings to speak of, except an altar, a row of pews and a pulpit.

The altar housed an array of white candles that glimmered in the gloomy light. The church was bare of any ornamentation and this pleased the man. He had given up wealth and position to become God's servant and believed everyone else should do the same.

A secret door opened and shut and the man turned to witness a lady enter the chapel. She covered her face with a veil which managed to protect her from the man's gaze. At first Germanus went to acknowledge the lady, then decided to bide his time.

'You are very prompt, your grace,' the lady advised.

To Germanus's surprise the lady's voice sounded like Guinevere's. Still he remained cautious. 'I did not expect to meet you in such a room as this,' the man admitted.

'You seem surprised?'

'Yes, it was not what I expected.'

'How so?' the lady asked.

'I was led to believe the Lady Ygerne was a pagan. I am therefore surprised to find she has her own private chapel.'

'Perhaps you have been poorly informed concerning the lady?'

Germanus acknowledged this remark by a smile and a slight nod of his head. He began to walk around the circular room. 'Indeed, it is hard to recognize one's friends from one's enemies these days.'

Ygerne approached the man. 'You have met the Lady Ygerne?' she inquired.

'I haven't had that pleasure.'

'You have something to report?' the lady asked,

Sensing the lady before him was not the Queen the man assumed it could only be Lady Ygerne.

Shifting his tone, Germanus spoke softly and with genuine concern. 'I would advise you and your family to leave this place at once.'

The secret door opened again and this time King Lot entered. He had his sword already drawn and proceeded to approach Germanus and Ygerne.

Germanus continued to speak to the Lady Ygerne. 'Guinevere will soon be here with a lot of men, so take this chance to escape.'

The lady started to speak, but Lot's sword was thrust at the man's neck. 'It is no good my lady, let me get the information from him. I have my own methods, methods that have been tried and tested over many years.'

The Lady Ygerne removed her veil and looked into the bishop's eyes. 'I don't doubt my son-in-law is very accomplished in certain forms of inducement.'

'Let me introduce myself, I am the bishop Germanus, the special envoy to Pope Celestine.'

Lady Ygerne smiled. She was surprised at the lack of fear in the man's eyes.

'I take it I am addressing the Lady Ygerne?' Germanus continued.

'You are indeed. Now tell me what you know of Queen Guinevere's plans?'

'I will gladly, just as soon as your henchman removes his sword from my throat.'

The lady looked at King Lot and the man dropped his sword to his side.

'That is better,' sighed the bishop. 'My warning to you was given with the best of intentions. The Queen arrives soon with an army and I suspect she will be in a jubilant mood.'

'Why is that?' asked Lot.

'She is ruthless in her determination to rid this kingdom of what she might call undesirables.'

Lot shot a glance at Lady Ygerne. She kept her eyes fixed on the bishop however and tried to engage what the man was thinking. 'An army,' the lady began. 'Tell me, whose army? It can not be my son's, so in whose name is this army formed?'

Without blinking an eye Germanus volunteered an answer. 'Why it is the Queen's army, of course.'

The tone in which these words were spoken alerted the lady to the realization that the Queen was planning and executing a deadly plan. If that were the case then Arthur had to be warned, for his life would be in danger.

Germanus seem to read her mind. 'I fear your warning might come too late,' he warned.

Lot had his sword thrust once more at the man's throat. 'Tell us, what she has planned for the King?'

Struggling to speak, the bishop nonetheless, managed a faint reply. 'I fear she plans the King's death, but I could not swear to it.'

Merlin became invisible again and stalked Frith and his two companions along the dockside, until they came to a broken-down shack. The cabin was black with grime and smoke and housed a dubious Saxon by the name of Targo. The man was well known in the criminal class of the area, his specialty being in the handling of stolen goods. He had persuaded Gallia to come there with a promise of a fat purse, but had decided to betray the lady instead.

Gallia however had taken precautions and sent someone in her stead. She had given a young woman of the street, two silver coins in exchange for her help. The young woman did not know why she was walking towards the shack, or what she would encounter. Gallia watched from a distance as the woman was suddenly surrounded by three men, who knocked her down and tore the pouch from her grasp.

Gallia saw everything and was thankful for her own good sense, although she wished she had compensated the woman more, for the men began to kick her where she lay. It was Frith who enjoyed this brutality the most, until finally Grim torn him away. Just as Frith looked into the pouch, Merlin appeared beside Gallia. His presence seemed to come out of nowhere and the lady let out a shriek of terror. Frith looked up and across, towards an old dock building where the noise had originated from.

Merlin put his hand over Gallia's mouth and pulled her back out of sight. He whispered. 'Do not be afraid, I have come to help you.'

Gallia turned her face and even in the darkness thought she recognized the man holding her. 'You,' she murmured.

Merlin let his hand loosen from the lady's mouth.

'What the hell do you want with me?' Gallia whispered.

'To save you from yourself,' Merlin said, smiling.

'Why? What are you, some kind of monk?'

'Yes, you could call me that.'

Loosening his grip on the lady, Merlin suggested they depart while they still had the chance. Gallia agreed and they both moved away from the shack and the surrounding area.

A short time later they felt safe and could rest, both were panting from lack of breath as they came to a bridge over a stream. Gallia's mouth and throat hurt, so she climbed down the bank to the water's edge and putting her hands together gave herself several handfuls of fresh clean water to drink.

Merlin followed her down the bank and drank some water from the stream himself. The lady was wary of her new friend's interest in her wellbeing and planned to escape from him whenever she got the chance.

'I take it the pouch Frith has, does not contain the artifacts,' Merlin inquired.

Gallia studied Merlin's face. 'Frith, what do you know about him?' she asked in a voice that was harsh and biting.

'Only what I could find out from dregs of this place.'

'How do you know about the artifacts?' Gallia asked.

'Let's just say I am a good listener, for the time being.'

'Or the devil himself,' murmured Gallia.

'You do not carry the items with you I see.'

'So that is your interest. Well the goods are safe and I shall not share their profits with you or anyone else.'

'The blood of others have touched these trophies, all that touch them now will be accursed.'

'You are a monk, or a sorcerer,' the lady conjectured.

'I haven't decided which yet.'

'I somehow do not think we have seen the last of our friend Frith,' Merlin advised.

'If you were rich, you could buy the treasure and I could execute my plan for escape.'

'Escape from what?' asked Merlin.

Gallia's piercing brown eyes studied the man before her. He was the same old man that sat beside her in the inn the night before and yet he looked different, younger, less tired, more interesting, and perhaps even a little handsome.

'I don't know who you are. You could be working for my enemies for all I know.'

Merlin shook his head. 'I had pressing business to take care of, but I was shocked by the company that you kept.'

'They are not a pretty bunch, are they?'

'Why are you involved with them?'

139

Gallia laughed. 'That's easy. I am a courier of stolen goods. Not wanting to boast, I am extremely good at what I do.'

'It's hardly a trade to be proud of,' Merlin commented.

'It's better than starving to death,' the lady snarled.

Merlin could taste the hate and loathing inside the lady, for he had lived with the same feelings for more than fifteen years himself. 'Let me help you,' he pleaded.

The lady threw back her hair and laughed. 'How often do you think I have heard those lines before? Men have a way of saving women like me, but the price is always just a little too high.'

Merlin tried to convince Gallia that his intentions to her were honorable, but the lady remarked that she had heard those words a little too often also.

'You still haven't explained, what you meant about your escape,' he asked.

The lady got flustered and began to climb back up the bank. Merlin helped her and they stood on the bridge for awhile without conversing. Finally the lady gave in and told the man a little about her predicament.

The air was getting cooler as Merlin and Gallia walked away from the town into the countryside. They walked for a good while, before Merlin realized how tired the lady was becoming. He put his arm around her waist and gave her support and the lady even laid her head slightly on his shoulder.

'You see now why I need the money?' the lady whispered.

Merlin sighed. 'I don't know what to say. I'm sorry about your troubles, but I'm not sure how I can help.'

'At least you listened and did not preach.'

'Once I finish my business, I will find you and help if I can.'

Gallia eyes looked up at Merlin. 'By then it will be too late.'

'You're worried about Frith?'

140

'Don't you see what his next port of call will be? If he tells my father how I make my money, it will surely break his heart. I fear the shock might even kill him.'

'I will not abandon you,' Merlin promised.

23

To his dismay, Gaheris's secret was out. His buried treasure had been removed from his hideout and his two loyal servants murdered. He was a day late to prevent this catastrophe from happening. The cave lay some distance from the village of Traunent and a good few furlongs from the Tantallon hill-fort of his father's. To his horror, his men had their throats cut. Their murderers had taken everything from the cave; gold, silver, an assortment of chalices, cauldrons, broaches, rings, maps and many other items of unknown origins, such as two small metal drums, the contents of which had remained a mystery.

Gaheris gave his men a Christian burial, before setting out in pursuit of Mordred. He was unaware as he travelled south past the Old Roman wall into Corbenic, of the events earlier that day. He was wary of travelling through King Pelles's lands for fear Pelles had made some deal with Guinevere.

His thoughts turned to the young lady he was so keen to see and wondered why he could not track her down. He knew his interest in finding her was now bordering on an obsession. Arthur had not given him direct orders to look for the girl, but he hinted that he would be pleased to speak with her and to find out what she knew. It was strange, he thought, to look for a complete stranger, someone you had never laid eyes on before, strange and extremely difficult. A good description and a crudely painted icon were not sufficient tools to bring about a successfully outcome it would seem, but he was a patient and resolute man.

He passed many villages in Corbenic and became aware of a feeling of tension and unrest. The day before, this tension was not present when he travelled in the opposite direction, so he wondered what had happened to suddenly bring about this change.

As he got nearer to Catraeth, a group of villagers suddenly occupied the main road, blocking his way. They all had some kind of weapon in their hands; some were carrying swords, others spears, but most were carrying makeshift weapons, such as pitchforks and spades. He slowed his horse down in case he had to make a quick retreat. They had a look of desperation about them and Gaheris saw that most were Angles or Saxons. A young man with flowing blonde hair, raced forward towards him. 'Are you the praeside from York?' he asked.

Gaheris inquired what had happened.

'We seek the praeside's help in tracking down the barbarians, who massacred the people of Haydon Bridge,' the man informed him.

'A massacre you say,' a shocked Gaheris recapitulated.

'The whole village was destroyed and everyone was killed.'

Again Gaheris couldn't believe what he was hearing. 'There must be some survivors,' he concluded.

The blonde man shook his head. 'Are you the praeside for this area?' the man inquired.

Gaheris knew the man they were seeking, but knew him to be corrupt and a fool to boot. A friend to King Pelles, the man was not interested in his work but lived off the fat of his land instead. He had often complained to Arthur about him, but the King needed to keep Pelles happy and did not remove the incompetent fool from office. 'I am not, but the praeside in this area is a drunkard and a fool, I doubt he will be of much use to you.'

A murmur of unrest circulated amongst the men, leaving a scent of anger.

'Do not fear, I will look into this matter and report directly to the King.'

The blonde haired man took hold of the reins of Gaheris's horse and glared up at him. 'And who the devil are you, sir?' he asked forcefully.

'I am the King's nephew, my name is Gaheris.'

The men murmured amongst themselves. It was the mention of the King's name that had precipitated the passionate discussion. Gaheris could feel their anger and animosity, although he found it disquieting that they should feel anything but love for their King.

It was not the thought that Gaheris was a relation to the King that finally persuaded the men to accept the young man's help, but the fact he was the son of their neighbor King Lot. To be fair on the people gathered on that lonely road, they did not know King Arthur, for he was as distant to them as any Sultan or Emperor from the East. King Lot however, was a man they knew well, he was a man they had dealings with before, a man they trusted and respected.

The men all listened to Gaheris as if he were the local praeside, or consulare. What he told them was to stick together, stay alert and to have a small council gather all the evidence of the massacre together. He on his part promised to report the incident to the King by the quickest means possible and to inform all his family and supporters also.

After talking with Gaheris the men felt reassured that swift action would be taken. By promising to look into the matter Gaheris was doing two things; he was taking upon himself the role that was not his, that of a law enforcement official, and he was making it possible to stay in Britain for the time being. He would seek out Morgan's help and at the same time take care of some of his own affairs, such as the gathering of all information on the possible sightings of the young girl he sought.

In the past such acts of barbarity might well be put down to raids from the Picts, but no one thought that the northern tribes were responsible this time. The area had been quiet for two years of violence, so it was disconcerting to think that perhaps old scores were now being settled.

As Gaheris was about to leave, the young blonde man came towards him. While he mounted his horse, the young Angle quietly spoke to him. 'Forgive me for doubting you earlier, but we are full of apprehension.'

'I understand. It's hard to believe anyone could commit such a crime.'

'There is one man capable of such an atrocity. King Pelles has spoken out against our kind.'

'You're not suggesting your own King is behind this attack?'

'Yes, I am suggesting such a thing.'

Gaheris leant forward from his horse. 'If the proof can be found, he shall pay for his crime, you have my word.'

The young man accepted his statement and bid Gaheris farewell.

'My lady,' cried Yvain. 'Slow down you will become unseated if you do not.'

Morgan eased her horse a little, but Yvain still had trouble keeping up with his mistress. Finally as day turned to night the lady slowed her pace and relaxed, much for the sake of the horses as for her own. Both rider and horse were sweating greatly and a thankful Yvain sighed. 'Lady, you must stop, you must consider your health.'

Morgan knew the young man spoke the truth, but she had such a burden to bear. She wanted to reach her brother before the fatal blow would strike him down. She did not know how he would die for the lady had not confided in her with the details. 'You are right, my friend. Forgive me if I have been poor company since returning to the mainland.'

They had reached the beginning of the country road that would take them to Winchester. She feared she could not possibly reach Dover by the next day and that she would be too late. It would make sense to rest up and perhaps get some sleep, but she was determined not to rest.

'Should we not make camp and get some sleep?' Yvain inquired.

'I can not sleep, but we must rest for awhile.'

They dismounted from their horses and sank to the ground beside the road exhausted. The horses were panting harshly, but the evening breeze soon cooled them down.

Yvain was frightened to speak in case it might upset his mistress, but after quite some time of quiet repose he ventured to approach her. 'We do not have wings, my lady, it is impossible for us to reach Dover by tomorrow. A normal journey would take us three days, not one.'

Morgan knew this and wondered for the first time, why the lady of the lake had told her about Arthur's impending death. With her pledge to save Elaine it seemed strange to Morgan that the lady of the lake had not offered to help her reach Arthur in time. What did she expect her to do? She could not possibly right all the wrongs of the world and yet the lady had charged her to try. She had not had time to consider the consequences of Elaine's rebirth. It would create quite a stir in her world when the lady re-emerged. 'You have not asked me about Elaine,' inquired Morgan.

'You will tell me, if I have to right to know,' the young man replied.

Morgan was still emotional after her encounter on Avalon and felt so alone that these words hurt her. She needed a confidant and the young servant was the most loyal person she had ever known. 'Of course you have a right to know, you are my friend.'

Yvain was taken aback by the statement, but was happy to believe the lady meant it. 'You know you can trust me with anything.'

'Yes I know that. I have great news. The lady of the lady has agreed to restore my sweet sister back to life.'

'That is wonderful, but when?' Yvain asked.

'Just as soon as I can bring her to Tintagel,' the lady replied.

'I am glad for your sister, but mostly I am glad for you, my lady. Your strength and determination has made this possible and no one deserves this happiness more than you.'

Morgan was pleased with her servant's reply and his loyalty. 'I was surprised you could bear to prize yourself away from your young girl. Are you not keen to spend more time with her?'

'My duty to you comes first,' the young man announced.

Morgan smiled. 'You will meet up with her again, I presume?'

'She can find me anytime that she pleases.'

'With her magic?' asked Morgan.

Shrugging his shoulders the man said he didn't know, but assumed so.

'You have a right to know why we break our necks in charging towards Dover,' said the lady.

Yvain explained it did not matter, but the lady wanted to justify her haste.

'The God told me that tomorrow my brother and our King will be killed. She did not tell me where or how, only that I could not stop it.'

Yvain should have been shocked by this revelation, but what transpired around this lady was never ordinary. His reaction was to offer to go on ahead and to ride on through without stopping so as to get to Dover as soon as was humanly possible.

'We ride together; we should not split up, but thank you. When some reality returns to our lives I will be honored to bestow upon you a substantial dowry, so you can marry your young sweetheart.'

Yvain had not thought about marriage, but of course he would be honored if Nemue agreed to be his wife. A sudden doubt struck at his heart. Did she feel the same passion as he did, or had her passion waned?

They rested for a little longer, and spoke sparingly before once more riding at great speed towards Winchester.

Most of the King's men had crossed the sea to Dover, leaving Arthur and a few of his friends the last to leave. Lancelot had taken control of all the sailings and had made sure that both he and his bodyguard, a man by the nickname Ironfist would travel with Arthur and Helena in the final boat to leave Calais. He did not have a clear plan, but he was determined his old friend should never make

147

the shores of his homeland alive. Lancelot had arranged everything. He had made sure that all the other vessels had left Calais and that the last boat to sail was only capable of carrying a handful of passengers.

The captain and first mate were the only crew aboard, leaving just five passengers; King Arthur, Lady Helena, Agravain, Ironfist and himself. No one was suspicious of the lateness of the King's departure after his ill health. The King was able to walk, but was still weak and needed help from Agravain. It was the young warrior who worried Lancelot. A sick man and a young maiden should not put up much of a fight, but a young and strong soldier certainly would.

Everyone's personal belongings had been put on board and the captain had informed his passengers that they would have to leave immediately or miss the tide. So Agravain helped Arthur onboard and found the King a safe berth down in the hatch. Helena joined the King, leaving Ironfist and Lancelot on deck with the two crew members. They moved to the stern of the boat and conferred quietly. 'What are we going to do about Agravain?' Ironfist asked

'What does it matter, one more will not make a difference,' Lancelot replied.

'We set out to kill the King, but now it has become four,' Ironfist complained.

Lancelot corrected him. 'Five, we can not allow any witnesses.'

'The lady too?' the bodyguard whispered. He said it as if he had only just thought about it. 'How long will the journey take?' he asked.

'Long enough', Lancelot said quietly.

Lancelot waited until the shores of Britain were in sight and as luck would have it an argument between the captain and his first mate ensued. The first mate was getting on in years and his reluctance to carry out his captain's orders was making his superior angry. The two men were ready to come to blows as Lancelot made ready his plan.

The captain yelled at his mate for the umpteenth time and once too often, for the man picked up a ship's hook and came forward to confront his skipper. Lancelot saw the whole brief fight. As the mate swung his weapon, the captain ducked and caught the man with a fierce blow into his ribcage. The blow hit the man hard and he staggered for a moment, before the captain followed up with a right hook that caught the man squarely on the jaw. The first mate closed his eyes and fell backwards as if he were dead. The captain cursed and return to the tiller, where Lancelot joined him.

'I hope you can manage without your mate,' Lancelot asked, pretending to be alarmed.

The captain laughed. 'Course I can, I only keep him on for sentimental reasons.'

Lancelot wasn't interested in what the man meant by his remark, for his chance had arrived. With his eyes looking straight ahead the captain did not notice Lancelot take out his dagger from his scabbard. The captain met his end quickly, for his assassin cut his throat with one silent thrust. Disposal of the body was easy, as Lancelot eased his heavy frame quietly over the side. He then did the same with the unconscious mate, before securing the boat the best he could by taking down the lone sail and tying the tiller.

He pressed his head down to see below into the hold. The space was small and the occupants would have faired better on deck with the sea wind than huddled together in a stuffy hold. 'Ironfist,' Lancelot bellowed. He could hear a certain stirring from below and his man opened the hatch door to see Lancelot lying on the deck a short distance from him. 'It's now,' Lancelot whispered to him.

'I have my dagger ready,' the man replied.

As they slipped down into the hold Lancelot whispered. 'I'll take care of Arthur and Helena and you kill Agravain.'

Ironfist had no time to protest, for the act of betrayal was enacted quickly and without delay.

The confined space and the poor light made assassination difficult, but the surprise element was in their favor. Arthur and Helena were asleep and outstretched on a hammock, while Agravain had his head in a bowl being sick.

Lancelot jumped onto the hammock, his dagger raised and stabbed several blows into the body of the King. Helena screamed and jumped down onto the ground. The bloody body of Arthur slouched forward until it succumbed and was tipped over onto the floor. Helena's brief hysterics came to an end when Lancelot turned his attention on her. With his knife still covered in blood, he lunged forward to stab the lady. She took a step to one side and somehow managed to parry his blow, although the blade did graze her side. Lancelot tried again and this time struck Helena high up on her shoulder where the blade stuck for a moment, before he pulled it from her body. Just as Helena screamed in pain Agravain came to her rescue and bear-wrestled Lancelot.

Ironfist was a big and strong man, but not nimble in his actions. He went to cut Agravain with his knife by swinging at his head, but the blade sliced only a part of the young man's ear. Agravain put his hands forward in protection for a second blow, but by the time the second came he had risen to his feet and caught hold of his attacker's wrist.

The blow lacked vigor and Agravain not only deflected it away, but forced Ironfist to drop his knife onto the floor. Agravain kicked out at Ironfist and managed to hit the man in between his legs making him yell in pain. His knees gave way as he groaned and slouched to the floor. Picking up Ironfist's knife, Agravain showed the man no mercy and stuck him through the heart with his own blade.

Helena tried to hide behind Agravain who put himself between her and Lancelot. As the men struggled to gain control over each other, they began swinging at each other with their knives periodically. Helena's legs gave way and she crumbled to the floor to watch the two men battle for supremacy. The fight was brutal, as two powerful men lashed out at each other and at times wrestled like prize gladiators. At one point Lancelot's knife was squeezed from his hand and landed not too far from Helena's reach.

The lady crept forward and tried to reach it, but every time it looked like she was going to get it the men's bodies got in her way. Finally Agravain was struck from a blow from Lancelot's head that knocked him back and almost off his feet. Lancelot followed up quickly, by grabbing hold of the knife on the floor and stabbing Agravain through the heart. As he watched his quarry die, Guinevere's lover realized he too might succumb as he looked over his blooded frame. The sticky fluid poured over the right side of his white tunic, covering it quickly in a crimson tide. He covered his wound with his hand and somehow crawled up onto the deck ignoring the fact that Helena was still alive and huddled in a corner.

The Lady Helena was barely conscious; she blinked and mumbled to herself in a desperate effort to stay awake. Her very life depended on her finding hidden strength from somewhere. She crawled over to Agravain and Arthur and tried to awaken them, but both men were dead. She sobbed softly to herself and listened in vain to hear what Lancelot was doing on deck. It was impossible for her to comprehend what had just happened. It did not feel real, it somehow wasn't possible.

Three men were stretched before her all dead, all sacrificed for no reason that she could fathom. What could have made Lancelot do such a terrible thing, she wondered?

She felt sick with the pain from her body, but at the same time she felt numb as if her pain was somehow outside her body. She knew he would be back to finish off his ghastly work and put an end to her short life. All the moments of joy and all the moments of sadness flashed into her head, as if she had to cram every single memory she had at her disposal, for one last lament before crossing over to another world. She was not a Christian and hoped that Lancelot knew this and would put a coin in her mouth or in her hand so as to pay the ferryman. He was a monster, so why should he care if she crossed the river Styx safely to the other world or not. If he had a pinch of integrity left she would beg him for this last wish.

Lancelot struggled like the lady to remain conscious, but at least on deck the breeze awoke his senses and he felt again clear headed. He found a chest with bandages and tried the best he could to halt the flow of blood. He was quite thankful to see the blood slow to a halt and he began to breathe a little more easily. He had suffered many cuts and abrasions in battles and his use of tourniquets had often saved his life. Again he knew from experience he would survive, but could he finish off his night's gruesome work. For a moment he began to weep like a child, and then he cursed the Queen's name over and over again. 'What have you made me do?' he cried? .He repeated the same question over and over, as he struck his hand against his blood soaked chest.

Having recovered his senses, Lancelot set about the task of finishing his plan. He would throw the rest of the bodies over the side and scuttle the boat, before swimming ashore to raise the alarm. His story would be a simple; the boat was attacked by pirates and everyone onboard had perished, by some miracle he had survived. The extent of the injuries inflicted on him and the blood he lost attested to the ferocity of the attack. He had little doubt his story would be believed. There would be great sorrow when the news of the King's death reached inland.

The sorrow would be real, but not everyone in the kingdoms would mourn. Arthur was a King who ruled from afar and many had never even set eyes on him, including members of the nobility. Lancelot felt that the King had delegated too much to others and had lost touch with his own people. The son of King Ban was an idealist, and although his deeds weighed heavily on his conscience, he could contemplate a better time ahead. A decent period of mourning would take place, after which he and Guinevere would announce their marriage and set about stabilizing the five kingdoms. New laws would set out plans the length and breathe of the country to build and rebuild in a grand scale, giving occupation and purpose to all. Many great towns would spring up as would castles, churches and aqueducts. It would be an age of enlightenment, where sculptors, carpenters, painters and masons would flourish. This was the man's dream, but it was only possible after one final act of barbarity. Lady Helena must die.

She might already have bled to death, if not he would have to give her the final death blow. With this thought in his head, the man returned to the hold and climbed down to find to his astonishment that there was no sign of the lady. He covered every spec in that small confined hold and followed a trail of blood that could easily have been his own, up onto to the deck. He presumed the lady had climbed up while he was berating himself and had slipped overboard unseen and unheard. If that were the case, then the coldness of the water and the severity of her wounds would surely have taken her life from her body. He crossed himself and thanked God for sparing him this final act of violence.

With his injuries still giving him great pain, he somehow managed to carry the bodies onto the deck of the boat. He then managed to tip them overboard one by one. Their bodies made little noise, as they hit the choppy sea. Lancelot began to cough up blood as he lay on the deck for a moment to recover. He found his body so weak that he waited to see if he could regain some strength before going over the side himself. He closed his tired eyes and fell asleep.

26

Merlin had purchased two fresh horses and had travelled with Gallia through the night heading for Londinium. They hoped to get to Cardinal, Gallia's father's villa on the shore of the Thames, before Frith and his men. As the morning sun rose and filtered much needed light upon the road, Merlin pleaded with the lady to slow her pace.

Gallia glanced over at her companion and eased her animal to a gentle canter. Merlin sighed. 'We have not seen a soul since we left Mucking, Frith could not possibly be on our tail.'

A smile formed around the lady's mouth, although it disappeared as quickly as it had appeared. 'You must play up before my father, I don't expect you to lie, just be careful with your words.'

Merlin could see the dread in the lady's eyes and reassured her. 'Lying is not a problem, it's the one thing I am good at,' he attested.

The faint smile returned. 'What other qualities do you have?' the lady asked.

'I am unreliable; I snore, suffer from foul breath and have a weakness for fallen women.'

Again the smile returned for a moment. 'You can say you are my boss, he believes I am legitimate trader. It explains all my comings and goings.'

Merlin declined his head. 'Your father's name wouldn't happen to be Philemon, by any chance?'

A gasp of surprise, told Merlin it was.

'Have we met before?' the lady challenged.

'I saw you once before, when you were almost of age, walking in the market square in Antioch with your father. We spoke, but I can not remember what we said. I remember how proud your father was as he declared to all present that his daughter was going to be a great scholar.'

Merlin's words pierced the lady's heart and made her eyes water, but her anger took hold. 'You have me at a disadvantage, you know who I am, but you are a man of mystery, a man that I have placed all my hopes on, but who keeps all his secrets to himself.'

'I am no one of any worth my lady, a simple man who has no kin and no one to care whether he lives or dies.'

'If you're such a simple man, how is it you appear from nowhere and know things that are not possible for anyone to know?'

Merlin put on his most innocent look.

'I suspect you to be a sorcerer, but I can not tell whether you mean me harm or good.'

'A sorcerer,' Merlin laughed. 'If I was, would I not just strike Frith down and free you from his hold on you?'

'Perhaps you are like the old Greek gods that liked to play and amuse themselves with their unfortunate human subjects.'

Merlin chuckled, but the lady's instinct was uncanny. He thought to change the subject. 'I do not remember your father being blind all those years ago.'

The look of sadness returned to her face. 'He was not. His blindness came because of the great earthquake. We survived although tens of thousands perished, but a fire took hold in our mansion and a piece of scorched timber struck him in the face. I, somehow with my servant, helped rescue him from the place. We lost everything that day, our property and our possessions.'

The tale the lady told was sad, but not uncommon in the harsh world that Merlin knew. 'His business,' Merlin asked. 'Did that perish too?'

'His partner swindled him of all the money he had. He was never a great judge of character. I think I take after him in that.'

'How did you survive?'

'With my wits,' the lady retorted. 'I used every man I knew, to get money to leave that accursed place. We arrived in Gaul and set up in a stall selling wool at the local market. I found I could not earn enough and look after my father at the same time, so I returned to using my body to acquire what we needed.'

The lady spoke with such candor that Merlin wanted to extend some comfort to her. But he knew the lady would not appreciate an outpouring of sentiment, so he was content to let her continue.

Gallia stopped her horse and lowered her voice almost to a whisper. 'I care not what you think of me, but even if I was tricked into working with Frith, I welcomed the benefits. So what does that say about me?'

Merlin moved his horse closer to the lady's. He wanted to caress her cheek with his hand, but found his resolve too weak. 'How were you tricked?' the man asked.

'My father and I went from one hovel to another, until I saw how disheveled he looked. I could not continue as I was, for I had degenerated into the most common of street whores. Then I met Frith one cold winter's night on the streets of Paris.' The lady halted her address and looking uncomfortable on her horse. She began to fidget and eventually decided to dismount.

Merlin dismounted too and helped her to the ground. The man saw for himself how light the lady weighed as he helped her down. The years of deprivation had taken its toll on her body. The man realized that she was little more than skin and bone and if the light was still in her eyes, it was due to her steely determination to save her father from ever knowing her terrible secret.

'Tell me how the blackguard tricked you,' Merlin pleaded.

They walked a little, holding the reins of the horses as they went. 'He persuaded me to carry certain items from one country to another. I do not look like a crook, so no one stopped me and from then on it became convenient for us both. I did not ask many questions for the money he gave me satisfied my needs. He used me, but I did not complain, because it suited me fine.'

For whatever the reason, the lady did not want to condemn the man. It was intolerable for Merlin to listen to her speak of him. 'You must see how he used you for his own purposes,' he pointed out.

Gallia smiled. 'I used him too, I knew what I was doing was wrong and yet I continued.'

'Have you ever committed any other crimes?' Merlin asked.

The lady's smile turned to a frown. 'What ever do you mean?'

'I would suggest a man like Frith has committed murder...'

Raising her voice, Gallia rounded on Merlin. 'How dare you suggest I have killed anyone?'

The couple stopped walking and a sudden impulse took hold of Merlin. He ventured to take the lady in his arms, but Gallia noticed his arms reach out at her and was quick with her response. She hit him across his face with her hand. 'I'm not some innocent maiden you can play with,' she told him.

Merlin jumped back and began to laugh. After a moment looking at each other, the lady laughed too. 'If I kill you, you would be my first I promise.'

'I'm glad to hear it, though I suspect you could tell me a great many gruesome tales about your employer.'

'Let me make myself clear. No matter what he has done, I would never betray him to the authorities.'

Merlin gestured with his head that he understood. 'Unfortunately, he does not know that.'

'His pride has been hurt. I've made him look like a fool before his colleagues and he's not likely to forgive me for that.'

'What are you saying?

'I've been useful to him, but not anymore.'

'You mean, he means to silence you forever?'

'He might give me one last chance if I returned his merchandise, but I have no intention of doing that.'

'Why did you go up against him?' asked the man.

'In my business you make contacts. I have in my possession an object that someone will pay a great deal of money for.'

'The chalice in your possession is not what you think,' Merlin informed the lady, 'although it is a nice object and quite valuable.'

Gallia pulled her dagger from her sheath and cursed the man before her. 'Who the devil are you?' she yelled.

'I'm not the devil, or some sorcerer, but a man who sometimes has more knowledge than is good for him.'

'Your knowledge is going to get you killed one day.'

'Yes, but not today.'

'How do you know about the chalice?'

'I saw Frith kill the man who had it in his possession...'

'That's impossible...you couldn't have.'

'He was a small man, with a beard. He looked like a Jew from the east.'

Gallia's breathing became heavy as she struggled to keep from passing out. 'You must be the devil,' she muttered, 'only he could know such things.'

Mordred was continuing on his journey in the pursuit of finding the Lady Morgan. After consultation with her mother, the young man believed the lady would be at Tintagel and so he intended to travel there as fast as he could. He left with Lady Ygerne and her family as they left Cadbury Castle to travel with King Lot to the safety of his lands in Lothian. This was a long and arduous journey, made worse by the precautions taken by the King to forgo all the main roads. They travelled with light supplies and no possessions, and found themselves crossing dangerous rivers and streams. Throughout all their hardships no one complained, not even Morgause who found Galahad's company compelling, much to the annoyance of her husband. Mordred parted from his kin at the town of Wells and wished them a safe journey before returning they way he had come. It was a straight-forward journey to Tintagel and he knew his way, so the young man felt carefree and a little careless. He drifted back onto the known roads and without thinking found himself on the road to Cadbury again.

A sudden thunder rocked the ground around him, as he watched hundreds of soldiers gallop pass. He moved onto the side of a path to keep out of their way, but was engulfed by the dust that nearly choked the life out of him. After coughing much of the debris from his throat, Mordred was pleased to see the road clear again and set his horse back onto it. A few moments later he saw a lone soldier approach, in the opposite direction.

To his great misfortune the disfigurement that had haunted him everyday of his life, made it easy for friends and acquaintances to recognize him. The soldiers under Guinevere's control were the unlucky ones that had not gone off to war with the King in Gaul.

One such friend of Gawain's, had spotted Mordred and had returned to see if the young man had any news of his brother. The man stopped by his side and immediately Mordred recognized him, his name was Kay. He was a good natured man with a tongue that chattered the whole time and a pleasing personality that was rather hard not to like. Mordred was pondering how to get out of his predicament when his situation became worse. Another batch of soldiers now approached, this time at a slow canter. In the middle of the group of soldiers, rode the Queen and by her side were Pelles and Ursien. Mordred feared being spotted and turned his head away from the passing throng. At first it looked like his precaution had worked, but then to his dismay he saw a lone soldier peel away from the main group and ride his horse up to where they were conversing.

Kay was jabbering on about the war and about his brothers, but Mordred's eyes were on the lone rider. The man came upon them and issued an order to Kay, that the Queen commanded them to join her at her table for supper.

Kay looked at Mordred. 'You are most fortunate my friend, it has been sometime since our Queen has favored me with such a request.'

Mordred looked less than honored and whispered that he did not wish to go.

The man looked amazed at his young friend and thought to reassure him in matters of etiquette. 'She makes a wonderful hostess and her cooks always prepare such wonderful food...oh the partridge is to die for. You do not even have to be careful what you say, for the Queen tolerates swearing. You will enjoy yourself, I promise you. '

Mordred continued to look apprehensive, but found he was riding by Kay's side towards the castle.

'This is wonderful,' Kay said. 'You can tell us all your news over the feast. Tell me about Gawain. How many men has he killed?'

Mordred pleaded his ignorance on the matter.

'Then how many woman has he taken to his bed?'

Again Mordred offered no answer. Kay was beginning to suspect supper was going to be dull affair, if he was seated next to his pious friend. He couldn't think what they would think of to talk about, if not battles or women.

27

The Lady Ygerne's castle was turned upside down with the
feast that was set before the Queen's special guests. The
tables were rearranged so that the dining and festivities
were more intimate. At the head of the table sat Guinevere,
wearing a green silk dress adorned with many sparkling
items of jewelry. Her manly persona had been put away, to
be replaced with her most elegant mask. To her immediate
right sat Pelles, on her immediate left sat Germanus and
beside him was Ursien. Kay and Mordred were seated next
to each other on her right hand side. The conversation was
as Kay had suggested at times coarse, but also loud and
merry. Although the Queen never contributed to the sexual
lewdness put before all assembled, she did not condemn it
either. She laughed with her men and seemed to be
enjoying their company. It was strange thought Mordred. It
was almost as if Arthur was sitting at the head of the table
ruling over the proceedings and not his wife. There were no
other ladies present only twenty men and the Queen.

Mordred wondered why she had asked him to the
feast and dreaded being interrogated before the others, but
so far the lady had only occasionally glanced in his
direction. It was Germanus who addressed him first.
'Young man, it is good to see you again, but I did not expect
to see you so soon. Did you not manage to deliver my
letters?'

A rather hesitant Mordred said that he had.

Germanus looked perplexed. 'I perceive you have
sprouted wings since I last saw you.'

The humor was lost on all those present.

'And did the Lady Morgan have an answer for me?'
Germanus asked.

Mordred was useless at lying, but pretended he had
seen the lady and that she had not given him an answer.

'And the King, you surely couldn't have seen him also?'

'No, I gave your letter to the lady to give to him.'

'I see, that was sensible of you,' Germanus replied. The bishop then produced both letters from a pouch by his chair and slapped them down on the table in front of everyone. 'It's quite remarkable how their seals have remained untouched,' he pronounced.

There was a sudden silence and most heads turned to face Mordred. Then an unexpected thing happened. The Queen got up from her chair and walked over to Mordred. The young man sat rigid, scared to move as Guinevere put her arms around him and gave him an affectionate kiss on the cheek. She looked at Germanus and gave him a cold stare. 'I will not have family treated in this way,' she thundered.

The whole atmosphere changed around the room as everyone wondered if the Queen was playing some game. The truth was that Guinevere did not tolerate failure and the bishop had failed her twice concerning Morgan and Arthur's son. It might have seemed a poor substitute to have Mordred instead, but the Queen was strangely fond of her nephew. He, like her, was seen as an outcast and hated by many in the land. His shape and his lack of social graces made him a source of laughter and ridicule. This angered the lady, for she knew his mind was sharp and more than able.

It did not take long for the good nature of the assembly to return and for everyone to continue with their merriment. Only Mordred and Germanus remained quiet as they glanced back at each other from time to time. Mordred wondered what would happen next and he was in for another surprise when the Queen announced all the people who would be sleeping within the castle walls and all those who would not. With the Lady Ygerne's servants sadly missing, there was a shortage of staff to take care of everyone. The best rooms went to the Queen and her immediate favorites. It was embarrassing for the young lad to be included in a list that included Kings and high

162

members of the church. Perhaps he should have felt honored, but all he felt was scared.

Mordred did not sleep and was trying to conceive a plan to escape, but this would not be easy. The guards stood at the end of every corridor and with several hundred men encamped outside, it was near impossible to flee unnoticed. He tossed and turned, got up and paraded around the room and listened to the sounds of the night. The men were indulging in their carnal lust, for somehow the Queen or someone else on her behalf had managed to procure a large number of young and willing women to satisfy their needs. This was uncomfortable for the young man, who had never lain with a woman before. To hear the laughter and moans of pleasure made him wince and firm up below. He could hear people coming and going along the corridor and he began to fear for his life.

Taking a dagger from its sheath the young man listened at the door, half expecting someone to burst into his room at any time. On the other side of his door was a figure, they had taken care to disguise themselves, for they were covered from head to toe in a white monk's habit. Another door opened nearby and a male figure exited, his nakedness paraded before the figure in the habit. The bishop Germanus was entertaining some young women when he heard a noise from the corridor and went to investigate.

Germanus had used all his charms and passion to try and seduce the Queen, but the lady seemed only amused by his attempts and flirted with others to annoy him. He knew his failure was tantamount to betrayal in the lady's eyes, but this did not make him despair for he had now employed a professional whose record in his field was unrivalled. He knew it would not be long before Galahad was in the Queen's possession and Christ's chalice was in his.

The faint hope went through the bishop's mind that the noise he heard in the corridor was that of the Queen coming to pay him a visit. So when he saw the figure he wondered if it was the lady. He never thought about his appearance or the fact he was already occupied, only that his time might have come. To his surprise the figure turned and looked long and hard at his naked body.

He began to smile, but his face changed when the figure pull the hood down to reveal their face. It was Guinevere, but she was not paying him a visit, but the young Mordred.

She took a key from under her habit and opened the door Just as she was about to enter, she smiled at Germanus. The man's hands clenched and his face went red through anger, as he watched her enter the room.

Once inside, the room was dark as pitch and the lady stood for a moment trying to get her bearings. She could not see that the young man was immediately behind her with his dagger drawn. Mordred feared attack, and in the faint light he thought the outline of the figure appeared to be a monk and thought Germanus had come to kill him. He was about to lunge forward and attack his intruder, when a soft female voice spoke his name. 'Mordred, do not be afraid, it is Guinevere.'

Just for a moment the young man thought about slitting his Queen's throat, but he breathed a sigh and returned the dagger to its sheath. The lady had heard his sigh and turned to face him. 'You do not have to fear me,' Guinevere told him.

It was so dark that neither could see each other's faces, but as Mordred offered to light some candles. Guinevere pulled him to her. 'It is better this way,' she whispered. The young man did not know what she meant, but he soon realized as the lady's arms went around his twisted body as she tried to kiss his face. The touch of the women's soft skin almost proved too much for the young man to resist, but he tried to pull the Queen away from him. Guinevere's hands caressed his body until she reached a certain place where the young man thought was inappropriate. Much to the lady's frustration he forced her hand away and an awkward kind of wrestling match ensued. Finally Guinevere stopped trying to seduce the young man and offered him an apology instead. 'You are right to refuse me,' she began. 'I only wish others would do the same. I am surrounded by sycophants, who bow at my feet and do everything I ask like scared sheep.'

Mordred lit a few candles and although the light was still feeble both parties could see each other's faces now. The young man's thoughts were confused as he tried to understand why any woman would want him and not just any woman, but the Queen, his uncle's wife. His thoughts turned to his own wretched existence and wondered if in the future he would look back and curse himself for missing out on an unforgettable experience.

Guinevere looked in no hurry to leave and continued to talk to the young man as if he was her equal. 'What goes on in your mind?' the lady asked.

'I do not know what you mean, my lady.'

'Most people just live for their basic needs, such as food, drink and carnal lust, but you do not.' Guinevere took hold of Mordred's hand and forced him to sit on the edge of the bed. 'You use your mind to better your understanding of the world around you.'

'I have to thank the Lady Morgan...'

Guinevere interrupted. 'No please, don't say the name of the one that hates me so.'

'No, I'm sure she does not.'

'I know things about the lady that would disgust you, but I fear to tell you in case you think me a liar.'

'I would not listen to gossip,' the man declared.

Guinevere grimaced as if a pain had struck at her body. 'Do you know what it is like to feel genuine hate?'

Although embarrassed by the question, Mordred had to admit that he did.

A haunting look crossed the lady's face. 'Then perhaps you can understand. I gave up everything to come to this land and start a new life. I was promised happiness with the greatest King of his age...and yet...'

Mordred found his attention focused on the woman beside him, it was as if she was a totally different person than the one he thought he knew. 'Go on,' he encouraged.

165

The lady fought back tears as she continued. 'On our wedding night I was prepared by all the women, washed, garnished with sweet smelling odors and adorned with petals of fresh wild flowers.' The lady paused and Mordred thought he witnessed a tear drop from her eye. 'I waited and waited...it was almost dawn before I got up from my bed. I put on a robe and went to explore my new surroundings in the hope I might chance upon my husband. I wandered around the castle without being challenged, until I came to a room at the end of a corridor. There were two guards there standing at attention, as I approached; they immediately took their spears and blocked my entrance, declaring that the King was not to be disturbed.

Mordred found the lady's hand was still in his and he managed a weak smile.

'Do you know whose room that was?' she asked him

The young man shook his head.

'Later that day I was given a tour of the whole castle by one of the stewards, a man who is still in the King's service. When we got to the room that I had been barred from, I asked the man whose room it was. He told me it was the Lady Morgan's.'

A few moments earlier the young man was ready to defend the name of the woman he loved as a mother, but some uncomfortable reminiscences entered his memory. This was not the first time that he had heard such stories, but this time he was hearing it from the point of view of the victim which left him much troubled.

The lady could see that her arrow had struck its mark and that the young man was fighting conflicting loyalties. The reason her story was so compelling was that every word she spoke was the truth. Even on her wedding night the brute was implanting another. No wonder she hated him. No wonder she hated them both, but revenge was at hand and soon she would hear the magic words....*The King is dead.*

If the pain of that first night was not bad enough, the next great pain was ten times greater. The Queen

166

fulfilled her duty to her husband and became pregnant. Their son was called Loholt and he grew strong like his father, until one day at the age of twelve the boy was allowed to accompany his papa on his campaign of war. On the first day of activities in his war against the Jutes, Loholt lost touch with his guards and became isolated. He and two other young soldiers perished amongst a barrage of thundering arrows and spears. Guinevere was quick to blame Arthur and vowed never to give birth again. She never forgave his carelessness and their relationship grew worse, more acrimonious by the day.

Mordred digested the Queen's statement and felt rather overwhelmed that she should confide in him. 'Have you ever told this to anyone else?' the young man asked.

Guinevere smiled. 'No I haven't and I never shall.'

Mordred found the Queen's hand grip his tighter. 'Why have you told me...I am hardly a person of importance,' Mordred said.

Guinevere wondered why she was attracted to this cripple of a man, was it just the thought of turning his loyalties so that she would have a confidant in the enemy camp, or was it more subtle than that. She felt his pain, his anger and frustration and most of all his lack of worth. That was exactly how she felt in the first days of her confinement at Caerleon. The whole place reeked of intrigue and everyone saw her as an outsider and a threat. It took her quite some time to come to terms with her new situation. When she did, she found she was a match for them all. If they wanted intrigue she would give them intrigue and if they plotted, her plots would be the better and more deadly than anyone's.

'You can be important and you shall be,' stated the Queen.

Looking flustered and uncomfortable the young man thought to ridicule himself. 'I don't blame anyone for despising me.'

'You shall never speak like this again,' the Queen insisted. 'Be guided by me, take my strength, take my advice and you will be one of the most powerful men in the land.'

Mordred could not conceive what the Queen meant.

Guinevere clasped her hands around his face and kissed him on the mouth. The kiss lasted only for a moment, but its impact would last for the rest of his life. 'You want me?' the young man stammered. 'You don't mean...'

With her hands still on his face she made her intentions clearer. 'I need a man I can trust, one without guile, a man who will put my interests before all others. Do you think you could be that man?'

After hesitating, Mordred said he wished to be the man she described.

'If you aspire to be, then you must first start believing in yourself.'

Guinevere pushed the young man down unto the bed. She threw off her habit and her naked body rested gently on top of his clothed. 'You have never been with a woman I assume?' the lady asked.

Still nervous, Mordred asked the lady how she knew.

He could see her smile, as her hand caressed his cheek. 'Never mind, after tomorrow no one will think that.'

Up until the age of fourteen the young man had a manservant help him undress. His twisted body had made that necessary, but even if it meant a night of pain he banished his helper and forced himself to undo his clothes, similarly in the morning he dressed himself although it was the custom for the hierarchy not to. He let Guinevere lift his tunic over his head without protest; next she set about releasing the buckle of his belt to let loose his trousers and his leggings. Her hands quickly disposed of them onto the floor, which only left his girdle. The devise was specially made to fit the contorted body of the man and was not easy to undo. With the lady's help Mordred tore away at the leather thongs. One by one they untied until the contraption lay stranded at the back of the young man's body. The lady lifted the girdle from beneath him and tugged it free unto the floor. Mordred gasped in pain.

168

'I did not mean to hurt you,' the lady said.

Mordred was quick to assure her she did not. Their bodies mixed together contorting in an effort to give each other pleasure. It was a pleasure the lady had only occasionally experienced with a man before.

28

The night had come and gone as the small boat moved by degrees further inland to the main port of Dover. By the time Lancelot awoke, the boat was surrounded by a multitude of men all trudging about its deck and its hold. Questions were fired at the man, as he tried to clear his head and answer them the best he could. The lack of crew and fellow passengers needed addressing and when the men saw the excess of blood on the boat, they pressed Lancelot for some reply. He stuck to his story that pirates had attacked the vessel and had killed all onboard. The blood contested to the mayhem, but some of the men knew the vessel and its captain and they appeared harder to convince. With his mind cloudy and his head hurting, Lancelot's impatience aroused still further doubt. He was helped ashore and given medical assistant by a ship's physician, who cleaned his wound and changed his bandage.

The news of the King's death spread like a wildfire and the incident of a sole survivor had everyone confounded. Morgan and Yvain heard the stories and were given directions as to where the boat now lay. She tried to push to the back of her mind the thought that she was too late. The boat was easy to pick out from the coastal road, for a mass of people surrounded it. The lady wondered how many had plodded around on it and whether any evidence remained.

Coming up close, the lady's presence was soon felt as she issued orders and took command of the situation. 'Who is in charge here?' she demanded to know.

When no one answered, Morgan took it upon herself to take charge. She asked if the Military Magistrate of Dover had been sent for. When no one answered her, she gave orders for the man to be contacted and brought before her at once. After a young man offered his assistance,

Morgan asked Yvain to go with him to make sure the magistrate was compliant. She ordered all the people standing around the boat to move away, before boarding herself.

Morgan took her time and examined everything in detail. She was struck by two things; the amount of blood, for there were signs that the occupants had put up a fight, and the evidence that people had been dragged up from the hold and thrown overboard. The blood trail indicated that the bodies were dragged by their heads and that their feet and legs trailed along the ground leaving quite obvious lines. There was blood on the several different places along the rail to indicate where the bodies had been tossed overboard.

Morgan heard a voice she knew and looked across to the quay to see Gawain with a small party of soldiers. 'I came as soon as I heard,' he told her.

'I'm glad you are here nephew. Can you tell me who was on board?'

Gawain climbed onto to gangplank and boarded the boat. His face grew greyer as he wandered from spot to spot, seeing the blood and taking in the ambience of violence. 'My brother,' yelled Gawain, 'he was the last along with, the King, Lady Helena, Lancelot and his servant.'

'The crew?' asked Morgan.

Gawain shook his head. 'I'm not sure, but I think there were at least two.'

The young man went below deck to see the blood splattered walls and floor of where his brother might have met his end. While there he spotted Arthur's great sword resting against the wall, unused and with possibly drops of the King's blood around its scabbard. He took the sword with him as he left the hold to go back on deck.

'Have you any idea what happened here?' Gawain asked the lady.

'I believe one man survived and is being looked after by a physician on shore, perhaps he can show some light on the matter.'

Gawain gasped with delight, but Morgan's eyes told him the man could not be his brother. 'The description told to me makes it likely to be Lancelot.'

Although the lady knew of Lancelot's possible betrayal of her sister, she was surprised to see the lines across Gawain's eyes suggest the young man was suspicious.

'I have seen all I wish to see here. Why don't we find out what the man knows,' suggested Morgan.

Gawain seemed more than pleased to do so.

Back on dry land, Morgan ordered two sailors to keep guard and paid them handsomely for their trouble. She told them where they were headed and issued them with instructions to bring the governor to her when he showed up.

The Inn was crowded as Morgan and Gawain were escorted to a back room away from the noise of the clientele. Sitting with his hands on his face was a bad-tempered Lancelot. He pulled his hands away from his face and got to his feet, when Morgan entered. He looked at his jailer, the physician who had bandaged his wound. 'This fool has kept me prisoner,' he complained.

'That was my doing,' admitted Morgan.

'Why, I'm surely free to go as I please.'

'Not until you tell us what has transpired here,' Gawain stated.

Lancelot offered the lady his chair but she declined. His face had regained its color and with his fresh bandage, he looked to be on the mend.

'What happened on board that boat?' Morgan asked.

'We were all in the hold trying to get some sleep, when we heard noises of people talking on deck. Then we hear a scream and the sound of two splashes as if two people had been thrown overboard. Ironfist and I went to investigate, but as I opened the hatch to the hold I was dragged to my feet by two ruffians who cut me with their knives. Ironfist was likewise pulled up and I fear was mortally stabbed for I saw him go down. I can remember nothing more except I thought I heard Arthur and Agravain scream from below deck, but then everything went dark.'

In the past listening to this story Morgan would quite probably have believed every word, but as Lancelot spoke she remembered Elaine and everything the lady of the lake had shown her. Without proof she could not condemn the man, but condemn him in her heart she did. To her amazement, she was not the only one who doubted the man's story.

Gawain had moved closer to Lancelot and studied the man. 'They killed all on board except you, why did they not kill you too?'

Shaking his head Lancelot could not explain why this was so.

Gawain continued. 'Tell me why would pirates attack such a small vessel, they could not possible expect a great prize.'

Again Lancelot had no answer.

'Unless they knew the King was onboard,' he offered eventually.

Lancelot looked at Gawain and then Morgan and wondered what they were thinking. He saw their eyes question his answers, and he felt uneasy.

'I've called for the Military Magistrate to come here and question you some more,' Morgan informed Lancelot.

So that's it, the man thought. You want to put me on trial and hope I will confess. He laughed nervously. 'Do you think I am guilty of something? he shouted.

'I think your answers are poor at best,' suggested Morgan. 'You might want reconsider them before the magistrate arrives.'

Lancelot went red in the face, his cool persona evaporated and he went into a rage. 'The Queen will hear of this, you can not hold me prisoner,' he screamed.

'I am a member of the High Council and intend to call a special hearing into this business. For now it will be up to the magistrate to decide to hold you captive or not, but I will strongly suggest to him that he should.'

Lancelot was confounded by the lady's attitude. He could not understand her hostility. 'I have urgent business to attend to,' he began. 'Wait until my father hears of this.'

'Nothing is more urgent than this,' Morgan assured him. 'It is quite possible you will be charged with both murder and treason.'

'That is ridiculous,' Lancelot spat. 'I am innocent of any crime...'

'If that is so, pray tell us the truth, for I do not believe a word you have said so far,' Gawain thundered.

Before Lancelot could reply, shouts were heard from outside, shouts concerning the King. All rushed from the inn and into the street to hear. The town crier was shouting from the top of his voice. 'The King is dead. Several bodies have been washed up on shore. The King is dead.'

Gawain moved towards the man and interrupted his shouting. 'Tell me what you know,' he demanded.

The man was quickly swamped by people, but Gawain held centre stage and asked the man again. 'Three bodies found so far, all within a furlong of each other, all males all in middle age. Someone has already identified one as the King.'

'Tell me where about along the shore?' Gawain asked.

The man turned to his right and pointed past a row of small boats to an inlet and to a large building resembling a castle. 'Two of the bodies were found over there, while the third is a little further past the inlet.'

Gawain thanked the man and found he had a large entourage following him in that general direction. Morgan and Lancelot followed also, but none could keep up with the young man as he sprinted like an Olympian runner towards the building.

By the time Morgan and Lancelot got to the inlet, the bodies had been taken ashore into the building. Entering this large and forbidding structure, they found a great many people in a state of panic. The building was once a castle belonging to King Ban, but after he moved his kin and courtiers to Benoic, the place had been used as a chamber of commerce and a place of work for the local magistrate and his lackeys. The magistrate was not present, and it was one of his assistants who showed them the way.

Morgan was shown into the room where the bodies lay and witnessed Gawain draped over his brother, distraught. The scene was mirrored by a young woman equally wretched beside the body of the King. She was small with a pale face and wore a flaming red robe with reddish-gold torc studded with red stones around her neck.

Lancelot stood at the entrance barring anyone else from entering, while Gawain and Morgan mourned their kin. Morgan touched Gawain's shoulder, in passing, but the young man barely acknowledged her presence. The young lady kept her hood covered as Morgan sat down beside her on the stone floor.

'You moan for your King?' she asked the maiden.

The young woman put her hand up to her eyes and wiped away a tear. 'I lied to gain an entrance, for I wanted to see him just once.'

Morgan introduced herself and the maiden at once offered her condolences.

'I must leave you to mourn your dead,' the young lady informed her. She raised herself to her feet and was about to leave, but Morgan touched her arm and with a weak smile asked her stay.

The maiden bowed and returned to the King's body, placing herself a little back from it, allowing Morgan pride of place beside her brother. Both maidens listened to the soulful mourns from Gawain near them. His sobs were interrupted ever so often with his curses of vengeance. 'I will find the bastards responsible and slit their throats, this I promise brother,' he yelled.

Morgan by contrast found her feelings hard to define as she laid her hands over his chest to examine her brother's stab wounds. Whoever had killed him did so with a degree of anger or strength, for the wounds were deep and around his heart. She could not be sure, but she suspected Arthur died immediately.

175

This did not make her feel any better and like Gawain she swore inwardly to avenge his death. She could not find the tears that she knew were just beyond the surface, perhaps later she would fall apart, but for now keeping her self-control seemed appropriate. She wanted to arrange a boat to carry his corpse to Avalon, but worried what others might think. She had the right to claim his body because she was family, but he was the people's King and they had certain rights too. She would need the help of Gawain whose powerful force within the army would ensure no one questioned her actions.

Arthur had decided to put a great distance between them, in the hope that their worldly love would dissipate. She had not seen him in some time and felt their love too have foundered upon his Christian beliefs. He feared the wrath of his one God, while she did not fear any Gods, or any man for that matter. She had come to realize he did not love her like a man loves a woman and was content to renew his brotherly love instead, but it was too late. Their rare meetings still carried a haunting guilt and the man went to lengths to find reasons to keep the distance between them. It was typical of the man to run away from his problems, and typical of Morgan to forgive him his faults.

The lady knew that much had to be done and was aware the direction she wanted proceedings to go. She would have time later to mourn, for now she was more concerned with justice. To arrest Lancelot she would need the help of the magistrate, with Arthur's army all around he would hardly disagree. She feared Lancelot was in league with Guinevere and might just slip away if the chance arrived. With this thought in her mind, she turned her head to see that he had in fact done just that. His large frame was no longer standing guard over the entrance to the room. She looked across at Gawain and shouted. 'Lancelot's gone.'

Gawain immediately got to his feet and gave chase.

29

The Lady Morgan searched her immediate surroundings for any sight of Gawain or Lancelot. She sighed and looked at the young woman who had accompanied her outside. 'Hardly the act of an innocent man,' she remarked more for her own benefit than for the maiden's. She did not expect an answer, but the woman whose name was Olwen offered up her opinion.

'The authorities will catch up with this Lancelot I'm sure. Until then we can not be sure of his innocence or guilt.'

The two women looked at each other and for the first time the maiden lowered her hood to reveal her face. Her hair was cut short and her complexion was whiter than her own making the girl look sickly. Morgan thought she must be a stranger to their lands, for she clearly had never heard of Lancelot. How strange then to mourn for a King that you did not know.

'You presume to give advice,' remarked Morgan.

'I hope you do not think it wrong of me?'

'If the authorities don't catch Lancelot, Gawain certainly will.'

'If he does, I hope he will not be too rash in his actions.'

'He wants justice, not vengeance.'

The words Morgan spoke were her own, for she had no idea what Gawain had in his mind. He was hot-headed at the best of times and had a habit of taking actions without thinking of the consequences. If Lancelot and Gawain found each other and fought, Morgause might well have two dead sons to mourn and not just one.

As the women were about to re-enter the building Morgan saw Yvain wave his hand in the air from some distance away. The young man had tracked the magistrate down and was rushing the over-weight man along the waterfront, much to the amusement of the throngs of people who had gathered to await further news. The man was red in the face and blustered that he was close to death himself, but Yvain kept him up to the task.

Much out of breath, the magistrate, who was loathed by the masses, begged his forgiveness when at last he was presented to Lady Morgan. 'My my, lady this is such a terrible day...terrible day,' he spouted. His name was Samson, which at first sight might have appeared appropriate because of his size, but unfortunately the man was all fat and no muscle, so the name had for him become something of a bad joke.

'I have told the magistrate all that I know of what has occurred,' Yvain told his mistress.

Samson nodded his head and began as he started, in repeating everything several times. 'A calamity, a calamity...to think he did not die in battle, but in some tragic accident.'

Morgan glanced at Yvain, who only shook his head.

'It was no accident,' Morgan insisted. 'It was murder and we had a suspect...but he has escaped. You must issue warrants for the arrest of Lancelot of Benoic immediately. Then you must...'

Samson's cheeks were ready to explode. 'Lancelot...Lancelot...you can not mean it. Not Lancelot, not thee Lancelot...'

'Yes, thee Lancelot,' shouted Morgan. 'He was found onboard and can not give a reasonable account of his actions.'

'Surely that does not mean?'

'My nephew Gawain has gone after him. I put his capture in your hands, do not fail me or your position here could well be in doubt.'

Samson continued to bluster and entered the building to put in motion what the lady had asked.

Yvain came closer to his mistress and whispered to her. 'You will never guess what the man was doing when I found him?'

'Oh, please spare me the details,' the lady told him.

Morgan re-entered the building and set upon making all the necessary arrangements. Her one thought was to get Arthur's body to Avalon.

Olwen remained at the lady's side and was helpful in giving her comfort, but Morgan still wondered about the girl. Why did she seek out the King? What did she want with him? Just as she was about to put these questions to the girl, a young man came up to Olwen and whispered in her ear.

Straight away Olwen sought Morgan out, to say her farewells.

'Thank you for your help and your kindness,' Morgan told the girl.

Olwen bowed her head and was about to move away, but Morgan's curiosity got the better of her. 'Please before you go, tell me why you sought out the King?'

Olwen glanced at John, who looked anxious as he approached the girl. He went to say something to Olwen, but the girl raised her hand to protest at his unspoken warning.

'I had hoped to ask for his help, my lady,' girl advised.

'What kind of help?'

'The type that requires strong muscles and a brave heart,' Olwen remarked.

Morgan was intrigued. 'Go on, tell me more.'

'I'm in need of warriors, but I have no money to buy them. I had heard the King was a good man, gentle in spirit and compassionate. If he had heard my tale I felt sure he would have offered me his help.'

With a possible civil war pending Morgan could not offer the young lady much hope of help. She listened a little more then promised Olwen to find time to talk later. John, who was always suspicious of nobility, whispered something in the young girl's ear and as Morgan moved away to badger the governor, he ushered Olwen away from the building. His protective nature had prevented Morgan from hearing the important piece of the tale that might have convinced the lady to offer arms and men to their cause. The young couple left Dover to go to Londinium in pursuit of another possible benefactor instead.

The rays of the sun dazzled the river, as Gallia and Merlin watched the sleepy dawn awaken Londinium inhabitants, of sailors, dockhands and merchants from their slumber. The business of the day was already well started, as the lady pointed to her father's mansion from King Arthur's monument. The couple faced east and saw the row of splendid Roman mansions including the Governor's palace directly below them. To Merlin's surprise Gallia's father's mansion rivaled the Governor's in size and grandeur. He turned to face the lady. 'I don't wonder that you love your home, but there are other wonderful places...'

Gallia interrupted. 'You forget this is the only home he as ever known since his accident.'

'I promise you he would love the Summer Country, with its rugged mountains and peaceful streams, or the Middle Kingdom with its lush fields and gentle valleys. He would make many new friends and become immersed in village life.'

'You make a good case for me to run and hide amongst the country you love so well, but no matter where I go Frith would find me and punish me for my transgression.'

'Yes Frith, we will need to take care of him, but you should leave that to me.'

They were both allowing their horses to rest and allowing themselves a moment's breathing space. 'Do you mean to kill him?' Gallia inquired.

'Only if I can not find another alternative,' Merlin replied.

The brow of Gallia tightened as she fought back some misplaced loyalty to the man. 'No, I can not allow that to happen.'

Merlin challenged the lady's sentiment. 'Do you really think he can be reasoned with?'

Gallia shook her head.

180

'Then it comes down to a contest of wills. Go back to him and be the lady that turns a blind eye to murder, or rid yourself of him once and for all and live a quiet and peaceful life with your father.'

'What about the authorities?' Gallia inquired.

'Why should they get involved?'

Gallia stared at Merlin. 'There is another way,' she stated. 'I take away the threat, by divulging my dirty secret.'

Merlin knew enough about the lady to know she could withstand the shame, but her father was a different matter. 'From the little I know of your father, I would not say he was a man of the world.'

Gallia accepted this statement as fact.

'You should never doubt your instinct. Your instinct told you that you had to keep your new life from your father. That instinct was not wrong.'

Gallia sighed. She pointed out the best way to approach the mansion, but Merlin contradicted her. 'We should take a small boat and use the marshland to reach it.'

'The road is quicker and much safer,' Gallia pointed out.

'Yes and if by any miracle Frith has beaten us here, he could see us coming from many furlongs away.'

Gallia's eyes questioned Merlin. 'You said he couldn't possibly arrive before us.'

'I said it unlikely, but I think the precaution to be prudent.'

Merlin paddled his small craft along the river towards the marshland and the bank nearest to the mansion. The thought of climbing through a bog to get to her home seemed ridiculous to Gallia, but she would soon be grateful for Merlin's precaution. As they approached from their unlikely position they could make out a figure stretched out on the Roman terrace.

Forcing the lady to the floor of the boat, Merlin peered over the rim to see a man lying on his back on a Greek Kline sofa, with his eyes closed enjoying the morning sun. He knew immediately who the man was. It was Frith and he had a triumphant smile upon his face. Merlin was in no doubt that the front of the mansion was well watched by his associates. Frith was celebrating a victory he could smell and almost touch, but had not yet won.

Merlin dropped to the floor of the boat lowered his head, until it was beside the lady's. 'Can your father swim?' he asked her.

Looking bewildered the lady answered he could, if she became his eyes.

He had little time to explain, and instead asked Gallia to trust him. The lady acknowledged that she was in his hands.

Merlin and Gallia left the boat and swam towards the mansion, until they found themselves waist deep in the bog and were forced to wade instead. The plant life of the reef hid them as they reached the edge of the marsh, where the muddy path reached all the way up to the villa. Here they stopped and Merlin whispered to the lady. 'You remain here and I will rescue your father...'

Gallia shook her head. 'He will not come with you, I must come too.'

Merlin accepted her statement. 'You will do what I say?'

The lady agreed.

Just as they were about to leave the safety of the marsh, they heard voices from the terrace.

An elderly man walked out from the villa and onto the terrace and addressed Frith. He was old but spritely and his face shone with a light of good cheer. His eyes were open and his surefootedness gave no indication that the man could not see. 'I fear you might be in for a long wait,' Philemon told Frith.

Frith turned his head and acknowledged the man's statement with a broad smile. 'I am enjoying your fine view. You are lucky, this is a wonderful villa and great place to retire away from the world.'

'I am most fortunate,' Philemon admitted. 'I must apologize for the tardiness of my servants, they are usually so attentive.'

'That is quite alright, I fear my colleagues might be taking up too much of their time.'

'I will see about getting you some refreshment...'

'That will not be necessary. Stay with me and tell me more about your daughter.'

The old man moved a little closer to Frith. 'I rather think you should tell me, for you see far more of her than I.'

'That's different, that is work. Gallia keeps her private affairs a secret. For instance, what made you come to this part of the world? I can hear from your accent that you're from the east.'

'You have a good ear sir, although I am devastated. I had hoped my accent had left me and that I now sounded like a native.'

'It's my job to pick up on such things.'

There was plenty of room on the sofa that was more native to the east than the west, but Philemon preferred to stand.

'There has never been a gentler angel set upon this earth,' the man began. 'She is responsible for all you see before you, without her I should never have survived.'

Frith looked interested. 'I know how hard she works, but tell me more about your time in Antioch.'

'You surely know about the earthquake?' Philemon asked.

'A terrible thing, you were there when it happened?'

Philemon put his hand up to his eyes. 'I got this when our mansion burnt to the ground.'

'How terrible, was Gallia hurt?'

'She saved me, pulled me free...but I believe her body got badly burnt in the process.'

30

Gawain tracked Lancelot along the narrow streets of Dover and saw him push his way through the crowd. Each time he got close, someone would get in his way and he would curse at them and cause quite a stir. Lancelot kept moving, but was aware his shadow would never give up. He had no plan other than to get clean away and reach Guinevere or her forces. For now he could not see Gawain and so he breathed easier and headed away from town.

Gawain found a livery stable on the outskirts of the Saxon settlement and inquired there if anyone had recently purchased a horse. The man confirmed someone had and verified the description of Lancelot as being the man. Gawain purchased a horse of his own and asked what direction Lancelot had taken. 'He took the Londinium road, sir. No doubt he has a long ride ahead of him, as do you if you were thinking of following.'

'If you had some water to spare I would be obliged,' asked Gawain.

The proprietor went into the stables and came back out with a black mare that was in good trim. 'This is my finest beast,' said the man as he paraded it in front of his young customer. 'Although not as young as she once was, she can still run as fast as any on flat ground,' he declared.

Gawain looked at the horse and found no fault in her and told the man so. The man then filled the young warrior's pouch with water and handed it to him. Gawain handed the man his purse of coin and mounted the horse. There was a considerable amount in it, but Gawain was not thinking of money, he was thinking of vengeance. The man looked inside and got a pleasant surprise. 'This is too much,' he shouted after the young man. Gawain never heard the refrain for he galloped away heading towards the road that would take him to Londinium.

Lancelot's horse cantered peacefully along that same road with the man himself seemingly unperturbed, despite the fact that Gawain would likely come after him. After glancing behind several times, the man took the view it was wiser to be safe rather than to be sorry. So he came off the main track and found a dirt path that edged around some forest land that was out of sight from the main road. This was a precaution, but the man felt safer than he should have. He did not think any in the land would believe him capable of killing the King, since he was Arthur's oldest friend.

The first he knew of any disturbance came when he heard a faint sound up ahead of him. He did not take much note, until a second sound rang out that sounded like a human voice. Lancelot slowed his pace, and eased his horse in the direction of the noise. In a clearing ahead he saw two men tied to a tree and four men engaged in badgering them with their swords and daggers. What seemed like the leader of the group of cutthroats carried two saddlebags in his hand and was keen to depart. His men had other ideas and were enjoying themselves, mostly due to the discovery that one of the men was in fact a woman. After forcibly removing their victim's headgear, the men witnessed that one of their captives looked feminine, despite the short hair and pale face.

It seemed hardly the time for Lancelot to go charging into a dangerous situation, but the man could not control his eagerness. A damsel was in distress and when he spied how the cutthroats had treated her he was incensed with rage. Blood was issuing from both victims, primarily from their mouths, but Lancelot could see several wounds also about their bodies.

Lancelot saw that time was not in his favor, for it was clear that some of the men wanted to violate the lady further. One man came up close to her and stuck his tongue close to her mouth, while unfastening first his belt, then his trousers. With a defiant look on the lady's face, she spat with a passion into his face. This brought a tumultuous laughter from all the outlaws looking on. As the man

185

slapped the girl across her face, his trousers fell to the ground in an action that was both comic and distasteful. This brought more raucous laughter and gave Lancelot his chance to charge. Coming from behind some bushes he yelled like a man possessed by the devil and cried his battle chant, 'Benoic, for the honor of Benoic.'

He screamed down on the men like a torrent, swinging his sword like an axe, and using its point he slashed his way through the men like a sheaf cuts through wheat. The first outlaw fell like a stone, transfixed through his throat. The second victim succumbed immediately after, when the power of Lancelot's blow cut almost the man's head clear off his shoulders.

The leader of the outlaws tried to escape with the plunder, but he did not get far though, despite mounting his horse. Lancelot came after him and, raising his sword over his head, swung it forward to strike the man in the back nearest to his neck. The sword came out of his hands and stayed registered in the man's body. The last of the outlaws also tried to mount a horse, but when he saw his comrades slaughtered ran instead into the forest as fast as his legs could carry him.

Lancelot got down from his horse to rescue his sword from the slain outlaw, before coming over to untie the captives.

'God bless you, stranger!' croaked Olwen, her lips black with blood.

'Any one would have done the same thing,' Lancelot suggested.

Olwen put her hand in his. 'We owe you our lives,' she told him.

Lancelot then untied John as well. The man was also complementary and patted him on the back.

'What may we call you, sir?' Olwen asked.

Neither Lancelot nor Olwen recognized each other from earlier. Lancelot had been too occupied thinking of his escape, while the maiden had kept her hood covering her face.

Nonetheless Lancelot hesitated about parting with his name. 'My name is of no importance,' he stated.

John rescued the saddlebags and produced a cloth and water to wipe clean Olwen's face and hands. Lancelot quickly saw how the young man cherished the lady and thought he knew why. She was striking in her naturalness; pale in color, her delicate features remaindered him of the fabulous statues depicting the Roman Gods he had seen as a boy in Ravenna.

After wiping his own face John introduced himself, but refrained from announcing the identity of his mistress.

Lancelot turned to face the young lady. 'May I ask your name?' he inquired.

The lady looked ready to comply, but John interceded. 'Like you, my lady's name is of no importance.'

Both Lancelot and Olwen smiled at John. The lady shook her head at him

'This will not do,' she complained. 'The man saved our lives, I own him at least a name.'

John stared at Lancelot and agreed with the faintest of acknowledgments.

'My name is Olwen,' the girl declared.

'A lovely name and not one I am familiar with.'

'I am a stranger here, we are strangers here.'

'That perhaps explains why you veered off the main road. I must beg your pardon for the conduct of some of our citizens; they are not at all typical of our entire race.'

'I am sure every land has its fair share of bandits,' the girl conceded.

John was anxious to move on, but first with some ointment he continued the bathe his mistress's wounds. The injuries inflicted were superficial and the lady made light of them. Once John had finished, Lancelot did the same for him, but again his cuts were not serious either. The bandits were not of murderous intent, but had simply enjoyed terrorizing their victims.

'If you are heading for Londinium, it would be safer to stick to the main road,' Lancelot advised.

'Thank you for your advice, but we prefer to stay away from prying eyes,' John replied.

This was a strange answer, but Lancelot was rather glad, for he too had no intention of taking the more direct route either.'

'I love the countryside myself,' Lancelot admitted. 'Perhaps we could travel together?'

John glanced at Olwen, who smiled and agreed.

Gallia had received her instructions from Merlin, but had decided on a different course of action. She weighed up all her options and had decided that her father's safety and welfare had to come first. Merlin might see her actions as a betrayal, but she could not help this. With the soothsayer desperate to distract Frith away, he had moved to the back of the mansion nearest to her father's and he crawled through the owner's land to reach the front.

The plan was for Merlin to distract Frith long enough, for Gallia to whisk her father to safety by swimming for the boat and then sailing away down the river. Like all quickly made plans, it sounded desperate and unlikely to succeed. Waiting still under cover, Gallia heard Merlin's assault and ran up the muddy track to the rear of her father's Mansion as fast as she could. Frith's reaction to the commotion was predictable as he got to his feet and began to move forward.

'Firth, hear me out,' she cried. 'I have come to make a bargain with you, but you must leave this place now, never to return.'

Her father moved forward towards his daughter's voice. 'Is that you, Gallia?'

'Bargain my lady? Is it not too late for such things?' Frith suggested.

'I have been a dutiful employee, have I not,' the lady stated. 'I can still be of great use to you.'

Frith walked towards Gallia. 'I've got to tell you, I did not see your treachery coming.'

Gallia glanced at her father and with a voice full of desperation, muttered a plea to Frith. 'Not here please', she whispered. 'We can sort this out without anyone getting hurt.'

The old man's voice took on a strange tone, 'Treachery,' he breathed.

Gallia's frantic efforts to save her secret seemed doomed, as Frith addressed the old man. 'You believe your daughter to be a trader, I believe?'

Philemon turned his head and faced the man. 'I know everything there is to know about my daughter...'

Gallia pleaded for the last time. 'I will do whatever you want...'

'You shall not,' shouted her father.

'Father please, leave this to me.'

'No I shall not.' The old man clenched his fists and verbally attacked his guest. 'How dare you come into my home and insult my daughter...you should leave immediately...'

The old man did not get a chance to finish his sentence, as Frith pulled a knife from his belt and put it up to the old man's throat.

He then addressed Gallia. 'I think this goes beyond a slight case of a misunderstanding, don't you.'

It was the sound of Gallia's voice shrieking in panic that brought Merlin running from the front of the building to the rear. With one hand around Philemon and the other with his knife around the old man's throat, Firth turned partly to see the new visitor.

Frith began to issue his orders. 'I want two things,' he said. 'One is the goods you stole from me and the other is a new understanding.'

'Please let my father go, I will give you the goods and anything else you wish.'

'Really,' spat Frith. 'There is nothing you would not do to save your father?'

'No, nothing,' she declared.

Merlin edged closer to Frith, but the man tightened his grip on the knife until a spat of blood appeared along Philemon's neck.

'You are among witnesses,' Frith declared to Gallia. 'You will swear on your father's life that you will do what I ask?'

Merlin tried to attract Gallia's attention, but she promised Frith whatever he wanted.

Frith sighed and made his surprise announcement. 'Then we shall be married this very day.'

Gallia gasped in complete shock. It took her a moment or two to recover her senses, in that moment two of Frith's henchmen had come upon Merlin and tackled him to the ground. They held him down in a locked embrace, and after hearing what had just transpired he seemed content to remain under restraint.

'You made your promise,' Frith reminded the woman.

Gallia bowed her head and agreed to his sudden proposal.

Frith let go of her father and the old man after putting his hands around his neck, spoke with vigor. 'You dirty swine,' he shouted. 'I'll never let you marry my daughter, I'd sooner die.'

Frith turned his gaze on the lady again. 'I trust your word on this matter,' he said.

'I will keep my word, but I do have a condition.'

Frith listened. 'Anything for you, within reason,' he suggested.

'You shall never return to this place and you will allow me to visit my father whenever I choose.'

Frith contemplated. 'That will be acceptable,' he said.

Philemon did not agree however and berated his daughter. She did not interrupt his tirade, but did her best to soften his anger. She could not fully explain her decision to her father, but it was strange, she thought, that Taliesin had not said a word on the matter.

The lady had convinced herself that the man had feelings for her, but she waited for one word of protest, of indignation that never came.

Merlin felt more human than he had ever done before in his life, but his emotions were so confused that he could make a decision. The lady had agreed to marry the most degenerate of men, a man capable of cold blooded murder. The words of Daphne resonated in his ear, '*Have you not learnt, after the last time.*' Clearly he had not learnt when it came to his dealings with women.

The lady took her father inside the house and called for the servants to bring her his medicine. One of the female servants brought this from another room and Gallia administrated it to her father. All the time the old man continued to grumble and made his case for having Frith forcibly removed from the place. Gallia wanted no violence and finally convinced her father that everything would be alright. The maid-servant helped the old man to his room and Gallia promised to visit him soon.

Frith had not forgotten Merlin and after the old man had departed, had his men bring him into the main living quarters where Gallia sat with her hands on her head. She looked up to catch the look of betrayal in Merlin's eyes, as he was forced to sit on the floor next to her.

'You shall let this man go,' Gallia commanded.

Frith sat between the two and whispered in Gallia's ear. 'He knows too much, what if he went to the authorities.'

'He has already given me his word that he would not.'

Merlin interrupted. 'That was to you my lady. I did not promise I would not go to the authorities regarding this scoundrel.'

Gallia sighed and tried again. 'If you turn in my husband, then you turn me in also.'

These words hurt Merlin, as much as any trained torturer could have by the turn of his rack.

The words were meant to sting, but they were also meant to appease Frith from his murderous intent.

Biting his lip, Merlin agreed to forget everything he had seen and heard. He knew this would not be enough for Frith, but his grip on living had become so weak that he really didn't care if he lived or died.

'Then I trust our paths will never cross again,' said Frith.

Merlin agreed it would be unlikely they should. The two thugs employed by Frith picked him up from floor and carried him towards the front entrance. Gallia got to her feet, glanced at the man. 'I want your promise he will not be hurt?'

Frith agreed. 'My men will take him far enough away, so that he will not return to spoil our wedding plans.'

'Can I speak with him for a moment?' Gallia pleaded.

'No, I won't allow that.'

Gallia put on a smile and lowered her voice. 'You can grant me this one thing. I only want to spit in his face for leading me astray.'

Frith shouted to his men not to leave just yet.

'So it was he who came up with this plan?'

'Yes, he persuaded me I didn't need you.'

'So it was never personal between you?'

'Strictly business,' Gallia assured him. 'Now that we are equal partners you can fill me in on all your other contacts.'

'Did I agree to make you my full partner?'

'That is what marriage is. If we keep secrets from each other then it will never work.'

Frith's eyes grew tense, but something about Gallia's close presence always made him feel inclined to give in to her. 'You can have your few moments but I want to see your spit on his face.'

'I want a little privacy,' the lady asked.

Frith told Grim and his associate to wait outside. As the men left, Gallia approached Merlin. Standing a little away from them, Frith kept his eyes on them the whole time.

It was an awkward encounter. Gallia whispered to Merlin and hoped Frith did not hear. 'Are you armed?' the lady asked.

Merlin shook his head.

'You must try and make a break for it,'

'What do you care,' Merlin queried.

'For what it is worth, I'm sorry. I have a bit of information that might be of use. Grim, that's...'

'I know who he is.'

'He keeps a spare dagger down in his left boot. If you fake a stumble you might be able to grab it and...'

'Why?'Merlin asked. 'Why?'

'I don't want your death on my conscience.'

Frith was looking anxious and Gallia knew her time had come to end their tete a tete. She had one last thing to do as she saw Frith approach. Completely without warning Gallia looked into Merlin's eyes and spat into his face. This brought about a laugh from Frith and smile from the lady. For Merlin it came as a wake-up call. He knew the lady was playing a part and he realized the safety of her father forbad him from taking direct action here and now. He would rescue her at her convenience and would kill the swine at his.

31

Gaheris must have missed his family as each travelled in
opposite directions. His father kept to the west and
travelled through Gore, while he travelled more inland
through the Humberlands and Mercia. Coming upon
Cadbury, he was met by a band of locals who had been
kicked off their land by the orders of Guinevere. Many of
these men were the same who had helped Accolon free the
Lady Ygerne from imprisonment. They were resentful and
loud in their protests, since now the lady had gone and left
them to their fate. Gaheris was known to one or two and
was warned of what was up ahead in the castle. He thanked
all those present for their information and gave them what
little coin he had. He further promised that their lands
would be restored to them in due course, brave words, for a
man with no powers and no way of knowing what was
going to happen next. Yet he spoke with such authority that
the majority believed him and waited for his return with
the King's forces.

Gaheris was heading south to where he thought the
King would be and that was likely to be Londinium. It was
the natural place for the large army to hold up and for the
King to stay. He had not heard the news that the King was
dead nor did he have any idea where to find the Lady
Morgan, or what had happened to Mordred. The lack of
communication was a great hindrance, but luckily Lady
Morgan's communication system had made it possible for
riders (early mail service) to carry messages to key posts
the length and breadth of the country. The man knew one
of these posts was nearby, so he headed there as quickly as
his horse would take him.

The outposts were basically little more than isolated
huts, situated in strategically important places, along main
roads, good communication lanes to major towns and
emerging cities. He reached the post on the outskirts of

Cadbury to find a rider there exhausted from delivering the tragic news that the King was dead.

The man told him that Lady Morgan had requested warrants to be issued for the capture and arrest of Lancelot on the suspicion of the King's murder. This news was shocking and all kinds of questions ran through the young man's mind. What he had seen recently all confirmed some kind of conspiracy and now he knew who was behind it all. If Lancelot was connected in any way to the death of Arthur, then the Queen his lover was really the one that was responsible. He thanked the young rider and was given a fresh horse by the man, something that was always at hand at these outposts. He headed for Londinium hoping to meet Morgan and to fill her in on the Queen's treachery.

The news reached the Queen by the latter part of the day, that the King was dead. This tragic news was greeted in different ways, by all the contrasting factions present at the castle, for some it was the news they had hoped for, but for others it would mean change and change was always unsettling. Some people, such as King Ursien feared a civil war, where Celt might slay Celt. Others, like King Pelles was preparing to grab the High crown before anyone else had a chance too. Germanus had no doubt the Queen would prevail, his only worry was that his own part in her plot would come out. Guinevere found it difficult to control her glee, but managed in public to put on a sober face of a grieving wife.

It was only Mordred and the common soldiers who felt the pain of the King's departure. The men were restless and made their discontent vocal in and outside the castle walls. It took the Queen to come out amongst them to quell their nerves. She spoke about her husband in regal terms, comparing him to past Roman Emperors and promised to have a full investigation into the circumstances of his death. Many were satisfied with this and felt moved by her eloquence, but a few were still restless and agitated that they wanted to go to where the King's body was held. The Queen felt she had no choice but to give in to their will and

195

ordered the majority of the forces present to accompany her on the journey south.

Arrangements had been put in place for the marriage of Gallia and Frith to take place at Cardinal. Gallia's father had refused to take part, but after much pleading from his daughter he finally agreed. A priest was summoned and arrived in time for supper which he was offered and gladly accepted. Even though Frith was anxious to complete the arrangement as quickly as possible, he was concerned about his two colleagues. They had not returned despite been given clear instructions to dispose of the body and to return at once.

The priest, whose name was Aidan, was old but jolly and seemed rather eccentric in his habits and table manners, he ate as if he had not seen food for days and stuffed his face as a pig stuffs his head in the trough. The man only stopped eating for as long as it took him to break wind, both from the mouth and elsewhere. Gallia and Frith kept him company, but they hardly touched their food. Philemon had refused to sit at the same table with the scoundrel who was to marry his daughter and ate alone in his room.

Aidan noticed the dark atmosphere at supper and after breaking more wind, commended on the lack of good cheer. 'For two people so close to binding their existence together, you both seem rather tense if you don't mind me saying so.'

Frith's eyes shot him a look that would have chilled the blood of many a man, but Aidan only smiled.

'Nerves can make anyone anxious,' the priest remarked.

'Keep your comments to yourself,' Frith told the man.

This rebuke failed to upset the priest. He turned his head a little to look at the lady sitting opposite him. 'You have picked out a nice dress?' he asked Gallia.

The lady stared at him, as if she did not understand his question. 'What do you mean?'

196

'The wedding dress?' he stated. Come to think of it, where are all your women?'

'There will be no women and no wedding dress,' Gallia stated.

The priest put down the chicken breast he had in his hand and shot a look of near panic at both parties. 'I must have come to the wrong place,' he stammered. 'And to think I've eaten all your food.'

Frith swore under his breath. 'You have not come to the wrong place...'

'Well, is it a case of the wrong ceremony? Has someone died and you want me to arrange a funeral.'

All present could hear Frith muttering. 'The only person that's going to die here is you, your blundering oaf.'

'My instructions were rather vague,' Aidan admitted.

'Just as soon as you finish stuffing your face, we can proceed with the wedding,' Frith stated.

'You have witnesses present?' Aidan asked.

Frith indicated Gallia's father would be present.

'And the others?' continued the priest.

'What others?' spat Frith.

Getting himself rather agitated, the priest put his hands in the air as if someone had broken one of the commandments. 'You can not have a wedding without people,' he said with astonishment.

'You surely only need two?' inquired Gallia.

The priest's anxiety seemed to increase. 'No my good lady, at least four people not including myself must be present.'

Frith had found the answer. 'A servant can be the other witness,' he declared.

Aidan gave a long passionate sigh. 'Good,' the man said. 'Now when were you thinking of attending the church?'

Frith got to his feet and looked ready to do violence.

'You were briefed that the ceremony would be held here, because of the health of my father,' the lady informed him.

197

Looking dim-witted the priest shook his head. 'Oh, that does pose a problem.'

Losing her patience, Gallia snapped at the priest herself. 'What problem?'

'Well, I take it you have the certificate in your possession?' he inquired.

'What certificate?' the lady asked.

'The one that allows marriage, outside a holy place of worship,' he said.

Frith's face was red with rage as he put his hand on the handle of his dagger. Gallia saw his action and tried to quell his anger. She got to her feet and whispered to him to leave the whole thing to her. He moved away from the table and sulked in a corner of the room.

'Where can we get this certificate,' she asked the priest.

'Any magistrate or praeside would give you one.'

'They will all have gone home by now,' said Gallia.

Aidan agreed. 'Yes that is true, but I know where the local praeside lives and he is a friend of mine.'

Gallia glanced over her shoulder. 'He says if we go to the local praeside we can get the certificate and be married there.'

'What about your father?' inquired Frith.

'When I looked in on him, he seemed awfully tired. I think this might be for the best?'

Frith, who was still in a bad mood, nodded his head.

Gallia said she thought it would save time.

'Okay, but perhaps the priest has a point. Why don't you find you most beautiful gown and wear it for the occasion.'

The lady agreed and hurried to her bedroom to change. This left Frith alone with the priest. He stared long and hard at the man, but assumed he was nothing more than a fool. Aidan compounded this idea by stuffing still more food into his mouth with the glee of a child.

32

The night air was cool and the lack of any real breeze gave a peaceful feeling to the small camp of King Lot and his family, as they rested just a day's ride away from Hadrian's Wall and the sanctuary of Lothian. All were tired and ready for sleep, all except Lot who stood watch as he had every night since they had departed from Cadbury.

Lot stared up at the sky and watched the stars shine their wondrous light upon the earth. He had always loved the outdoors and the freedom the country life gave him. He hated sleeping indoors and would often leave his castle to wander around his people and share in their everyday lives. He would sleep in barns or fields and be up with the dawn without fail. Morgause was right to call him uncouth, vulgar, a peasant, all these things were true, but he was also pure in spirit and one with nature.

He hated politics and everything to do with the court and especially the intrigues and plots of the other Kings. He heard footsteps approaching and quickly jumped to his feet. He pulled out his sword which was lying on the ground beside him and made ready to challenge whoever approached. He recognized the figure that moved towards him, as his wife. He returned his sword to his sheath and heaved a sigh of relief.

'You better be careful you don't run one of us through with that thing,' the lady informed him.

Lot remained standing and wondered why he was being so honored by the lady's presence.

The tone in his voice sounded scornful. 'To what do I owe this pleasure?' he asked.

Morgause came up to her husband and by the help of the stars looked upon his face.

'You're not still in one of your sulks?' the lady inquired.

Lot thought this was extremely rich, coming from a woman who had spent the last fifteen years in one long sulk.

'I don't know what you mean, I never sulk, ask any of my friends or servants.'

'Perhaps I should ask all your lovers?' the lady quipped.

'Lovers,' the man scoffed. 'You do like to exaggerate.'

'I'm sorry, I thought it would safe to suggest more than one.'

'I will not discuss such things with you.'

'Perhaps that is why our marriage is the state it is in.'

'I don't know what you mean? Our marriage isn't in any kind of state,' Lot grumbled.

Morgause sighed and agreed. 'That is true.'

Lot asked his wife to sit beside him and she did.

The man tried to remain relaxed, but being beside his wife he could not be sure he could remain calm.

'I just wanted to ask you what you make of our young friend Galahad.' asked Morgause.

The King was immediately on the alert. 'I don't know what you mean?'

'Well, don't you find it bit strange, my sister asking you to do what you did?'

'I was only too pleased to carry out her instructions.'

'Yes, and you never questioned her about it?'

'No, why should I?'

'Oh, you can be obtuse sometimes.'

'What about him?'

'My sister and her secrets,' murmured Morgause. 'I was just wondering who he really was and why this family is connected to him.'

'What makes you think the family is connected to him?'

'Well there must be some connection.'

Lot shrugged his shoulders. 'You will need to ask your sister yourself.'

'My god, you know something.'

Lot denied knowing anything about the boy and was getting worked up again.

'I am your wife, you can tell me.'

Lot disagreed. 'I can not tell you anything.'

'I'm also Morgan's sister. She would not expect you to keep her secret from me.'

Again Lot refused to budge. 'I gave the lady my word.'

Morgause gave a huge sigh of frustration.

'Returning to the subject of lovers, I never expected you to become chaste for my benefit. I mean fifteen years is a long time, but...'

The lady failed to finish her sentence.

'What are you trying to say?'

Morgause bit the top of her lip. 'Well, I guess I'm trying to say, have you found someone special in that time.'

'I can with all honesty say that I have not.'

The man spoke the truth, it was never his intention to replace his wife, just receive comfort and passion elsewhere.

Morgause lowered her voice to almost a whisper. 'I would like to believe that.'

Lot took his wife's hand in his. 'You can,' he breathed. He then chuckled. 'I even miss our fights,' he admitted.

'You like women throwing things at you?' she asked.

There was a comfortable silence as husband and wife lay with their backs to a tree and relived their past passionate encounters.

'You never took a lover?' the man asked some time later.

'Who said I didn't?' Morgause queried.

'I was only curious. You're a fine looking woman.'

'I never expected you to give up so easily.'

'I guess I just got older, slower at ducking.'

And now?' the lady asked. Do you want me to return to the matrimonial bed?'

The man's voice suddenly became passionate. 'Nothing would please me more,' he admitted.

'I will, but on one condition.'

'Anything,' pleaded the man.

'You allow me to take a lover. I have been a dutiful wife and mother, but I crave a little excitement now. I wish to indulge in romance for pleasure's sake, just like a man. I do not want to wait a moment longer either, for I fear I will soon be too old. I don't mind telling you I have picked out the man I wish to seduce.'

Lot looked at his wife and thought she must be joking. 'I find your jest offensive.'

'It is no jest. I wish to know what it is like to have a lover. Is it exciting knowing that you're cheating on your spouse?'

'I have a good mind to take you over my knee and smack you hard.'

'Why don't you try, it would be the first exciting thing that has happened to me in fifteen years.'

Lot got to his feet, his face blazing with anger. 'Have your blasted affair, see if I care.'

He stormed past his wife, to look for some dumb animal to kick. It should have been his wife that he aimed his blow at, but his honor forbad him from laying a finger on a woman.

To continue riding in the dark on an old dirt track, might have kept them hidden, but Lancelot knew they could easily lose their way altogether and end up getting completely lost. John had a similar view and broached the subject with Olwen first.

'We must go back on the main road, my lady,' he said.

'Why?' asked Olwen.

'It's too dark to see where we are going.'

Lancelot pitched in. 'Your friend is right, we could be going around in circles.'

Olwen seemed to listen more to Lancelot's council and agreed to his suggestion. They turned to their right and ventured forward hoping to find an opening that led to a main road. To their dismay they did not find an opening and before long were truly lost.

Both men offered to take the blame for their misfortune, but Olwen would have none of it. Instead she suggested they make camp and rest until morning.

'It is not safe to rest here,' ventured John.

Lancelot disagreed and promised to keep a watch the whole time, while the others slept. John argued some more, but Olwen agreed and a camp of sorts were made. John lit a fire and brought from their saddlebags food comprising of cold meat, bread and water. This was much appreciated by Lancelot who praised the meal as the best he had ever eaten.

A simple bed was constructed for the lady, consisting of John's saddlebag for a headrest and Lancelot's blanket from his horse. The smell was perhaps a little strong, but it soon disappeared. Olwen lay down to sleep unaware that both men were preparing for a long night of guard duty.

Lancelot looked up at the stars, while listening in case anyone, including Gawain might stumble across them. He thought John must be in love with his mistress, for the way he guarded her and watched over her like a dutiful dog. He glanced behind to see to his amazement that the man he had praised slouched to one side, fast asleep. As he faced forward again to look at the stars, he heard a noise behind him. He turned his body around to see the Lady Olwen coming towards him.

The lady looked suitable rested and came and sat beside him. She spoke softly in case she woke John. 'I wish to ask you something my lord, which might seem indelicate?'

'You can ask me anything you wish,' Lancelot replied.

'Are you a great lord?'

Lancelot wondered why the lady asked such a question.

'My father is a great lord, in fact he is a King. Not of this land, but across the water in the land of Benoic.'

'You are a great warrior then, so you must have sufficient funds to allow you to do whatever you wish.'

'My days of plunder are hopefully over, but certainly I should never go hungry.'

'I do not mean to pry, but I am in need of warriors and funds to make an expedition to a most dangerous place.'

Lancelot was intrigued, but feared that the Queen's business had to take precedent over everything else.

'I am not as free as you might think. I have obligations to another I'm afraid.'

It was Olwen this time who was intrigued.

'Is she prettier than me?' the lady asked.

Lancelot doubted that anyone was prettier than the girl before him, but he implied that she was indeed good looking.

'I am not tired now, why don't you tell me about your good lady.'

Lancelot could not utter the Queen's name and certainly was not going to open his heart to this girl. 'I'm more interested in you,' the man said.

'I think I am uninteresting and will only tell you about myself if you agreed to lead my expedition.'

'This I can not do.'

It was when Lancelot and Olwen were engrossed in conversation that Gawain had heard their gentle prattle. He quietly got off his horse, took the King's sword and moved like a snake, slow and cunning towards his prey.

Gawain knelt and peered through a break in the trees to see before him the man who was his quarry, sitting enjoying the night air with a lady who seemed oddly familiar. He hesitated to pounce before Lancelot, in case the lady got hurt in the process, but delay might mean failure so he extended Arthur's great sword and rushed upon the couple.

The clatter of swords soon awoke John from his slumber and he got to his feet to come to help. Before he could reach his sword he witnessed in the gloomy light a figure of a warrior rein down his sword with an almighty vigor on Lancelot. Each swing of his sword was followed by an almost unearthly cry of anger that chilled the blood. 'You murdering swine,' Gawain shouted. 'I will avenge my brother and cut you into tiny pieces.'

Olwen moved out of the way of the fight and watched with her eyes half open and half shut as both men fought like men possessed. She whimpered for the men to stop, but to no avail.

John got his sword and made to venture into the fray.

Lancelot shouted. 'This is personal. It is not your fight, stay out of it.'

Sword in hand the man stood and watched, what was becoming a battle between two titans.

Lancelot was forever being forced backwards with the sheer power of Gawain's efforts, but he hoped in time the young man would tire. There was no sign of that, if anything Gawain seemed to be gaining more momentum and was becoming aware of Lancelot's defensive moves. The straight cut and thrust of his early attacks were being modified to incorporate more sophisticated blows. He used techniques he had learnt from his time in the east to shaken and to keep Lancelot guessing of what blow was to come next. Somehow Lancelot managed to stave of his attacker, but with his wound reopening from his exertions, he realized it was only a matter of time before he succumbed to younger and fitter man.

If it hadn't been for the bravery and foolhardiness of Olwen, Lancelot would have died at the hands of Gawain that night. She raced forward as both men continued to strike and counter strike at each other. It was the sword of Gawain's that graced the lady's arm and made her shriek in pain.

Immediately the two men stopped their dual and were joined by an animated John, who ran to his lady in a panic. He tore away a piece of cloth from his shirt that was big enough to put round the lady's arm and tried to attend to her wound.

To John's surprise both men helped him, for his hands trembled and could not work efficiently. They were better equipped to stop the bleeding and it was Gawain who made an effective tourniquet for the lady's arm.

'I'm sorry, so sorry,' he pleaded over and over again.

Olwen and John could see this was no cutthroat, but a soldier like the man who had rescued them.

'I don't know what all this is about, but surely there is a more civilized way to deal with your squabble,' Olwen attested.

Gawain looked at Lancelot and then at the lady.

'You do not know what this man has done. He has killed the King and others, including my brother.'

Olwen looked at Lancelot.

'You are Lancelot?' she asked the man.

He acknowledged he was.

The lady then addressed Gawain. 'This man saved our lives this day. But for him I believe we both would have perished in the forest.'

'That does not excuse his crimes,' said Gawain.

'I have committed no crime,' Lancelot insisted.

'You will accompany me to the nearest gaol and await the authorities then,' asked Gawain.

Lancelot could see in their faces that Olwen and John were undecided about the charges put before him.

'And if I do not?' asked Lancelot.

'I will forcibly restrain you and take you there myself.'

Lancelot thought that the balance of suspicion lay with him and if he made a break for it, his new found friends would help him to escape. He was wrong in this assumption, even though the lady might have given him the benefit of the doubt, John had decided that the charges were too great to ignore. He had been suspicious of the man from the first and his attacker's anger seemed honest and heartfelt.

John suddenly took hold of Lancelot's arms, allowing Gawain to tie them behind his back with a piece of rope. Gawain then relieved the prisoner of his sword and gave it to John for save keeping. Lancelot studied Olwen's face to see that the look of anguish gave him at least some hope. They were closer to Londinium than Dover and he assumed they would ride there, but not until the morning. The rest of the night might still provide him with a chance to escape.

33

Gallia and Frith were in the priest's hands as the rather dotty cleric sauntered his way through the streets and lanes of Londinium. They began to worry when he guided them into the seedy district, of the Island of Thorns. The whole area was surrounded by water; the great river carved a path through two strips of land on either of its sides. On the left bank of the river lay the infamous marsh that Merlin and Gallia crossed successfully in daylight. To try such a journey at night would be tantamount to committing suicide. The other bank was safe, although the water often spilled over onto the land, flooding the large warehouses on occasions.

Frith, who had said little up on till now, began to curse the fool who had led them to this dangerous area. 'Are you trying to get all our throats cut,' he chided.

'Oh, do not fear attack my friend, I can handle myself quite well,' replied the priest.

'And the lady?' inquired Frith.

'Oh, I will protect her.'

'I'm sure she feels a lot saver now.'

The party stopped outside one of the biggest warehouses and to Frith and Gallia's surprise, Aidan brought out a key from his cloak and opened the door.

'You are not telling me the praeside likes here,' grumbled Frith.

'Oh no, of course not,' said Aidan. 'Didn't I say?'

'Say what?' Gallia asked.

'The man has duties too attend to in these warehouses...'

'For God's sake,' swore Frith. 'We are not getting married in a bloody warehouse,' he shouted.'

'Well no quite, he will marry you in his home I presume.'

'Presume? I'm beginning to think you are not even a priest. You're some madman let loose from some madhouse.'

The priest laughed. 'You will have your little joke.'

Frith's face thundered. He took a dagger from beneath his cloak and held it by his side.

Aidan saw the knife and the look of panic on Gallia's face. 'At last, here we are,' he said. 'The praeside should just be over here...'

'Damn the praeside, who are you?' screeched Frith.

'I am the local priest at St Mary's...'

'You're a bloody liar.'

'Now is that any way to address a holy man...'

Frith had his knife extended in his hand, ready to cut the man before him.

Gallia sensibly moved a slight distance away from the men and addressed Frith. 'Don't be a fool. They'll surely hang you if you murder a priest.'

'He's no priest. Tell us who you really are?'

Smiling, Aidan agreed. He removed some padded cloth from his stomach and threw it down on the ground. This took away the illusion of fatness and replaced it with a scrawny frame. Aidan scratched his stomach and sighed in relief. 'That's better, it did itch terribly.' He then tore away additional hair from the side of his face and wiped away red and white powder from his face with a cloth he produced from a pocket. All the time he was transforming his image, both Frith and Gallia stared at him in amazement. Finally he covered his face with his hand for a moment, before taking it away to reveal the face of the man they both knew as Taliesin.

Gallia sighed in relief and put her hands up to her face. 'God be praised,' she shrieked.

Frith look at one then the other, as he clenched his face in hate. 'So that's it, lovers after all.'

Merlin shook his head and continued to act as the priest. 'May God forgive your vicious mind,' he said.

Frith leapt forward with his knife and swung it at Merlin, first one way and then other. The swish of the blade made a terrifying sound, as Gallia gasped in alarm. Merlin moved to one side then other and did not look unduly worried as his attacker missed his mark again and again.

While dodging the blows from Frith, Merlin glanced in the direction of Gallia.' Do you still wish me to spare him?' he asked her.

The lady hesitated. 'Do what you have to do.'

Frith hissed like a snake, before rushing at Merlin with the hope of wrestling him to the floor. His hatred blinded him to reason and this made his judgment poor, but Frith was battling no ordinary human. The dexterity that Merlin showed was not normal and no matter what his attacker tried he was unable to even touch the man. In fact his knife was useless and after awhile the man looked exhausted and ready to give up.

From the corner of his eye, Frith kept his eyes peeled to where Gallia was. The lady quite sensibly had moved to a corner of the room well away from the fight. Without drawing attention to the fact, Frith moved himself closer to her. Merlin had enjoyed the charade up until now, but he knew he had to finish it soon. He would rather not dispatch the villain into the next world in close sight of the lady. 'Gallia, go outside,' he charged her.

The lady was startled and shook her head.

'Please,' Merlin pleaded.

As she turned her back to depart, Frith made a rush for her. Merlin put out his hand and with the power of his will forced the man to stop in his tracks.

Gallia turned her head, to see the man frozen in time. She looked at Merlin and her eyes stared at him aghast with horror. 'You must be the devil to do such a thing.'

Merlin came towards her, but the lady turned and ran out of the warehouse. He decided not to go after her, but to depose of the villain once and for all. He unfroze the man with the wave of his hand and with that same hand pressed it down on Frith's head. The man dropped to the ground slowly, screaming in agony as if his brain was on fire. The end was quick after this, as the man fell back unto the floor dead.

Gallia ran back the way she had come, her mind confused with the images she had seen. It was not long before the lady got lost and found herself walking in the vilest streets imaginable. The air was heavy with smoke and the smell of urine reeked from the shacks all along the waterfront. Many people were outdoors, drinking and eating for the night was dry and the air was sweeter outside than their stinking hovels. The atmosphere seemed hostile towards the newcomer and many people glared at her as she walked through their neighborhood. She thought about asking directions, but found the locals so unsympathetic that she decided to walk on as fast as she could.

Some time later, the usual self-assured Gallia was in a panic as she scoured her immediate surrounds for an image or marker that would lead her on the track to her home. She walked north thinking that after awhile she would encounter a main road and that would take her back into the town centre. Without knowing it the lady was close to Arthur's monument, the place where she and Taliesin had spied her father's mansion earlier that day. Although the lady lived in Londinium, she rarely ventured from her father's mansion. She preferred to spend all her time at his side in an effort to make up for all the times she was forced to work away from home.

The sound of laughter and foul language alerted the lady that she was approaching some Tavern or Inn. She thought it likely, that someone there would be able to help her find her way. The Inn was out of the beaten track and was not dissimilar to many the lady knew from her past position as courier, come thief. She had become used to the noise and coarseness of such places and was not surprised when the level of noise dropped appreciably when she entered. She looked around the establishment to find the landlord; an old man with a craggy face and a limp. He dragged his person over to the table where Gallia had sat down. 'We don't get many visitors here,' he grumbled.

211

'With such a warm welcome, I'm not surprised,' remarked the lady.

'If you're looking to shift some cargo, Patrice will not be here until later.'

'That is good to know, but I was only looking for directions to the Governor's mansion.'

'Shh...Are you mad?' the man cried.

Gallia asked the man what he meant.

The man moved closer to her and whispered. 'If they think you're from the authorities, you'll never get out of here alive.'

Gallia found herself whispering too. 'I'm not, but I just need to get home to my father.'

'You're telling me you are just lost?'

'Yes,' the lady replied.

Unconvinced the man shook his head and offered her some advice. 'You better not leave straight away, it will look suspicious. I'll bring you over something to drink.'

Before the lady could reply, the man had turned and moved away. He returned with a goblet of ale and left it on her table. The lady was just about ready to burst into tears, when a man approached her table. She looked up to see a face she recognized. The man was an acquaintance of Frith's and a smuggler of some note by the name Judas. 'What are you doing here?' he asked her.

The last thing she wanted was to be recognized and by a known associate. Looking suitably miserable the lady thought up a story. 'I have broken my association with Frith and am on the look out for some new contacts.'

Looking pleased, Judas brought over a chair and sat next to her. 'That's interesting. You could be the answer to my prayers,' the man told her. 'I am in need of someone who can get me into one of our great castles.'

'Not by climbing its walls I take it,' Gallia mused.

Judas laughed. 'You have the right contacts. There's a banquet expected there on the first night of the new moon.'

'Whose castle are we talking about?'

'Do you know the present Duke of Mador at all? He has a castle in Cirencester.'

'Yes I know of it.'

'He is marrying his youngest daughter to some nobleman. It should be quite a grand affair.'

Gallia didn't look all that interested, but Judas pressed her.

'I hardly think I will get an invitation to the wedding.'

'Do you not know one or two people of some note in the nobility?'

'Yes, I do, but unless my contacts are friends or family I doubt they'll be invited either.'

'Well, could you not make some inquires?'

Gallia reluctantly agreed she would. 'Why this castle, what's so important?'

Judas bit his lip. 'No more Frith?' he asked.

The lady assured him, he would never see them together again.

'I'm not greedy like some; I am quite willing to cut you in on the spoils. I will give you a quarter of the share of the profits made from the haul.'

'And how much would that be?' inquired Gallia.

Judas bent his head forward and lowered his voice to whisper. 'Enough for us both to retire for good,' the man vouched.

The lady looked more interested and asked why the treasure amounted to so much.

'A ladies' maid who works in the castle witnessed the arrival of crates at the dead of night. She could not see the contents, but both Mador and his wife were present to organize their storage.'

'Most odd I admit...'

'She slipped out of her room and found that only one man was entrusted with the goods' safe keeping. He was their most trusted and long standing servant. He physically had to carry the grates down into the bowels of the castle himself. She assured me it took the man all night and he was so exhausted he fell asleep on one of the stairs.'

Gallia was dazed and didn't know what to say. If the man's information was correct, she would never have to worry about money again. She and her father could find some paradise away from prying eyes. She could finally be free.

She felt the hand of Judas on her arm. 'What do you say? Can you get me into that castle?'

'I don't know,' the lady replied. How long before the wedding?' she asked.

'The wedding's in three days time I believe.'

The lady's hand caressed her own neck. She was unbelievably tired and her brain was stale from all that had gone before. 'Where can I get hold of you?'

Judas's finger touched his lip. 'Its better I get in touch with you. Are you still living with your father?'

'Yes, you can find me there, but I'd rather we met someplace else.'

'I understand. I'll send word; I won't suddenly turn up and frighten the neighbors.'

'I'll try and make progress as soon as possible.'

Judas nodded. 'Three days doesn't give us much time?'

'No that's true, but maybe that's a good thing.'

'Why is that?'

'If we had time to think about it, we would probably come to the conclusion the whole enterprise is reckless.'

Judas chuckled.

'Now, can you escort me part of the way home?' the lady asked.

'You don't have to worry now that we've talked, everyone in the place will be happy to call you friend.'

'I'm kind of lost; I could do with you accompanying me as far as Arthur's Monument.'

'I'll gladly escort you.' The man laughed. 'They'll all think my luck's changed, going about with a real lady.'

Gallia laughed at herself. 'I gave up being a lady a long time ago. If I ever put on airs again, pinch me hard.'

'With Frith out of the way I might just do that,' the man suggested.

As they were leaving, Gallia noticed some men nodding their heads and winking at the happy Judas. The atmosphere had changed again to a friendly easy going one. Many men came towards Judas, but he shook his head and they walked away and sat back down again.

'You seem popular,' suggested the lady.

'This is one the best thieves dens in London.'

A thought came into the lady's head. 'You wouldn't happen to be Patrice by any chance?'

The man looked embarrassed. 'You can never have too many names in my business.'

'What is your real name?' the lady asked.

'Damned if I know, but I'm pretty sure it isn't Patrice.'

34

Waiting until the darkness was at its height, Yvain and Samson carried the body of the King on their shoulders down to the boat on the shore. The decision was taken to sneak Arthur's body out by the back of the building, so that it would correspond with a statement given by a spokesman at the front. The statement told the populace extremely little and was purely a diversionary tactic to let Morgan spirit the King's body away without detection.

She could not get a sea captain or hand to help her guide the boat to Avalon. The general seamen feared going anywhere near the small group of Islands. They believed the Gods would strike them down if they came anywhere near their shores. Many stories of shipwrecks and missing boats convinced the seafaring men it just wasn't safe. The lady did not believe their tales of disaster, after all she had ventured there unhindered and would do so again.

Samson was sweating greatly and stuttered his disapproval of the lady's actions. Morgan didn't care what the man thought and kept him up to the mark.

'Have your warrants all gone out?' she quizzed the man.

'Yes, yes...all the magistrates, praesides and consulares have been informed and Lancelot I am sure will be arrested soon.'

Yvain had a wonderful surprise when he lifted the King's body onto the boat, for sitting at its stern was his sweetheart. Nemue gave him a big smile and opened her arms. It did not take him long to embrace the girl and smother her with kisses.

'Did you miss me,' the girl asked in a most serious tone.

Yvain touched her face with his hands and whispered.

'I missed you every waking moment,' he told her.

216

Still teasing, the girl pretended to be less than overjoyed. 'Only the waking moments?' she queried.

He laughed. 'I can not believe I'm on my way to Avalon, the island of the Gods.'

'You are not. We are only going as far as Tintagel. Morgan will travel with the pixies the rest of the way with Arthur alone.

Yvain looked disappointed. 'Who would have believed me anyway?' he joked.

'Never mind, someday I will get permission for you to come to Avalon and meet my lady.'

Yvain looked puzzled. What did she mean by my lady? he pondered.

Lancelot waited his chance and whenever he glanced over at Olwen, he was sure the lady was on his side. No one got much sleep that night and all were relieved when the sun rose to provide the much needed light to escape the path and find the road to Londinium. With his hands tied behind his back, Lancelot rode without the reins of his horse. This made travelling by necessity a slow business. He was situated between John and Gawain, Olwen followed in the rear. Gawain had him in his sights at all times, making his chance of breaking away from the group difficult. If only the lady could invent a piece of drama to provide him with a distraction. His hopes rested with her gratitude and possibly in his good looks and manner towards her. Did she dare risk helping him he wondered?

Gawain voiced thundered into his ear shot. 'Did you murder the Lady Helena too?'

'I have no idea what became of Lady Helena,' Lancelot replied.

'When the pirates raided you mean?'

'Yes,' Lancelot answered.

'You were too busy saving your own skin to help save the lady?'

Gawain was hoping the lady was listening to their conversation, just in case she was contemplating helping the prisoner.'

'I was struck and left unconscious.'

'Liar, you killed the lady just like you killed my brother.'

Lancelot almost gave into a laugh. 'If you think you can goad me into making a break for it, so you can cut me down, think again.'

'Did they suffer, or did you strike them down when they slept?'

'We were once good friends.'

'Do not rely on old friendships, they mean little when murder is involved.'

Lancelot tried to turn his body to look at Gawain. 'We fought in many battles together; surely you don't think me capable of such a thing?'

Gawain paused. 'Everyone knows you bed the Queen...'

'More lies,' Lancelot barked.

'There's barely a man or woman in the land that does not know it. You didn't think the King was ignorant of the fact.'

Lancelot tried to contort his body again. 'I confess to an attachment, but I swear I have never lain with the Queen.'

Olwen thought to enter into the conversation by addressing Gawain. 'What has the Queen got to do with the crimes you speak off?'

The young man did not answer her.

Lancelot did. 'He thinks the Queen wants her husband dead so that she can rule in his stead.'

Olwen looked confused. 'Doesn't she rule here, when her husband is away fighting his wars?'

'Exactly,' Lancelot said with an air of triumph.

'It still makes better sense, than a raid on a small boat by a group of blood-thirsty pirates.'

Lancelot knew it would not be long before they reached their destination and his chance of escape would be gone. It was almost as if Gawain could read his mind, he rode up beside him with his sword unsheathed and pointed at his lower body. The movement corresponded to the sight of a farmer and his small herd of cows hurrying onto the road from a side track. It was now or never thought the captive.

Olwen did not let Lancelot down. Her horse suddenly began to misbehave and reared away from her. If the lady engineered this move it was a dangerous thing to do, particularly with so many cows in close attendance. The lady's beast burst forward and sprang past the men and bolted towards the cows. John immediately responded and was close to catching her runaway, when Lancelot kicked his own horse into action and raced it down the side track. Gawain who thought about going after Olwen changed his mind and sprinted after his quarry instead.

Lancelot kicked like a madman into the poor horse's side, but with his hands tied he could not control the beast from wandering. The horse veered from side to side and nearly stumbled several times, before Gawain on his own horse came along side. The young man jumped from his horse onto Lancelot's horse and pulled the man down from his mount. The two clattered to the ground and as Gawain got to his feet he used the butt of the King's sword to slash a blow across Lancelot's face. The blow was of such force that the sound of the man's bones cracking was clearly heard. Lancelot fell back and did not stir.

John was a fine horseman and even with a melee of excitable cows he managed to take hold of his mistress's horse and bring it to a halt. No words were exchanged between the two, but the lady smiled, a smile of gratitude.

They retraced their steps until they saw Gawain lift an unconscious Lancelot unto the road and smacked him down on the dirt. He quickly retrieved his horse, but saw that Lancelot's was long gone.

'My lady is not hurt I trust?' asked Gawain.

'Thankfully she is not,' John answered.

'I'm glad to hear it.'

Olwen gasped. 'Have you killed him then?'

'No, he was knocked unconscious. He'll live to answer his accusers.'

35

They were all in attendance. Londinium was awash with dignitaries, the Queen and half of her army had descended upon it like a plague. Morgan with her supporters numbered a great deal less, but nonetheless Gawain, Gaheris, Mordred were present. All the Kings had been summoned and all, but King Ban of Benoic and King Lot of Lothian had arrived. To Morgan's surprise Merlin had returned to her in a morose state. He apologized, but did not go into details of what had befallen him. They were all there for one purpose and that was to take part or bear witness to the trial of Lancelot. He was to be judged by the High Council, along with Guinevere, who insisted on representing her dead husband and the domain of the Middle Kingdom.

It quickly became clear that the council had two camps, those who supported the Queen and by association Lancelot, and those who believed the man to be guilty of the crimes he had been indicted for. It would be a few days before the trial would begin and that gave both camps time to prepare their cases. It also gave Morgan a chance to catch up with family members and hear their stories. Everyone had tales to tell; Gaheris on witnessing the aftermath of the massacre at Haydon Bridge, Gawain in capturing Lancelot and his encounter with Olwen, and Mordred with his tale of being spotted with Kay and being forced to eat at the Queen's table. He did not go on to tell of his more intimate meeting with the lady later that night.

No one noticed Mordred's more confident nature, except Morgan. She was pleased to see it, for she felt it was about time he stepped from the shadows and found his true position in society. Morgan could not be sure if King Lot would bring her son, but rather hoped he would not. She had enough to do in preparing her case to have her mind disrupted with thoughts of an awkward reunion. That time would come, but for now the lady had to concentrate on getting justice for her brother and nephew. The body of Helena had never been found and the assumption was that the lady perished like the rest. Morgan had taken special care to find Gaheris alone and in his quarters.

On entering his room, Morgan noticed the icon of Olwen lying on top of his dresser and picked it up to look at the pretty face of the girl she thought she recognized. 'I know this girl,' she proclaimed.

Gaheris who had just finished dressing came from behind a screen to challenge the lady's statement. 'You know her you say, how? Where have you seen her?'

Morgan looked at her nephew and was surprised at his reaction. It was clear the lady meant a great deal to the young man. 'Is she your sweetheart?' she asked.

'No, I've never even seen her, but I must find out where she is.'

'Never seen her and yet you have a painting of the lady?'

'I know it seems strange, but I need to find her.'

Morgan thought Gawain would be the person to ask as he had seen the lady only a day earlier. Gaheris made ready to see his brother, but Morgan put her hand on his arm and addressed him in a tone not normal for the lady. 'You will kindly tell me all about the treasure you and my brother stole from Avalon,' she demanded.

The man knew he had no choice and agreed to tell the lady everything.

'I should tell the full story. It is a strange tale and you'll think I exaggerate it when I tell it.'

Morgan made Gaheris sit on a hardwood chair and she sat on another close by. 'I need the treasure to return it to Avalon. I made a promise to the Gods that I would.'

Gaheris face looked pained. 'I do not know where it is. It's been stolen and I have no way of knowing where it is now.'

Morgan sighed and put her hands on her head. She slowly raised her head to look at her nephew. 'You wouldn't lie to me?'

'I swear I do not lie. I believe it to be in the Queen's possession now.'

'That bloody woman again,' Morgan cursed. 'I wish it were her on trial and not Lancelot.'

'She is behind everything evil in this land,' concluded Gaheris.

'Don't exaggerate. Now tell me your tale and leave nothing out.'

'Do you remember the time I abandoned my duties?'

'Were you on some quest for the King?'

The man nodded. 'I was, but now it has become my own quest.'

He paused a moment and his eyes glazed over before he continued. 'It was two years ago, going by the Roman calendar,' he began. 'The King gathered a select group of soldiers to go on a special mission with him. He swore us to secrecy.' The man was reluctant to break that promise even now, the lady could tell. She took his hand in hers and began to plead with him to continue.

The man did so. 'The King picked a raiding party of twelve men and we travelled to the Islands of Avalon. We knew it was forbidden to go ashore on the Gods islands, but we went because our King asked us too.

The King told his men nothing of his plan, until we reached the first of the islands. He told us that at a particular time each day the Gods were all occupied and that their treasures were left unguarded. How he knew this we did not ask.

Arthur and I led the small boats onto the shore, as the sun fell behind the mountains and the moon's light filtered strange shadows against the trees and rocks. We wore no armor so as to make no noise and we carried only knives for we wanted no violence. Arthur led us, as if he had mapped out every step beforehand, straight to the Gods' hoard.

We entered a large cave and had walked only a short time before our eyes were astounded by an array of gold, silver and precious jewels. Many of our men picked up these treasures with the intension of plunder, but Arthur was preoccupied in his hunt for a single item that he allowed the plunder to happen without question.

I later found out the object he was looking for was a silver chalice. A humbler drinking vessel you could not have found, but when Arthur set eyes on the object he fell to his knees in exultation. For the King this was what he had come for, but for many of his men the lore of such wonders became too much for them. Many helped themselves to all manner of valuables, though I swear I did not, good lady.'

A slight nod of her head assured Gaheris he was believed. 'Did Arthur not see this plunder?' the lady asked.

'He did not seem to care what the others did, for his eyes were transfixed on this one object. He seemed to be in some kind of trance as I pulled him away from the cave and dragged him back to the boats.

It was when all the plunder were loaded that the first sign of life appeared from the Gods. A figure, with a frame of oxen and the head of a snake descended upon us. He opened his snake like mouth and fired a salvo of flames across our bows.

Arthur and I pushed one of the boats free from the bank but the rest of the men were still loading more precious items into their boat, when the God belched destruction down upon them. The flames engulfed our men and they roasted like boars on a spit. Their screams were terrible, like the cries of the damned, but we could not help them and I made Arthur realize this.

Having choked back a few tears, the man continued, although his voice lowered. 'There is more to tell, lady,' he stammered. 'The beast then turned his sights on us and showered down more thunderbolts. My one abiding thought was to save the King, so I covered our bodies with a blanket and persuaded him to take our chances in the water. I heard our men screaming as the flames engulfed them.'

'The flames, even on the water, were so intense that I feared we would perish. A great wind blew us by some miracle, along the river until we reached a river bank. Still fearful of the Gods, I remained in the water, while Arthur climbed ashore with the chalice still in his grasp.'

'What happened to the other treasure?' Morgan asked.

'The boat drifted our way and rested just a short distance away. Arthur dragged it onto the shore. He told me that the Gods rarely visited this place for this was the dreaded Island of the Dead. It housed the insane and the dead, whose souls would roam forever in torment.

I still resisted Arthur's hand as he offered to pull me ashore. Fear gripped me and I almost abandoned my King. Finally I gave in and he helped me on to the bank. The island at first looked empty and its vegetation looked much like our own. I stayed near the bank and warned our King not to venture further. Arthur showed no fear. He took the satchel with the chalice and placed it inside his shirt.

Morgan looked gripped by the tale as Gaheris continued.

'We encountered many strange creatures on that hellish place, but none more bizarre than Ysbaddaden. He was a giant, big in size, but quiet in nature who spoke softly almost in a continuous whisper. We had come to a huge derelict castle and despite hearing desperate cries from within we decided to enter. We were met at first with ghosts of white and black mist as they formed and dissipated before our eyes. They all cried or screamed obscenities at us but none kept their form for long. I was petrified and although he hid it well, I could see the King's fear for the first time. Reason told us the creatures we assumed were all phantoms could not hurt us. However, if our physical bodies were safe, our minds could be in mortal peril. Fear and the uncertainty of losing our minds prayed on our thoughts. We feared we would go mad if we stayed in that terrible place for any length of time.

'Several living beings approached us in that miserable place, but we threatened them with our knives and managed to keep them at bay. There was one however, the huge figure of Ysbaddaden that we found interesting. He was in a large chamber, the best and the only room in the castle that housed a fire. He was slouched down on the ground near the blaze, muttering mournful utterances to himself when we entered. 'Come in,' he said. He did not move or turn his head to see us, but stared into the fire. 'Are you dead or are you one of the living?'

We looked at each other before Arthur uttered a rather pitiful reply. 'We are still alive.'

The giant groaned. 'Then you must be like me, a hostage to fortune.'

The King's eyes met mine again, as we walked further into the room. The light of the fire had a great effect on us both. Not only did it give us much needed light, but it also warmed our hearts. I hadn't stopped shivering from the cold of the water and from the fear of my surroundings. I ambled to the fire, kneeled down and warmed myself. Arthur slowly followed, but sat nearer to the giant than to me and began to question him about the island and its occupants.

The giant told us his name and we told him ours. It is hard to describe the giant, without stating the obvious. He was just like any Celtic man of middle to old age, only four times as big I suppose. He wore a beard that was going grey and his hair had flecks of white running through the black. Arthur looked comical beside him as I watched him compel the giant into telling us his story.

'What do you know of the Gods?' he asked Arthur.

'Not much, only to fear ever crossing them.'

'You are right to fear them,' he said. His voice fell into a lamentation. 'They can be cruel, I should know. They have broken both my legs as a punishment, so that I should always be a prisoner in this hellish place.

Arthur pressed him for a reason for their cruelty, but his thoughts seem to make him sad. We watched the giant's tears fall down his face and land on the ground next to us. Arthur jumped to one side to miss the large drops as they fell, but I was not so lucky and got drenched in them. Ysbaddaden apologized, as I tried to dry myself. Arthur wanted to learn more so the giant told us the story of his daughter Olwen. 'She is the embodiment of everything

225

good,' he told us. 'She has a way with her that beguiles everyone, not just young men, but everyone who sets eyes on her.'

'Is she also a giant?' I asked.

'No, she is no bigger than you are,' he replied.

The giant continued. 'Goodness has been her downfall,' he complained. 'The Gods heard of her kindness and they visited her one night and beguiled her to their island. I thought I would not see her again, but she managed to slip a note to the death oarsman to take a message back over to our world. From his hand he gave it to a merchant who managed to get it to me.'

Ysbaddaden took from his right sandal a piece of parchment and began to read from it. 'Dearest father, they will not release me from this dreadful place. Please come and rescue me. The Gods are not what they seem. They care not for any human, but use us to do their dangerous work. Many have died from a strange disease. The victims' bodies are covered in boils and they become so sick that the can not eat or drink. They die a terrible death and I have to prepare them for burning. I am now feeling weak myself and fear my own death. Oh, father what have I done to deserve this?'The giant began to cry again, this time I got to my feet and let the salt water pass by me. I was moved by the lady's words and went to sit near the giant and to offer him a kind word of comfort.

'You are kind sir, but that is not the end of it,' he said.

'He told us he travelled to Avalon by boat, but fearing observation he left it and swam ashore without being seen. He sought his daughter and found her sick in a filthy cabin from a fever. He bathed her, gave her fresh water to drink and covered her body with an ointment that he had brought with him. He tended her for two days and in that time did not see single soul. The Gods had left her to die, but on that third day two men came to the cabin. They came to burn it down with his daughter still inside. He fought the men, who were strangely clothed, but he got the better of them by striking them down with a tree branch.

He then carried his daughter to a boat, and paddled the boat for all his worth away from the island.'

Gaheris continued. 'They travelled on their boat without disturbance until a God appeared before them at the corridor of their world and ours. The God looked no different he said than many a warrior with his scars and chainmail. So he fought him. The God was smaller than the giant, but that did not matter for he had magical powers and the strength of ten giants. Again and again he said he was knocked down, but came back and continued the fight. He was determined to save his daughter at all cost, so in an unselfish act of bravery Ysbaddaden stepped away from the boat and engaged with the God in the water. The sea water came up to his mouth, but that did not matter, for as he glanced behind, he blew with all is might and saw the vessel slowly glide towards freedom.

Poor Olwen screamed, as the boat glided away from the fight and try as she might to stop it, it continued on its course through the corridor and into our world.

'You mean the God did not try to come after her?'

'The giant kept him busy for as long as he could, but eventually he tired and was knocked unconscious.'

Morgan looked at the icon again

'So this girl's the giant's daughter?'

'Yes I had it painted from the description Ysbaddaden gave me.'

'Then the giant did not lie, the girl is just as she appears in this painting.'

Gaheris was full of passion and he did not even know it. Morgan saw his eyes fill with emotion every time the girl came up in the conversation. She wanted to assure him, he would not be disappointed when he finally set eyes on her.

'I now know why she wanted to see Arthur,' said Morgan. 'I believe she means to obtain men and weapons to try and rescue her father.'

'If that is the case, then I must do what I can to help her.'

'You must speak with Gawain and find out what he knows. Then I can give you two days to look for the lady, but I need you back here by the time the trial gets underway.'

Gaheris agreed and could not contain himself a moment longer.

Morgan caught hold of his arm. 'How did you and Arthur escape from the Island?'

Gaheris smiled. 'That's for another day, my lady.'

36

The Duke of Mador had been summoned to Londinium by the Queen to give her his support. He left behind a belligerent daughter who refused to do what she was told. Her wedding day had been put back because of recent events, which was a great relief to the lady. Mador hoped she would see reason and give in, so that some of the young man's land would come into his hands. The land was not large, but would increase his presence into Lady Morgan's territory. This would be beneficial to Guinevere if ever a war between the two ladies came about, as many were now predicting.

The ambitious Duke still held out vague hopes of marrying the Queen, despite the problem of his own wife being in the way. The Queen had confided in him and sought out his help in securing a safe place to hold her secret treasure. This made his position, he felt, unique, although she showed no sign of physical interest in him, other than to comment how fine his daughter looked. Was this her way of suggesting his manhood could provide her, even at this late stage, with a possible child. If not a husband he could become her lover he thought.

The Lady Megan was confined to her room, a prisoner in her own home. She was not ready to surrender her virginity and was quite prepared to run away or even kill herself to prevent it. It was because her father knew her so well, that he imprisoned her and set her horrid step-mother to watch over her.

Hester was only six years older than her and yet she felt no compulsion in seeing her offered up to some old man, like a human sacrifice. She thought her step-mother might have taken her part, but she only meekly followed her husband as always. She had not eaten in two days as a protest, but her belly now rumbled and she was desperate for something to fill it. The thought of creating another scene only wearied her, so she took a different tact. She called out to her step-mother that she was ready to be reasonable and was ready to eat something.

It was not Hester that came to open her room, but one of the servants, a young girl roughly of her age, by the name of Rose. The girl left the door open and went to get Megan some food. The young maiden wondered why her step-mother had not come and feeling rather aggrieved, left the confinement of her room to seek her out. Her first port of call was Hester's own room, which was on the other side of the castle. It never occurred to Megan why her father and his recent bride should keep their bedrooms so far from hers.

The far end of the castle was blessed with plenty of sunshine and the sun was flicking into Hester's room, as the lady pleaded with her maid to do what she wished. The lady was spread-eagled flat on her bed with her dress opened at the back, revealing her bare skin. The maid had a vial of ointment in her hand, but her hands were shaking as she stooped over her mistress ready to apply the healing balm.

'Come on, its not you that will feel its sting,' the lady complained.

'I know, but I do not want to hurt you, my lady.'

'The hurt's been done, so just apply it as gently as you can.'

The maid took her time and barely touched her mistress's body with the balm. Her gentleness eased much of the pain for Hester, but just as she thought the maid had finished the girl touched a particularly sensitive wound. Lady Hester shrieked in pain.

Megan heard the shriek and burst into her step-mother's room unannounced. She saw Hester faced down on her bed getting treatment for the many scars etched across her body. The scars looked new with their red lines cutting into the milk white flesh of the lady's back. Megan put her hand up to her mouth and held back a scream. She muffled her cry and approached Hester with a look of distress upon her face. The lady did not take too kindly to this intrusion and yelled at her step-daughter to get out. Megan came up close to Hester anyway and to the latter's surprise began to cry.

The two women, one merely a child, had never taken to one another. Each of the ladies mistrusted the other, fear and loathing sprung from their lack of communication. Neither of the ladies had tried to see the other's point of view and because of that, only tension and suspicion grew between them. In fact the young women had a lot in common, both suffered at the hands of a cruel and ambitious man. Hester dismissed the maid and allowed Megan to have a good look at her father's handy work. Megan was appalled and cursed her father, not just for this one act of brutality, but for all the acts of cruelty over the years dished upon her person too.

'When did this start?' Megan inquired.

Finding it hard to look upon the girl, the lady admitted it had started on their wedding night.

'Tell me why? What makes him do such things?'

Hester did not know, but assumed he got some kind of pleasure from it.'

'Pleasure,' shrieked Megan. 'It must stop, I will...'

Hester put her hands around Megan's body and made the girl look at her.

'You must never speak of this...not to anyone...do you hear me?'

'But you can not put up with such treatment.'

'I have no choice,' she the lady. 'He would put me out on to the streets and I should starve.'

'You can earn money...'

'By doing what?' asked Hester

'You can sew and run a household...'

'I can do nothing of any use. If I was tipped out onto the streets, I would either have to beg, sell my body, or become a thief to survive. My life here is a purgatory but at least I am fed, clothed and when we entertain, I am treated with respect.'

'Respect,' yelled Megan.

'I am content to live this life, just like you must give in and marry Lord Lionel.'

'Never,' cried Megan. 'I would rather die.'

'Would you, I don't think so? In any case he might be a kind man and treat you well.'

'Or he might be a monster, like my father.'

Megan began to cry. She was crying for many reasons, some selfish, some pure in heart. She wiped away her tears with her hand and made a promise. 'From this day forward we will be friends. We will be like sisters, always looking out for one another.'

Hester agreed. 'I fear you wish me to interfere on your behalf, but it would be a futile course, for your father has made up his mind...'

'I haven't given up, but I know now why you did not speak up for me.'

'I wanted to on many occasions...'

'I'm glad I've found out his ghastly secret.'

Megan put her arms around her step-mother and kissed her on the cheek. It was the first time in a long while that anyone had shown the lady any kindness and the emotion came flooding out. She clung on to Megan and began to cry herself.

Rose had left food in Megan's room when she returned to find the lady gone. She did not go looking for her, but descended many stairs until she reached the courtyard. With her master gone and the head cook busy, she managed to move to the back of the courtyard towards the guard tower. No one was watching the rear of the castle so no one saw her enter the gatehouse. One man was there his head covered with a cloth cap, lying on the floor beside him was a guard. The man was Judas.

'You didn't need to do that,' said Rose.

'The man was in my way,' Judas explained.

'How am I to explain it?'

'With your master away, does it need explaining?'

'I'll think of something.'

232

Judas looked impatiently at his accomplice. 'Is it on for tomorrow night?' he pressed.

'Yes, everything's in place, I will let you and your men in by this gatehouse at the changing of the guard.'

'When will that be?' an anxious Judas asked

'You will just have to await my signal, but it will be late, when the sky is at its blackest.'

Judas nodded that he understood. He could not keep his joy from his face, but Rose issued a word of warning.

'Many things can go wrong in this undertaking.'

Judas just smiled. 'Nothing is going to go wrong, I feel it.'

'I still do not know why you recruited this woman.'

'Such treasure will need to be fenced and she has many wealthy contacts.'

'Is that the only reason?'

'Yes, of course. She will pay her way, I know her to be reliable.'

'She is coming tomorrow?'

'Yes, she can help us pick the best pieces.'

'Just as long as she knows that you are mine.'

Judas kissed the young woman. 'Everyone knows how I love you.'

'Liar, the only thing you love is gold and silver.'

'And the only thing you love is precious jewels.'

'That's good to know, we understand each other then.'

37

King Lot left his family well secured at his castle in Peebles, to travel to Londinium. The night before a strange occurrence had taken place in the room that housed the body of Elaine. Morgause who slept in the same room woke with a start and went to check on her sister, to find her body gone. The whole household was alerted and search parties were arranged to scour the land, but before all this could take place a maid came running out from the hall to announce that Elaine had suddenly returned. The whole family gathered around her bed to witness the lady stretched out before them as before, but with a subtle difference. After murmuring together, Morgause stated her sister had somehow changed.

'Changed?' cried Ygerne.

'Yes. Her smile is different. It was never so pronounced before.'

Everyone laughed, but after close inspection many agreed with the lady that a change had indeed occurred. No one could explain this and everyone present agreed to take turns in watching over Elaine both day and night.

Sextus was a man of many disguises. He had been born a bastard and grew up with the Roman army in Constantinople as a kind of regimental mascot. He never knew his mother and father, but when he was six years of age the commander of the comitatus troops there took him under his wing and brought him up as if he was his own. His adopted father was called Varos and his legion was much praised for its courage and steadfastness. Tragedy struck Varos and his men when a great illness swept across the land killing more than half of his regiment. The neighboring towns and cities succumbed also and by the end of that summer tens of thousands had perished.

The young man was by then fifteen and able to look out for himself. So he took the decision to leave his adopted army, which he had never signed a paper of consent, to travel abroad. His adopted father had left him some money and a few possessions, with these he travelled across the continent until he crossed the sea to Britain. After his money ran out, he found work at first as a blacksmith, then as a laborer, until finally he put forward his services as mercenary, a kind of jack of all trades. He would do odd jobs for a wide variety of clients, sometimes dangerous, often illegal. His reputation flourished amongst the criminal fraternity of the kingdom.

He made contact with a man whom he assumed was a priest, by the way he dressed, and agreed to carry out a task for him. The man was Germanus and he offered Sextus a large amount of silver if he would kidnap a young man by the name of Galahad.

Now this was not something uncommon, the man had been asked to do far worse. He had killed many men and women in his time and his conscience had never bothered him. To kidnap some young pupil of God sounded straightforward and profitable, so he immediately accepted. Germanus had found out that King Lot had taken Galahad to his castle in Peebles and so Sextus headed there with due speed.

The castle at Peebles was well fortified and well guarded with Lot's men both inside and out. This made the chance of entry dependent on a good disguise and an even better excuse. It had taken him two days to perfect his masquerade, but his costume was now flawless and his mannerism was now skilful enough to fool most. When a priest called, looking for donations to help his church, at the approach of the castle no one thought anything was out of the ordinary. The guard had been given strict instructions not to let anyone enter unless they recognized them, so the guard told the priest to move away. It was done with some discourtesy and was overheard by Galahad who was strolling about the castle's battlements.

'You down there,' the young man shouted at the guard. 'Why have you sent the good father away?'

'My master gave us strict instructions...'

Galahad was incensed with outrage. 'Let the father come into the castle,' he demanded.

'But young master, I can not go against my instructions.'

'You shall do as I say,' Galahad insisted.

The man grumbled, but gave the signal for the large gates to be opened. The priest walked into the castle, looked up to see young Galahad descend quickly from the battlements to greet him.

'Forgive our unfriendly welcome, father,' he said. 'This is still a land full of heathen customs.'

'Do not apologize young sir, you have made me most welcome.'

'I am always pleased to meet a servant of God. Please follow me and I shall introduce you to the others.'

'The others?' inquired the priest.

'Yes, I am but a guest here. This is the home of King Lot and his kin as perhaps you already know.'

'I am new here, my name is Father Mathew.'

'My name is Galahad, and I too wish to join your ranks and serve God.'

'How interesting, Tell me more, have you studied much?'

'Yes, at the Church of the Virgin Mary in Glastonbury.'

The father seemed impressed. 'My, you must have good contacts to manage to study there.'

The two men passed through the courtyard and up a good many stairs to the private housed rooms that belonged to the family of King. Just before Galahad entered the main hall, he questioned Father Mathew as to why he was here today.

The priest hesitated, but said he was looking for funds to rebuild an old church outside of town. This seemed a good cause to Galahad but Sextus worried the lie might not fool the others who knew the area better.

As the two men entered the hall, they saw several servants running about making preparations for the forthcoming meal. Immediately the young man offered the priest a chance to eat with the family. Although Sextus was counting on such an offer, he did not want to appear over eager.

'It is very kind of you, young sir,' he began, 'but should you not ask your hosts first?'

'Call me Galahad; it is a name some have told me is suggestive of foreign climes.'

'Indeed it does sound unusual.'

'I am sure our hosts will agree for you to stay.'

'I'd hate to put them out.

'Nonsense, I'm sure they'll love to speak to you.'

Galahad was in his element and sought out Lady Ygerne to introduce her to the priest. This was the moment of truth he thought, but to his surprise the lady suspected nothing and could not have been more kind. With some time yet before supper, Galahad escorted the Father from one end of the castle to the other. By the end of the tour the man was exhausted and bored beyond words, but that did not matter for the first part of his plan had been successful.

Gaheris cautiously advanced toward the river, he had followed Gawain's suggested trail and have finally caught up with his goal. It had taken him nearly two years to track down the lady, but now he felt apprehensive about finally setting eyes on her. Could she be as beautiful as her father suggested? Could he conceal his true feelings for her? He spotted John first; he had been told about this fierce guardian and was conciliatory when he approached the man. He made his horse come to a halt, nodded his head in acknowledgement to the man. 'I have come to speak with your good mistress. Her name I believe is Olwen.'

John took his sword from his sheath and stared before answering. 'There is no one here of that name.'

Gaheris stared back at the man. 'I come to speak with her concerning her quest.'

'Quest?' inquired John

'I understand your caution, but I have just come from Lady Morgan. My name is Gaheris...'

Olwen came out from behind a tree and stood next to her servant.

'It's alright John, I believe him to be a friend,' she said.

Gaheris dismounted from his horse and slowly walked towards the couple. John's face remained stern as he approached, but Olwen seemed to offer him a warmer welcome.

'You are Lady Morgan's nephew I believe?' inquired the lady.

'One of many,' the man replied.

John remained cautious. 'How do we know you are who you say?' he quizzed.

Olwen turned her head to look at her protector. 'John, don't be rude, of course he is who he says.'

Gaheris walked back to his horse and from his saddlebag withdrew the small icon of the lady that he had commissioned. He brought it to the couple and put the picture into the lady's hands. Olwen studied the painting, staring at it with curiously.

'Is this meant to be me?' she asked.

'It does not do you justice, my lady, but I had nothing to go on except your father's description...'

'My father,' the lady cried. 'You have seen him? Is he still alive?'

Olwen was beside herself with emotion. She began to tremble and Gaheris wondered if she was going to have some kind of seizure, but John managed to calm his mistress by holding both her hands and whispering softly in her ear. The lady took a couple of deep breaths and seemed much calmer.

Trying to force a smile, she asked Gaheris if he had travelled far.

Gaheris wanted to tell her he had been searching for her for the last two years, but only stated that he had left Londinium earlier that day.

John addressed the man. 'You mentioned the lady's quest...'

'Yes, I know all about it...'

Olwen took a couple of paces forward and offered her hand to Gaheris.

'Pray tell me everything that you can about my poor father.'

'Gladly my lady,' he replied.

The man took her hand and they walked slowly towards the river. John lodged his sword back into its sheath and walked a few paces behind.

'Unfortunately it has been nearly two years, since I saw him.'

Olwen looked startled, almost incredulous. 'But you saw him in the flesh in that dreadful place?'

'Yes my lady, he was well although a little disheartened.'

Olwen tried to force back some tears. 'I have let my father down,' she sobbed. 'I could not get sufficient funds to stage a rescue and I have taken too long.'

As the tears came, Gaheris offered her some hope. 'Fear not, you have at your disposal every gold tremisses I have in the world and the promise of every man I can muster.'

The young lady gasped in exultation. 'You mean we can rescue my father at long last.'

It did his heart good to see the lady change from despair to happiness so quickly. 'We will begin planning immediately,' he suggested.

Olwen turned to look at John. 'Do you hear that John, we're going to find my father and rescue him away from those beasts?'

John looked doubtful. He addressed Gaheris sternly. 'You do realize the dangers,' he suggested. 'We're not going up against normal beings...'

'I know that, that's why we must plan our strategy carefully.'

John still looked unhappy and Olwen began to stare at him with a look of disappointment. Then she remembered all the times, he had kept her strong when despair had almost crushed the life out of her. She came up to her faithful servant and kissed him on the cheek.

'Dear John,' she said, 'still looking out for me I see?'

'I just don't want you to be disappointed again.'

Gaheris interceded. 'The lady will not be present when we attack of course...'

Olwen interrupted. 'I shall, you can not stop me...'

John laughed. 'She will not be persuaded from this point, my friend.'

'It is too dangerous for you.'

'It is my father and my fight. You can not expect me to wait when others risk their lives.'

'That is exactly what I do expect.'

A heated argument between Gaheris and the lady then ensued and it was John who became the peacemaker. 'There's no point discussing this, until we make plans.'

They both listened to his good sense and calmed down.

Gaheris wanted to bring up another matter, but he found himself more hesitant now. 'Your father suggested that you had knowledge concerning the Gods that many people might find shocking? He suggested they are not what they appear.'

John put on his most protective face. 'Can't your questions wait,' he suggested.

'No John, I want to answer. I saw things on their island that convince me the Gods employ forced human labor. I also saw countless men and women die from a strange disease. I nearly perished myself from their terrible plague, only my father's medicine and his good care saved me.

John had taken the lady's hand in his as they walked along. His touch seemed to calm the lady again, for she had broken out in a sweat and her voice had indicated how excited she was becoming again.

Lowering his voice to a gentle murmur, Gaheris hope to reassure the lady of his commitment. 'When we rescue your father, perhaps we can rescue others too. Who knows perhaps, we can expose the Gods for what they really are?'

Looking anything but convinced John put in his oar. 'Perhaps we will all be killed. That is a more likely scenario.'

38

Yvain tried anxiously to bring up the subject of marriage to
Nemue, but his lady seemed not to want to discuss the
subject with him. He had no choice but to hold his fire, in
the hope that the lady might warm to the idea. The truth
was the lady feared the simple life of a wife and mother.
She could not see herself with babies and feared this would
mean the loss of Yvain's love. She wanted something more;
she wanted excitement, power and the influence that only
magic could give her. Her ambition was so overpowering
that she wondered if Yvain fitted in with her plans at all. He
was inclined towards the simple life and wanted nothing
more than to live on a small farm with her by his side. She
knew this was not what she wanted, but she could not bring
herself to tell him so.

They had been given a new assignment by Lady
Morgan, one they could achieve together. They were to
bring back from Gaul someone of interest in the Lancelot
case. They traced the person and although the woman was
reluctantly at first, after a little persuasion she came with
them back to Britain.

Sextus continued with his act and feigned from eating
much at the table of his hosts. There was plenty of food on
offer, such as rare delicacies like venison and partridge, but
he declined these to nibble at some bread and cheese to
further define his character. He was more interested in the
family's conversation and found to his surprise that the
ladies spoke quite clearly on matters of state. Lady Ygerne
was after all the King's mother and had a wealth of
experience in the running of the country. She spoke freely
and condemned the Queen outright, calling her a traitor
and a murderer to everyone present. To hear her speak
with such candor shocked the man, but as he listened he
also watched all the others around the table.

The Lady Morgause sat next to Galahad and behaved liked a spoiled girl in search of her first kiss. The young man seemed to return her affection, but did not respond to the lady's hand when it accidently touched his leg. He would quickly repel it, while looking embarrassed while he did.

The Lady Ygerne turned her head to look at the priest. 'Father Mathew, how can we help you in your affaires?'

'Oh, a simple donation will be quite sufficient,' he remarked.

'Yes, but perhaps I can arrange for some of our workers to lend a hand.'

Looking suitably humble, the man thanked her for her generosity.

'Tomorrow, I will arrange a small group to accompany you to the site.'

Sextus was not particularly happy at the prospect, but what could he do.

Morgause tore her attention away from Galahad to make a comment. 'It is strange, but I can not remember any such church,' she remarked to Sextus.

'It was once an old pagan site, but it came into disrepute and it was your kind husband that gave the land to the local diocese. They have been slow to make anything of it up until now, but with my new appointment I pushed for a new church to be built on the old site.'

Morgause looked reassured and did not further pry into the affair. When the subject of the conversation continued on religious matters, the lady got quickly bored and suggested everyone went for a walk around the grounds. Since it was a calm evening all agreed. As they strolled Sextus hoped to speak in private with Galahad, but he was thwarted at ever turn by the Lady Morgause who refused to let the young man out of her sight.

He had been offered a bed for the night and had accepted Lady Ygerne's kind offer. As night descended, he waited until everyone was asleep before leaving his room to wander around the corridors of the castle in an attempt to find a clue as to what room Galahad might be housed. Towards the end of a corridor Sextus stopped and listened, as he thought he had heard voices. Sure enough the sound of a discussion was taking place within one of the rooms. He crept forward to listen at the door. What he heard was the voice of a man and a woman debating the merits of celibacy.

Sitting up in his bed was a flustered Galahad. He wore a white shirt under his tunic and his hands clutched at his bedcovers in attempt to stave off revealing the lower part of his body. Beside him sat Lady Morgause, who likewise wore undergarments but nothing else.

'You are not a young boy anymore,' observed Morgause.

Galahad defended his actions. 'I know that many in the echelons of the church do not abide with the notion of celibacy at all, but I believe all young monks should take the vow...'

The young man did not get a chance to complete his statement. 'You are not yet a monk and have not yet taken such a vow.'

'No, but I intent too,' Galahad assured the lady.

The light in the room was poor and the young man stared at the lady as she bowed her head and seem to weep. He immediately placed his hands on hers and whispered. 'Please my lady, do not be upset.'

Morgause whimpered. 'I have made a fool of myself coming to you like this. What must you think of me? I am old and ugly, while you are young and noble.'

The tone in Galahad's reply warmed the lady's heart. 'You are beautiful and make such an intelligent conversation.'

'But I am old?'

'You are not. You must turn many a young man's head...'

'Not yours, it would seem.'

'You do not know what it has been like for me the last few days.'

244

Morgause moved her position on the bed to get even closer to the young man. Their hands remained locked together as their faces almost touched each other. 'Tell me what you mean,' whispered Morgause.

'I am not use to speaking with women, I thought I would find it awkward, but I did not find it so with you.'

'Why do you think that was?'

'You are so alive and clever. I did not know women spoke or thought as you do.'

Not knowing if this was a compliment or not, the lady asked for clarification.

'I watched you on our journey here,' he said. 'You never complained not even when we were knee deep in mud, or when it rained so hard that we were all soaked through. You were as strong as any man could be in both body and mind.' Galahad chuckled. 'It's as if I'd known you all my life, like you were my own sister or something.'

Morgause gave a passionate response. 'Don't you see my love? That is not the reaction of a brother; it is the reaction of man who is in love with a woman.'

Galahad gasped. 'Is it really? 'I thought if I ever fell in love I would feel different.'

'How so?' mused Morgause.

'I don't know, they say you can't eat or sleep.'

'Who says such nonsense?'

'Everyone, well monks and priests...'

'Do they know anything of life, these priests?'

'Well, they claim to.'

'They know nothing,' whispered the lady. 'I will tell you everything there is to know.'

Morgause took her hand and caressed the young man's face. She reached forward to kiss him on the mouth, but the young man pulled away again.

'What is it? What's wrong?' Morgause asked.

Galahad wouldn't say, but the lady suspected.

'Is it because I am married?'

The young man lowered his head.

Morgause smiled. 'We have an arrangement,' she informed the man. 'We have not slept together for more than fifteen years. He takes his lovers...'

'I can not be your lover, my lady. I'm not worldly...I fear God's wrath...'

'My marriage to my husband is over and has been for a long time. God does not want us to be celibate, Galahad,' the lady pleaded. 'It is not natural and I fear members of your church has mislead you to think that it is.'

'No. I have studied the matter and I feel Christ must have been celibate.'

'I have studied it too. I am convinced that Jesus was married and might even have had a child.'

'Nowhere have I found evidence to suggest this.'

'Was he not a rabbi?' the lady questioned.

'Yes, but...'

'Isn't it a fact that under Jewish law, all rabbis must marry?'

Galahad pondered. 'Yes, I believe so.'

'By the Roman records we have found, Jesus was well into adulthood when he died.'

Galahad agreed.

'Don't you see? It would have been unthinkable for a rabbi not to be married by this time.'

Galahad digested this information and had to agree.

'When you think about it, everyone would have remarked upon an unmarried rabbi.'

'You amaze me,' exclaimed Galahad as he stared into the lady's eyes.

'Let me amaze you in other ways,' the lady said quietly.

Morgause was just about to kiss the young man, when he put his hand up in front of his face to stop the embrace.

'Not here,' the young man whispered.

'Why?' the lady asked.

'This is your husband's castle and I am his guest, it would be wrong...'

Morgause agreed it would be unseemly. 'Where then can we be alone?' she inquired.

Galahad thoughts were cloudy. 'I can not say.'

Morgause had an idea. 'We are surrounded by countryside in this part of the world, we could conveniently get lost.'

'We have to accompany the priest tomorrow...'

'Perhaps we can wander away from the main party and find a secluded place to be together.'

The young man hesitated, as if he was having second thoughts. 'Is our love not wrong?'

Morgause smiled. She had heard a word that hinted at her success. 'Our love can not possibly be wrong, for I feel it so strongly,' she whispered.

The lady finally kissed the young man on the mouth, but then thought it prudent to withdraw.

Sextus had heard enough and thought his chance would come tomorrow, so he too withdrew, hoping to avoid the lady's departure. As Morgause exited the room he managed to turn a corner out of her sight, just in time.

39

Sextus called a halt to the procession to announce their arrival at the old church. He dismounted and talked with the master builder on the structure that was set before them. The church was really a villa left unoccupied since Roman times. It was in much need of repair, its walls were crumbling with many of the stones loose and whole walls were near to collapse. The builder walked with him into the villa and started to make observations, jotting some things down on a piece of parchment. When all this was going on, Sextus feared the lovers might take their chance and make their escape. He could not stop the endless chatter from the builder as he sized up the scale of work that would be needed. He finally made an excuse to leave the man and went in search of the lovers. He scoured all the surrounding countryside and talked to some of the men, but they all said the same thing, that they did know where the couple had gone.

The man did not despair, for he was a good tracker and could easily pick up their trail. He left instructions for the master builder to use the men to clear out all the unwanted debris from the villa by the end of the day. He told the man he would be back later and went looking for his prize amongst the radiant countryside of Lothian.

Morgause held a bunch of wild flowers in her hand. She picked the petals off the snowdrops, just like she had done when she was a child when the whole world seemed innocent and safe. She was acting immature in an effort to appeal to the young man's innocence.

Galahad was admiring her frivolous activity and feeling for the first time the gentle agony of love. He had wanted to feel something and now after his sleepless night his wish had come true. His head hurt, but his heart raced and his senses responded to the lovely surroundings and the lovely lady sitting next to him.

'I used to do this when I was young,' Morgause remarked.

He smiled and paid her a compliment. 'You are still young, my lady.'

The lady returned his smile.

Galahad had unleashed in her an inner passion, a need for joy that had always eluded her. She no longer felt alone in the world, she no longer felt worthless. To her surprise she felt happy, for she had something of her own, something that did not come with obligations or duty. She had become something more than just Lot's wife, Gawain's mother, or Morgan's sister. She had found something tangible for herself.

Sextus tracked their horses to an open field where he dismounted to study their movements. They were outstretched on the grass, playing like children blowing flowers into the air and staring into each other's eyes. He had with him a substance that would render them both unconscious within an instant. This would allow him to carry the young man away without force. He tied his horse to a tree and carefully approached them. With their backs to him he could see the couple's every move, as he moved slowly down the gentle incline towards where they sat.

The couple were so caught up in themselves that they did not hear the man approach them. Sextus sprinkled the contents of the vial over a cloth and quickened his pace. The last few steps brought danger of discovery, but luck was on his side for the couple had just engaged in a passionate embrace.

The last person Gallia wanted to see was standing in front of her father's villa clean and by his standards well-dressed. She was preparing for her return to crime and did not want to be disturbed, yet her conscience bothered her. He had saved her life, even if he was some kind of demon or the devil himself. She came out to the front of the building and offered Merlin a chance to stroll with her around the grounds. He accepted and offered her the flowers.

'Is this some kind of peace offering?' the lady inquired.

'I did not know we were at war,' the man replied.

Gallia took the flowers, put her nose up close to them and breathed in their aroma. 'They smell like the morning wind, fresh and clean.'

They walked round the small area that surrounded the villa in deep contemplation.

'I do not want to know the details,' the lady emphasized.

Merlin studied her reaction and found it bewildering. 'Tell me you are not sorry he is out of your life?'

'I'm glad to be free of him, but that does not mean I am glad he is dead.'

'As long as he was alive, you would never have been free.'

'That is true, but you were not the first to rescue me. He saved me from a life of prostitution.'

'To a life of crime, hardly a great improvement,' admonished the man.

'Who are you to sit in judgment of me, or of anyone else?'

Merlin apologized. 'What will you do now?' he asked.

'You need not worry, I can look after myself.'

With a rueful smile Merlin remembered. 'You still have the booty.'

Gallia had forgotten about her earlier spoils. 'Of course you should take the prize, it's only fair.'

'I don't want your plunder.'

'Then what do you want?'

The question hit the man like a dagger threw his heart. What did he want from the woman; love, praise, redemption, maybe a chance to have a life worth living again?

His hesitation fascinated the lady. Surely he did not expect romance, not at his time of life. She no longer belicved in such nonsense and doubted the man did either. Yet he wanted something from her, she could feel his need.

'I want to be of use, I want to help you...'

'You want to be my conscience?'

'Well, maybe something like that...I just want to be around you...'

'I have a father and I have no need for a lover...'

'And you have all the friends you could ever need?'

Gallia shook her head. 'No. No one can have too many friends.'

Merlin smiled. 'Then let me be your friend?'

The lady paused, looked away for a moment before returning to look in his eyes. 'On one condition,' she stipulated.

'Anything,' he cried.

'You never try to kiss me again,'

He agreed.

'Your father is well?' asked Merlin, as they re-entered the villa.

'Yes, but I have to leave him alone tonight, there's something I must attend too.'

'I could keep him company,' the man offered.

'There's no need, there will be a servant on hand.'

'I would like to, it will give me a chance to find out more about you.'

'You can't believe a word he says. He is totally biased.'

'Where is he now?'

'He's taking a nap. He always takes one at this time of the day.'

'When do you need to leave?' asked Merlin.

'Not for awhile, but why don't you come back around supper time and we can all eat together.'

Merlin welcomed the invitation and said he would return before nightfall.

The moon was blocked by the density of the clouds and the night was as dark as Judas and his associates could have wished for. They waited patiently for Rose to let them in at the rear gatehouse, but so far the girl had not arrived. The cold air was making many impatient, including Gallia. 'How much longer?' she asked Judas.

Judas addressed everyone. 'Not much longer. She will only let us in when everyone except the night guard has gone to bed.'

The three men and Gallia rubbed their hands to keep warm and glanced up at the gatehouse every so often, their thoughts preoccupied with greed. Gallia wondered if she had jumped prematurely into this venture. Her emotions were raw when she had agreed to become involved. She was free from obligations for the first time in a long while and feared she was putting that freedom in jeopardy. She approached Judas and whispered to him. 'Do you really need me with you on this part?'

Judas looked at her with suspicion. 'I thought you would have been keen to see the stuff straight away.'

'My experience will come in handy later, when I appraise the items.'

'What if we have to leave some stuff behind?'

'Three strong men can surely carry away a few crates.'

Judas bit his lip and agreed. 'You can stay here if you wish.'

Gallia thanked the man.

'If I didn't know you better, I would say you were losing your nerve.'

Just at that moment, a voice whispered down from the sentry position in the gatehouse. Rose had opened the door the men were free to enter.

Led by the lady, the three men were escorted down to the lower levels of the castle to where the dungeons lay. Rose gave Judas one lighted torch and kept the other for herself. They went down fifty or sixty steps until on the lowest level of all they reached a dungeon that housed three medium-sized crates. Rose showed Judas the cell gate and the lock that barred their way.

'You're the expert, you boasted you could open any lock. How difficult is this one?' she asked.

Judas peered at the locks and grinned. 'A child could open it,' he announced.

As Judas took a fine tool from his pocket and began to tamper with the lock, Rose looked about her. 'Where is the lady?' she queried.

'She is waiting outside the castle walls,' replied Judas.

The woman smirked. 'Scared to get her hands dirty, eh?'

They all heard a click and saw Judas pull the cell gates open. He glanced at everyone and beamed a smile. The men pounced on the crates and began to force open the lids, using their knives. Each of them placed their hands inside the crates and rummaged around expecting to find some loot. All they found was an excess of straw and rags. They all turned to complain to Judas, but as they turned, they saw the man staring past them all.

A powerful woman's voice rang out. 'You don't think I'd let you steal my treasure, do you,' the lady cried.

Judas stared at the woman on the other side of the cell. Coming out from the shadows the lady had six soldiers by her side; five of the men had their swords drawn, while one of them had his knife around the throat of Rose. The woman who had spoken stepped forward into the light and stared at the bandits standing like frozen statues. Only Judas recognized the woman standing before them. It was Queen Guinevere. He thought about kneeling before her, but his arms and legs seemed unable to move.

'Do you not bow before your Queen,' the lady roared.

One or two bowed, but the rest continued to stare with their eyes wide open.

'Who is you leader?' Guinevere asked.

Judas let his tool drop and walked a few paces forward. 'I am,' he said.

Guinevere studied the man. 'Give me one good reason why I don't have all of you hung this very night?'

Judas reacted with a cold indifference. 'I can not think of any reason, except perhaps I could be of use to you.'

'How so?' the Queen queried.

'If you ever needed a job done that required a man with no conscience, then I would be your man.'

The Queen laughed. 'Prove your loyalty to me. There is one amongst you that has betrayed me. She must die. Thrust a knife through her heart before me now and I'll consider sparing your contemptible life.'

Rose tried to speak, but the soldier who had the knife round her throat covered her muffled cries with his hand. It was Guinevere that offered Judas the knife to commit his murder. He took it without question and with a look as cold as the winter wind, stabbed the lady through the heart without hesitation. Rose dropped from the soldier's grip onto the ground dead. A quiet hateful silence followed.

Judas looked to the Queen for her reaction. Guinevere's smile was replaced by a frown. 'My, you weren't joking when you said you had no conscience.'

'In my profession you can not afford one.'

Guinevere acknowledged his remark with the slightest of nods. 'In my profession you can not afford one either.'

She turned to her soldiers and addressed them. 'Kill them all. Cut this man's heart out and bring it to me when you have finished.'

The thieves considered they had nothing to lose and began to charge the solders. It wasn't a contest, as one by one Judas's men were felled down by experienced warriors. Judas was last to fall. He lunged forward towards the Queen, but Gruffydd blocked his way with his huge frame.

The bodyguard put his broad arm around Judas's neck and began to squeeze the life out of his body. Before long Judas's face had changed to a dark purple color and he stopped breathing.

Lady Hester was talking to the Queen, expressing her loyalty and praising her daughter for her quick thinking. The Queen listened intently glancing ever so often in the direction of the young maiden. Megan sat a little away from the adults, listening to what they were saying.

'It was Megan who suspected something was wrong, when she found one of the guards unconscious. She feared that with my husband away the treasure might be at risk...'

A stern looking Queen stared at Hester. 'She knew about the treasure?' she asked.

Megan thought to interrupt, but Hester shot her a glance of reproach.

'She does not know anything really, only that some of your possessions were in our keep.'

'I thought Rose looked deceitful,' Megan propounded.

Hester frowned at her step-daughter, but the Queen looked directly at her. With her hand, she ushered the girl nearer to her. Megan moved from her chair to sit opposite the lady.

'I am most grateful to you,' expressed the Queen. 'If there's ever anything I can do for you?'

Megan glanced at Hester, the latter shook her head, but the young lady ignored the gesture.

'Yes your grace, there is something.'

Hester began to intervene, expressing her opinion that the matter could wait, but Megan responded by stating categorically that it could not.

'Come, you do not want to bother the Queen with our little problems,' stated Hester.

'No, continue. If I can help I shall.'

'My father has promised my hand to a local nobleman, who is twice my age.'

'How old are you?'Guinevere asked.

'Thirteen, my lady,' the girl replied.

The Queen glanced at Hester.

'It is not my doing, your grace.'

'I am not ready for womanhood,' declared an adamant Megan.

Guinevere agreed and seemed shocked at Mador's lack of concern for his own family.

'Can you do anything?' the girl pleaded.

Guinevere smiled. 'Do not fear. I promise you shall not be forced to marry this man.'

Megan could not withhold her joy. 'Oh your grace, how can I thank you?'

Hester however remained pensive. 'My husband will not be pleased,' she stated.

'Do not worry about the Duke, I have plans for him. He will be informed of my decision when I return to Londinium.'

Hester bowed her head.

Guinevere's instinct told her there was more to the tale. She could see that both women seemed afraid of the Duke. For the moment Megan seemed relieved, but Hester remained frightened.

'Have you someone who could look after this place for awhile? 'she asked.

'Yes, we have an able head steward.'

'Excellent. Then you shall accompany me on my journey.'

Megan was overjoyed at the suggestion, but Hester pleaded to remain.

Guinevere would not hear of it. 'I have not made myself clear; I want you both to become members of my household.'

The young women looked shocked and excited in equal measure.

'What about my husband?'

'I wish for you both to become my ladies in waiting.'

'Oh, your grace, what an honor,' Megan gasped.

'I do not think my husband will be pleased...'

'Do not worry about that. He is not in a position to object.'

The two young women embraced each other as Guinevere looked on. It would seem their imprisonment was over. Just what was ahead of them they could not know, but a better life was surely likely in the court of the most powerful woman in the land.

A soldier entered and whispered in the Queen's ear. Guinevere left the happy women to accompany the soldier. The warrior took her down some stairs until they entered a small chamber off the dungeons. In the chamber sitting on a stool, with her hands tied behind her back, was Gallia. She looked up to see Guinevere standing over her. She ventured to her feet and bowed in acknowledgement to her Queen.

'We found her outside the castle walls. She could be their lookout,' the soldier whispered?'

'What were you doing outside the castle walls?' asked the Queen.

Keeping a calm head, Gallia explained she suffered from an affliction that allowed her to walk in her sleep unawares where she was going.

Guinevere looked unconvinced by her statement, but listened anyway as the woman explained her affliction in more detail. She did not seem like the others, in fact there was something familiar about her. Had their paths crossed before she wondered?

'That's enough chatter,' the Queen decided. Looking at the soldier, she issued her orders to him. 'I do not believe this woman is part of band of bandits, but I also do not believe her story. I have no time to interrogate her now, so she will have to accompany us on her journey back to Londinium.'

'Yes, your grace,' the soldier acknowledged.

A noise from the behind the Queen made the lady turn to see another warrior approach. This soldier had an item in his hand that brought a gasp of alarm from Gallia. In the soldier's right hand lay a human heart, its blood still issuing from its severed arteries. This showed a strange mixture of red and flesh colored slime that overflowed onto the floor.

'Your grace, your trophy,' the man announced.

The Queen looked hard at the object, but showed no kind of emotion. 'So that is what a human heart looks like?' she murmured.

No one spoke and the atmosphere grew heavy with apprehension.

Guinevere studied the object as it crumpled in the man's hand. 'Not much good to anyone, now,' she said.

'What will I do with it?' he asked.

'Throw it to the dogs,' Guinevere commanded.

40

With the preliminaries over and the charges announced, the six members of the High Council took their seats before a select audience of nobles in the old Roman Forum. All sat on throne chairs, signifying their right to be addressed as a King or as a Queen. The thrones were not elaborate with one exception, that of the central throne, where the High King sat. This had a higher than normal back and contained some beautiful carving along its arms and spine. A great woodcarver had carved goblins and nymphs along the arms of the chair, while on its back he carved a symbol of a great dragon to represent the Pendragon name. Sitting on this throne was Arthur's wife, Guinevere. Despite protests from her rival, the lady persuaded those present that it was her right to sit on the High King's chair and take her husband's place as the Council's leader.

The proceedings began with wrangling over procedure and protocol. It quickly became a battle of wits between two strong minded women as to what would be allowed as fact and what was deemed conjecture. Morgan started by questioning some of the troops who had last seen the King alive before his fatal journey. In her questioning she brought out the question of the King's poor health and seemed to indicate that his weakness might have been brought about by poison or bad food. To her surprise neither Guinevere nor any of her supporters objected to this line of questioning.

'Did the King ever complain about his food?' Morgan asked Gawain who was standing to give his evidence.

The young man said that he did.

'When was this?' she asked.

'Twice that I know about; one time I remember him forbidding his men to eat some meat that had made him sick, declaring it unfit for humans.'

King Ursien interrupted. 'Did the King not have food tasters with him?'

Gawain nodded. 'He did, but they would only eat a little and it was often some time later before the King would show signs of being unwell.'

'They did not?' Ursien queried.

'No, they showed no signs of ill health.'

Guinevere put forward an explanation. 'The King always did over indulge himself at supper. I often scolded him about his appetite for red meat, but he would never listen.'

Morgan turned again to Gawain. 'The second time?' she inquired.

Gawain looked a little uncomfortable as he stood before such an array of powerful dignities. 'Yes, that was when he had eaten some fruit. He complained of a sore stomach a little time after.'

'When was this?' asked Morgan.

'The day we sailed,' the young man said. 'It was because of this latter attack that his departure was delayed.'

'Was this the reason he was last to leave Gaul?' Morgan asked.

'Yes my lady, it was felt he was too ill to travel the day I departed.'

'Who organized the party to accompany the King on his final journey?'

Gawain glanced to his right to see Lancelot. 'Lancelot took charge of all sailings including the King's.'

Once Morgan had finished with her questions, the other Kings interrogated Gawain: King Ursien wanted to know if the young man had noticed anything suspicious on the day of his departure, King Bors wanted to know if the King had ever mentioned any fears of assassination. King Lot wondered why his son had accompanied the King and not young Bors, and King Pelles brought to everyone's attention the fact that the young Helena of Benoic was at the King's side the whole time. Only Guinevere failed to ask anything of the young man.

The first day of the trial dragged on with little resolved and a great deal of ill feeling, as Morgan hinted at conspiracies and grand plots but could not produce a single item of real proof. The second day would be soon enough to hear Lancelot's lies, for by that time her surprise witness would be present.

Merlin scoured Londinium from the Saxon settlements in the north to the Dover road in the south, but to no avail. Gallia had just vanished. She had not returned and he feared for her safety. He used his powers of invisibility to gain access to many buildings and private chambers, but gained no news of her whereabouts. He ventured into seedy areas where the thieves and cutthroats lay in wait for many an unsuspecting traveler, but again learnt nothing of use to him. It was when he was returning, amongst the crowded streets around the Roman Amphitheatre, that an object struck him on his temple. He clutched his head, before bending down to see the object lying at his feet on the dusty ground. He picked it up and saw that it was an old Roman bronze coin, depicting Romulus and Remus being suckled by a sea-wolf. Such a coin was rare and was no longer used in Britain for trade. Perhaps someone had kept it as a lucky charm the man conjectured, hoping in his heart it was his lady.

With the coin in his hand the man surveyed the area about him, hoping to find where the object had been thrown. He looked upwards and scanned from right to left, but failed to see anything of note. Shutting his eyes in an effort to block out the din around him, he listened with the faint hope of hearing his lady's voice. Almost as if by magic, the words seem to descend from the heavens. 'Taliesin, Taliesin,' he heard, spoken like a whisper. Following the direction of the voice, Merlin opened his eyes and stared upwards. He saw a light, or a white cloth moving slightly from side to side from a slit high up in a building on the opposite side of the road from where he stood.

The building was part of a complex, of which it was the largest. The other structures around it where all newly built and stood fresh with timber and hatch, while the old Roman baths basilica stood out rather like a faded but grand reminder of the country's old conquerors. It still incorporated the masonry walls of basilica, but had been reinforced crudely, by blocks of timber to secure its safety. The upper part of the building housed a series of small rooms, or antechambers. The room on the corner of the building was where Merlin saw the white flag and he acknowledged the occupant with a wave of his own.

The man moved across the street to stand directly beneath the room. Gallia threw a second object at his feet. He picked it up to see it was piece of jewelry, a small broach, designed with Celtic markings. His fingers seemed big and clumsy as he tried to open the broach. Inside he found a small piece of parchment, which read simply, '*be careful the building is being watched, I am a prisoner.*'

The Lady Morgause was in mourning for the loss of three men, two of whom were her kin. She had lost her son, Agravain and her step-brother Arthur, killed by the traitor Lancelot, probably by the orders of the Queen. It was likely that it was by the same woman's orders that her new love had been abducted. She did not know whether he was dead or only held against his will. No one could understand the reasoning behind the Queen's actions in this matter. What did she want with the innocent young Galahad?

Locked away in her private bedchamber, the lady paid little attention to the grief suffered by others, including her mother and her sons. The special relationship a mother feels for her sons, did not quite translate to Morgause. The pain she felt for the loss of her new lover seemed to hurt her more than the loss of her own child. It had been several years since she had even set eyes on Agravain and feelings between them had never been particularly strong. He was a virile man much like his father and did not have much time for anything other than fighting. Still he was fine warrior and loyal to his King, right to the end. What mother could ask more from her son than that?

Some of the family had gathered in Lothian to bury and have a service to commemorate the lives of their loved ones. There were some notable absentees, namely; Lady Morgan, King Lot, Gawain and Gaheris who were in Londinium fighting to expose the truth and punish the perpetrators for their crimes. Agravain's body had travelled home to the place of his birth by wagon and a small escort, but no one knew where the body of the King had gone.

Gawain had told Mordred something of the truth concerning Morgan's desperate trip to Avalon, but even he did not know what transpired there. Being the only son present, a lot fell upon young Mordred's shoulders. Much to his mother's and grand mother's delight, he organized a great deal of the proceedings and showed a great deal of maturity in addressing those present.

Having not eaten for days, Lady Morgause rose from her bed to go in search of food and human companionship. She wandered the corridors of the castle in search of guards or servants. Grumbling to herself, she wondered whether the family had gone ahead and started the ceremony without her. She was headed for her mother's room, when she heard voices directly below her coming from the great hall. She went to investigate what the clamor was all about.

As Morgause reached the great hall, she became aware of the presence of the whole family including all the servants. Running towards her was her own ladies maid, Ina. She had her arms outstretched ready to embrace her mistress. 'Mistress, it is a miracle,' the young woman exclaimed excitedly.

Feeling sick and retched, the sight of a happy person made Morgause want to scream, but as Ina stopped short of a full embrace, another lady burst forth before her. Was it the light, or was it the delirium, but the figure standing before her resembled her dead sister Elaine.

'Do you not recognize me sister, have I changed that much?' Elaine asked.

Morgause moved a few paces forward and stared. 'Oh sweet Jesus, have the Gods brought you back from the dead?'

Elaine smiled and nodded her head.

The two sisters embraced and began to cry tears of joy.

'How is it possible?' asked an emotional Morgause. 'What can you remember?'

'I remember nothing. It is as if I had just been sleeping. I awoke suddenly to see mother standing over me with her mouth open.'

Morgause glanced at her mother.

Lady Ygerne clapped her hands to draw everyone's attention to her. She made an announcement. 'This sad day has ended with the joyful return of our beloved Elaine. We all have many questions to ask her, but for now we must bury our dead and thank God for relieving our sorrow. I must ask you all to make me a promise that no one present will divulge Elaine's return for now.'

Everyone present agreed to this, but with a dozen people in the room, Lady Ygerne was anxious that someone might speak without thinking and that news might somehow reach the Queen. Guinevere would be quick to accuse the whole family of witchcraft, for what else could explain Elaine's resurrection from the dead?

After receiving a great deal of attention and goodwill, Lady Elaine began to feel tired. Her face began to look pale as she wandered over to the fireplace to sit down nearest the fire. She had listened to eloquent speeches and fine eulogies concerning her brother and nephew, but now all she wished for was to shut her eyes.

Elaine could hear the lady of the lake whisper instructions in her ear, as if she was in the room with her. Her mind cleared and emptied of all other thoughts as she concentrated on the God. To her surprise her thoughts had never been more concise as she quickly realized her mind worked faster than before. It was as if she had been given someone else's personality. In truth she had, for the lady of the lake had empowered her with some of her own gifts; invisibility, the ability to move objects with her thoughts, the ability to strike her enemies down with a single wave of her hand and most importantly perhaps, the ability to read other peoples minds.

In her semiconscious state she began to listen to the thoughts of all present at the funeral. One by one she heard what was in their heads; all immediate family was thinking of Arthur or Agravain, all except one, Mordred. As Elaine's mind entered his, she found her sister's son's thoughts were on Guinevere. This was a surprise for in the past the young man had always been in awe of the lady. More surprises followed. His thoughts were of a sexual nature, she could almost feel his passion wrap around the lady's body.

Even in her passive state, Elaine's body twitched as if she was sharing his sexual experience with him. His thoughts were on their next encounter with the lady, whenever that was going to be. Elaine, God willing, would be present if not in body then at least in mind when their paths next crossed.

'Wake up, wake up,' shouted Ygerne.

Ygerne was shaking her by her arms. She could feel her touch and hear her voice, but she was still under the spell of the lady of the lake.

Morgause then touched her with a little more force. Her voice sounded more powerful and this released her from the spell. She awoke with a start and asked where she was. Morgause assured her she was safe and offered to take her to her bedchamber. Elaine yawned and thanked her sister. She saw a change in Morgause also, a change for the good and yet she sensed her sorrow was for someone other than her dead kin. As they walked upstairs to her bedroom Elaine saw a face of a man she had never seen before. The man was Galahad and, like her sister, she was much taken by his looks. Morgause must love this man she thought, otherwise why would she be so overpowered by his aura.

41

Morgan saw how all the Kings were getting impatient with the proceedings and thought it was time to bring forward the only witness to the carnage of that day. Her testifier was frightened and had changed almost beyond all recognition from the self-confident young lady known by many in the chamber. Yvain and Nemue had persuaded her to journey to Britain with them, but it was Gawain who had coaxed her to give her testimony. The young man had surprised Morgan with his kindness and understanding in dealing with the young maiden.

There was a lot of chatter amongst the audience as most thought their time was being wasted on such a feeble trial. The Queen look jubilant, almost as if she believed Lancelot was about to be released. She began to relax and tell amusing stories to the two Kings on either side of her, King Pelles and King Ursien. The tension that Morgan had tried to generate had been released somehow and had been replaced by a revelry that seemed wholly inappropriate to her and to all her family.

Morgan interrupted the crowd's chatter, to summon the next witness. 'I call the Lady Helena of Benoic,' she shouted.

The noise levels dropped immediately, as everyone present thought they had misheard. Guinevere flashed a stare in the direction of Lancelot. The man shook his head at his Queen and looked as astonished as anyone else with the announcement.

Helena was escorted to a chair next to the Lady Morgan, by Gawain. She looked frail and walked unsteadily holding onto the young man's arm at all times. Her skin had an ugly tint of yellow which made her look older while her face had lost all its innocence.

She stared at Lancelot as she passed him and he stared back, as both seemed fearful of each other. Helena had to pull herself away from the gaze of her attacker, to look up at Lady Morgan who was standing over her.

'State your full name for the record,' requested Morgan.

'My name is Helena of Benoic, niece to Lord Bedivere of Benoic.'

'Where you present when King Arthur and Lord Agravain were murdered while onboard a boat travelling to Britain?'

'Yes I was.'

'Can you name the person, or persons responsible for the murder of our King?'

'I can and I shall,' the lady calmly stated. She got to her feet and pointed her finger at Lancelot. 'Lord Lancelot and his servant, the one they called Ironfist, attacked the King and Agravain while they rested below deck. Lancelot killed the King outright before he could get to his feet, but Agravain killed Ironfist, before being killed by Lancelot in a short knife fight.'

There was an outcry from some of the audience. '*Murderer,*' they cried from their seats at the back of the forum. Guinevere called for quiet and interrupted Morgan's questioning to address Helena directly. 'May I ask you a question?' stated the Queen.

'You will get your chance shortly,' Morgan remarked.

'All I wanted to know is why the Lady Helena looks such a ghastly color?'

Helena, who was still on her feet, tore part of her dress away to reveal a terrible scar just below her shoulder and above her heart. The scar was easily recognizable as a wound from a sword or a dagger, for all present had seen plenty of them over the years. Not many had seen a lady bare such a gash and many gasped in shock. The scar looked fresh, its line was still red and broken and if you were to put your finger across it, it would cover almost perfectly the size of the wound.

Once the audience had calmed down, Morgan continued to question the young woman. 'Did Lancelot do that to you?' she asked.

'Yes,' Helena replied.

The crowd clamored some more.

'What happened after you were stabbed?'

'I thought he would finish me too, but he was wounded and climbed on deck, I suspect to get away from the awful sight of carnage below.'

Morgan looked puzzled. 'He knew you were still alive?'

'Yes. He was covered in blood, his own and others and...' Helena paused and glanced at Lancelot.

Morgan tried to regain the young woman's attention. 'Go on...finish what you were saying.'

'I think he hesitated, perhaps he feared God's wrath or maybe it was the smell.'

Morgan inquired what the lady meant.

'The smell of blood was sickening. I almost passed out from it.'

'What did you do?'

'I crawled forward to where Arthur lay and saw that he was dead, likewise I did the same with Agravain. I listened to hear what Lancelot was doing on deck, before climbing the ladder from the hold.' Helena took a break and began to scour the room to see if her words were being believed. To her surprise the majority looked sympathetic and on tenterhooks.

'I saw Lancelot near the front of the boat. He was putting a bandage around his wounds and cursing.'

'He did not see you?' asked Morgan.

'No, he never turned around.'

'You said he was cursing. Could you hear what he was saying?'

'Oh yes, he was shouting out...'

'What was he shouting?'

'He was shouting the Queen's name, over and over again.'

'Can you remember exactly what he said?'

Helena glanced to her left to see all the Kings' eyes upon her. She could see Guinevere's too; her eyes were cold and black, just like her heart must be thought the girl.

'He said...Guinevere, Guinevere what have you made me do.'

Noise thundered around the room, as gasps of disbelief echoed from all parts. King Lot and King Ursien were on their feet and stared at Guinevere. The Queen was the only one present who did not react to this startling evidence.

Once the noise died down Morgan continued. 'What did you do next?'

'I managed to crawl to the stern of the boat and forced myself overboard.'

'You are a good swimmer?' asked Morgan.

'Yes, but the water was cold and quickly I began to lose the feeling in my legs. I struggled to keep hold of the side of the boat and finally I was washed away from it.'

'Clearly you did not die, how did you survive?'

'My muscles hurt so much, that after a time my arms gave out and I began to sink down below the water. I blacked out only to awaken onboard a fishing vessel, with the skipper pushing me in the back and speaking in a strange language. He pumped out water from my insides and brought me back to life.'

'Truly remarkable,' shrieked Guinevere.

Morgan persuaded Helena to go on.

'The fishermen took me to their small village and looked after me. They were kind, giving me food and clothing to wear and I was content to stay with them...'

'Surely it was your duty to come forward and tell your story,' pleaded Morgan.

'I was unwell and frightened. Every night, I dreaded falling asleep for I would have terrible nightmares. And then I...'

'Yes, and then...'

'I feared if I ever stepped foot in Britain again, I would be killed by Guinevere or Lancelot's forces.'

'So it was the fear of death that kept you from telling your tale?'

'Yes, it was that and that alone.'

If the place was still being watched he could not tell, but as luck would have it Merlin had not been spied upon the previous evening. The man was confident that even as he approached the building in broad daylight, no one would stop him from entering. He was confident for another reason, for he did not appear as himself, but as a completely different person. His disguise was so perfect that he was positive of fooling anyone who came upon him. He felt his powers returning along with his boldness of old. The building looked empty, at least of people, for only one man sat on the steps leading to the entrance. That man was Guinevere's most trusted servant Gruffydd. As Merlin approached, the man jumped to his feet in surprise. 'Your grace, I thought you would still be at the trial,' the man declared.

The figure of Guinevere stared at the man and in her most listless voice answered his question. 'I've never been so fatigued. I could not listen to the witch prattle on a moment longer.

Gruffydd chuckled.

'Has she told you anything?' the Queen asked.

'Nothing, she still holds to her preposterous story.'

'Well, maybe the preposterous story is true.'

The statement made Gruffydd wish to query his mistress, but he only asked if she had more instructions for him.

'Yes, release the woman immediately.'

The man looked shocked and hesitated. 'Your grace, are you sure. Remember the lady has seen the treasure, or at least their containers.'

'Why do you question my orders,' Guinevere snarled.

Gruffydd could not remember a time his mistress had addressed him in such a manner. He was suspicious, but the woman before him looked like the Queen and her

270

voice sounded like the Queen. Yet something about her manner alerted the man that something was not right.

'I did what you commanded, but the woman is tougher than she looks.'

'You have not harmed her?'

'I spared her face, but the torture was of no use anyway.'

Gruffydd turned and walked into the building. Merlin followed as they climbed two storey's together in silence. They reached the room were Gallia was housed.

'Is she much weakened?' asked Merlin.

'The lady has seen much hardship, but she has an inner strength that is surprising.'

'She can walk I take it?'

'With a little help, yes I would say so.'

Gruffydd stood back and allowed Guinevere to enter first. What Merlin saw shocked him, for the lady was chained by iron manacles to a stone wall. Somehow she had managed the previous night, to reach close enough to the window to throw down her coin. It must have been a pure fluke that the shot hit its target. She was barely conscious and her face and hands were dirty with dried blood.

Merlin sighed and turned to look at Gruffydd. 'Undo the manacles and bring some water and a cloth. We need to make her look respectable.'

The man took a key from his pocket and undid the chains that tied Gallia. Gruffydd looked annoyed, but left the room to fetch the items his mistress had asked for. While he was away, Merlin kneeled down beside his lady and whispered in his own voice. 'Your ordeal is almost over my lady, I will soon have you out of here.'

Gallia stared at the woman beside her and made a jest. 'Fancy being married to you, you'd go to sleep beside a man only to wake up beside a women,' she complained.

'Is that a proposal?' he queried.

Gallia tried to laugh, but she was in too much pain. 'I suppose if I told you to go to hell, you'd leave me here.'

'Most definitely,' he replied.

Merlin helped Gallia to her feet and steadied her against the wall. They looked into each other's eyes. 'There's no getting rid of you,' the lady remarked.

'I intend to be around you for the conceivable future.'

Merlin was keeping an eye on the entrance fearing Gruffydd was taking too long.

'If that is to be the case, then you must stop changing your appearance all the time, it's very disconcerting you know.'

'As soon as we leave here I will be glad to revert back to the way I was.'

'You don't have to become boring, why don't you settle upon a nice looking man like Lancelot?'

'If all goes well, in the next few days that man's head will be parted from his body.'

Gallia frowned. 'Don't talk like that.'

Merlin heard footsteps and turned his head to look at Gruffydd standing in the door frame. The man had not brought water, but two colleagues who like himself had their swords drawn. 'I don't know who you are, but you are not my queen,' he stated.

Merlin sighed.

Gallia's weary sigh eclipsed her friend's. 'Wave your hand and make them go away, I'm tired,' she asserted.

Merlin didn't need to do that. His physical form underwent a metamorphosis before the three men eyes. They watched with their mouths open as Guinevere transformed back into Merlin. They did not wait to see the full transfiguration as they bolted from the building like scared rabbits.

Merlin turned to look at Gallia and smiled.

'Don't look so smug, just get me out of here,' she instructed.

He wrapped his arms around her and descended steadily together towards the street.

'You did agree to marry me,' the man whispered to her.

Gallia looked confused 'Did I, I thought I agreed to marry Lancelot.'

42

It was Guinevere's turn to question Helena now. She seemed in no rush, as she left her throne chair, to pace up and down the room. It was getting late, but what she had in store would keep everyone awake. Lady Morgan was not the only one who had a surprise witness, but for now her purpose was to throw doubt on everything that the young maiden had just said. 'Your parents are both dead is that so?' asked Guinevere.

'Yes,' Helena replied.

'How did your father die?'

Helena looked tentative, reluctant to answer.

'You do know how he died?' the Queen inquired.

'I was not present, but I have heard the tale.'

'Tale?' the Queen questioned. 'A tale implies something other than a fact. Do you believe the facts against your father were wrong?'

'Yes, I believe so.'

'Then, please tell us this tale perhaps you can persuade us to rewrite the past.'

Helena was biting her lip and looking towards Lady Morgan for some kind of assistance.

'My Lords, what has the death of Lady Helena's father got to do with the murder of our King?' Morgan questioned.

King Pelles looked over the Queen. 'I too, I'm wondering, your grace?

'It will become apparent shortly,' Guinevere assured the Kings.

They agreed to allow the Queen to continue with her line of questioning.

Guinevere flashed a smile at her rival and continued. 'I am not aware of this tale and perhaps many present are not either, so please enlighten us.'

Clenching her hands over the arm of her chair, the lady sat more upright and glared at the Queen. 'I was only a child, so my memory is vague and I am reliant on other people for my conclusions.'

Guinevere was getting impatient. 'Perhaps I can set the scene for everyone. It was ten years ago and the land was beset with petty squabbles. Arthur was forced to quell a rebellion in the north from the Angles and at the same time stop the Saxons in the area we are in now, from driving out many of our own people. He called on his supporters in Benoic to come and assist him. King Ban sent Lancelot and three hundred of his best warriors, King Bors, also sent his son the young Bors, with two hundred men, but your father sent no one.'

Helena rose from her chair, her hands still clinging to the chair. 'You accuse my father of disloyalty?'

'My dear, many accused him of far worse, many accused him of treason.'

The young woman had tears in her eyes. 'He was mourning the death of his wife, my mother.'

'That might well be true, but why did he not send some men?'

Crying, Helena shook her head and said she did not know.

Morgan went towards her witness. 'My Lords, perhaps this is a good time to call a halt to today's proceedings?' she suggested.

'No, I must defend my father's honor and rebuke the allegations made at his trial,' Helena pleaded.

'They were more than just allegations; he was found guilty of conspiring with the Saxon leader Hengist and hung for his crime.'

'He was innocent of any wrong doing and those responsible for his death are all in this room today.'

Looking suitably shocked, Guinevere asked the girl to point the wrong doers out.

Helena pointed to two individuals seated in the room, first was Lancelot and the second was her uncle

Bedivere. 'They both benefitted from my father's ruin,' she attested as she sobbed.

'His land was giving to these men and you were casted out onto the street like a pauper?' asked Guinevere.

With her head bent low, Helena wiped away some of her tears and addressed the question. 'No, Lord Bedivere took me in and gave me his protection.'

'I think he did more than that?'

'Yes, he was kind. He treated me like his own child.'

'He provided you with wealth, enough for you to be educated.'

Helena agreed.

'He has even given your land of your own, so that you are not forced to marry for lack of money.'

Helena agreed again. 'He has been kind and I appreciate all that he has done...'

'It hardly seems that way, if you stand here and accuse him to be behind the death of your father.'

Helena looked exhausted and shook her head pleading she did not mean to attack anyone.

'You attack Lord Lancelot by accusing him of the murder of our beloved King.'

'I was present when he attacked us without provocation.'

'So you say, but you also say Lancelot and Bedivere plotted to kill your father. Is there anyone else in this room you want to accuse while you are here?'

Helena sat back down in her chair. She was being goaded by the Guinevere into mentioning her by name, but she calmed herself and became passive in an effort not to fall further into the Queen's trap.

'Why would I make up such a story?' queried Helena.

'That is a good question. May I suggest you did not, but others have put you up to it?'

Helena shook her head.

'Did you come here voluntarily or were you coerced?'

'I came here of my own free will.'

'Did not people track you down to your small village in Gaul and plead with you to come here today?'

Helena hesitated for a moment before agreeing this was so.

'The people who came, who were they?'

'One was a servant to Lady Morgan and the other I had never seen before.'

Morgan was on her feet and addressed the Queen. 'I hope you are not suggesting I am part of any conspiracy,' she raged.

Guinevere was adamant in defending her rival of any such thing. 'As I am aware the young man is no longer in your service. There is no evidence that you were responsible for finding Lady Helena, or of bringing her here.'

Morgan sat back down again, but glanced at King Lot whose face was as phlegmatic as ever.

'The other person was a young maiden, was it not?'

'Yes, she was about my age.'

'Was it the young maiden who did all the talking?'

'Yes, the young man listened for the most part.'

'Did she tell you her name?'

'Yes, she said her name was Nemue.'

'Nemue, yes it might surprise you, but I have heard this name before.'

The atmosphere in the chamber was at its most sombre as everyone was engrossed with Guinevere and her performance. The lady was a great orator and was having a great time twisting her rival's tale and seeing her suffer.

King Ursien asked the Queen who this Nemue was.

Guinevere was happy to oblige him with an answer. 'She is a witch of some notoriety. She was thrown out of an Irish settlement in Dalriada, after some men began to disappear. Even her own father, who is here today, has condemned her as a sorceress.

Moans of discontent echoed around the hall. Helena was still sitting awaiting more questions, but everyone's attention had shifted to Guinevere. Everyone was awaiting some further revelation from the lady.

'You have proof of what you say?' asked King Pelles.

'Yes, I can call the maiden's father to give evidence and others from the settlement.'

'This will all take time. I suggest we continue tomorrow,' Morgan again suggested.

Most of the Kings were weary except Pelles and Ban who declared they wanted this matter settled as soon as possible. Pelles was aware that his ally had taken the initiative, while Ban was anxious to get back home away from all the intrigues that he hated so much.

'We will hear from this man, bring him forth,' shouted Pelles.

Morgan, Lot and Ursien all complained of feeling fatigued, but Pelles insisted the truth could not wait. 'If necessary I am prepared to be here all night,' he declared.

The doors to the chamber opened and Capa came into the room, his head turned from side to side as he tried to absorb the atmosphere and the splendor of the surroundings. He was escorted to a seat near Lady Helena.

'Please state your name for the record,' commanded Guinevere.

The man looked petrified and seemed not to understand the Queen's command. It was Morgan who approached and repeated the request to the man in his native tongue. It was clear the lady was going to have to act as interpreter, much to her regret and frustration.

Through her, the man told his tale of terror at the hands of his own daughter. He told them of his own injuries inflicted by her, but also of the fear that everyone in their camp felt. 'People would stay clear of her, often crossing themselves whenever she pasted.'

Guinevere wanted to know why they did not banish her sooner.

'No one dared. She had a terrible temper.'

The man told them about the disappearance of MacRoth and the assumption that Nemue and Yvain had killed him. His testimony painted a black picture of his daughter as a practicing witch. A woman from the camp followed and told a similar tale.

278

When the villagers were finished, Morgan insisted on putting an end to the trial for the day as Lady Helena looked ill. Her face was grey with fatigue, while her eyes were ashen from lack of sleep. All agreed. Although Guinevere was annoyed at the interruption, she could afford to be generous and wait to drive home her advantage the next day. Lancelot's position had looked bleak, but now the man could almost taste his freedom. This was all down to the Queen and her meticulous planning.

Morgan sent out scouts to trace Nemue and Yvain in the hope that she was wrong and they were not ensnared by the Queen. She could not find them about their dwellings and regretted ever giving them a leave of absence. They could both already be arrested for murder. A steward entered her room to announce a visitor. The lady asked who it was and was told it was a man called Taliesin who had some good news to deliver.

Although weary, she recognized Merlin's other name and hoped his news would improve her faulting spirits. 'Show him in,' she told the steward.

The man entered, but he was not alone. He had with him, Gallia whom Morgan thought looked as ill as Lady Helena. She too had a grey look to her skin and the lady wondered if some epidemic was about to strike the whole populace. The physician in Morgan came to the fore, as she got to her feet and helped the lady to a sofa. Without them exchanging words the ladies seem to take to each other in an instant. A tonic was given to Gallia which revived her, making her skin regain a little color. Merlin stood patiently waiting for a chance to impart his important news. His eyes met Gallia's. 'Can I tell her now?' he inquired.

'Of course,' she replied.

Merlin outstretched his arms and gently forced Morgan to sit beside his love. 'We have it,' he exclaimed.

His voice was jubilant, but Morgan did not understand.

Gallia intervened. 'He means we know where the God's treasure is.'

Morgan jumped to her feet. 'How...? Where...?'

'Not far, but I suggest you move quickly before the Queen has a chance to spirit it away again.'

'The Queen,' cried Morgan.

Merlin grinned. 'Who else,' he proclaimed.

Morgan, who had rented out an entire inn across from the forum, summoned her compatriots, Lot, Gawain and Gaheris to her room.

'If you don't mind, I would like to stay here and rest,' said Gallia.

Morgan and Merlin concurred.

'Gallia has given me precise directions.'

'Trust a man to forget the introductions, it is good to meet you, Gallia,' Morgan stated, as she kissed the woman on both cheeks. 'You have no idea what this means to me. My name is...'

Gallia kissed Morgan in return. 'I know your name and what you represent.'

Morgan wasn't sure what the lady meant, but she never got a chance to find out for the men quickly entered the room.

Arrangements were made to raid the old armory which was now in the predominantly Saxon settlement called Fleet. For once Morgan chose not to be subtle, but allowed Lot to take as many men as he thought necessary. Fifty of his men embarked for the small Island or mud flat known by the Saxons as eyots, taking with them Lady Morgan, Merlin and Gawain. Gaheris and Olwen were given the task of looking after Gallia and Helena until their return.

43

The Queen with a small army crossed the bridge at Blackfriars, heading towards the area called Fleet Island. She saw in the distance a trail of smoke approaching her from the north. Guinevere feared she was too late and that her enemy had taken her prize, but she still had hopes of taking it back by force. She had fifty trusted solders with her, men who would gladly lay down their lives for her. She whispered to Gruffydd to ride on ahead and find out who was approaching. The man immediately obliged, taking with him another soldier. The two men rode at speed towards the smoke of dust in the horizon.

King Lot spotted the two riders approaching and issued a warning to Lady Morgan. 'My lady, I assume it is Guinevere that is up ahead. What do you want us to do?'

Morgan did not want bloodshed. She feared an encounter now could easily lead to a civil war. She asked Lot's opinion as to what should be done. He pondered for a moment, but came to only one conclusion. 'We must fight, unless you want to give up the treasure voluntary.'

Morgan was adamant she could not. 'Is there not another road out of here?' she inquired.

'It's possible to go back the way we came, pass the Saxon settlement towards Silchester, but that will take us further away from Londinium.'

'I think it might be prudent...'

Lot who had never ran away from a battle, disagreed. 'By the time we turn around, the Queen's force will almost be upon us. They will simply chase us down and attack us from behind.'

Morgan said she understood, but still insisted that the man came up with a solution that did not mean Celt killing Celt.

'It's possible that Guinevere will not want a confrontation either,' the man suggested. 'The trial would be abandoned and Lancelot would not have a chance to clear his name.'

'It would seem I must negotiate with the lady then, see if we can come to some agreement.'

'You would negotiate with a snake?' the man questioned. 'Do you think that is such a good idea?'

'Go meet with the riders approaching. Tell them I will rendezvous with the Queen on the road, half way between our two forces.'

Lot agreed, but gave his sister-in-law a look of displeasure. He took Gawain with him and reached Gruffydd and his companion quickly. Morgan could see the tiny figures up ahead of her stop and confer. The riders went back to their own camps shortly after.

Lot rode up close to Morgan to tell her that the message was given and the meeting was likely to take place.

The two women, whose hatred was legendary, met each other on a dusty road approaching Blackfriars, as the crows bellowed in another day. It was still dark, although soon the daylight would bring forth enough light for the two armies to fight one another. Friend would come up against friend and without thinking would try and kill each other.

It was Morgan who spoke first. 'I need the treasure to return it to the Gods,' she stated.

Guinevere seemed not to care what her enemy wanted. 'A lot of the objects belong to us or to our previous occupiers, the Romans, what right do these beings have to them?'

Morgan could not answer this. 'I have not looked at the treasure, but all I know is that the Gods want what was stolen from them.'

'What will they do if they do not get it?' Guinevere asked.

'I do not know, perhaps nothing.'

'I also need the treasure or at least one item from it.'

282

Morgan hesitated, was she suggesting a compromise? If so, it was unlike the lady. Could she be trusted this half-breed of Celt and Roman, or was she planning some double-cross.

'You needn't look at me with such mistrust, I can keep a bargain. All I want is the chalice. The rest of the valuables are of little interest to me,' the Queen asserted.

'There might be more than one,' Morgan announced.

'Yes I'm sure, but we both know what chalice I am talking about.'

Morgan knew the item, because Mider had described it, otherwise she doubted she would know one from another. The deal was generous and Morgan stated as much to her rival.

'You need not get sentimental about it. Is it a deal?' inquired Guinevere.

'We have a deal. I will find the chalice and meet with you back here shortly.'

Guinevere agreed and both parties returned to their men.

It did not take long for Morgan to find the chalice, which was encased in a velvet pouch, and return with it to the designated spot. She gave the drinking vessel to her rival, who looked at it closely and smiled.

The Queen accepted the vessel as genuine, but seemed reluctant to move away. Morgan dismounted from her horse and requested the Queen to do likewise. Guinevere dismounted and the two women began to converse as they strolled beside the road.

'Why do you hate me so much?' asked Morgan.

'Oh, I don't know, perhaps I find hate the only truthful emotion,' the Queen replied.

'I know you had Arthur killed, but I don't understand why?'

'Either you're exceedingly stupid or you take after your son,'

'What do you mean by that?' yelled Morgan.

'He is quite naive, but I like him just the same. He is quite well by the way, but he does not send his love.'

'If you harm one hair on his head...'

'Why would I do that, I find him charming. We share the same Christian beliefs and often talk well into the night on such matters, although he has trouble with the Lords' commandment to *honor thy father and mother.*'

'I want to see him,' pleaded Morgan.

'I will try and intercede on your behalf, but I would give him some time to overcome his shock.'

Morgan could see her pleas were useless and decided not to allow her rival to twist her tail further. She had other questions she wanted to ask the lady anyway. 'Why do you protect Lancelot?'

Guinevere was somewhat taken aback with the question. 'I am loyal,' was all she replied.

Morgan stared at the Queen. 'Perhaps I am asking the wrong person, but why did he kill my sister?'

The lady was shocked by the question; Guinevere assured her foe that the man did not kill the lady.

'I know he did, I have proof.'

'I hope your proof is more reliable than the proof you produced earlier today.'

Morgan could see the lady did not lie when she denied Lancelot's involvement in Elaine's death. She began to wonder if the lady of the lake had tricked her with her vision.

'It's my turn to ask you a question,' Guinevere announced. 'How was my husband in the matrimonial bed?'

Morgan looked reluctant to answer the lady.

'I could ask many of the young maidens he deflowered, but I'd rather hear it from a woman and not some silly child.'

'I have not slept with Arthur in almost ten years,' Morgan proclaimed.

'You have not forgotten?'

'Why bring this up now?'

'I was only curious.'

'You mean you and your husband never slept together?'

'Only the once, but after that I think he feared he might not awaken the following day.'

'Is that a confession?' Morgan smirked.

'I can hardly murder someone from another country, though I hear you have powers that can make such a thing possible.'

'I have no such powers,' insisted Morgan.

'The days of witchery are over in this country, I warn you not to get caught practicing such evil rituals. Your young protégé is almost certain to be found guilty and punished.'

The lady knew the Queen was referring to Nemue, but did not mention the girl's name. Her thoughts turned to another young maiden and her weakened health. 'You will not subject the Lady Helena to further questions I hope,' she pleaded.

'Are you asking me to make you a promise?' asked Guinevere.

'Yes, the girl is unwell and I am worried about her health.'

'You should have thought about that, before you brought her here.'

'There have been too many deaths already...'

'I can't believe I'm hearing this; do you not want Lancelot's head on a spike on some castle wall?'

'For his crimes he deserves to die.'

'And the Lady Helena's crimes, does she not deserve the same?'

'She has committed no crime.'

Guinevere laughed. 'I suggest we both get some sleep, if we are to commence hostilities again so soon.'

'And the Lady Helena?' pleaded Morgan.

'I will not ask her another question, if it pleases you.'

44

Everyone in the forum was struck by the sincerity of Lancelot, as he gave his evidence of a pirate's raid upon the King's boat. After stating his facts to Guinevere, the man had to contend with a barrage of accusations from Morgan and one or two other awkward questions from the Kings. In the end though, it all came down to whether you believed in Lady Helena's story or in Lancelot's story.

The Queen had one last witness to produce. 'I call Lord Bedivere to give his evidence,' she announced.

The audience must have wondered why the nobleman had been called. He approached the same chair that his niece had given her evidence on the previous day. Helena was not present in the forum and was resting under the careful eyes of Gallia and Olwen in the inn across the street. The Queen began with the usual introductions, getting the man to state who he was and what connection he was to all concerned. 'You have become like a father to Lady Helena, have you not?' she asked.

'Yes. I felt it my duty to take care of the girl after she lost both her parents.'

'She was your sister's child, is that correct?'

'Yes, although I did not approve of my sister's choice of husband, I believed the child was adored by both parents.'

'There is much in the young maiden that reminds you of your sister, in fact?'

'They could well have been twins, they look so alike.'

'You would not wish any harm to come to your niece?'

'No, I would not.'

'Has her upbringing been easy?'

After a little hesitation, Bedivere stated it had been difficult.

'Can you tell us why that was?'

'We tried not to spoil her, but the damage had already been done. She needed to be the centre of attraction at all times, going into tantrums whenever she did not get her way.'

'Did you or your wife not try to discipline her?'

'We did our best, but neither of us had it in our hearts to scold the girl after all she had been through.'

Morgan got to her feet and complained. 'What has this testimony to do the case? So the lady was a precocious as a child, so too was half the audience here.'

King Ursien laughed and agreed. 'We need facts, your grace,' he said addressing the Queen.

With a slight nod of her head, Guinevere accepted the instruction. She turned again to her witness. 'We must move on to particulars,' she told Bedivere.

'Was there a time when the lady got herself into trouble with the authorities?'

Again the man hesitated. 'It never in the end got that far...'

'I'm not sure I understand?' Guinevere queried.

'There was an unfortunate incident last summer, but I feel I must point out that the lady was probably innocent of the charges put against her.'

'I feel I must ask you to relate this incident.' Guinevere turned her head to look at all the Kings. 'These men need facts, my lord.'

'The facts are not in doubt. A young lord in Benoic by the name of Brevet, son of a courtier of King Ban played court to Lady Helena. They had a brief romance it would seem and the lord proposed marriage, but the lady refused him.'

'Was that the end of the matter?'

'No, the young man's family claimed the lady had enchanted the young man with a love potion.'

A few people in the audience sniggered.

'Go on my lord, what then transpired?'

The man began to sweat and look uncomfortable. 'A most terrible thing happened. The young man took his own life, and his mother claimed...'

287

Bedivere stopped and lowered his head. 'His mother claimed she found a witch's enchantment under his bed.'

The audience stirred with gasps of shock.

Bedivere continued. 'She claimed a pendant belonging to Helena had been entwined in mandrake and tied to the base of his bed by a witch's knot.'

Guinevere looked bewildered.

Bedivere thought to clarify his statement. 'I later found out that witches use hexes or charms in such a way. The lady further claimed there was a scroll with a curse written inside the pendant, in Helena's hand.'

'Do you know what words were on that parchment?' asked the Queen.

'I still have the pendant with the inscription.'

'I don't understand?'

'I purchased the object along with a promise from the family not to mention anything about this whole affair.'

Sounding surprised, Guinevere asked if the mother agreed to this.

'Eventually, after a great deal of persuasion on my part, she did.'

'I take it the sum was quite considerable?'

'Indeed it was more than two years profit from my estate.'

'Can you recite the words?'

Bedivere did better than recite them. He took from his pocket the actual pendant and offered it to the Queen.

Guinevere took the object into her hand and saw that it was in a shape of a heart, with thorns entwined around it. It was made of silver with small red jewels that sharply protruded out from the thorns. She opened it and looked inside to find a piece of fine blonde hair tied in a knot. Guinevere took the hair out and walked over to the Kings to show them. After Morgan had examined it also, the Queen returned it to the pendant and took out a small piece of folded parchment. She opened the tightly folded scroll and tried to read it, but she had trouble making out the Celtic writing and looked to Morgan to decipher the contents.

The lady again felt obliged to help out her foe and read out the words to the Kings. 'My heart is held strong by passion and is wrapped in dark bliss. I bind our hearts together for eternity, never to release you from your promise of everlasting love.'

After the words were spoken there was an eerie silence. It was Morgan who broke the quiet. 'This is harmless, a worthless charm made by an impressionable young woman in search of love. Surely no one here takes this seriously.'

Looking about the room, Morgan saw that everyone believed in the love enchantment and its power. She suddenly felt the whole proceeding lurching away from Lancelot's innocence or guilt, towards a full blown witch hunt. The emotions around the room were becoming tangible and even a sensible woman like her, feared the frenzy and anger of a mob. She still remembered the witch trials from her childhood, where she saw how easily crowds were manipulated into a senseless fury.

Guinevere returned the pendant to Bedivere and continued to question him. A somber atmosphere now engulfed the forum and everyone seemed morbid in their curiosity. The man had one last revelation to impart, but the Queen was clever in keeping everyone waiting. After exhausting the subject of Lady Helena's early life, Guinevere finally asked Bedivere to reveal a conversation that he had with his niece the night before Arthur went to war.

The lady's stare seem to jolt the man into answering. 'The night before the King's departure I found Helena preparing to receive Arthur in her room.'

'How do you know this?' asked Guinevere.

Bedivere coughed. 'I observed them during the feast, their eyes met and there was a definite attraction between the two.'

The man exchanged a glance with the Queen. He saw the lady's cold stare of indifference as she prompted him to go on.

'I was alarmed for the lady. I had seen many other young maidens throw away their maidenhead in such away.'

King Lot rose to his feet and bent forward to address Bedivere. 'You are aware you are speaking of the High King?' he thundered.

Guinevere smiled and turned to look at Lot. 'I am aware of the countless lovers of my late husband,' she stated. 'I can assure you it does not embarrass me at all, so it should not embarrass anyone else in this room.'

Lot sat back down again. Guinevere turned her attention to Bedivere again.

'I pleaded with her not to have a sexual encounter with the King, but she only laughed at this. She told me that she was about to change the course of history.'

'What did she mean by that?' asked the Queen.

'She would not say, but I noticed a cauldron filled with a strange brew and I asked her what was in it. She got angry and told me to leave.'

'And did you leave?'

'No, I picked up the cauldron and was about to taste its contents when the lady grabbed my arm and swore at me. This made me fearful for the life of our King and I wrestled the bowl away from her. I asked her to tell me what was in the vessel, but she would not. We argued until the lady broke down in tears and confessed she wanted to kill the King to take revenge for the death of her father many years earlier.'

Lady Morgan was up on her feet. 'I protest this testimony is hearsay, we have only this man's word this conversation ever took place.'

King Ursien addressed Morgan. 'The lady must be allowed to come forward to refute these allegations of course, but for now I am intrigued to hear the rest of the tale.'

After a little prompting from Guinevere, Bedivere continued. 'I heard footsteps approaching and feared it was the King, so I took the cauldron with me and left by a secret passageway.'

'Was it the King?' asked Guinevere.

'I believe so, but I did not witness him.'

'The King was healthy the next day?'

'Yes, he was quite jovial in fact.'

'It's wonderful how a night of passion can rejuvenate one,' mocked the lady.

After the sniggers and muffled laughter the lady continued. 'Is there more?' she inquired.

'Yes, sadly I gave the cauldron to a hungry pack of hounds a short time later and all fell sick. One died the following morning.'

'Are you saying you saved the King's life that night?'

'Yes that time, but I feared for his safety so I stayed close by his side.'

'I take it the lady did not depart with the troops the next day.'

'No, but she managed to follow the trail of the army and join the King some time later.'

'I know my late husband well enough to know he would not be pleased to see a lady in the midst of a battle.'

'That is true, initially he was angry, but when he became sick he was grateful for the lady's attention.'

'You are implying, are you not, that the lady was responsible for the King's illness?'

With a mournful sigh the man agreed he was. 'There are plenty who witnessed his poor state of health.'

Morgan approached Bedivere and asked him a question. 'The King was not killed by poison, but by several blows from a dagger. You are not surely suggesting the lady had anything to do with that?'

'I have no proof of that, but I fear with the failure of the poison the lady became desperate. There are many dangerous criminals along the coast of Calais who are willing to earn money for services rendered.'

Morgan laughed. 'I'm afraid I will have to take your word for that,' she said.

'May I continue?' interrupted an impatient Guinevere.

Morgan glanced at the lady and whispered as she passed her. 'You have him well prepared.'

Guinevere did not answer.

More damning evidence from the man put doubt in the minds of all present that King Arthur must have been under the young woman's spell. He told those present how she criticized the soldiers for their treatment of prisoners. He hinted that she was behind the release of several Roman prisoners and implied she was in love one of them. To the credit of his coach, his performance was so brilliant that almost everyone in the room believed in his story.

On the previous day, a certain amount of doubt had arisen concerning the lady's testimony. After her uncle's performance, only Morgan and her supporters now believed her account. Morgan tried to catch the man out in a lie, but many of the soldiers were present and could attest to his statement that the girl was critical of the treatment of the King's enemies.

Fearing defeat, the lady passed word along for Accolon to warn the others at the inn, to make ready for a quick departure. She feared Helena was going to be arrested and assumed Nemue and Yvain were already at the Queen's mercy in some dungeon in the town.

With all the witnesses finished and all the testimony done, it was left to the four Kings, Guinevere and Morgan to decide Lancelot's fate. With nothing more to be done, Morgan put up little opposition to the inevitable and all the rulers pronounced Lancelot innocent. On the Queen's instructions, warrants were issued for the capture of Lady Helena, Nemue and Yvain on charges of witchcraft, murder and conspiracy.

As one side celebrated victory, the other thought of ways to escape without being seen. Having risked Helena's life in coming forward, Morgan could not abandon the lady. She knew she could rely on her family and friends to stand by her side. Already her forces were somewhat depleted for she had sent Gaheris and Merlin ahead with a small group of soldiers to escort the Gods' treasure to

Tintagel. From there she intended to inform the fairies to tell the lady of the lake of its capture and immediate return.

45

Thousands of soldiers lined the streets drinking and carousing, many of them Lancelot's supporters celebrating his release. On the other side many of King Arthur's supporters were unsure as to the innocence of the Queen's champion and were not in the mood for celebrating. Resentment hung in the air and possible recriminations were bubbling just below the surface. Fights began to break out, many of them fists fights, but as the night progressed more violent confrontations took place. Several deaths had already taken place, by the time Morgan had arranged to spirit Helena away from all the praesides and marshals surrounding the roads in and out of Londinium. More officials had been drafted into the area, no doubt by the instructions of the Queen. Any escape attempt would be fraught with danger, for anyone helping a fugitive could be charged with treason.

King Lot accompanied by a few of his soldiers had made a reconnaissance of the surrounding area. They found that all the bridges and places along the river that were passable by horse had men on parade, ready to apprehend anyone who might give them cause to suspect they were wanted fugitives. He returned to Morgan with the bad news and told her that his men were ready to smash their way through any lines if need be.

'Let's try not to cause a war,' the lady calmly stated.

'The way my men feel right now, I fear it is already too late to stop that.'

'We must keep cool heads. I have had reports of deaths, stupid confrontations...'

'Many have died and I fear many more will follow, so the sooner we leave the better.'

'We are ready now. Gallia and Olwen have Helena in their wagon and will try to cross the river near Blackfriars.

If your men ride a good distance behind to keep an eye on their progress, we can hopefully avoid bloodshed.'

Lot was not an admirer of the plan and told the lady so. 'Let me ride with the ladies,' he pleaded.

'No men. This way there is less chance of violence.'

'Sometimes violence is necessary. If they are stopped and arrested, it might be too late before my men can reach them.'

'They have their merchandise loaded on the wagon. They will tell anyone who asks them, that they are on their way to Silchester for a market fair.'

'At this time of night?' cried Lot.

'Their animals are old and take a long time to get anywhere.'

'It doesn't convince me and I don't see it convincing any of the Queen's men either.'

'She has employed her own men?'

'Her loyal guards are everywhere.'

'I have made up my mind it has to be this way.'

'Very well, I will ride with my men a good distance behind. We have no time to lose though, so we must leave now.'

Morgan then surprised her brother-in-law. 'I'm not leaving with you, I must stay awhile longer.'

Lot tried to convince her come with him.

'I will be quite safe. The Queen would not dare to arrest me.'

The man had no time to convince the lady, so he left her behind to follow Gallia and Olwen's wagon as they made their way through the overcrowded streets towards Blackfriars.

The night was as dark as pitch, as the Lady Morgan and Accolon walked towards the Governor's Palace. The servant had confessed of his dealings with Guinevere, but strongly asserted that he never once told the lady anything of importance. He had received information that Yvain and Nemue were kept prisoner below stairs in the cells.

Wearing a disguise, Morgan took on the appearance of a maid-servant and was shown into the servant's quarters.

'I could be leading you into a trap, my lady,' whispered Accolon. He was about to leave his mistress to report to the Queen.

'You think me a bad judge of character, my friend?'

The young man shook his head.

'You saved my sister with your quick thinking and your bravery,' Morgan attested. 'I know you are loyal and will remain so.'

Accolon almost had tears in his eyes as he thanked the lady. He gave her a quickly sketched plan of the cells beneath and went to deliver his report.

No one challenged the lady despite the fact the staff being overburdened by work. She slipped away and found the stairs that led down to the cells. She became aware of a strange aroma, it was strong, sweet and musty and somehow familiar to her. She had smelt the same aroma just before the fairies had came upon her on Tintagel. The lady wondered if the tiny creatures were here. She glanced from side to side just as a beast flew around her face. It was Eros, accompanied by some of his kin. 'Go back my lady, go back,' he shouted. Before she could react to his statement several of the Queen's guards rushed up the stairs with their swords drawn. They brandished them at the lady's head, but Morgan turned and ran upwards only to be met by more soldiers descending.

Morgan was taken down to the cell, where she was met by jubilant Guinevere. 'Put her with her servant,' the Queen ordered. One of the guards turned the lock in the cell and opened it. Morgan was pushed in and the cell was shut and relocked. Guinevere stood on the other side of the bars and began to mock her enemy. 'You have too trusting a nature...do you really think loyalty can not be bought?'

The lady did not reply. She had a quick glance around her new surroundings and witnessed only one other occupant. Yvain's right leg and right hand were in irons in the corner of the cell. The lady could see he had been beaten; dried blood surrounded his mouth and around his lower lip a scar was visible, his cheeks were blown up considerably around his eyes, to the effect that his right eye was partially closed all together.

'This man gave you nothing,' challenged Lady Morgan.

The ladies looked at each other again.

'True, he is more stubborn than a mule, but young Accolon is a coward and cowards talk their heads of when you threaten them with death.'

Morgan nodded her head. 'I see,' she said. 'You must be pleased with the outcome of today's proceedings?'

'This is one of the happiest days of my life. I never knew victory could taste so sweet,' the Queen admitted.

'You can afford to be generous, my lady. Please allow me some water, a cloth and some medicine for my friend.'

Guinevere agreed and gave the order for the items to be brought.

'I'll be leaving you shortly, I have guests to entertain, but don't worry, I'll send you supper down in a short while. Bread and water I think, how does that sound?'

'It sounds just fine,' the lady replied.

A guard came with a bucket of water, a cloth and some ointment and opened the cell gate. He put the items inside the goal and relocked the cell.

Everyone left with the Queen, except two guards who remained in plain sight, a little away from the cell.

Morgan bathed Yvain with great care before asking him questions. Eros buzzed around the lady's head trying to get her to pay him some attention. 'I failed to warn you, my young mistress will be cross with me,' he said.

'Young mistress?' asked Morgan.

'Nemue escaped when we were ambushed, I think she will have some plan for our escape,' advised Yvain.

Eros did not like to be interrupted, but he realized the man could not see him so he was forgiven. 'Nemue has come up with a brilliant idea and with my band of helpers we should have you free in no time,' stated the fairy.

Morgan turned her head and looked up at Eros flying around the cell. 'I think I would like to hear what this plan is.'

Yvain wondered who his mistress was talking to. He watched as she got up from the ground and went over to the lone slit in the wall.

'This plan,' Morgan whispered. 'I hope it does not involve magic.'

Eros put his small hands in the air and gave the lady a look of shock. 'Of course it involves magic. We are creatures of magic after all.'

'I do not want people killed.'

Eros smiled. 'Ah, that will not happen. The lady has bewitched all the food and drink in the mansion. After awhile when all the dignitaries have gorged themselves, we will simply walk out of the place. Brilliant don't you think so?'

The lady did and managed a smile. She turned to face Yvain and saw his face stare upon her. He looked worried and asked the lady if she was feeling alright. 'Do not worry my friend. I feel you will be reunited with your love before the night is out.'

The lady turned to Eros and whispered something concerning the two guards outside.

'My children will sprinkle their magic dust upon them and they will sleep like babies until the morning.'

'When will this all take place?'

'The lady is amongst them now, in disguise of course. I'm sure it will not be long.'

Nemue was having a merry old time. She was seated a few seats away from the Queen, but the lady did not recognize the maiden for she looked remarkably like Lord Bedivere. Having taken the man's place she was not expecting so much praise and homage made towards her, considering the man was regarded as the biggest bore in the land.

Lancelot caught Nemue's attention. 'I owe you a great debt my lord,' he said as he bowed his head in her direction.

'Do you?' a surprised Nemue replied in the voice of Bedivere.

'I know it must have been difficult to betray your own niece.'

Guinevere stared at Nemue and offered a consoling word. 'It was for the good of the five kingdoms.'

Nemue smiled. 'This will allow you to raid more villages and slay more children,' she suggested to the Queen.

Those around the Queen's table stopped talking to listen to the sudden petulance of the feeble Lord.

Lancelot turned his head to look at Guinevere. 'What the devil is he talking about?'

Pelles intervened. 'The man is clearly drunk and does not know what he is saying.'

Guinevere studied Bedivere closely. 'Oh, I think he does. Why don't you enlighten Lancelot on what you refer to?'

Nemue was most anxious to do just that. 'I refer to the sickening incident at Haydon Bridge, where some Angle children were slaughtered like helpless sheep.'

'You have evidence as to who was responsible?' asked the Queen.

'We both know who were responsible.'

'Indeed I would love to know, so that I could pat them on the back and offer them my best wine,' joked Guinevere.

Pelles and others laughed and the whole subject took on an air of jest, but Nemue noticed Lancelot did not find the subject amusing. She felt if she could forge a wedge between the two, it might prove of use in the future. She glanced around the room and saw many of the men and women yawning and closing their eyes. It would not be long now before everyone in the place would be fast asleep. With only a short time left she wanted to blacken the Queen in Lancelot's eyes still further.

'How is your conscience my lord?' she asked Lancelot.

'If you are referring to Lady Helena, I will not feel guilty. If the lady uses magic then she has only herself to blame, when the law catches up with her.'

'You believe she should be executed?

'I do not feel qualified to answer that.'

'And what about Lady Morgan, do you feel she should also lose her life?'

Guinevere swore under her breath. 'Since when have you championed the lady?' asked the Queen.

Lancelot blinked and said the Queen's brew was awfully strong and fought to keep his eyes from closing. 'No one wants to kill Lady Morgan,' he uttered.

'No. Then why is she being held captive in the cells below us?' asked Nemue.

King Ursien staggered to his feet and looked at the Queen. 'Is this true,' he demanded.

Guinevere like everyone else was starting to feel groggy. 'I don't think I like your tone,' she suggested.

Lancelot closed his eyes and put his head forward to rest on the table. Guinevere looked at him and then all around the other tables. Only one or two men were still awake. Ursien, and Pelles had join Lancelot and were fast asleep. The Queen stared at Bedivere. 'Who the devil are you?' she mumbled.

Taking great delight, Nemue transformed from Bedivere to her own self and bellowed out a laugh. 'I don't think I have ever enjoyed a night so much.'

'You mean to kill us?' asked a semi-conscious Guinevere.

Nemue got to her feet. 'That will depend on what the Lady Morgan decides.'

Guinevere was the last person in the room to succumb.

Nemue ran from the room, down the stairs to the cells below. She was met by Yvain and Morgan and an exuberant band of fairies. 'You could not wait for me to rescue you?' asked the maiden.

'We were starting to get worried,' replied her young man.

They all headed up the stairs, stepping over many guards on the way. Lady Morgan was about to leave by a side door, but Nemue ushered her along a corridor to the great hall. When they entered they were met by a strange and saturnine sight. Thirty men and one woman were slouched over tables and chairs oblivious to everything around them.

Nemue moved over to where the Queen and Lancelot were huddled together and addressed Morgan. 'This is your chance to take revenge on your enemies,' she said. She took a dagger from her belt and held it around the neck of the Queen. 'Just give me the word and I will rid this world of this evil woman.'

Yvain stood watching the whole proceedings wondering who this young maiden was, who spoke of killing with such relish.

Morgan came towards the girl. 'Put down your dagger, there will be no killing here.'

Nemue let go of the head of the Queen and turned to Lancelot. She lifted his head from the table and with her dagger placed it around his neck. 'He killed your sister, do you not want revenge?'

'No I want justice. I will see both this murderers hanging from a jib when they are found guilty of their crimes.'

Nemue obeyed her elder, more for the sake of keeping her lover happy than anything else. The fairies were rejoicing with them all, so Nemue said a few words and Yvain saw the tiny creatures fly and engage with the humans for the first time. His eyes nearly popped out of his head as they swarmed around his head in joyful merriment.

Morgan walked around the tables and chairs looking at ever face she could. Yvain approached her. 'Are you looking for someone?' he inquired.

'He does not seem to be here. It's time we left anyway,' she said to the others.

'To Avalon?' suggested Nemue.

'I will go to Avalon alone, but first we must avoid detection. I suggest we travel to Colchester, they will not suspect us going in the wrong direction.'

They all agreed, but as they were about to leave Yvain came across Accolon and spoke to his mistress. 'Should we take him along?'

'We should not let the traitor live,' snapped Nemue.

With an air of frustration, Morgan told them to leave him be.

46

The cart jostled along the ragged road towards Blackfriars Bridge, with its occupants alert and ready for anything that might transpire. King Lot had moved ahead of his men and rode a short distance behind the wagon, shadowing him was Gawain. Every person was being stopped and in many cases searched at each end of the footbridge. The cart was covered in fleeces of wool. Hiding below these fleeces was Helena, just a little forward from her sat Gallia and Olwen. With the reins in her hand, Gallia shouted encouragement for the sad looking mule to increase its pace. The beast could not respond so the cart continued to bump along at a slow boring tempo.

One man put out his hand in the air to stop the cart, while another came forward to address the ladies. 'Where are you going this time of the night?' he asked.

Gallia told him they were on their way to market and stipulated they wanted to be first so as to steal a march on their rivals. Used to telling lies, the lady was quite convincing, nonetheless the man looked over the women with great care. He asked them both to get down from the cart, so as he could study their faces in more detail. The ladies did this and the man, hand on his face, swept his beady eyes over them before shaking his head at his colleague. He called for the other man to let the cart through. The ladies got back onto their cart and began to move forward, but the second man seemed to have some doubts for he shouted for it to halt again.

He then moved behind the cart and started poking his fingers into the fleeces of wool. He jabbed and prodded at the first bale, then the second without discovering a thing.

King Lot had gotten off his horse and had sneaked up unseen by the side of the road. He was just about in striking distance of the man, when the first marshal came up to his colleague and berated him for wasting time. He waved the ladies on and Gallia coaxed the mule to go forward onto the bridge proper.

Sensing the danger was over Lot retraced his steps and went back to his horse. Now a good distance away, the man was in no position to help when a yell went up from the other side of the bridge to signify the ladies were in trouble. He quickly waved his soldiers on towards the bridge to lead an assault. The front of the bridge was well guarded by the Queen's guards and only a few of Lot's men managed to make it onto the bridge. The sound of swordplay rattled through the cloudy night as the two forces battled each other. A few of Lot's men made it to the other side include Lot and Gawain. What they found was an upturned cart lying on its side, with two of its fleeces beside it. A further two were floating down the river, away from them, but no sign of the women. Then one of Lot's men pointed to the fleeces in the water and asked everyone to listen. In the distance faint cries travelled through the air. 'We are safe and over here, but they have taken Helena,' cried Gallia. She pointed to her left and Gawain mounted his horse and raced through the crowd in that general direction.

Lot set two of his men to swim after the ladies to make sure they were alright, while he and his remaining few men battled their way through a crowd of onlookers. They looked in the direction that Gawain had headed but did not see the Lady Helena. They were quickly swamped by marshals and the Queen's guards. There was nothing left to do, but to fight their way through the bridge and save as many of his own men as he could. The larger group of his men was signaled to advance and join up with their King. Most made it through although a handful perished at the hands of the well trained guards.

The two parties met up along the Holborn River and exchanged their stories. The ladies had battled with their male attackers and had sustained a collection of small cuts and bruises around their wrists and hands. Helena was too weak to put up any resistance and was quickly bundled onto a horse where a soldier rode her away from the scene.

Gallia scratched the face of one of her attackers and seeing the bales of wool lying near the bridge wall, threw one onto the water below. Olwen did the same and both ladies jumped into the water and luckily onto the bales to their freedom. They drifted down stream, until the wool began to sink and Lot's men caught up with them to bring about an end to their excitement.

Lot sent everyone on west to head for Tintagel, to await the arrival of Lady Morgan. He put his faithful commander Caius in charge of their safe keeping. Gallia offered to come with him to show him the last place she had seen the lady, but the man refused to risk her safety. His mission was likely to fail, but perhaps his reconnaissance could be put to good use later. In any case he was worried for his son. He had only just lost one son and did not want to lose another.

Three days later, Queen Guinevere was walking in what used to be Lady Ygerne's garden in Cadbury. She looked serene as she picked a variety of wild flowers and placed them in a wicker basket beside her. When footsteps approached her, she turned to face Germanus standing with his usual insouciant expression before her.

'Now this is a rare treat, to see the fully feminine side of the great lady. Is this perhaps Lancelot's doing, has he brought out all your finer feelings?'

'Enough of your sarcasm,' scolded the Queen. 'We are here to do business.'

'You are pleased with the gift of the boy?' the man inquired.

'He is a fine scholar and seems intent to stay with me and learn all about my world for now.'

'You've not added him to your lovers too by any chance?'

'You have a filthy mind. Let's discuss our business. I want certain assurances that you can produce the men you say you can for the forthcoming war.'

'I have waited long enough for my reward. It is time you gave me what you promised.'

Guinevere smiled, reached down into the basket and pick up the silver chalice. It did not glitter in the sunlight, for it had a brown, drab looking coat to it.

Germanus went to take the object from the lady's hand. She moved her hand away before he could touch it. 'This does not look like the chalice I expected,' the man complained.

'The one you search for is an illusion, I do not believe it exists anymore, but this chalice contains a great deal of power.'

Germanus looked interested. 'Power,' he jested. 'Do you think it can make people disappear?'

'Perhaps it can, I do not know how to enhance all its power. It was stolen by Arthur from the Gods. Like you I think he assumed it was the last drinking vessel of our Lord Jesus.'

'What is then, if it is not that?' the man asked.

'I don't know, but I must warn you when you touch it you will be in for a rare experience.'

The bishop looked skeptical. Guinevere handed the man the chalice. He took hold of it and stared at the object, until his eyes began to burn like red hot irons. He felt the power drain from his body as if someone had opened all his veins and drew off all his blood. The Queen grabbed the chalice from his grasp and threw it down on the ground. The man followed the object as it hit the grass about the same time with a thud.

Guinevere splashed water and slapped the man around the face, before he regained his wits. 'What was that?' he asked the lady as he came out of his daze.

'I don't know, but already I have mastered some of its power. Just think how we could use such intensity.'

The man raised himself up with a little help from the lady. 'You realize this is not God's work.'

'What God are we talking about?'

'There is only one God, the God you champion everyday.'

306

'I am only interested in power, no matter what God gives me it.'

'Why am I not surprised?'

'Now let's get back to our bargain. Will the Franks join with me?'

'I believe so, but the bargain was the Holy Grail, you have not found it after all.'

'I have found something far greater. Don't you see together we will conquer not only the west but the east too?'

'You are ambitious my lady, but can you control it?'

'In time I will master it, but in the meantime I have business with a certain lady to take care of.'

'What do you intend for Lady Morgan?'

'I have devised a special kind of torture, just for the lady.'

47

With the sun at his back, Gaheris watched his lady at play enjoying the late autumn sunshine. She was collecting butterflies along with Gallia and Elaine in the pleasant pastures of Traunent, on his father's estate in Lothian. The ladies all played like children, giggling and falling to the ground in comic ineptitude as yet another painted-lady, managed to escape their net. Olwen fell short of another dazzling specimen as she jumped forward, net in hand, to witness the beast fly upwards, away out of her reach. She picked herself up, looked at her new friends and began to laugh. 'I can't remember the last time I enjoyed myself so much,' she stated.

Elaine came over to her and kissed the lady on the cheek. 'This is your new home now and we are your new family.' The lady glanced at Gallia and repeated the statement to her.

'You have made me so welcome, but I have affairs of my own that I must attend too,' stated Olwen.

Elaine's face grimaced. 'No, you can not leave just yet, I will not allow it.' She saw Gaheris watching and called out to him. 'Tell her she must stay awhile longer.'

Gaheris smiled at the three ladies, but addressed Olwen. 'Everyone obeys my aunt, it safer that way. She has such a temper. You do not want to see her anger, it is truly terrifying,' he stated.

'Oh, you beast,' Elaine replied.

Gallia and Olwen chuckled.

'Do either of you ladies have brothers?' asked a playful Elaine.

The ladies said they did not.

'You are lucky, mine think I am still a child. I am a grown woman, am I not?'

Elaine although middle-aged, was still childlike in her simplicity and innocence. She may look a mature lady, but Gallia thought Elaine was still a child at heart.

'Of course you are,' replied Olwen.

'My brothers are so protective...'

'You are fortunate. I wish I had someone like Gaheris to watch over me,' Gallia announced.

Olwen turn her head to look at Gallia. 'You have my lady, Taliesin is your protector.'

The Lady Olwen then turned her head to look upon Gaheris. 'I wish I had someone too.'

Elaine smiled. She now had the ability to look inside people's minds and see their thoughts. She could tell that Olwen was in love with her brother and that he felt the same way about her, yet the man's pride was stopping them from being together. Sensing the lady wanted to be alone with her sweetheart Elaine took hold of Gallia's arm and whispered something in her ear. The two ladies then moved away from Olwen, towards the middle of the field.

The young lady seemed ready to take a rest and sauntered over to Gaheris and lowered herself to the ground. They were alone for the first time in quite some time and both young people seemed awkward and ill at ease in each other's company.

'You were watching me the whole time while we played in the field,' Olwen stated.

'Is there some reason I should not?' the man answered harshly.

With an air of disappointment the lady shrugged. 'I have studied the map you made while you visited Avalon and I'm sure the third Island is the one my father is being held captive.'

'I agree, I remember its contours from my first excursion there.'

'You still refuse to take me with you?'

'It is too dangerous, my lady.'

'I have no riches to bestow upon you, only my undying gratitude.'

The lady had meant to say love, but at the last minute she faltered. She could not be sure if the man loved her or not. The longer he said nothing, the more likely she thought he did not love her at all. She would pretend a little longer in the hope he would suddenly take her in his arms and announce his adoration.

The man raised himself to his feet and turned his head away to look upon the other ladies in the distance. His coldness left Olwen in little doubt, that the love she felt for him was not returned. Perhaps his love could only be expressed in terms of a brotherly affection. She would have to be content with that, but it seemed such a shame for she knew she could never love another the same way.

Gaheris was unused to ladies and did not know how to express his feelings in their company. As a man he had been taught to be strong, never to show emotion and so now his manly instinct told him to be cautious around even the girl he knew he was in love with. 'I have to wait on the return of Lady Morgan before I can act.'

'I can be patient a little longer.'

'I have not seen John these past few days. I hope you have not sent him away?'

Olwen looked puzzled. 'Why would I send him away?'

'He never usually leaves your side.'

'I have given him some time to himself, so he can explore the beautiful countryside around here.'

'I understand. He loves you a great deal it is clear to see.'

'I adore him of course, without his help I would have died.'

Gaheris suggested rejoining the others.

'Not yet, I need to know something first.'

The man still had his head turned away from the young lady.

'Since I sat down beside you, you have not once looked upon me?

Gaheris joked that the lady was mistaken.

'Why are you scared to look at me?'

There was a moment's silence. Then the lady flung herself down on her face and burst into tears.

Shocked by the incident, Gaheris went to her side immediately and lifted her up. He took her in his arms and kissed her on the mouth. With a mixture of salt tears and sweat from the man, the lady felt his warmth and passion upon her lips. When they had finished with their embrace, the man finally looked into her eyes.

'Can't you see it now?' the lady asked.

'I have always seen it. I just couldn't quite believe it.'

Olwen smiled. 'I must make you understand, that I would only ever let you take me. I have sworn that no other man will ever touch me that way.'

Morgause could not be more miserable, despite the return of her sister Elaine. She took to wandering alone in the fields beside the River Tweed a good furlong away from her husband's estate. She looked a desolate figure as she crossed over a subsidiary stream, to find a good place to lie in the cool grass and soak up the pleasant sunshine.

As she laid back the sun's rays made her close her eyes, but as she did this she became aware that an object had blocked out its beam. She opened her eyes to see her husband looking down at her, his large frame had a threatening quality to it.

'Have you been following me?' the lady asked.

'It would appear so,' was his sarcastic reply.

'Could you at least move to one side so as not to block out the sun?'

The man did so, but offered his hand to his wife. She reluctantly took it and the man pulled her to her feet. The couple stared into each others eyes.

'I suppose you have come to scold me?' the lady said.

Lot offered to walk with her and so they strolled along the river barely speaking.

'If you've come to gloat, I wish you would get on with it,' said the lady.

'As always you wish to portray me in a bad light.'

Morgause shook her head. 'No,' she replied. 'I just wish you'd show some emotion.'

'Like taking a stick to you and beating you with it?'

'It might show me you cared.'

Lot shook his head this time. 'Perhaps I ought too; a man has some rights over his wife after all.'

'Like adultery,' suggested the lady.

The man sighed. 'Be honest, can you blame me. I never wanted to look elsewhere.'

'It is my fault now you can't keep it in your trousers.'

'Yee Gods,' the man cried, 'I've a good mind to teach you a leason.'

'I know about your bastards, sir,' the lady stated.

'They are innocents. Please don't use them against me.'

'I would never condemn the girls, for their father's sins.'

'In any case you have had your revenge.'

'How so?' asked the woman.

'You and the young man...'

'We did nothing together. I was teasing him...'

'You were punishing me.'

'I wished to make you jealous, but I failed...'

'You know you did not fail. I had been wretched.'

'You conceal your wretchedness well...'

Lot took a firm grip of his wife and turned her over his knee and smacked her several times on her bottom. When he had stopped, the lady jumped up and came at him with her hands outstretched, ready to tear at his face. He wrestled with her, taking hold of her arms, as they struggled together with the lady's uncontrollable rage.

A short time later, with Morgause exhausted, the couple stood looking defiantly back at each other. Memories of their past came flooding back, as they both remembered the fire and the passion of their earlier encounters.

'You always did have the claws of a wild-cat.'

'And you always did kick like a mule.'

The man reached forward with his arms and forced the lady's head back, and for once the lady gave into her husband. He forced his mouth onto hers and the couple kissed so passionately that the lady fell back onto the ground with a thud. The man fell on top of her and began to rip at her clothes.

Morgan was in conversation with the lady of the lake on Avalon. The God was content, for her two cylinders had been returned and with them her future. 'I have given the rest of the treasure to the others. I had no need for it,' she informed the lady.

'So Mider is appeased?' asked Morgan.

'Yes he is quite overcome with gratitude to you and your followers.'

'My followers?' question the lady.

'You are their leader. In times ahead they will rely on you and you must steel yourself for the fight ahead which will be long and hard.'

'I have no wish to lead anyone.'

'Nonetheless they rely upon you.'

'The vision you showed me where Lancelot killed Elaine, I find that I question it.'

'The vision hinted that the man killed her, but we only saw a pair of hands, perhaps they belonged to another.'

'Are you saying your visions can not be relied upon?'

'I am saying I do not have to defend myself to you.'

The lady of the lake did not like the lady's tone and was quite curt with her as the remaining discussion unfolded.

'I do not like to complain, but I feel I must bring to your attention the increase in power that Nemue now possesses.'

'That is my doing, the young maiden learns fast.'

'It is dangerous. Anyone using magic in the five kingdoms will be arrested and will be hung.'

'You do not think I'd let my protégé be harmed in anyway.'

313

'I fear the increase in her power has changed the maiden.'

'I have no doubt it has, but that is a good thing. We need her power to destroy Guinevere and her allies. She told me of your mercy in the mansion. I hope you will not regret that decision, when the five kingdoms are steeped in blood.'

'Your prophecy can not be correct. The Celtic peoples would not go to war with each other again.'

Sounding exasperated, the lady of the lake offered to the show the lady in the pool. Morgan shook her head. 'What must I do to stop this?'

'You can not stop it, but you can come out the winner.'

Morgan sighed. 'I am tired, I have no wish to fight anyone.'

'To defeat Guinevere you will need more allies. At the moment you have too few men to win a long lasting confrontation. So you must make alliances.'

'The Queen has made all the Kings her ally except Lot...'

'Not so, King Ban is not keen to fight at all. He is content to stay in Benoic, but in time his excuses will wear thin. Until then you do not have worry about him. As for King Ursien he longs to disassociate himself from the Queen. He also yearns for a wife.'

Morgan stared at the lady, her eyes shone like daggers. 'I don't think I like what you are suggesting.'

'With his forces on your side, the Queen might reconsider her rashness in going to a civil war.'

'I do not even like the man.'

'What does it matter, if it saves countless lives?'

'He is old and licentious.'

'I'm not suggesting you bed the man, just take his name and his power.'

'Everyone knows the man wants a son.'

'So lay with him once, it can not be that bad.'

'I do not want another child,' raged Morgan.

The lady of the lake could feel Morgan's pain. 'Once your son meets you he will see past all of Guinevere's lies and come to love you.'

'I have no right to his love.'

'I am not a mortal, but I have it on good authority that there is no greater bond between humans, than the bond of love between a mother and a son.'

Morgan looked at the lady and saw she meant to be kind. 'Is there no other way, but to marry this awful man?' she asked.

'I do not believe so, but take heart. I have seen a vision where you share great happiness with your son.'

Morgan was tempted to look at such a vision, but she had vowed not to be tempted into looking at the future. She felt it wrong and harmful, for if she knew something was to happen, wouldn't she try and stop it. So by definition the future unlike the past could be changed. Such knowledge was never meant to come to mere mortals.

Lady Morgan left the lady of the lake with her entourage of fairies to travel back by boat past the Isle of Mona towards the coast of Lothian. She had much on her mind, not least a lonely old King.

TO BE CONTINUED

5323259R00175

Printed in Great Britain
by Amazon.co.uk, Ltd.,
Marston Gate.